*Sooner or later, he'd get a handle on the problem.* The problem. Even at the best of times, it took everything he had to let the name of that problem enter his brain.

"Barcina's xylopoiesis," he said aloud. The words came out as a croak. They seemed to bounce around the room and repeat themselves endlessly. Once again, so as to never lose sight of his goal, he forced himself to review the problem. Maybe he'd come up with an idea on how to fix it.

Barcina's xylopoiesis. An extremely rare disease, so rare that very little research had been done on it. Giulio Barcina had identified it and given it the name that was partly his and partly a description of the disease itself. Even though Laslo's firm researched and fabricated drug therapies for genetic defects, he'd never heard of Barcina's until he'd found out more than two years ago, entirely by accident, that Zelimir would die from it.

Barcina's xylopoiesis. The disease was dormant in his son's body, ready to burst inside him, waiting for the right trigger. Laslo knew the symptoms by heart. First, incoordination of voluntary movements and aphasia—the loss of the ability to articulate ideas or comprehend spoken language. Then, gangrene and blindness.

He rubbed his eyes. Zelimir's nerve endings would begin to die, starting with the toes. Their muscle cells would transform into wooden tissue then rot, forcing the surgeons to amputate. The mutation would creep up to the torso, where it would attack the major organs, shutting them down as it invaded.

To extend Zel's life expectancy, surgeons would excise the rotting parts, piece by piece, until all that was left of him was a trunk with a head. Death would come soon after, the pain excruciating, his son blind, unable to express what he felt.

Also by M.D. Benoit

The Jack Meter Case files
Metered Space
Meter Maid
Meter Destiny (2007)

# SYNERGY

BY

# M. D. BENOIT

ZUMAYA OTHERWORLDS                                                                  AUSTIN TX

2007

This book is a work of fiction. Names, characters, places and incidents are products of the author's imagination or are used fictitiously. Any resemblance to actual persons or events is purely coincidental.

SYNERGY

© 2007 by M. D. BENOIT
ISBN 13: 978-1-934135-13-6
ISBN 10: 1-934135-13-5

Cover art by Moor Dragon
Cover design by Martine Jardin

All rights reserved. Except for use in review, the reproduction or utilization of this work in whole or in part in any form by any electronic, mechanical or other means now known or hereafter invented, is prohibited without the written permission of the author or publisher.

Look for us online at http://www.zumayapublications.com

Library of Congress Cataloging-in-Publication Data

Benoit, M. D., 1957-
 Synergy / by M. D. Benoit.
    p. cm.
 ISBN-13: 978-1-934135-13-6
 ISBN-10: 1-934135-13-5
 I. Title.
 PR9199.4.B466S96 2007
 813'.6--dc22
                                2007008074

For Daniel

"Logic doesn't apply to the real world."

> Lee Marvin Minsky
> "The Mind's I—fantasies and
> reflections on self and soul,"
> 1981
> Hofstadter and Dennet, eds.

# FOREWORD

*Extract from Ezekiel Sartre Longmere's "A sociogenetic study of the Mundial Genetic Revision Committee in the Twenty-first Century," Lunar Sky Publishing, 2175*

AT THE BEGINNING OF THE SECOND DECADE OF THE TWENTY-FIRST CENTURY, THE thinning of the ozone layer, an increase in radiation fallout from the Indo-Pakistani nuclear war, a worldwide protracted drought and the spread of environmental pollution forced Earth's population to turn to genetic engineers for their survival. For two decades, scientists fought a constant race against the extinction of species. They concentrated their efforts on the development of mutation-resistant strains of crops and livestock and devised more effective techniques for organ cloning and transplants.

This single-minded fight to survive justifies why the medical community ignored the sudden outbreaks of salmonella poisoning, cholera and plague that cropped up across the planet. For those who treated the sick, however, the manifestation of the diseases was baffling—within a few kilometers' radius, the disease would appear while other areas would remain untouched. The diseases were extremely resistant to treatment and close to one hundred percent of affected people died. The obvious connection was not made for almost half a century.

In 2046, Dr. Ishiko Katmura proved that bio-terrorists were responsible for these epidemics. She advanced that they were testing genetically altered bacterial preparations. Her theory was confirmed a few months later when, on 20 September 2046, the nihilistic Aum Shinri Kyo cult announced responsibility for a smallpox epidemic in the European States. This epidemic was particularly devastating since no vaccine for that disease had existed for the previous twenty-five years and no medical treatment existing at the time proved effective. Two million people died in that epidemic. The disease was successfully stopped under severe quarantine conditions.

Panic descended on the world. Biotech companies began to fabricate protective bio-suits for the civilian population. Their costs were prohibitive, however, and only the rich could afford them. The cry of unfairness and elitism led Government Mundial to subsidize the development of early detection equipment such as bio-electronic chips and fiber-optic tubes lined with light-emitting antibodies which responded to the presence of bio-weapons and had the potential of saving a greater number of lives at one time.

These preventive measures addressed the biological aspect of this form of terrorism, but not its genetic component. At the conclusion of the Third Synod, Government Mundial officials opted for a major intervention. On 30 December 2047, Government Mundial passed two major bills. The first one, called the "Genetic Privacy Bill," decreed every person's inalienable ownership of their DNA and made it a crime to use unauthorized genetic material for any type of research. The second bill, the "Genetic Control and Monitoring Bill," made it a legal requirement for every scientist involved in biological and genetic engineering to register their projects with Government Mundial.

These bills set the stage for the establishment of the Mundial Genetic Revision Committee (MGRC) which, by 2050, controlled every aspect of genomic research, including most genebanks. The MGRC consisted of a group of scientists and politicians divided into Research Evaluation, Enforcement and Prosecution. The Enforcement Branch had a police structure and similar powers; the Prosecution Branch applied Government Mundial's guidelines with zeal, inflicting stiff penalties ranging from loss of license to life imprisonment.

In response to public pressure, genetic research was limited to a minimum for the next ten years. These restrictions came with a price. Soon, mutations due to environmental fallout began to proliferate. To limit future inherited defects, MGRC authorized the sterilization of any person with a severe mutation. When the decree turned into a witch-hunt, MGRC rescinded its policy. The sociological effects of this form of eugenics, however, were considerable, the least of which was an increased demand for genetic privacy.

Genetic therapy, through pharmacogenomics, was re-established in 2080 on a limited basis, and still with stringent monitoring and control processes. In 2090, MGRC instituted a secret research group to try to limit the number of mutations across Government Mundial.

By 2095, despite efforts to contain them, mutations had increased in severity and strangeness. Rumors began to circulate that, despite MGRC's efforts to eliminate genetic terrorism, it had become a reality again, and in a more virulent form.

# Chapter One

H E GRINNED. HE THOUGHT OF HIMSELF, SITTING IN HIS OFFICE MOTIONLESS, A VIDSTILL in his hands. It never ceased to amaze him how he felt himself move as if he'd taken his body along when he knew only his eyes and his mind did the walking.

Torver blinked then glanced behind him. Damn, he thought, I skipped five years. He did an about-turn and ran his eyes along the girl's lifepath to the place-time he wanted. He focused on it, felt the slight disorientation of his body catching up. Then, he was there.

The spot he'd selected expanded like a flat-screen vid to reveal the scene he'd glimpsed a few seconds before. Immediately, he saw the child, the only splash of color in the dining room. The walls were covered in white silk, the floors with white marble, the table and chairs were white plasmer. Even the woman, whom he almost failed to notice standing beside the child, wore a floor-length white caftan that blended with her white hair, making her face appear as if it floated above the little girl.

The child sat at the table in a higher chair made for her size, her black hair shining blue against the white surroundings, wearing a dress—a pink combination of frills and lace—that, somehow, looked wrong on her. She swung her white shoes and pink socks, repeatedly hitting the underside of the table.

The woman beside her bent at the waist and intercepted a leg with a sharp shake of her head and pressure from her hand. The girl slid the woman a resentful glance and hooked her feet around the chair legs. She plunked her elbows on the table, laid her chin in her hands and glared at the pink-and-white-frosted birthday cake in front of her. It had five unlit candles on it.

The woman pulled the girl's elbows off the table, at the same time pushing against the girl's lower back with the flat of her hand.

"Sit up, for heaven's sake," the woman said. She had a slight Italian accent.

"I hate this stupid dress," the girl said. She yanked at the hem. "It's ugly."

"Daddy likes it when you wear your pink dress."

"He won't come."

"Of course, he will." The woman's face hardened. "He promised."

"He promised before and he didn't come. He likes his stupid subjects more than me."

A white-uniformed man appeared in the doorway. "Excuse me, ma'am."

"Now, darling," the woman said to the girl in a distracted tone, "you know that's not true." She straightened and turned towards the man. "Yes, Jakes?"

"Comm for you from the Philharmonic," Jakes said.

The woman's face cleared. "Darling, I won't be a minute. Please try not to get wrinkled." She rushed out of the room.

Torver shut off the scene and moved his eyes a fraction along the path. He'd become quite good at reading lifepaths, slowing the flow to a specific time then to a specific scene with barely a conscious effort; but he never had as much control as with this child. The images of her life were sharper, more detailed than any others—except maybe his parents'—and he could focus for several minutes without feeling he'd lose his own self if he stayed longer.

That sensation of fading invariably brought him out, sometimes gasping, as if he'd spent long minutes under water. With her, he sensed he could travel her lifepath for as long as he wanted.

He refocused on the thread at a place only a few minutes after the mother left. It expanded to reveal the girl still sitting at the table. She was back to rocking her feet. One of her shoes had fallen off. A woman—a maid by the uniform she wore—hovered in the background but didn't move to replace the shoe. The girl's aloneness hovered around her, a shroud ready to fall and smother her. Like him, she was an abandoned child.

The mother came back into the room. She hesitated, then strode to her daughter and placed a hand on her shoulder. The girl looked up.

"It was Maestro Klausser," the mother said. "He wants me to play for him. What we call an audition."

"I know what an audition is. You explained it."

"Yes. You see, Mummy practiced a lot for this audition. It's very important to her."

"You have to go play for him now, don't you."

"Yes, darling."

The girl started her legs swinging again. Her other shoe dropped to the floor.

"Daddy will be here in a few minutes," the mother continued. She glanced at the maid, who still stood in the corner. "You'll be all right with Rita until then."

The girl's eyes remained fixed on the cake with its unlit candles. The mother hesitated for another moment then kissed the top of the child's head. She motioned for the maid to follow her. They left without looking back.

"Nuke rad," Torver said, consciously using his favorite childhood expression of disgust. "If it were me, little girl, I'd want to get even."

The girl's head jerked up. She tilted it slightly to the side, as if searching for something, then looked straight at him. After a few seconds, she gave him a broad smile. He smiled back.

Then he frowned. "Stupid, she can't see you."

She slid from her chair. Carefully, a bit of her tongue sticking out between her lips, she slid the cake from the table and carefully set it on the white marble floor. She picked up her shoes and set them neatly under the chair, took off her socks and shoved them into her shoes.

She tilted her head to the side in a repeat of her earlier gesture, scowled, circled the cake, backed away to study it from a distance. The result seemed to satisfy her, and she nodded decisively. Then, bare feet together, she whooped and jumped on the dessert. Chunks of it gushed to the sides. She stomped her feet a few times then spread icing and cake over the floor with her hands. With a laugh she rolled on the mess until her dress stuck to her body. She rose, smiled at her sticky self and the shambles she'd made, then up in Torver's direction. She giggled and clapped her hands.

Torver shut down and stepped off. Immediately, he was back in his office, the girl's vidstill in his hand. He dropped it as if it had burned him, more shaken than he wanted to admit.

Impossible, he assured himself. He'd been witnessing events from twenty-five years ago. She couldn't have been aware of him. He shivered. *But she looked straight at me, and she did exactly what I would have done.*

He needed to know if what happened was simply a coincidence, or if the girl had seen him. He picked up the vidstill and prepared to re-enter her eyes. He'd replay the scene but this time keep his thoughts to himself. Surely, the child would jump on the cake all by herself.

He mulled over this idea for a moment. What if he'd influenced the events forever? How could he determine that she hadn't been conscious of his presence, and that the scene was now imprinted on her lifepath?

*Unless I find her in real time and ask her if she saw me.* That possibility sounded quite interesting. He wondered how he'd approach her.

A loud bang on his door jerked him from his thoughts.

"Dr. Lockwood, are you in there?" Barton's voice came through the thermoplastic door, sounding high and thin. Torver turned on the internal comm.

"What is it?"

"Open the door, Dr. Lockwood, unless you want me to do it."

Torver made a face. Barton probably saw it as a personal affront that someone had dared code-lock a door in his building. Torver wondered what color Barton was today.

He placed his right hand on his bionet reader's metal plaque and sent a mental pulse to the Identichip in his palm to uncode the door. The door glided open, and Dr. Barton, resentment and something like expectation plastered on his face, rushed inside.

The CEO of DyneMed wore brown-tinted hair piled high on his head and an expensive brown silk stretch-suit that matched his hair and the color of his brown-tinted irises. Although the unified color scheme was meant to make him appear taller, it made him look like a lump of mud.

Torver's boss waved, and a man and a woman followed him in. The door glided shut behind them.

"Dr. Lockwood," Barton said with a smile, "these are Mundial Genetics Revision Committee Officers."

The woman was dressed in the black-and-white MGRC uniform. She was shaped like an inverted triangle on sticks topped with a gaunt, pointed face that gave her a permanent sour look.

The man, more than two meters tall, loomed over all of them. As opposed to the uniformed woman, he appeared casually at ease. The pale gray suit he wore intensified the ebony of his skin and gave him a quiet air of authority. He moved past Barton and extended long, graceful fingers. Torver stared at them for a moment before he rose to his feet, slipped the girl's vidstill into his coat pocket and shook the man's hand.

"Audit-Inspector Jethro Alim," the man said. He motioned to the woman as he walked over to the bionet reader. "This is Officer Martin." Alim placed his hand on the reader's metal plaque; his credentials appeared on the vidscreen. Officer Martin followed suit then inserted a disc in the bionet slot. A document bearing MGRC logo appeared on the vidscreen.

"Dr. Lockwood," she said in a rough voice, "your genetics license is hereby suspended until further notice."

Torver stared at the screen then back at Officer Martin. She gestured for him to acknowledge the summons. He shook his head and retreated from her until the edge of the seat hit him behind the knees. He sank onto the chair.

Barton was grinning.

"Let me see," he said. He scanned the vidscreen. "Yes, you are suspended, Lockwood."

Torver ignored him. Jethro Alim frowned at Barton then at his colleague.

"Dr. Lockwood," he said in the soft, melodious voice that contrasted with Officer Martin's harsh one, "your suspension is effective immediately. I am sorry."

Torver turned to Barton. "You called them?"

"No." Barton chuckled. "You're fired, by the way."

"I made you a lot of money in the past eight months."

"You're a renegade, Lockwood. We don't need your kind at DyneMed."

"Dr. Barton," Alim said, "Dr. Lockwood has not been accused of anything at this point, except maybe of bad judgment. A leave of absence—"

"The decision is final." Barton whipped up the clutch of plasteene he'd kept at his side until then. "Dr. Lockwood sent this request to MGRC without my knowledge. DyneMed is a law-abiding company and does not condone the kind of research Dr. Lockwood wishes to conduct." He shuddered theatrically before he turned to Torver. "The idea of mixing plant and animal genetic material in that manner is repulsive. You should be lobotomized."

Alim cleared his throat. "We will complete this interview without you, Dr. Barton."

Barton glared at Torver for a few more seconds then nodded once. "I want you out of here in an hour," he said to Torver. He shoved the plasteene pages into the recycler and left.

Alim sighed. "My apologies."

Torver stared at the document on his vidscreen. Suspended. He'd expected a reaction from MGRC when he'd sent his request, but not one that extreme. A wave of panic flooded his brain, making his body dissolve into sweat. His thoughts raced faster than he could catch them. An acrid smell rose from his skin like a noxious vapor.

Without his license, the only kind of work he'd be able to get would be doing chemical analyses for a biotech company. That was if MGRC even let him that close to anything related to genetics. And he had no recourse. No lawyer would take him on as a client, however wrongfully MGRC had treated him.

He lifted his eyes towards Alim, who still stood in the center of the room.

"Do you really believe you can produce a living creature that can resist droughts and pollution?" Alim said, a speculative look in his eyes.

Torver saw the trap just before he was about to fall into it. "It's something I'd like to try, Inspector Alim."

Officer Martin moved to stand beside Alim. "You've gone against the system once too often, Dr. Lockwood."

"It's been forty-five years since the last bio-genetic terrorists were crushed. Haven't we earned a bit of latitude?"

Officer Martin gave him an incredulous look. "You can't be that out of touch. Haven't you been watching the news?"

"I know you've caught some group trying to replicate the old bio-genetic weapons." He shrugged. "They couldn't have the knowledge, let alone the facilities, to do much. You guys control everything."

"Even if that were true, you believe they were justified in trying it, Dr. Lockwood?" Officer Martin's voice was becoming harsher.

"I believe in finding solutions. Genetic diseases, mutations, are getting worse. Only a blind bureaucracy can continue to deny there's a problem." Torver swallowed the rest of his harangue. Martin was obviously trying to goad him into giving away incriminating evidence.

He rose from his chair and leaned against the counter. "Apart from this request, what else do you have against me?"

"Rumors, mainly," Alim said, "but it's our duty to investigate."

"I have to work."

Alim shook his head. "MGRC doesn't want any surprises. Consider this just a break in your activities. A holiday."

"I don't need a holiday. I'll go nuts if I don't have a challenge facing me."

"And therein lies the problem," Alim murmured. "Our investigation will be based on facts, Dr. Lockwood. If we find no evidence of illegal activities, we will reactivate your license." He pointed to the screen. "Your acknowledgement, please." When Torver hesitated, he continued. "It doesn't make a difference. We'll go ahead even without your assent."

Torver placed his hand on the reader and sent the mental pulse for his Identic. "If you don't mind," he said, "I have to pack and get out of here."

Alim retrieved the disc and signaled to Officer Martin. "I'll request that they give you a few minutes by yourself. We'll keep in touch."

The door swished closed on the officers' retreating backs.

Torver reached under his desk to retrieve the empty box he hadn't bothered to discard after he'd set up his office and began to put in it the few possessions he'd brought to DyneMed. The girl's vidstill jangled in his pocket when he knocked it against the desk. He retrieved the picture and stared at the serious face.

"I don't even know your name," he muttered. She only stared back.

He remembered her glee after she'd squashed the cake. That's what he needed, a release. A bit of revenge. He grinned back at her. He'd never liked Barton anyway. Time to reveal a few secrets. He moved to his comm and requested a channel.

Torver left a short time later, followed closely by the security chief who'd searched his box to make sure he didn't carry company secrets with him.

It was near the end of the afternoon, the June air hot and filled with the choking dust of unceasing pedestrian traffic. The security chief pushed him into the stream of people, and he began walking, afraid he'd be trampled if he stayed stationary. By sheer luck he'd turned in the direction of the right bus stop.

Thirty minutes later, he stood on a bus, the box with his possessions clutched against his ribs, unable to really believe he wouldn't be able to work. Genetics had been his anchor, his salvation, the world in which he had a purpose.

They wouldn't find anything, he assured himself. He'd been careful, more so since he'd lost access to the university holonets after he graduated. He'd scattered his data throughout countless protocols and banks. Alim wouldn't be able to link the research because he didn't know how it all fit together. At least, he hoped so.

"Hey, you! End of the line!"

Torver started and looked up. The driver stared at him from his rearview mirror, a frown on his face. Torver looked around and realized he'd not only overshot his stop, he'd ended up at the other end of the city in an empty bus. He'd been so lost in his thoughts and his panic he had noticed nothing.

"Are you going back downtown?"

The driver shook his head. "This baby's going to the garage. You'll have to take another bus." He tapped his vidscreen. "Next one's in forty-five minutes, unless you want to walk to the corner of Carp and Juanita. Buses run more regularly there."

"How far is it from here?"

"About half a klick."

Torver sighed. The day wasn't getting any better. The sun was going down, and he had no interest in waiting in a nearly isolated area. That meant he was walking.

"All right, thanks."

It took him another three hours and two bus changes. The sun had set an hour ago. He felt hot and filthy and pissed off.

His parents' house was dark; as usual, they hadn't thought to leave a light on for him. He fumbled to connect with the lock then made his way to the back of the house as quietly as he could. As he was about to unlock his bedroom door, he heard a shuffle behind him.

Torver turned the hall light on. His father hovered at the entrance to his room, blinking in the sudden glare.

"Some people came here to see you tonight," he said. Torver could feel the anticipation simmering in him. "MGRC officers."

"Really."

"Maybe they came to arrest you."

"Or you."

"Me?" His father paled. "What did you tell them?"

"Nothing. Relax."

His father stared at him. "As long as you live in my house—never." He turned on his heel and disappeared inside his bedroom.

Torver uncoded his door, deposited the box on his desk then recoded the lock with a new brain pulse. He thumped his head on the closed panel, thankful that no one, barring the dismantling of the house, could enter his room. If Alim and Martin searched it, they'd use the secrets contained in there to put him away forever.

He moved to the cage set on a small table. Its resident mouse sniffed the air.

Not for the first time, Torver told himself he lived in the wrong century. One hundred years ago, in the face of the incontrovertible proof in front of him, he'd have been celebrated as a genius, a miracle worker who'd achieved the impossible. Today, if it were discovered, he wouldn't survive this tiny mammal.

In all respects but one, his mouse—Family—Muridae, Species—Mus musculus—had developed normally to the adult stage. Psychomotor behavior, organs, nervous system and musculo-skeletal structure, all were standard.

Torver picked up the mouse and caressed it with a finger. Unfortunately, its singular anomaly could never go unnoticed. The mouse had moss-green fur.

It had sprouted thick and cropped and felt velvety to the touch. It smelled wet and earthy, making Torver imagine shaded streams and dappled light. Up close he could see flecks of black and yellow in it, but from afar the fur was a rich, vibrant green that could never be reproduced artificially. Still, it was fur, although it had all the characteristics of moss.

Not that he would know what moss looked like, except from a vid. What did it matter? He'd searched DyneMed's gene banks for an extinct plant genome and happened first on the moss. The genetic code had served its purpose.

Torver let the mouse run up his arm. It lodged on his shoulder and squeaked in his ear, demanding food. Torver presented a pellet. It grabbed the food with its front paws and started munching.

"What am I going to do, mouse? I don't have a job and I don't have a license. I should get rid of you. You're evidence, you know."

The mouse squeaked and shuffled around his neck to his other shoulder. Its toes and tail tickled his bare skin.

His chest tightened. "I have to work, mouse, I just have to." Fatigue washed over him.

He secured the mouse back in its cage then flopped on his bed. Before he even thought about undressing, he was asleep.

# Chapter Two

D EMETRIA SLID THE WAFER OF HER TACTILE HOLOGRAPH VIEWER OVER THE VID interface implanted under the skin of her right temple. When it connected, she swiveled the thin tungsten wire to match the eyepieces to her irises. The metal plate on her desk glowed white, and the space above it shimmered.

"Petrie project," she said.

A varicolored graph appeared above the plate. She studied the picture, dissatisfied with the presentation. The diagram summarized her entire report on the feasibility of mining Ganymede's ice crust. She'd had to support her conclusions by making the various alternatives she'd painstakingly constructed into a three-dimensional picture. She smiled to herself. Making sense of the data she'd been given might have been a daunting task if not for her talent with predictive statistics.

She still remembered that jolt when, in university, she'd realized that what she understood so clearly appeared as a chaotic jumble to most others.

Demetria considered that her affinity for numbers had been an unaccountable piece of luck in her otherwise rotten life. She'd been able to mount a profitable business. That she'd also gained a reputation as an eccentric only made her services more attractive. These days, she thought with satisfaction, clients came to her.

She picked up the left corner of the graph and rotated it down and away from her. Yes, she liked that overall view better.

"Replay graph description." She listened to the text that accompanied the image, trying to hear it with a neophyte's ear. Several times she stopped, changed a word, a phrase, an expression, until she was satisfied the Petrie LunarSat board of directors would understand the results.

She shoved the eyepieces of her tactile holograph to the side.

"Save and send, Dympna," she said, "with the usual letter."

"Very well, Demetria." The disembodied lilt of her Exalink Perceptron—or EP, as everyone thought of them—floated around her. "Shall I also indicate that you completed the work well in advance of the estimated date?"

"Sure. Don't brag, though. I want a quiet, serious tone. Their best experts attacked the problem for six months before they called me. I may not be popular in some quarters."

"Do you want to approve the letter before I send it?"

"Just go ahead. I trust you." She yawned.

"Very well. While you were working, Dr. Francis called. I told him you would call him back."

"I wonder what he wants. Maybe he just wants to tell me how the board greeted that report I prepared for him. He said his entire budget increase depended on it."

"Dr. Francis seems to appreciate your abilities."

Demetria laughed. "Vincent knows how to use talent. Why do a job if someone else can do it better and faster? I don't mind helping him once in a while."

Besides, she thought ruefully, she owed him. She was the one who'd broken off the engagement. Despite her change of heart, he'd stuck by her, ignored her protests to leave her alone. He'd weathered her depression, her anger, her grief, and when all encouragement had failed, he'd plied her with vintage wine.

"Put Vincent through, will you, Dympna?"

"I could, but he might not be pleased to hear from you at two in the morning."

Demetria looked up at the clock. "I didn't realize it was so late." She got up and stretched. The jumpy feeling she'd had all day came back. She shivered. "Is it cold in here?"

"It is exactly twenty-one-point-five degrees Celsius. You have complained of the cold often today. Are you feeling sick, Demetria?"

"Not sick. Odd. I'm too wired to sleep. I'll do some vocal scanning before I go to bed."

"Petrie has acknowledged receipt of your report. They will contact you in five days to discuss if need be."

"That was fast."

"I suppose. I am glad you are finished with them. Their EP is such a snob."

"Are you sure you don't like her because she's more advanced than you are?"

"Of course not. She may be faster and slicker, but I am older, I have more experience. When her neural net is as developed as mine, she might begin to feel superior. Right now, she is just an infant."

"With the arrogance of the young, Dympna. I remember the first year I acquired you. You knew everything."

Dympna made a sound that resembled a sniff. "I'll take care of packing the Petrie records for you."

Demetria smiled. Dympna hated to be reminded of her early days as Demetria's Perceptron. Her EP had learned very quickly but in the process had acquired a cranky personality. She didn't really know why she'd chosen to give her EP the name of the Irish patroness of the insane—it just seemed to fit.

"I'll go clean up while you do that," she said. She got up from her chair and entered the decont cubicle.

She passed her hands under the spout installed over the counter and felt the tingling that accompanied the cleansing and decontamination. She used the extension to clean her face and her hair, all that was needed since she'd already taken a whole-body decont that morning. Once the machine beeped, she took out a sealed container from the medicine cabinet, opened its lid then turned off the light.

She waited a few seconds in the dark, gathering her courage, hating the inevitable. Get on with it, she told herself. With swift, practiced movements she pressed the tiny switch embedded at the base of her left ear, which disengaged bioelectric connectors, then peeled away the skin that covered the left half of her face and neck. The feel of it, something like thin, wet paper, repulsed her. She let the prosthesis fall into the preserving solution and sealed the cover. She sagged a little against the counter, relieved the procedure was over, already dreading the reverse process she'd have to go through in the morning.

Demetria raised her head and saw the darker outline of her body in the mirror. She longed to look at her face the way it used to be, the way she remembered it. How could she have known the appearance of one small sore on her cheek would devastate her life so thoroughly?

She'd gone to her doctor, mildly worried that the small patch of cancer would leave a scar. What a joke. By the time she'd received the diagnosis, the lesion had grown to the size of a mini-disc. "Brett's dermophagia," they'd whispered around her, like a curse.

She thought about her mother, who needed everything so perfect, so pristine. When Demetria had told her the genetic mutation had been caused by ingestion of toxic engineered food while she was pregnant, Carlotta had stared at her daughter in horror and left. They hadn't spoken since, which had been a relief for Demetria. She'd had enough to cope with. She didn't need her mother around as a reminder that, once again, as a daughter she'd failed some unwritten test.

Week after week, she watched the skin of her face rot away, leaving muscles and tendons exposed. The disease also produced a plasma-like film that covered the denuded area; it didn't run but glistened in the light like a pane of glass. It prevented her muscles and tendons from drying out but it also gave her the look of a damaged automaton.

The pitying looks, furtive stares, whispers and insults had sickened her. She'd had enough of gawkers to last her a lifetime. Better to avoid public situations.

She stared at her outline. The earnest face of her doctor superimposed hers in the dark mirror. She saw him tell her she was lucky because, with the slow progress of the disease, her nerve endings would adjust and she would live pain-free. And in her case, he'd added, her genetic abnormality was mild enough it would affect only one side of her face and neck. A prosthesis would hide most of the damage.

Demetria rubbed the top of the sealed container. *Most* had been the operative word. They hadn't been able to match her skin tone exactly, so the fake side, a shade darker than her own pale skin, stood out. Then there was the seam that ran along the middle of her face, like a rift zone. When she'd looked at herself she'd seen two people, neither someone she recognized.

It was ironic, she thought, that even though she hated it she felt whole only when she wore the prosthesis. All she had to do was avoid looking at herself in a mirror.

Putting the skin on was always harder on her nerves. She hated the slightly uncomfortable sensation, a feeling between a slight electrical charge and bugs crawling under the skin as the bioelectric connectors matched the receptors installed inside the muscles. Five years ago, preoccupied with a complex work problem, she'd rushed through the motions then turned on the light. The skin, badly anchored, had fallen off. For an endless moment she'd been faced with her own ugliness.

No, she decided, it was more than ugliness. It was an insult to harmony, a gothic step into the horrible, a cleaving of yin and yang. She'd recoiled. Then, with morbid fascination, she'd examined every inch of the marred tendons and bone, the rictus that uncovered her teeth on that side of her face when she smiled, the muscles that tied the orb of her eye to her skull. She shuddered. That was the first and last time she'd seen her face uncovered.

What had kept her sane—apart from Dympna and Vincent—what had helped her reshape a life for herself, was her vocal scanning. With these unwanted memories invading her mind, she needed it more than ever.

She turned away and walked to her bedroom. While she undressed and slipped into a silk caftan, she hummed quietly, a low continuous note that drowned her thoughts.

"Sound-proofing, Dympna."

Her humming took on a muted, internal quality. She sat cross-legged on the floor and began her light toning, the usual low *aaah* that focused her mind. Once it settled, she began modulating her voice, sliding from low tones to high. Her breathing deepened and lengthened, her range increased. Her body began to feel light, as if the Earth's gravity had lessened.

Then part of her, what she thought of as her consciousness, shifted outward and sideways and found itself in a gray no-man's-land, neither dark nor light. She knew that if she twisted around she would see a filament floating from her body into the void. If she tugged on it, it would bring her back to her physical self. She waited in that place until she saw the door that would open and let her cross into a different world.

This time an old-fashioned door appeared, one with a handle instead of a wall plate. She approached it. Her eyes were level with the handle. She raised her hand and saw it had the pudginess of baby fat. She followed the hand to the rest of her body; it was dressed in a pink-and-white dress with the hated white shoes and pink socks. She was a child of five again.

Demetria pulled open the door and walked in, unsurprised to find herself in her mother's living room. The familiar silence—allowed to be broken only by her mother's music—surrounded her. She moved further into the room. The polished surface of the white Steinway grand flashed with the sun that poured through the windows. A summery breeze caressed her cheeks and stole through her hair. Demetria frowned. Her mother never took the filters off the windows, even on a rainy day, and certainly never let in the outside air.

Something twinkled in the sun in the corner near the piano, something that had not been there when she grew up. She approached it. It looked like a twisted ladder, its styles red and its rungs a combination of blue, yellow, orange and purple. Its slow spin filled her with dread despite its colorful appearance.

She heard a noise behind her and whipped around. A boy, no older than she was, sat on her mother's couch, his bare knees up to his chest, his dirty shoes on the white linen. She walked over to him.

They stared at each other in silence. The boy's hair was as dark as hers, but the resemblance stopped there. His eyes, a deep Prussian blue that reminded her of a fifteenth-century painting, stared at her over bent legs that ended in shoes seemingly too large for his body.

She disliked him immediately, more for the way his eyes made her feel—electrified, squirrelly inside—than for the obvious arrogance of his sitting position.

Then he squinted, and even from where she stood, she saw his pupils contract. She squirmed, feeling invaded, unable to break his gaze. That made her angry, and she glared back, mentally pushing him away. He jerked his head to the side, his cheeks flushed. When he turned his face back to her, there was a surprised look in his eyes.

Demetria planted her fists on her hips, feet solid on the ground in challenge. His eyes were laughing now, and a smile tugged at his mouth. All at once she wanted to laugh, too, as if the whole silent exchange had been a game, and she'd won.

"You're not s'posed to put your feet on the sofa," she said instead. He didn't move. "Did you hear me? My mother will be angry. She'll tell the butler to kick you out."

"I'm only doing what you've always wanted to do," he answered. "Try it."

She shook her head. "Who are you?"

"I know you." He rose and stepped from one sofa to the other, marking each cushion with a muddy footprint. She wanted to tell him to stop but every mark, so clear against the white, fascinated her. He stopped on the last cushion and turned to her. He pointed beyond the piano. "Did you see the double helix?"

"What is it?"

"The first true representation of the human race. Its past, present and future."

"You talk funny."

He didn't answer but continued to point at the colored ladder. It spun faster. The walls on each side of it lost definition, as if they'd begun to melt. The helix spun even faster, and as it did, the space close to it contracted and puckered, moving into the spin like cotton candy around a stick. Demetria felt herself pulled forward.

"It's sucking us up. Stop it!"

The rungs of the ladder split in the center and some of the broken rungs changed color.

"Oh," the boy said. "It doesn't work very well. Are you going to help me fix it?" He laughed. The sound reverberated off the walls.

Demetria strained against the pull. The boy seemed unaffected. He stood on the end of the white sofa, his cobalt eyes full of mischief.

Suddenly, she was in her adult body. She grabbed the edge of a heavy metal coffee table, but it began to slide towards the spinning helix. She remembered the door through which she'd come. All she had to do was go out the same way. Where was it?

Her gaze skittered across the twisted walls until she spotted it, farther away than before. She pulled against furniture, inching her way to the door. It kept backing away, and she barely had any purchase on the floor. She heard a loud crunch and glanced over her shoulder. One of the sofas was halfway inside the helix.

She strained forward, stretched her arm as far as she could. The air whistled in her ears. She felt a tug and stumbled; the edge of the carpet had caught in the helix. She scrabbled at the rug until she could stand on the marble floor. The stone began to crack around her white shoes.

She pushed off the floor and reached behind her. She got a firm hold of the filament in her back.

"Come on," she yelled to the boy. "Come with me." She turned, but he was gone. She tugged and was wrenched through the door.

Demetria slumped to the floor. A nice, unmoving floor. She was back in her bedroom.

"Demetria," Dympna said, "are you okay? My monitors went crazy. What happened?"

She pushed herself up. Her ears still rang with the whistle of the wind and the boy's laughter. Her hand ached, and she raised it to her eyes. The corner of the coffee table was imprinted in her palm.

"I don't know, Dympna. Something went wrong with the scanning." She shivered, thinking of the boy with the blue eyes. Had he been crushed by the helix?

"Your heart rate was erratic and your blood pressure elevated," Dympna said. "Another thirty seconds and I would have brought you out."

Demetria bit her lip. "I'm not sure you'd have been able to. This vision was different, as if..." She shook her head, got up and left her bedroom. She'd been about to say as if the vision had originated outside of her.

Slowly, she crossed through her living room to the kitchen. She took a bottle of white wine from a cold cupboard. Never had she felt so shaken after a scanning session, even at the beginning when she'd had to deal with visions of her own death. During her directed sessions at the Assembly of Sound, she'd been able to reach another plane, to focus her energy. That control had helped her gain a handle on how to deal with her disease. When she returned from there, she felt at peace for a while. She'd been able to continue the same routine on her own, with the same success. Until now.

She opened the wine and poured a glass. It was halfway to her mouth when she remembered she'd taken off her prosthesis. It was impossible to drink without it. She stared at the golden liquid, wishing she could drown in it. She poured the wine out, stashed the glass in the recycler then wandered to her office to stare at her desk. Maybe, she thought, working at night wasn't such a good idea.

"Dympna, why don't you print me the provenance for that dresser I'm thinking of buying? If everything's in order we can confirm delivery." A single sheet of multicycled paper slid out of a slot in her desk. "That's it?"

She picked it up and scanned it. In the middle of the page, a name jumped out at her.

"Are you sure this information is correct?"

"Of course. Unless the dealer's bionet made a mistake, which I doubt. I could ask."

"Don't bother." There had been only three owners for that dresser. The last one had been Vincent Francis, her ex-fiance.

She read the provenance again, unable to believe Vincent had disposed of the dresser. Why had he not offered it to her? He knew her passion for antiques.

"Contact Mr. Putnam in the morning, Dympna. Tell him I want the dresser delivered as quickly as possible."

"Very well, Demetria. There are still a few hours before he is open for business, you know."

"If that's your way of telling me I should go to bed, I agree." She rolled her shoulders. "If I can't drink, I might as well sleep."

It took her forever to fall asleep. Every time she closed her eyes, the face of a blue-eyed boy hovered at the edge of a nightmare.

# Chapter Three

"So, Dad, what do you think?"

Laslo Radic smiled at his son, whose face floated above the comm plate. "I don't know, Zel. A whole gang of you loose in my factory—it sounds pretty dangerous for us."

"Aw, come on, Dad, say yes. This would be my best show-and-tell yet."

"You're eleven. You're too old for show-and-tell."

"You know what I mean."

"Sure. You'll bring your class here and let my staff do your homework for you."

Zelimir grinned. "At least I thought of it all by myself."

His son's beaming face reminded Laslo of the first time Zel had ensnared him with that smile. It had been an ordinary morning like any other, a few months after Zelimir was born. He'd come into the baby's room to say goodbye to Jelena, his mind already at the firm, when he glanced into the crib. The baby gurgled and squealed. There was his son, arms and feet jerking up and down, a broad smile on his face and recognition in his eyes. Laslo had picked him up, inhaled the baby smell, nuzzled the delicate skin of his neck, caressed the gold fuzz on his head.

My son, he'd thought, and his gut twisted.

"Dad?"

"I'll think about it."

"But, Dad..."

"I said I'll think about it."

Zelimir made a face. "I was sure you'd say yes."

"Does that mean you've committed me already?"

"Well..."

"Zel." His son's sheepish face didn't fool Laslo. "Fine. But you'll give me a report of everything you've learned during the tour." He raised his hand when he saw him about to protest. "Take it or leave it, Zelimir. You can't have everyone do your work for you."

"You do."

Laslo chuckled. "That's not quite how it works, son. Talk to Satah to set up your visit. He'll arrange everything for you."

"Thanks, Dad. Will you be here for dinner?"

"I doubt it. Let your mother know, will you?"

Zelimir nodded. "Love you, Dad."

Before Laslo could answer, Zelimir had turned off the comm. Laslo pushed away from his desk and leaned into his chair. For a minute there he'd forgotten. He'd laughed as if nothing were wrong with Zel. At least his son didn't know. He deserved a normal childhood, like any other kid, even if his chances of reaching adulthood were slim.

Not if I have something to say about it, Laslo vowed.

His eyes burned, and he blinked quickly. He didn't know how long he could go on faking it, acting as if everything was fine. Because it wasn't.

A year of research had yielded nothing. Time was flowing away, each minute irretrievable and useless. He wanted to throw something, vent his anger; but he gripped the arms of his chair instead. His heart beat so fast he thought it would bore a hole through his chest. *Focus on the moment.* If he gave in to his fear, he'd start to feed on it and never stop, and he'd end up crazier than a Star user. Although, he brooded, the white junk might give him some relief from obsessing about his son.

Sooner or later, he'd get a handle on the problem. The problem. Even at the best of times, it took everything he had to let the name of that problem enter his brain.

"Barcina's xylopoiesis," he said aloud. The words came out as a croak. They seemed to bounce around the room and repeat themselves endlessly. Once again, so as to never lose sight of his goal, he forced himself to review the problem. Maybe he'd come up with an idea on how to fix it.

Barcina's xylopoiesis. An extremely rare disease, so rare that very little research had been done on it. Giulio Barcina had identified it and given it the name that was partly his and partly a description of the disease itself. Even though Laslo's firm researched and fabricated drug therapies for genetic defects, he'd never heard of Barcina's until he'd found out more than two years ago, entirely by accident, that Zelimir would die from it.

Barcina's xylopoiesis. The disease was dormant in his son's body, ready to burst inside him, waiting for the right trigger. Laslo knew the symptoms by heart. First, incoordination of voluntary movements and aphasia—the loss of the ability to articulate ideas or comprehend spoken language. Then, gangrene and blindness.

He rubbed his eyes. Zelimir's nerve endings would begin to die, starting with the toes. Their muscle cells would transform into wooden tissue then rot, forcing the surgeons to amputate. The mutation would creep up to the torso, where it would attack the major organs, shutting them down as it invaded.

To extend Zel's life expectancy, surgeons would excise the rotting parts, piece by piece, until all that was left of him was a trunk with a head. Death would come soon after, the pain excruciating, his son blind, unable to express what he felt.

Laslo shuddered with a loathing partly directed at himself. He and Jelena had given the grisly genetic disease to their son. He wasn't supposed to know it, of course, but how could he have acted differently? After his cousin called, saying his own children were affected, Laslo had had his family's DNA secretly tested. The chances that Zel would have Barcina's had been astronomical; Laslo was stunned when he saw the analysis results. He didn't know what was worse—that his son had the disease or that he would have been diagnosed too late, simply because of MGRC's genetic privacy laws.

Every day, he went home and searched for the telltale signs. If his son tripped, or if he forgot a word, Laslo's fear crept up his spine until it was almost unbearable. He found himself stalking Zel, following him around the house, outside with his friends, back and forth from school.

He'd have to tell Jelena eventually. Sometimes he caught her staring at him with a puzzled expression on her face. She knew him too well. He worried her, but she didn't ask what bothered him, as though she sensed she'd hate the answer.

A soft chime warned him someone waited outside his office. He got up, rolled his shoulders and stretched his neck then sat back down. "Come in."

The door panel glided open. Gerry Sinclair stood in the entrance for a second then stepped into the room. The door closed silently behind him.

Gerry cleared his throat. "You've seen the results."

"Yes, I damn well saw the results." Laslo leaned his forearms on his desk. He pointed to a chair across from it. "Sit down, Gerry."

Gerry moved from his spot near the door and folded his lank frame into the seat.

Laslo leaned back in his chair and studied his chief scientist without speaking. As President and CEO of GeneTech, Laslo could say he had a handle on pretty much everything that was going on in his firm, except for detailed research matters. He'd left that responsibility to Gerry, who had the scientific knowledge to troubleshoot most problems. He was also known for having occasional touches of brilliance, and a certain *flexibility* with matters that fell slightly outside the law.

This arrangement had worked perfectly for years, but now Gerry had given up on finding a cure for Barcina's, and Laslo needed to understand why.

He already knew a few things. For one, he had given Gerry only five genetic samples to work with, and that made the process more difficult. Then, the literature on the disease was scarce. They were dealing with a polygenic recessive illness—the disease involved more than one gene. If two people carried the genetic elements of the disease, and those elements mixed in the proper combination, the offspring—offspring, hell, his son—developed the disease. If he'd married someone else, the defect in Zelimir would have been dormant, or not present at all in his genetic makeup.

Gerry rubbed his bald pate and pulled at an earlobe. "There's nothing else I can do, Laslo. Believe me."

"What's blocking you?"

"I can't pinpoint the exact biological pathways of the disease, or all of the ways the genetic defect can express itself. The problem is linked to dystrophin, a protein that plays a key role in muscle cells. For some reason, whatever dystrophin is produced by the faulty genes suddenly doesn't work well with other proteins in the muscles. I've confirmed two of the primary genes that influence the disease, but there could be up to twenty more, either on one primary gene or the other or on both, especially since it affects organs as well as muscles.

"I can also find an influence on another part of the chromosome that normally would prevent the development of the disease. I've tried a series of drug combinations to correct the defects in the two main genes, but as soon as I touch them, other problems spring up. Accelerated decrepitude. Cell necrosis. Overproduction of proteins. You name it, you have it."

"So, what's our next step?"

"You want my advice?"

"Not particularly."

"Drop the research. It's a lost cause. As awful as this disease is, the number of people who are affected by it is negligible, and even if I could find the cure, what could you do with it? You'd have to apply to MGRC for a research permit after the fact, and I guarantee they'd refuse you because you wouldn't be able to tell them you already have the solution."

Laslo pursed his lips. In different circumstances, he would have agreed with everything Gerry said. He couldn't fault his chief scientist for wanting to direct his energies elsewhere.

"I'm not prepared to stop the research at this point. What do we need?"

Gerry sighed and shook his head. "A different strategy, that's for sure. Drug therapy won't work. Geneng is what you want to do, and for that you need a molecular biologist. You'd need to have access to several kindred families with complete pedigrees, as far back as you could get them, starting from the latest identified case of Barcina's. That means getting permission from MGRC to access their genebanks. Once you have that access, you'd want to find an analyst who can map out the kindred's genetic combinations down the line, hundreds of thousands of combinations with only a few that will give a clue to the development of the disease. Lastly, and most importantly, you'd need a researcher who can sort out the connections between the genetic variations and then devise a way to repair the genetic defect without affecting the rest of the genes."

Laslo grunted and leaned back in his chair. "That's it?"

Gerry raised his eyebrows. "I thought that would be enough to discourage anybody."

"I don't give up easily."

"We're already up to our ears in illegal activities just by using the five DNA samples you gave me. You don't want to attract MGRC's attention by requesting access to the genebanks. They might want to come for a visit."

"You let me worry about the Mungers."

"I don't mind a certain amount of risk, Laslo, but I like my freedom. We could spend the rest of our lives in prison for this."

"When you're prevented from finding a cure to a deadly disease, I say genetic privacy has become an aberration. The MGRC policy is wrong."

"Jesus, is that what it's all about? A matter of principle?"

Laslo thought about Zelimir. "Don't worry, Gerry. I'd get you the best lawyer."

Gerry rose. "You're going to break into the genebanks, aren't you."

"It's not your problem. You said yourself you've done all you could."

"Say you find a way to tap into the genebanks without MGRC's knowledge and you get enough material to find a link. Where are you going to find someone who can manipulate that much info and make sense of it? I don't know any biometrician who could do it."

Laslo pondered that problem for a moment, then remembered the budget-forecast report he'd received from the Greater Ottawa Metropolis Health Center the day before. He'd thought at the time that its author must have had help—brilliant help—to come up with predictive numbers like those he was using to draw his conclusions.

"Maybe genetics training isn't necessary. What I need is someone who can handle statistics, right? I'll look into it. Now, about that scientist I need..."

Gerry glanced out the window then back at him. "I might be able to help you with that."

"You have someone in mind?"

"Did you hear about Barton at DyneMed?"

"No."

"The MGRC arrested him today. His company produces genetically enhanced mice for drug therapy research. It seems he's been copying more than defective DNA segments. He's been replicating entire DNA maps and selling them on the black market."

"What are the maps used for?"

Gerry shrugged. "People will pay a lot of money to have a defective gene replaced by a healthy one. With all the environmental mutations cropping up, the black market is flourishing."

"So, why are you telling me about Barton?"

"Just before the uproar at DyneMed, Dr. Torver Lockwood, a molecular biologist working there, had his license suspended. Barton fired him, claiming the man was a degenerate. Shortly after, MGRC received a detailed account of Barton's activities. Barton is screaming that Lockwood set him up."

Laslo raised an eyebrow. "A degenerate?"

"Apparently, Dr. Lockwood sent a request to MGRC to mix plant with mouse DNA to make a fallout-resistant animal. That's what got him suspended. He's your man, Laslo."

Laslo waited until the door closed then got up from his chair to stand at the tinted window. He watched a biobot work the earth in the tiny patch of garden that was his pride and joy, the symbol of his success. The flowers, their splash of yellow a surprise amid the metal and concrete complex, flourished around a sculpture that imitated a flowing fountain.

He'd made a good decision when he'd decided to build GeneTech around pharmacogenomics. Genetic engineering was a fact of life today. Who ever stopped to think that food, energy or information wouldn't exist without genetic engineering? He didn't care that without geneng the changing weather patterns, the increase in pollution, the depletion of water and energy sources would be uncontrollable and mean the death of millions. The technology had become cheap as dirt, and those who'd invested during the boom now struggled to make ends meet. Therapeutic drugs were a different matter. The need was often desperate, the development custom-made, the product always expensive.

What bitter irony that, with all his wealth and technology at his disposal, he couldn't save his son.

He'd tried to limit his illegal activities to the use of his close family's genes, something he hadn't bothered to tell Gerry. If he decided to tap into the genebanks and enter the netherworld of genetic manipulation, it would be through a one-way door.

Zelimir's face shimmered on the glass of the window. What choice did he have?

Access to the genebanks would be easy—he'd kept a few rogue channels open from his younger days. His old friend would provide him with what he needed.

He didn't know why he was so reluctant to explain himself to Jelena, Gerry or anyone else. He had the uneasy feeling, although he admonished himself it was totally irrational, that by telling others about his son—his beautiful, happy Zelimir—he would trigger the disease.

Maybe his grandfather's Old World superstitions had rubbed off on him. Or maybe he just sensed that Zelimir's time was running out.

## Chapter Four

DEMETRIA WOKE UP EXHAUSTED, THE PREVIOUS NIGHT'S SESSION VIVID IN HER MIND. She dragged herself out of bed, put on her prosthesis and took a full decont, then downed two cups of what now passed for coffee, adding extra stim. Once done, she felt less tired but skittish inside, as if the sucking winds of the vortex threatened to pull her back into her vision.

What she needed, she thought, was a friendly voice. She checked the time then picked up the telephone and placed a comm to Vincent at his house.

"Hello," he said, his voice hoarse with sleep. She heard a few rapid taps then, "Demi?"

She laughed. "Good morning. Did I wake you?"

"I knew it was you when I couldn't get a face on the comm. What time is it?"

"Nine-thirty. I thought you'd be on your way to the center, by now."

"I worked late last night."

"Something serious?"

"I think so." He yawned. "What's up?"

"I just wanted to know how we did."

"Did? Oh, the report. Sorry, I meant to call you, then I got sidetracked in the lab. Then when I remembered to call, you were in the zone. We got the fourteen billion."

"Congratulations."

"I couldn't have done it without you. Listen, have you had breakfast, yet?"

"No."

"I'll be there in half an hour."

"Sure." She remembered what she'd wanted to ask him last night. "Before you go, I bought a dresser from Putnam's Antiques yesterday. Guess who it belonged to before."

Victor was silent a few seconds. "I'll never understand your fascination for old junk," he said, his voice belligerent.

"It's because you live surrounded by it. You don't even notice it anymore."

"Yeah. See you in a while."

Demetria hung up. She wondered why Vincent had sounded so aggressive when she'd talked about the dresser. He knew she coveted that nineteenth-century house of his. Each piece of furniture, every molding and knob had an undefinable energy. Her own collection was paltry compared to the treasures in Vincent's house.

She meandered through her living room, glancing at the twentieth-century Canadian paintings covering her walls, peering into the two glass cases that contained her precious bric-a-brac. Her fingers skimmed the ancient furniture, its glossy wood cool and soft like satin on her skin. She stroked the padded chintz of a wingback chair, picked up a velvet cushion and hugged it against her stomach.

She thought about her mother's house. Growing up there, the unrelenting white had sapped her will; she'd escaped as soon as she could. Demetria glanced around her. *You won't find a speck of white in this place, Mother.* She looked down at her black shirt and pants and smiled.

VINCENT SCRATCHED HIS HEAD AND YAWNED AGAIN. GOD, HE WAS TIRED. FRUSTRATED, TOO. Maybe talking with Demi would clear his mind. Every time he used her as a sounding board, he ended up with a clearer understanding of his problem.

He got out of bed, worried about the dresser she'd bought. If she only knew, he thought. He was profoundly relieved that Demetria refused to use a vidcom. That way, she couldn't see what he'd done with the house she loved so much.

He wasn't lying to her, he assured himself. He only omitted to tell her that not only had he sold the dresser to Putnam but he had emptied the entire mausoleum in which he'd grown up, then had it demolished. He'd built the home of his dreams on the same spot.

He looked about his new house with a sense of overflowing pride. The avant-garde architecture, the ultramodern furniture, the post-contemporary art gave him unending pleasure. Demetria would hate it.

He remembered her reaction at seeing the old house. She'd been mesmerized, enthralled. She and his father had become great friends, sharing their passion for the past. There had never been a good time to tell her,

Vincent reasoned. When he'd made the decision to tear down the house, Demi had been going through hell trying to cope with the middle phase of her dermophagia. It hadn't seemed right to talk about his plans. Then she'd broken off the engagement, and why would he tell her at that point? He still didn't have to. Okay, maybe he'd have to explain about the dresser, but the less said the better.

DEMETRIA OPENED THE DOOR TO A SMILING VINCENT. HE HANDED HER A COOLING BAG.

"Got a surprise in there as well as the bubbly," he said.

She dug into the bag and brought out the champagne, then a sealed jar. "Lox? Where did you get smoked salmon?"

"I hope you have cream cheese and capers."

"I have the cheese anyhow. What about the salmon? You can't afford it, even on your salary."

Vincent took his time popping open the bottle and pouring the golden liquid into the flutes she had set on the dining room table, all the time grinning broadly.

"My team helped deconstruct the latest whitestar conformation. This guy, who owns a hatchery, was so grateful to be able to clean out his son he gave everybody some salmon." He presented her with a glass. "To fourteen billion."

She smiled. Vincent's grin always put her in a good mood. "Cheers."

They clinked glasses and sipped.

"Thanks for your help with that report," Vincent said. "Now I'll be able to buy more equipment and get my people some advanced training." She saw him hesitate. "By the way, the day after I did my presentation, one of the board members asked me who had helped me with the data. I gave him your name. He said he needed a good analyst." He took another sip. "I'm not sure you'll want to work for him, but all you have to do is say no, right?"

"I can always use another client. Who is it?"

"Laslo Radic. He's the CEO of GeneTech."

Demetria's good mood evaporated. "You know I don't contract out to genetic engineering firms."

"Come on, Demi. The guy just voted in favor of my budget increase, even made a little speech in support of it. What was I going to do? Besides, you're a big girl. You can turn him down yourself."

She frowned at him for a second then decided he was right. She shook her head. "It's a good thing you brought champagne."

"Don't forget the salmon."

She chuckled. "Let's have breakfast."

She brought out the cheese and bread and gestured to the chair facing hers at the table. For a while all she did was savor the rich taste of cream and smoke and fish and grape. With the silence, she finally noticed that Vincent's features were drawn with fatigue.

"You said you had a late night?"

"I did. While I was with the board, we received two DOAs. They were kids, Demi. Fourteen and twelve. I performed the autopsies."

"Aren't you concentrating on tracking down new developments in street drugs?"

"I am. Both kids had their gray matter fried on brain dust."

"I thought brain dust wasn't even addictive, let alone lethal. It's the drug of choice, ever since it came out."

"You're right. Brain dust isn't addictive. You can't overdose on it. It's the safest drug on the market. That doesn't mean it doesn't kill."

"What do you mean?"

"Dustheads either do something foolish while under the influence or they commit suicide when they realize the dust has changed them so much they don't even recognize themselves. I'm not only talking about the physical changes—the gauntness, the red irises, the black tongue—but the personality changes, too, which are totally unpredictable. These deaths are different, though."

"In what way?"

"It's the dust that killed them."

"But—"

"I know what I've said. We've had ten such deaths in the last month."

"So, what's different?"

"I don't know. That's what I was trying to find out yesterday."

"I take it you haven't had any luck."

"No. I went back a year, studied the results of the autopsies for all of our dust cases. The drug chemistry began to change radically only in the past two months." His eyes glazed over. "That's what strange, Demi. The drug doesn't work. It kills. If you're a drug dealer, you don't want to kill your users. Plus, it makes the police very nervous when kids start to die off. When you think of it, there's only one thing that makes sense. They've been experimenting, and they're using dustheads to test the changes."

"Maybe you're looking in the wrong place."

He focused back on her. "I can only work with what I have."

Demetria shook her head. She stood up, picked up their plates and headed for the kitchen. "I mean, maybe it's not the chemistry that's changed," she called out. "Maybe they added something, something you're overlooking because you don't expect it to be there."

He didn't answer. She deposited the plates on the counter and retraced her steps. He sat there, a stunned look on his face.

"Vincent?"

He turned his head slowly towards her. "Something I overlooked. Of course." He jumped from the chair, foregoing his usual complaint about how uncomfortable it was, grabbed her shoulders and soundly kissed her on the mouth. "I knew if I talked to you I'd get a new perspective. Thanks, Demi, got to go."

Before she could say anything, he was gone. Demetria shook her head in bemusement then burst out laughing.

It was past seven when Laslo arrived home; he let himself in. No one came to greet him at the door, but he hadn't expected it, and particularly not Jelena. In their fifteen years of marriage, she'd given up on having a normal household.

He could hear Zelimir in the kitchen, saying something in his still-childish voice. Jelena answered, and he could hear the teasing in her tone. He stayed in the hall for a moment, listening to the laughter, wondering if he should join them. He knew that if he did the joy would transform into a polite reserve from Jelena and a shy anticipation from Zel.

He walked into the living room.

His house filled him with as much pride as his GeneTech garden. He loved the white marble of the foyer, the top-quality acrylic flooring, the expensive art and furniture. He'd wanted to laugh when he'd seen the size of the Cluny holo in Dr. Francis's office—*his* Cluny covered almost an entire wall.

He was also proud of the curving stainless steel staircase, a metal almost impossible to find nowadays. He'd even had lighting installed that imitated sunlight so the metal would glisten like a mirror.

He directed his steps towards the crystal decanter that held his twenty-year-old scotch. He heard a rustle behind him before he'd reached the carafe.

"Dad?"

Laslo turned. "Zel. How was school today?"

"Okay. We already had dinner."

"Don't worry about it." He poured a good measure of scotch then sat on the couch. He studied Zel's movements as the boy came to sit beside him. No awkward or jerky gestures. Good. He felt himself relax.

"Are you all set for the visit to the factory?"

"Yes. The whole class is going."

Silence, the peaty smell of scotch and the feeling of heat on his hand from Zel's skin as he sat close to him, warmed his insides. Laslo smiled and leaned his head on the back of the couch.

"Dad?"

He rolled his head towards his son. "I take it you have something else to ask me."

"Friday is the end of classes."

"Already?"

"Yes." Zelimir made an impatient gesture, as if he were irritated at having to explain everything. "You know Graeme Dillon? He's my best friend."

"I thought someone called Jonathan was your best friend."

"That was last year. His parents moved away, don't you remember? Well, anyway, next week Graeme is going to this really neat summer camp. Can I go, too?"

"I don't see why not. What—"

Zel let out a whoop and stood up. "Thanks, Dad. This is great. I'll go tell Mom."

"Zel." His son stilled. "What kind of camp is it?"

"You know, summer camp. Camping."

Zel inched away from his father towards the door.

"I thought it was a science camp at school or some such."

"It's on Manitoulin Island. There's a firepit, and tents, and we can swim in the lake and fish and everything, Dad."

"Out of the question."

"But, Dad, I've never even seen water in a lake. It's just for a week. You won't even notice I'm gone."

Laslo felt suddenly angry. "Zelimir, I said no. You're not leaving this house overnight, and that's it."

"But why?" Zel wailed.

Laslo stared at the anguished face of his son. For a moment, he was tempted to tell the child the real reason. What if the disease manifested itself while he was away? What if his father was not there to take care of him? Apart from "You're going to die and I want to make sure I'm with you when you do," what reason could he give? "You're only eleven. You're too young for camp."

"Graeme is eleven, and his parents are letting him go."

"I don't care what Graeme's parents permit him to do. You're my son, and you'll do what I say."

Zel straightened and took a deep breath. "There will come a time, Father, when I won't have to do what you say. Even if I am your son."

Speechless, Laslo watched him leave, stunned by the parting comment. He'd expected a tantrum, or at least endless pleading. Instead, Zel had bowed to the unjustified decision. When had his son acquired this maturity? It scared him. In Zelimir's eyes, Laslo had seen the realization that, one day, he'd have the power to ignore his father.

"He's becoming his own person, Laslo," Jelena said from the doorway. "He needs breathing space." She entered the living room. "In less than six years, he will gain his majority. Don't let him feel he's gained his freedom."

Laslo clenched his glass between both hands. "I don't want to talk about it."

"You're getting more protective as he's getting older. Shouldn't it be the opposite? You need to let go, Laslo."

He stared into the depths of the golden liquid. "I told you, I don't want to talk about it."

"Fine." She sighed. "I'm going to clean up in the kitchen. I've got dinner there for you if you want."

He heard her leave but didn't lift his head. He was too absorbed in the problem of his son. He had no idea when the disease would be triggered. It could be tomorrow or four years from now. He was banking on the hope that Zel had a few years to go yet.

He wondered what fate would be worse—seeing his son die slowly or seeing his son's love change into hate.

# Chapter Five

"Jenny," Torver said above the noise of the restaurant, "let's pick up dessert at that little shop in the Market. What's it called?"

"Sweet Revenge."

"That's it. You can choose something decadent." He grinned. "We could eat it at your place."

"I don't think so."

His gaze fell to her mouth. He recalled all the things she could do with that mouth, the least of them eating dessert. The way her lips parted slightly when she listened to him was enough to give him a hard-on. When her tongue darted out to lick the corner of her mouth and she smoothed her lower lip with her ring finger, her eyes briefly glazing over, it made him swallow and be grateful he'd chosen a restaurant with long tablecloths.

He thought of the dozen men she'd slept with, or at least the dozen of them he'd seen when he'd walked her lifepath. From his point of view, Jenny hopped into bed at the drop of a hat. He hoped he was next in line.

"Why not?"

She leaned towards him, her voice low and intense. "I don't bring men I barely know back to my place on the first date."

"That never stopped you before," he said. He saw the shock in her eyes and cursed himself for letting his lower body do the talking.

She straightened. "What?"

"Come on, Jenny. I'm attracted to you, and I thought you felt the same way. So why not act on it?"

"That's not the point, is it? Is that why you went out with me? You thought you'd have a good chance of getting laid?"

"Forget I said anything."

She threw up her hands. "You don't even deny it."

She pushed away from the table. Before she could get up, Torver stretched across and grabbed her wrist. She looked at his hand in surprise.

"Let go of me."

He squeezed a little harder and pulled her to him.

"What about you, Jenny? Who was it that said, 'He kinda gives me the creeps but do you know how much geneticists make these days'?"

She paled and tugged at her wrist. "I never said that."

Torver tugged back. "Sure you did. Last Friday, before you strutted into my office on a flimsy pretext. Everything has a price, Jenny." He yanked her closer. "Of course, that was before I was fired. But what the hell, at least you got a free meal out of it. Isn't that what you said?"

Jenny wrenched her arm from his grasp and shot to her feet.

"Well," she said, her face flushed crimson, "I was right in the first place, wasn't I? You are a creep. You know what you can do with dessert." She turned on her heel and stormed through the door of the restaurant.

Torver closed his eyes and pinched the bridge of his nose. A waiter rushed to his side, fussed over the table—removing Jenny's place setting, mumbling about the water left in her glass. Torver ordered a double brandy and brooded about his situation.

Not the best finessed situation—he never knew when to keep his mouth shut. He knew he held an unfair advantage over the people he met; in the blink of an eye, he could learn more about them than their own mothers or partners knew. Walking along people's lifepaths had become something he did without even thinking, and lately his knee-jerk reactions had landed him in more trouble than he liked.

It also meant he'd spend another night alone. He looked around him at the other patrons, who seemed to have already forgotten Jenny's outburst. In a corner near the window, a man and a boy of maybe five sat across the table from a woman. The boy said something and laughed, his head thrown back. Both parents smiled then chuckled.

A family. Torver swallowed brandy along with his bitterness. He couldn't remember ever laughing like that with his parents. The few childhood stills his father had taken had long been stashed away somewhere or erased. He vaguely recalled a vid of himself at one and a half in which, with a look of concentration on his face, he was reciting a long poem in front of a small audience. Another one, when he was three years old, showed him bent over a chessboard. He couldn't think of any stills where he simply played, or laughed, like that little boy in the corner.

At five years old, he began to notice people staring at him wherever he went. "Such deep blue eyes, such black hair," his mother would croon to him. "And such a brain. You're just perfect." His parents loved him, he thought, and he would feel this warmth in his chest.

Then they began to show him off, to bring him out and ask him to recite a poem, to beat a champion at chess, to solve a calculus problem. He could cry and protest as much as he wanted; in the end his parents would get their way and exhibit him.

Until he discovered his talent.

That day was clear in his mind. He was six years old, and Eva and Nevik had taken him to the doctor's office. He'd been suffering from dizzy spells that made him fall and left him bruised and scared.

They were seated in the waiting room with several other parents and children. Across from him a little girl was squeezed in between her parents. She was very thin; beneath translucent skin, a web of blue veins ran along her arms and neck. Her parents were thick-skinned and huge, so big they took up part of her seat on each side of her. The mother talked to the girl nonstop, her head tilted sideways, her eyes focused on Torver.

Torver stared back. The dizziness started, but this time he didn't close his eyes. There were layers to the woman's gaze, one behind the other, as if her eyes spoke of different things than the words flowing out of her mouth. He wondered at those things, wondered when she'd learned to hide them with words.

He probed deeper, pushed past the words lined up in front of her like a perceptible barrier. Abruptly, they gave way, and he was yanked through her eyes. There he stood, gasping, in a space neither dark nor light. In front of him, as far as he could see, stretched a glowing thread. Today, he wondered why he hadn't been frightened. Instead, he'd felt only a deep curiosity seated in satisfaction. The white-hot thread fascinated him. He tried to touch it, but it was as elusive as a light beam.

He remembered the hidden things in the woman's eyes. At that thought, the thread rippled, and a long way off, bent into a loop. He squinted at it, and all at once he was at the fold. It opened up as soon as he set his eyes on it, like a square vidscreen. On it was a beautiful little girl the same age as he, with blond curls and blue eyes, standing in the middle of a room, obviously frightened. She looks like an angel, he heard voices say. He felt sorry for her, thinking they probably showed her off, just like him.

Suddenly, she dove under a bed, screaming. "No! Please, please, I'll be good, I promise."

A big man bent and tried to grab her. He looked mad. "Come here, you. I'll teach you to show respect."

"I'm sorry. Please, don't!" Her last words ended in a squeak when the man grasped the edge of the bed and pulled it away from the wall. The little girl cringed in the corner, pleading. Tears streamed down her face.

"Stupid bitch. Did you think your bed could protect you?" He dragged her up and slapped her, over and over again, until she went limp in his hands.

The vidscreen collapsed on itself, and Torver blinked. He was out of the woman's head and back in the doctor's office. His dizziness was gone, and the woman was still talking and ogling him.

He understood it all. The little girl was this woman at his age. Did she see herself when she saw him?

"I'm sorry the big man hit you," he said.

The woman stopped in mid-word and frowned.

"When you hid under the bed," he continued, eager to explain what he'd seen. "Was he your daddy?"

The woman gaped at him. She turned white, then red, and then white again. Her eyes rolled around, and she fell down in a dead faint.

In the rush to revive her, his comment was ignored. Torver was glad. He knew he'd discovered something very important but troubling. Could he do it again, go inside people like he had? If he could, would everyone react like the fat lady? Maybe he shouldn't have said anything. Maybe it should have been secret. His secret.

After his parents brought him home from the doctor's, he sat quietly in his room and continued to think about what had happened. Even with his immature mind, he understood that, somehow, he'd entered that lady's past and witnessed a part of her life. He tried to remember how he did it, but all he had left was this memory of the dizziness and standing beside the wispy thread. The more he forced himself to go over the events, the more they became blurred, and the more anxious he became.

Finally, he came to a decision—he had to know if he'd imagined it all or if it had been real. He had to try again.

Torver went in search of his mother. He found her in the kitchen, sipping a cup of strong tea, a rare indulgence. She was gazing into the steaming liquid, and he realized for the first time she always had this manner about her. Defeated, he called it later, when he was old enough to put names to feelings.

He stood in the entrance until she noticed him. "Baby, come here," she said in a tired voice. "You want a cookie?"

"Okay." He sat in the chair beside her. She handed him a plate with two small soy cookies. He took one then raised his eyes to her.

It was easier to get inside this time, maybe because he knew what to expect, or because of his familiarity with her. He followed the gossamer ribbon with his eyes until he saw a bulge. His gaze stopped there, and he was facing it. The growth pulsated like a heart. Slowly, it opened to reveal a scene.

A woman sat in a chair, the clasped hands on her thighs white at the knuckles. Torver stared at her with a sense of recognition. This was his mother, but in another time, a before. She looked like his mother, but her features were smoother, her hair brown instead of gray; and she wore a sort of tube around her legs he had never seen her wear. She was upset, he knew. She frowned in the same way she did when he threw a tantrum.

He scanned the room where she sat. It was an office, fairly ordinary, with a desk, two chairs, a case full of vidbooks. Only one peculiar thing stood in the corner—a twisted ladder with multicolored rings.

He had almost forgotten why he was there when a man in a brown coat burst into the room and sat across the desk from his mother. In the way he leaned towards her, Torver knew the office belonged to the man and that his mother had been waiting for him.

"How are you, Eva?"

"I came so my parents would stop nagging. I won't listen, Thaddeus." She pressed her lips together so tight they disappeared into a slash across her face.

The man in brown joined his fingers at their tips and pointed them towards her.

"Mrs. Katto says you told her she'll be developing a tumor on her kidney."

"She will."

"Then you told Jay Putter, in front of witnesses, that he lied when he said he fought in the clone revolt."

"He did lie. He would have never passed the physical. He has Palladin's syndrome."

"That's not the point, Eva. This is a small community. You're scaring people."

"I can't help it if I see inside them."

"Maybe not. If only you kept it to yourself."

Her eyes widened. "You would prefer that Mrs. Katto die?"

"You are not her doctor." Thaddeus leaned forward. "You're missing the point, Eva. People are calling you a monster."

Eva paled. She shook her head, mute.

"Your parents and I think it'd be best if you left. Make a new life elsewhere, where people don't know your ability."

Eva closed her eyes. When she opened them, Torver could see the pain. "And Peter?"

Thaddeus shook his head.

Fat tears rolled down her cheeks. "I thought he loved me."

Thaddeus rose from his desk and came to stand behind her He placed his hands on her shoulders. "You know his parents will never allow you to marry. If you stay here, one of the villagers will call in MGRC. If they can prove you can read other people's DNA, you'll be lobotomized. Do you want to take that risk? I've known you since you were born, Eva. What we're offering you is a chance to live a normal life."

"So, I'm banished?"

"Even if you stay here, you'll end up an outcast. You already knew that before you came into this office."

Torver's mother shrugged off Thaddeus's hands and stood up, her back so straight it curved backward. For a second, Torver thought she'd tell Thaddeus she was staying. Then she moaned. She extended a hand to grasp the back of the chair while the other clutched her midsection. She stayed there, panting.

The man moved, and at the same time the scene collapsed on itself. Torver faced his mother again in the present. She was gazing at him with a puzzled frown.

"Mummy," he said, "can you still see into people?"

Her expression changed from slack to intense. She grabbed him by the shoulders and lifted him out of his seat.

"What did you say?" She shook him. "Who told you that?"

"You!" His teeth clacked. "I saw it!" He started to cry.

She dropped him as if she'd touched acid. "Oh, God." She closed her eyes.

Torver cried louder. "I'm sorry, Mummy, I'm sorry."

Eva grasped his arms. "Listen to me, Torver. Secrets are not for sharing. You mustn't do that again, whatever you're doing. Do you hear me?"

He nodded, promised. She let go of him and sat back in her chair.

"If your father knew…Oh, God, Thaddeus was right. I passed it on to you." She rose and ran out of the kitchen.

He had thought it safe to share what he saw with his mother, but he'd been wrong. He felt betrayed, adrift. He couldn't look at her the same way. When she told him she loved him, he couldn't be sure it was true anymore. Although she still hugged him and held him, she wouldn't look directly at him.

He also noticed a change in her attitude. She made fewer demands on him. She began to take his side against his father. She rarely asked him to show off his talents and kept watching him when she thought he wouldn't notice.

But the lure had been too great, and he'd broken down one day after he'd been pulled aside by the school bully. He'd gone in, picked out a secret, used it. The bully had dropped him as if he'd been burnt. The sense of satisfaction had filled him again, and he decided then that he couldn't leave this talent of his unused and unpracticed.

It took him years to become proficient at traveling through people's pasts. He thought about how his mother had given up on her talent, and he thought he understood why. Like her, exploring his gift had begun as a challenge and had ended up a curse. These days, twenty-five years after the incident with the fat lady, he was likely to step into someone's lifepath without thinking, like scratching an itch or blinking. He often found himself idly traveling someone's past, sampling several years of their existence before he even realized what he was doing.

It hadn't been like that in the beginning. Then, it had been exciting, frightening, exhilarating. To hold secrets—grown-up secrets—gave him power. Most of all, power over his father, by knowing his deepest secret. Torver sighed. Twenty-five years was a long time to blackmail a father. Their emotions had become blunted, tired. Their hostility continued more through habit than real feeling.

The little boy laughed again, wrenching Torver from his thoughts. He noticed the waiter hovering close to his table. He signaled for another brandy. The waiter approached him with the bottle.

"Are you Dr. Lockwood?" he said as he poured.

"Yeah. Why?"

The waiter pointed to the bar area. "Two gentlemen would like to speak with you, sir."

Two men, one short and stocky, the other tall and thin, nodded to him. More Mungers, he thought. "Tell them to get lost."

"But, sir—"

Torver peered at the man's name tag. "Listen to me, Louis. I've just been dumped in front of the entire restaurant. This is not a good time. So tell the Mungers to go away."

"But, sir—"

"Are you deaf?" He groaned inwardly when the shorter man approached his table.

"Perhaps I should introduce myself." The man smiled slightly. "Laslo Radic. I'm not with MGRC, Dr. Lockwood. I'm the President and CEO of GeneTech. Perhaps you've heard of it?" Without waiting for an invitation, he pulled back the chair Jenny had vacated minutes ago and sat down.

Torver studied Laslo Radic. The chair could barely cope with his stocky, square shape, the self-molding material stretched to its maximum. Not that Radic had a gram of fat. His flat stomach and muscular thighs pushed at the fabric of his clothes. He looked about forty-five. Even though he smiled broadly at Torver, his gray eyes were flat. Radic made Torver think of Janus, the Roman god of gateways and beginnings. The lower portion of his face gave the impression of a jovial man; the eyes hinted at darkness. Despite himself, he was intrigued. He pushed past the orbs. Nothing happened.

He gaped at the man, stunned. He'd been brought to a standstill, as if he'd hurled himself against a solid door. For the first time since he'd discovered his ability, someone's lifepath was closed to him.

He blinked and watched the second man approach his table.

"How did you know I was here?"

"Your father. We went to your house first."

The tall man sat down.

"He seems distraught that you lost your job," Radic said. "And your license."

"I haven't lost my license yet."

"True. In the meantime, you might need a job."

Torver took a sip of his brandy. He turned to the other man and looked into his eyes. He was relieved to feel no resistance. The man's lifepath stretched ahead of him. He pulled back.

"Do I know you?" he said to the tall man.

The man shook his head. "I'm Dr. Gerry Sinclair. I work for Mr. Radic."

Torver turned back to Laslo Radic. "So, you're here to offer me a job. There's not much I can do for you without my license."

Radic leaned forward. "Oh, I think there is. If you're as good as your reputation." He straightened. "I'd rather talk about this in a more private place, though."

Torver pushed the button near his right hand, and his bill came up. He reviewed the entries then placed his hand on the reader and sent a mental pulse to accept the total and pay. He swallowed the last of his brandy and stood up. Radic and Sinclair rose with him.

"Mr. Radic, the last few days have been difficult for me. Right now, I only have your word you are who you are. For all I know, you could be Mungers trying to entrap me. I'm going home."

"You'll never find anything as interesting as this offer, with or without a license. I suggest we meet again in a few days, after you know for certain if your suspension is indefinite. It'll also give you time to research me."

"Forget it."

Radic grunted. He didn't look happy at all.

"Today's Monday. If you change your mind, come to GeneTech on Thursday. One o'clock."

Torver nodded and left, troubled by the granite in Laslo Radic's eyes. There had been too many shocks in his life lately, and tonight the only thing he could always rely on, his ability, had failed him. Only with Radic, though.

He had to admit Radic had sparked his interest, but he wasn't about to go into a discussion of his future with someone he knew nothing about and whom he couldn't read. Before they met again—if they did—he'd know who Laslo Radic was and why the man had taken the trouble to track him down at a small restaurant at eleven o'clock at night.

What would make Radic desperate enough to want to hire him? Torver smiled. Radic had promised him a challenge. Maybe the real challenge was Radic himself.

## Chapter Six

LASLO STARED OUT HIS WINDOW AT THE HEAT SHIMMERING UP FROM THE CONCRETE IN rolling waves. The day had started hot, close to thirty-two degrees Celsius; he figured it had now reached over forty. It was a wonder his garden could resist so much heat. He shifted in his seat. He hated waiting. It plunged him into brooding over his accomplishments, which suddenly seemed puny and insufficient.

He clenched his teeth, disgusted with the direction his thoughts were taking. He knew the pattern. Soon he'd feel sorry for himself and wonder what it was all about. Then, if he didn't get hold of this mood, he'd become mired in his own melodrama for days, unable to make a decision, drinking too much, sleeping little. He turned away from his garden, impatient with its cheeriness, and stared at the wall instead. If only something around him finally would go right.

He'd approached Lockwood from the wrong angle. He shouldn't have believed Gerry when he'd said Lockwood would be desperate, should have waited for Mahoud's report before he made overtures or offered the job. It wasn't like him to mishandle a situation. I'm slipping, he thought. Instead of bluffing Lockwood into taking the job, I've shown my hand.

Lockwood's appearance had surprised him. From a distance, the scientist looked like he belonged on vid ads, modeling underwear or cologne, not in a lab poring over DNA structures. Then he'd met Lockwood's eyes. Their dark blue color might make girls swoon, but when Lockwood had turned his gaze on him, Laslo had felt as if he'd been slammed against a wall. Five seconds after impact, he had forgotten Lockwood's physical perfection.

All the time they'd talked, he'd been buffeted by that gaze. He shuddered. Whatever else he might be, Lockwood wasn't vacuous or stupid. He'd even managed to put Laslo on the defensive. Maybe that was the reason for the botched deal. Now all he could do was wait. He hated waiting.

His thoughts shifted to Demetria Greyson. He'd spent a day tracking down and speaking with her clients. She was definitely the one he needed. It seemed almost an omen that she lived in the Metropolis instead of halfway around the world. Unfortunately, he hadn't been able to get past her EP to talk to her. He pursed his lips. The EP was a surprise. If Greyson could afford that kind of help, she must be doing all right, work-wise, which meant she wouldn't need the money, which would make it more difficult to bring her on board.

A red light blinked on his desk. He passed his hand over it, and the face of his chief of security appeared on the vid. Ashar Mahoud smiled, his teeth a slash of white against his olive-brown complexion.

"Talk to me," Laslo said.

"Nothing much about Lockwood. He lives with his parents, goes to work when he has a job, lectures at conferences. A typical tech-head."

"No bits of information I can use?"

"The only rumor going around is that he's the one who fingered Barton at DyneMed. Apart from that he's clean, although nobody likes him much." Mahoud looked down to consult his notes. "Now, the other one, Demetria Greyson, is interesting. Her mother is Carlotta Danterini, the world-famous pianist; her father is Dr. Charles Greyson, the evolutionary psychologist. Both come from families—along with the family fortunes—that can be traced back to the Renaissance."

Laslo whistled. "She comes from exalted stock."

"She's estranged from her parents. Ms. Danterini is currently on tour in the European States and Dr. Greyson is in Africa somewhere."

"How about Greyson herself?"

"Before she completed her studies," Mahoud said, "three universities wanted her and she got job offers from five multinationals, including Lunar Ex. She became a freelance stats guru instead."

"Her clients say they've never seen her, although she does sterling work. All their dealings have been through her EP. I wonder what it'll take to persuade her to come work for me."

"I doubt she will. I dug up something that's not widely known." Mahoud paused. "She has Brett's dermophagia."

Laslo blinked, surprised by the emotion that rushed through him. He pinpointed the feelings, anger mixed with panic, then pushed them away. What was left was euphoria. Just yesterday, GeneTech scientists had finished working the last glitches from an improved prosthesis for Brett's. The artificial cells merged better with the live ones, minimizing the appearance of the seams. Its development was very expensive, though. The new prosthesis would make a nice sign-on bonus for Ms. Greyson.

"Well done, Ashar. Send me anything else you have."

"Mr. Radic."

Laslo's hand hovered over the stop-call button.

"Is there anything you wish to tell me?"

He hesitated, wondering if he should let Ashar in on his plans. He didn't doubt the man's loyalty—Ashar had given it to him twenty years ago when Laslo had bought him a new identity and given him the job as his chief of security instead of turning him over to the Mungers in MGRC's Clone Management Office. It wouldn't be the first time Ashar had assisted him with less than legal operations, but he was reluctant to have another person involved in his personal business.

"Not yet," he finally said.

He terminated the comm then called up Demetria Greyson's number. A female voice, and not that of the EP, came on line. It sounded irritated.

"I must say you're very persistent, Mr. Radic."

"I presume I'm speaking with Ms. Greyson?"

"Who else?"

"I hope your EP has relayed my messages. My project is urgent, Ms. Greyson."

"All my clients say that, Mr. Radic."

"I was impressed by the report you wrote for Dr. Francis. I need a good statistician."

"Did he tell you that I don't work with genetics-related companies?"

Laslo swore silently. Francis had omitted that tidbit, and Ashar hadn't dug it up, either.

"Only fools never change their minds, Ms. Greyson. From what I hear, you don't fit the category."

"I'm not the right person for the job, Mr. Radic."

"I think you are. So do your clients. Besides, you haven't even heard about the project."

"I see."

Demetria Greyson's voice had suddenly chilled. She'd replaced her face on the screen with a moving fractal that seemed to mirror her mood. The fractal's motion had slowed down with the coldness in her voice. He pictured her in his mind—serious, even grim-looking.

"The standard procedure is to ask for a list of references, Mr. Radic."

"Everyone gave you glowing recommendations."

"Everyone?"

Laslo chuckled at her sarcastic tone. "Those who matter gave you high marks." He sensed hesitation, maybe even curiosity. He grinned when she asked, "What's the job?"

"I'm not prepared to discuss it over the comm channels, Ms. Greyson. The project is highly sensitive."

"I never meet my clients onsite, Mr. Radic. Call it my idiosyncrasy."

"Even if that means losing a very lucrative contract?"

"I've done it before. My EP is programmed with a highly sophisticated commsec system. If that's not sufficient for you, I'll get back to work."

He let the silence stretch. He got up and contemplated his garden. The yellow sunrays seemed to absorb the heat around them and reflect it back.

"Connection terminated," a mechanical voice said.

He raised an eyebrow. The woman didn't intimidate easily. He liked that. She'd have to work from home, then. On further reflection, limiting contact between her and Lockwood might be a better solution. Yes, he'd use the old balkanization method—keep them hostile and rule. All he had to do was convince Demetria Greyson to take on the job, and he had a trump card to do it with.

He re-established the communication. She came back online.

"I apologize, Ms. Greyson. Had to change comm. Seems to have a conflict with your system."

"Do we still have something to discuss, Mr. Radic?"

"Of course. And call me Laslo."

"Mr. Radic, I suggest you get to the point."

"I need you to analyze genetic data."

"I'm not a biometrician. My field is comparative statistics."

"That's exactly why I need you," Laslo said. He explained, in broad terms, what he wanted her to do. She listened without interruption. "Of course," he said finally, "the geneticist in charge will tell you more specifically what he needs. What do you think, Ms. Greyson?"

"Wouldn't I need special authorization to access the genebanks?"

"You'll have it by the end of the week." He heard the hiss of silence at the other end.

"I heard it's virtually impossible to get that kind of carte-blanche from

Government Mundial."

"Then you'll understand why you'll work on a need-to-know basis. MGRC insists that we give out as few details as possible." Laslo paused, coughed once. "I can promise you this much. Success in this project will mean saving children's lives, Ms. Greyson."

"Surely a biometrician..."

"My chief scientist assures me I need someone like you. Your lack of genetics knowledge is immaterial, since you'll have a geneticist to direct you." He hoped Lockwood would agree with him.

"I'll have to think about it, Mr. Radic."

Laslo took a deep breath. "While you do, think about something else, Ms. Greyson. Very few people know why you refuse to meet your clients, or why you don't have a vidcom."

Silence.

"More to the point, I am in a position to facilitate your life, Ms. Greyson. My company is in the final stages of developing a new prosthesis that can be matched seamlessly to your own skin. If we could help each other, maybe—"

"Connection terminated," the mechanical voice said.

Laslo blinked, astonished at Greyson's reaction. He thought she'd jump at the chance to get a better prosthesis. That was the second time he botched a job offer. Things weren't going well.

He'd give her a day or two then call her back.

He checked his watch. It was three o'clock. Now that he had Lockwood and Greyson almost lined up, he needed an authorization code. Only one person could help him with that. He wondered if Stan remembered his old debt.

LASLO PUSHED ASIDE THE STAR USER HUNCHED IN THE DOORWAY HE'D CHOSEN FOR HIS observation post. The mainliner blinked up at him then, as if his head had become too heavy for his neck, let it fall back until it hit the door. Laslo threw him a disgusted glance then sidled as much of his body as possible into the shadows of the recessed alcove.

Most of the streetlights were broken along the drag but enough light flooded through the windows of the bars, pawnshops and tattoo parlors that opened at sunset to make it possible to see.

Leave it to Stan to choose one of the worst parts of town to meet, Laslo thought. He watched a couple of dustheads buy dust right under the nose of a patrolling policeman who looked too young and too scared to do anything about it. A Whitestar user sat against a wall and hypoed a shot. The kiddy cop turned his back to him and speedwalked down the street.

Stan had suggested they meet at the Lickspittle Bar at twelve, before the crowds became too rowdy. Laslo checked his timepiece—eleven forty-five. He liked to arrive early and check out his surroundings. Old habits died hard, he supposed. He squinted to bring the bar entrance across the street into focus. So far, no one had come in or out.

The night air was stifling. The city's concrete had absorbed the day's heat and was giving it back like a dark sun. Laslo's sweater stuck to his skin; sweat rolled between his shoulder blades down to his waist, where it pooled like a second belt. The dry, dusty wind blew the smell of puke and piss and rotting garbage down the street and made him queasy.

He ought to go in, get a table where he could wait for Stan. Except he wasn't sure where it was more dangerous, outside or inside.

He remembered when the joint opened, eight, ten years ago. It had started out as an oxygen-and-water bar and had become instantly popular with bored rich kids who thought that sniffing $O_2$ in a rough neighborhood gave them status. After a couple of them had been beaten up and one killed, they'd left the bar to those for whom it had been intended.

He had heard that over the next few years the Lickspittle had evolved into a place where one could buy anything, from the latest drug cocktail to very specific information. He had to admit that, even though he wasn't too happy with the spot, his activities fit right in.

The rumble of a powerful engine distracted him. From the right, a black limo glided to a stop in front of the Lickspittle. Laslo flattened himself into the dark corner. Only a few people drove those kinds of cars into this neighborhood, and none of them belonged to polite society. The back door opened, and three heavily muscled men came out, one of them a giant.

"Wouldn't want to face him in a dark alley," a voice beside him whispered.

Laslo jumped and started to turn around. A hand on his shoulder held him in place.

"Let's just keep still for the moment," Stan murmured. "I don't want to attract attention."

"Friends of yours?" Laslo said.

Two of the three muscles entered the bar. The giant leaned on the car, arms crossed.

"Nah. These guys are into drugs and brute force. We leave them be, they do the same for us." The hand on Laslo's shoulder dug deeper. "Don't move. They never stay long. Wait until they're gone, then come on in."

Laslo turned his head, but he was alone. Stan was playing his disappearing game again. He'd forgotten how annoying he found it. Movement from the Lickspittle drew his attention. The muscles were coming back out with a scrawny-looking man sandwiched in the middle.

He pressed his body against the door. He knew the thin man very well. What in the world did Gerry Sinclair have to do with these people? He watched as the giant pushed away from the car and said something to Gerry. Gerry lifted his hands in a pacifying gesture and shook his head. The giant opened the door and motioned Gerry inside. He hesitated until one of the heavies gave him a tap in the back that made him stagger. He got in quickly, followed by the three men. The door slammed shut and a few seconds later, all that was left of them was a smell of exhaust.

Laslo stared in the direction they'd gone. He thought he knew enough about Gerry. He'd obviously been mistaken.

There was no one around to see him cross the street to the bar. Inside, the large room was dim and full of smoke from the hookah smokers lining one wall. He saw Stan at the back. He wove his way to the bar through scarred acrylic tables and broken self-molding chairs paralyzed into awkward shapes. Dark trails ran along the burn-dotted plasmer rug. The concrete floor showed under it. Behind a gleaming similiwood and copper counter, a squat woman with a flat face and a nose that had been broken at least once stared him up and down then scowled.

"Whaddayawant?"

"Trocadero." While he waited for the woman to pour his drink, he examined the few patrons. He wondered if Gerry had been talking to one of them. No one seemed lucid or sober enough. He must have been waiting for the guys in the limo. Laslo picked up his beer and walked over to Stan's table.

"What took you so long?" Stan said.

Laslo ignored him and sat down with a grunt. "Christ, I'm tired. I'm too old to do business at this hour."

Stan grinned and took a sip of the rocatini in front of him. "You want my help."

"Why'd you pick this place, Stan? You know I don't come into this part of town anymore."

"I thought it would bring back memories. A couple of decades ago, a place like this would have been quite posh for us, wouldn't it?"

"I suppose." He took out his handkerchief and mopped his face.

"What do you need?"

"An MGRC authorization code." He stuffed his handkerchief back into his pocket then swallowed some beer. Stan whistled softly. "I need an all-purpose code," he continued, "one that will allow me access to several different genebanks across the Mundial Network. And I want it transferable."

"Quite a challenge."

"Are you saying you can't do it?"

"Anything's possible." Stan's eyes glittered. "It'll cost you." Laslo shrugged. "When do you want it?"

It was Laslo's turn to show his teeth. "Yesterday."

"A week. Payment on delivery, of course." Stan chewed his olive. "This cancels the debt as well."

"Yes." He swallowed the rest of his drink, grimaced and got up. "There's another item I'd like you to look into. That man who left here with the two heavies..."

"The tall, skinny guy?"

"His name's Gerry Sinclair. He works for me. I want to know why he's taking a ride in a limo that belongs to a drug lord."

"You'll have the info at the same time as the code."

"Good." Laslo walked to the bar and placed his hand on the metal plaque embedded in the top. "My friend's rocatini's on me."

The woman behind the bar nodded and punched an amount. He verified it then sent a mental authorization.

He came out of the Lickspittle slowly. Even though the activity in the street had increased, he didn't sense danger. He'd risen in class over the years, but he'd kept his instincts honed.

He ambled down the street to the exec-bus service. He'd be home in an hour. Tomorrow, he'd convince Lockwood to work for him. Friday, he'd speak with Demetria Greyson and change her mind. Next week, he'd have all the pieces in place.

He thought about his son. Maybe it wouldn't hurt to let him go to camp. After all, what difference could a week make?

# Chapter Seven

STRINGER TAPPED TWICE ON HIS DESK, AND A VID OF THE CITY SPREAD OVER ITS SURFACE. In the corner, the thermometer indicated forty-five degrees Celsius. In the inner city, it would feel at least ten degrees hotter. The image rotated slowly, giving him a view around his compound.

The metropolis had a sleepy, oozy look to it, as if the buildings were melting under the heat. Even the omnipresent buses rolled more slowly down the streets, the excess of solar energy reducing them to sluggishness. Grey haze, caused by the dust they raised, swirled in their wake and climbed higher, engulfing the sun in a shimmering, choking halo.

He slapped off the vid with clammy hands. He loathed summer. The sun scorched the roofs and permeated reinforced concrete and steel. Even though he maintained his rooms at nineteen degrees, the outside heat stretched its tendrils to choke him. He could sense the sweltering haze rising from the streets like miasma from a swamp, the sun pounding from above, the heat seeping inside his building through microscopic cracks in the walls. The many folds of his body overheated, his clothing chafed, and the sour smell that emanated from his pores repelled him.

Each day of the endless summer, he dreamed of submerging himself in cool water. A dream he would soon bring to reality. All he could afford at this time was enough water to grow his precious plants, keep goldfish and drink tea. It wasn't enough.

Sweat trickled down his face into the crease of his neck, where it pooled. He moved his head, and a little waterfall dribbled down his chest. He shuddered and wiped his face and neck with an already sodden handkerchief.

One day—soon, he hoped—he'd have his own water supply. In five years he'd have the means to buy his own desalination plant. His mouth dried at the thought of so much water at his disposal.

He had a plant in mind, tucked up north on an island in Hudson Bay. He was already positioning himself to buy the company that owned the pipeline system that shuttled the water from the plant to the metropolis. Then, once he controlled the transport of the water, the plant owners would be forced into selling. There was no sense producing it if you couldn't send it where you could sell it. Takeovers were so common these days no one would pay attention until it was too late.

He pursed his lips. It would be strange to enter the legitimate world of business. Water was more precious than gold these days, but it wasn't monitored like drugs or genetic engineering. The MGRC didn't give a damn about water. Too bad for them, because soon they'd find themselves with a big problem on their hands. Within ten years, right under Government Mundial's nose, he would have gained a stranglehold on the water resources of the entire Northern States. Five years after that, he'd control the United Central and Southern States' water sources as well. He'd be a financial power to contend with.

He'd done his stint with the drugs, but it was a high-risk field and he wasn't getting any younger. There was too much competition these days, anyway; curbing the newcomers was getting too expensive and time-consuming, and it was cutting into his profit margin. One last big job and he could start buying. Unfortunately, he had to depend on someone else for the success of this last project.

Gerry Sinclair better deliver what he'd promised, and soon. Stringer was running out of patience. A year ago, when Sinclair had approached him with his offer of creating a new drug, it had sounded almost too easy. Sinclair's brain dust had tripled his profits, and had permitted him to activate his plan to buy water resources two years ahead of schedule. Stringer knew how to reward performance, and Gerry Sinclair was now a richer man for it.

Then the scientist had come up with his brilliant idea of changing the dust to make it detox resistant. The risks were astronomical; the payoff would more than equal the risks. If it worked.

Stringer liked to gamble, though this time the stakes might have become too high. So far the cops had pretty much ignored the dust, since it wasn't considered addictive. Now that dustheads were dying, they might start paying attention. If the cops involved the MGRC, they'd hunt until they found him. That would definitely cut into his plans.

He heard a sharp knock, then his office door glided open and Argus walked in without waiting for an answer. Stringer smiled slightly. He gave Argus these small privileges to indicate to others that he had a higher status and the boss's full confidence, and Argus availed himself of them at every opportunity. It was true that Argus was family, but the man had also taken on the responsibility of acting as Stringer's arms and legs, since moving around had become increasingly difficult in the last few years. Argus had earned those few advantages.

"Well?" Stringer said.

"It'll be difficult to get the dust off the streets. Most of our distributors have gone underground because of the heat. I know where they hole up, but they're scattered across the metropolis. I'll need more men."

"Take as many as you need. I don't want any more deaths because of the dust."

"How about Sinclair?"

"Get him back here. It's time I impress upon him the principles of business."

"Do you think he can pull it off?"

"He'd better, for his sake." He saw Argus hesitate. "Do you have something else in mind?"

Argus swallowed. His face took on a mutinous look. "I don't trust him."

"Your point being?"

"You leave yourself vulnerable. If he gets caught, he'll finger you, that's for sure. The cops have spent years looking for an excuse to put you away."

"They have their own problems to worry about. With all the personnel cutbacks they suffered this past year, they have to pick and choose their targets. They'd rather go for the terrorists, like those Hongfeng. Drug use isn't as visible politically. Besides, the anti-addiction drugs the Health Centers keep designing regulate the market. Even if they knew I was the one who put the dust on the market, they wouldn't go after me."

Argus barked out a laugh. "That's because they don't know what you've been up to."

"And you'll keep your trap shut about it, too."

Argus flushed. "They won't hear it from me. You can't be so sure about Sinclair."

Stringer tapped a few keys on his desk. A 3D image popped up from the middle of his desk and rotated slowly. "Look at her, Argus. The water plant near Green Bay. If Sinclair succeeds, I'll be able to buy four of those, plus the pipeline company."

"That's if you can sell Sinclair's formula."

Stringer chuckled. "Don't worry. I'll have no problem selling the formula, believe me. There will be enough buyers around to auction the product. It should make things interesting."

Argus shook his head. "Look what happened to el-Barrhad in Saudi. They never found all the pieces. The Mungers don't always settle things in court. And the other organizations don't play fair, either. You'd better cover your back if you deal with them."

Stringer stared at him in silence until he began to shuffle from foot to foot. "You're the son of my mother's sister," Stringer said then, "so I'll ignore your interfering this once. You want out, Argus? You tell me, right now, and you're gone. They're waiting in line to take your place."

Argus was shaking his head. "No, no. That's not what I want. I was just concerned about Sinclair. You're the best."

"You question my actions again, it'll make me unhappy. You clear on that?"

"I am. I swear."

Stringer studied him for a moment then nodded. Argus knew very well that those who left his organization left feet first. That minimized the leaks, and kept the rest of the riff-raff in line.

He waved him away. "Get out of here. Get me Sinclair. Oh, and bring me Pill as well. He and I have a difference of opinion we need to settle. I can impress the urgency of the situation on Dr. Sinclair at the same time."

As soon as Argus left, Stringer pulled out his handkerchief and mopped his face. He'd begin to groom someone else to take Argus's place, he thought, someone with fewer brain cells. Maybe he had let Argus take too many liberties, after all.

His comm chimed. The desk screen blinked twice then filled with a black rose. The Dooley brothers. He tapped a key to acknowledge the call.

"My clients have authorized me to buy the modified drug," a male voice said. Since it was most certainly comp-modified, Stringer didn't try to recognize it. The rose floating over his desk was identity enough. "If it ends up working, that is," the rep continued.

He felt a jolt of satisfaction. The stakes were rising if the Dooleys were interested. "The prototype is still in the trial stage. I'll need another month before we even think of putting it on the market. Then we'll see. The Black Rose isn't the only organization interested in our product."

"We're aware of another bidder and we're prepared to top any offer. Plus, we guarantee purchase of all further product." There was a pause. "My clients are not patient people."

Stringer patted his lips with his damp handkerchief. "We want to make sure the product works one hundred percent of the time before we turn it over to our clients. And believe me, when it works, people will buy it in droves. Your bosses will recoup their money and a hundred times more."

"We're wondering why you're not keeping the product for yourself."

"I have other plans. I'm bowing out of the drug trade."

"But not the design of it."

Stringer smiled. "As I said, I have plans. I guarantee they won't overlap with the Black Rose's."

"My clients will be glad to hear it."

"I'll keep them in mind when the product is ready." He tapped a key on his desk, and the black rose flickered out. He breathed a sigh.

He was almost tempted to change his mind and keep the dust for himself. What he'd said to the Rose's rep was true—they'd rake in billions with it. The market was more than ripe for a new designer drug. The exodus from the coasts may have stopped, but people were sitting on top of one another. Jobs were scarce, and most of those who held one worked long hours for meager pay. The heat and dust were intolerable in summer, winters were frigid. Kids were born with all kinds of weird mutations, the MGRC was cracking down on any genetic research, and with crops dying in the Midwest and in Asia, there were rumors food supplies might be short of demand again.

So many people who needed to escape their reality. The brain dust made them happy; they saw, heard, felt beautiful things. They'd want it, even if there was no cure for the addiction. And they'd keep buying it, because going back to their dreary lives would be like stepping into a nightmare. Once they realized they were hooked, it'd be too late. But even knowing there was no possible detox mechanism, he knew human nature. Flying had always been a dream.

He sighed again. No, better not derail from his goal. The discreet word he'd sent out was beginning to bear fruit. So far, two supply organizations had shown interest in buying the dust. He could simply pit them against each other, but he was convinced that in a month's time he'd have more than the two of them on side; he'd be able to start a nice bidding war.

If only his future didn't hang on the success of one man. Gerry Sinclair had the advantage over him, and Stringer had never liked handing control over to someone else. No one, however, was irreplaceable. If Sinclair couldn't deliver, there were other scientists with shady morals and greater abilities who would.

He'd wait to hear what Sinclair had to say before he decided on his approach. He grinned. If anything, Pill should provide them with a good show.

He picked up a dry handkerchief. He tapped on his desk and dropped the temperature a few more degrees.

# Chapter Eight

Torver entered the kitchen and passed by his father on his way to the fridge. Nevik sat at the table littered with bits and pieces of equipment. His toolkit lay open at his feet like a gutted animal.

"Vid on the fritz again?" Torver said as he opened the fridge and contemplated its contents. He was hungry, but he wasn't sure what he wanted. There was no trace of last night's meal, since Nevik, as usual, had polished off the dinner leftovers. It was a game his parents played. Eva put away the food and left; Nevik took it out and ate it quickly, standing up, in case she returned unexpectedly. Eva never asked about the missing food.

Nevik grunted and rummaged in his kit. "Did you borrow that equalizer I had?"

"Nope." Torver picked up some cheese-flavored tofu and smelled it. "Why don't you replace that vid? It's been acting up for a while."

"Are you nuts? It's almost brand-new. Ah, there it is."

Torver threw the tofu back into the fridge and closed the door. Maybe he wasn't hungry enough. Nevik fiddled with a micro component, muttering under his breath. The magnifying goggles made him look like a laboratory frog.

"I got a job offer Monday," Torver said.

Nevik stilled. With precise movements, he deposited the equalizer and the circuit on the table and removed the goggles. He looked up at Torver, who returned his father's gaze without entering his lifepath. Both knew there was nothing in it left for either of them. "Did you take it?"

Torver smiled slightly. He knew what his father was thinking. By law, Nevik couldn't throw his son out of the house, so he was stuck with him. If Torver left of his own accord, though, he couldn't come back, so Nevik was hoping the new job would pay enough he would want to leave. Never mind that he wasn't supposed to work while his license was suspended. Maybe Nevik hoped Torver would take that job so he could rat on him to the Mungers.

"Getting hopeful, Dad?"

Nevik rose from the table, poured himself a glass of water and swallowed the contents in one gulp. He set the glass on the counter but held on to it. His shoulders slumped a little and he turned his head towards Torver.

"What do you want from me?"

"Not a thing."

"You just enjoy taunting me. That's sick."

"No more than what you did."

Nevik straightened. "Don't give me that bullshit. Whatever dirt you get on people, you use for your own profit."

"Just following in dear dad's footsteps. Any means to an end is acceptable. Just like selling fetuses to buy a house."

Nevik paled. "I did what I had to do."

"Yeah, right." Torver stuffed his hands in his pockets. His stomach roiled. Suddenly, he had had enough. "If the job pays enough, I'll be moving out. So you better start praying." He walked to the kitchen doorway. "Tell Eva I won't be in for dinner." He left his father standing beside the table strewn with broken pieces.

Outside, sunlight blinded him; the heat assaulted him and cut off his breath for an instant. He stood motionless until the photofilters in his corneas adjusted to the light and the cooling cells of his suit adapted to the temperature. He pulled the hood of his unisuit over his head when he felt the sun burning through his hair. Even with the cooling cells, the heat was almost unbearable. The sweat already pooling at the base of his spine gave him a perverse pleasure. Only fools or people with a mission were out at this time of the day, and he wasn't a fool.

Torver hurried from his father's house through a maze of narrow alleys that led to the main street and the bus stop. He'd been told that a hundred years ago each house had its own plot of grass with trees on it. Now, dwellings stood on every portion of ground, sometimes stacked one upon the other like crates, so packed together that the concrete, windowless walls on each side of him made him feel like his green-furred mouse running through her maze. Reflexively, he looked up to see if some alien being observed him from above the roofs.

Torver hated the closed-in feeling. His place would have windows, he vowed, and a view. He wouldn't be content to live like a rat.

He climbed onto the bus that had just rolled to his stop and sat down near a shaded porthole. The research he'd done on Radic proved the CEO of GeneTech was genuine. He'd promised an interesting job, even though he knew of Torver's suspension. That meant the offer might be genuine, also, but not necessarily legal.

He shrugged. As long as he could work, he didn't give a damn about the rest.

The first thing he noticed when he was ushered into Laslo Radic's office was the huge bay window made of polycrystal glass. The sun poured into the room in a splash of yellow light, glinting on the copper surface of the desk, making him squint until his photofilters kicked in.

"Dr. Lockwood," Radic said from behind the desk. "Have a seat."

Torver glanced around the room. Except for the two chairs in front of him, it was empty. The bare walls were the same polished copper as the desk. There were no vidcases, no comm console, no fake plants. He blinked and looked back at Radic.

"Nice sunny day."

Radic chuckled. He touched something on his desk, and the crystal darkened.

"I wasn't sure you'd show up." He looked past Torver's shoulder and motioned for someone to approach. Torver turned to see Gerry Sinclair enter the room. They nodded to each other in greeting, but Sinclair looked quickly down, and Torver couldn't make eye contact.

"Shall we start?" Radic said.

Torver sat down and propped one ankle over his knee. He tried to read Radic and still couldn't. That fact made him unsure and edgy. "So, what's your project?"

Radic grinned, eyes cold. "I like someone who comes right to the point."

"I looked up your company, Mr. Radic. The thing is, I'm not desperate enough to get a job as a mechanic."

"Of course not, Dr. Lockwood. That would be a waste of your talent." Radic shifted forward. "But before we start, I want to make it clear that anything we discuss here will stay here."

Torver gave him a short nod. The older man seemed to be satisfied with that.

"Good." He looked to Sinclair.

The scientist cleared his throat, looked down at his hands. "Dr. Lockwood, have you ever worked with polygenic defects?"

Torver held his breath. He stared at Radic, then at Sinclair, then back at Radic. Excitement rippled through him. "It's not MGRC-allowed research. In most cases, anyway."

Radic said nothing. Sinclair fidgeted in his chair but also stayed silent. Torver shook his head quickly.

"I haven't worked on polygenic material in any of the positions I've held. If you've done your research, Dr. Sinclair, you'll know that the reason for my suspension is because I submitted a request to perform just that kind of research."

"With the added kick of mixing plant and animal genes," Radic said. "Did you think you could do it, or was it just for the excitement of trying something that has never been done?"

Torver pulled at his lower lip. What the hell, he thought. "Let's say that I have unofficially used various research facilities to study polygenic functions."

It was Radic's turn to look surprised. It was only for a fraction of a second, something that passed quickly in his eyes; but used as he was to burrowing into people, Torver saw it. So, he thought, Radic's wall was fabricated rather than a natural one. The man intrigued him even more.

"Would you care to explain, Dr. Lockwood?" Gerry said.

"Leave off the 'doctor' bit, please. Makes me feel ancient." He took a deep breath then let it out slowly. "There's always some leeway in any job. A bit of unused space on the bionet, a temporary access to a genebank, that kind of thing. I've taken advantage of that to pursue my own projects."

"Like mixing animal and plant DNA?" Gerry said.

Torver turned to him and nodded. "I've already made inroads in that direction."

Sinclair blinked at the admission. For an instant, he stared directly into Torver's eyes. Swiftly, Torver entered, zoomed in on a spot and watched. Next moment he was out; Sinclair was examining the ceiling, and Torver felt slightly nauseated by what he'd just learned. He wondered if Radic knew about his chief scientist's past.

Radic's chair creaked. "When you come to work for me, you'll restrain those urges, Lockwood."

He shifted his gaze to Radic. "I haven't accepted the job, yet, Mr. Radic."

"You will."

"You're that certain."

"You say you've studied polygenic defects. How about some proof?"

Torver paused an instant to consider Radic. "What do you know about polygenic expression?"

"The same as anyone on the street and certainly less then Dr. Sinclair, here."

"You do know that some traits are expressed through single genes, others through a combination of them? Our body shape, for instance, is regulated by the genes for size, bone density, muscle formation, metabolism and a host of others." Radic opened his mouth, but Torver raised his hand to stop the interruption. "I'm coming to it.

"In a polygenic combination, the genes, or portions of the genes, influence each other, but they also have an effect outside the group. With single-gene therapy, you insert a vector with the corrective gene and it's done. In a polygenic disease, if you've identified the defective genes and you use the same procedure, you can end up correcting your initial defect but creating a brand new set of problems, most of the time fatal."

"Yes," Gerry said. "There's a symbiotic relationship between the polygenic combination and the rest of the genetic code."

"Exactly," Torver said. "So, you can't just exchange the portions of the affected chromosomes for the correct sequences. You have to identify the defective genes' qualitative effects on other portions of the DNA and vice-versa then modify each gene so their effect on each other becomes the appropriate one. The more genes involved, the more complex the interaction, and the more difficult the solution."

Feeling nervy with what he knew was coming, he straightened in his chair and glanced out the window. He looked back at Radic in surprise.

"You have a garden?" He peered through the tinted crystal. "A garden." He shook his head.

"Forget the garden, Lockwood," Radic said. "Get on with the lecture."

Torver waited a second for dramatic effect. "De-evolution."

Gerry straightened. Radic frowned.

"That's just a pie-in-the-sky theory," Gerry said. "Nobody's been able to regress genetic information."

Torver kept his eyes on Radic. "I have. At least in theory."

"I've never heard of regressing genetic information," Radic said.

"Genetic mutations," Torver explained, "are passed along to the next generation only if they end up in biotypes that can reproduce. If a gene impedes reproduction, or is deadly for the carrier before it can be passed on, the mutation dies out. This system is more complex for polygenic combinations. The theory is that the mutations developed and refined themselves over generations as part of the evolution process."

"You mean human beings are evolving through these mutations?"

"That's exactly what happened when the family tree evolved from *Homo antecessor* five million years ago to *Homo sapiens* today," Torver said. "The changes in bone structure, brain size and eating habits all stem from genetic mutations. Why should we stop evolving?"

"You call some of the deadly diseases produced by mutations an evolution?" Radic sneered as he said the last word. Torver stared at him. Suddenly, without even going inside, he knew this conversation was very personal for him.

"No," he said, "but there are no biological laws that established all mutations must be beneficial. They're a hit-and-miss process over hundreds, thousands of years. You also have external causes, such as radiation, that can cause unhealthy mutations."

Radic grunted.

"Anyway," Torver continued, "I started from the premise that polygenic mutations were evolutionary in nature. The corollary to it is that, by tracing the genetic composition backwards, I'd be able to separate all the pieces of the puzzle, one by one, identify the interactions until I get to clean DNA, add each correction in to rebuild the genes, then switch the defective bits for ones that existed before the mutations began."

"What would you use for replacement DNA?" Gerry said.

Torver cleared his throat and fixed his eyes on the yellow patches in Radic's garden. "Fossilized hominid DNA."

The only sound in the room was the soft whistling of the air recycler. Torver could feel the astonishment of the two men ripple towards him. His heart beat against his ribcage. If his instincts were right, he'd get to do groundbreaking work. He smiled slightly.

"One of the major advantages of using ancient DNA," he said into the thickened silence, "is that it isn't controlled by MGRC. I worked with it in grad school and have a source where I can obtain more." He didn't add that the source was himself. He'd known then that keeping for himself some of the ancient DNA he'd had to work with would be useful one day. It looked like that day had come.

"What...?" Gerry's voice squeaked. "What would be your strategy?"

"It's twofold. First, I'd have to trace which genes need to be changed and how, and then, from that ancient DNA, fabricate a defect-specific combination. Most of that task should be done using probability theories rather than actual tests. Second, I'd have to test the compatibility of the rebuilt DNA with current DNA. I'd use geneng mice for that. If it works, then I'd test on human cells."

Gerry bounced up and paced. "This is incredible." He paced some more. "If it works, it's brilliant."

"This theory of yours," Radic said, "have you ever tried it out?"

"Of course not. I did modeling only, and even that was extremely risky."

Radic stood, walked around his desk and leaned against it in front of Torver. "I have a lab for you with the latest equipment. I'll give you half a mil a year in salary to start, plus an unlimited budget for the project. Officially, you're working on a new protein. What you'll really be doing is testing out that theory of yours."

"Why?"

"My reasons are not included in the deal. You have thirty seconds to decide."

Torver raised an eyebrow. "What makes you think I'd be prepared to perform illegal research?"

"You already have."

He thought about his mouse. "Sure, but I've covered my tracks."

"From what I've learned about you, Dr. Lockwood, you enjoy a challenge. Would you rather use that brain of yours for original research or for playing vidgames while you're waiting for the Mungers to clear you?"

He stared up at Radic for a few silent moments then sighed. "You know the answer to that."

Radic smiled and returned to his chair. "There are three conditions to this job offer. Security will be a premium. You'll wear a tracking biochip. You got a problem with that?"

He shrugged. "I guess not. What are the other conditions?"

"I get to pick the mutation. If it doesn't fit the profile, the deal is off."

"What is it?"

"Barcina's xylopoiesis."

Torver whistled. "You sure know how to pick them."

"You know about it?"

"I know it's very rare, although not as much as some geneticists might believe. May I ask why you picked this one?"

"No. The third condition is that you develop your corrective technique as gene therapy."

He stared at Radic. "You want it to work on humans rather than germ cells." It would've been much easier if he had been able to work with human sex cells. Now he'd also have to design a means to get the treatment into an already formed human being.

Radic, his eyes even more closed than before, returned his stare. If Torver had doubted there was a personal element in all this for the man, he was certain of it now. He began to understand why he couldn't go inside. Radic was hiding a secret so great he'd closed himself off completely. And what could be greater, Torver thought, than carrying the disease he wanted Torver to study? His own mother came to mind. He wondered if Radic had children. He looked away.

"It's not a bad choice, actually," he said. "The disease is recessive, which means I can study the genetic combinations and permutations." He frowned. "I'll need a biometrician."

"Can't you do without one?" Radic said.

"No. I realize you'd like to keep the involvement to a minimum, but I can't trace the mutations backwards myself. I warn you, you'll need a first-class analyst to do that."

"Gerry mentioned something to me about kindred and pedigrees," Radic said. "We can get you those."

Torver leaned his elbows on his knees. "What I need are the results of the analyses from kindred so I can get a clue how the mutations developed. In the case of polygenic disorders, the offspring inherits one set of defective genes from the father, another set from the mother, and it's the influence of one set of genes on the other that creates the disease. We call it gene penetrance. That's why I said that Barcina's is probably more frequent than most geneticists might think. Different gene penetrance will create various related mutations creating different symptoms, some milder than others."

"Which means that cases of Barcina's could have been misdiagnosed," Gerry said, "maybe confused with another disorder, seen as an environmental mutation or even an aberration."

"Exactly. The analyst will be checking each stripped combination to compare it with similar cases."

"What does that have to do with kindred?" Radic said.

"Members of the same family may have passed on part of the mutation without being affected themselves. Their offspring transmit the same combination in some of their own offspring, and so on. Each time, however, there might have been a slight difference in genetic composition, which meant that, when two carriers themselves had offspring, the disease evolved."

"That's why it's so rare," Gerry said. "The odds that two carriers would meet and produce offspring are fairly low."

Torver kept his eyes riveted on Radic's face. "Yes, although I can think of a good scenario. I've heard of communities or colonies that willingly segregate themselves, because of religion, culture or lifestyle. The members actively resist immigration into the their community. Marriages occur only within it. Even with a fairly large population, after a few hundred years everyone would end up related to each other because the community was segregated at the onset and the genetic pool was limited to whatever numbers they started with. Over the years, they'd avoid some mutations from the population at large, but some unique differences in their genotype would develop. Also with time, and possible migration from portions of the inbred population, you could end up with a large enough family for carriers to intermarry without them even knowing they are related to each other."

Radic pushed away from his desk and turned to the window. Torver was surprised how sure he was about his insight into the man's life.

"You start from a specific offspring who has the disease," Gerry said, "then move up the lineage and search for patterns."

"Not only up," Torver said, "but sideways. If, for instance, you find a family connection between the parents, then you have to study both sides of the couple. If there's another familial relationship, you study that as well. You look at the mutations in carriers and at those in bearers of the disease, then you compare. That's how you start finding connections."

"What good will it do to find out all this?" Radic said, turning back to him.

"To select the proper polygenic combination, I need to know how the mutation developed. Once I've established the pedigree as far as I can go, I'll start looking for a linkage between a certain form of a gene and the mutated gene. This gives a clue to the path of descent of the disease. Once I've patterned the linkages, then I'll start figuring out the influences."

He got up and stretched. "Let's say you can provide your biometrician with a kindred of three hundred people. He'll take these linkages, fit them into the bionet and assess which connections can explain the inheritance of the disease. The genome has more than twenty-five thousand genes. Take three hundred people, each with a different combination of genes that have their own natural variation. Can you even start to imagine the scope?"

"I still don't understand why you'd need all that information."

"One hundred years ago, they had to use people's blood samples to get enough DNA to analyze, and even then, it took years to learn what to look for. Now, we have all the DNA at our disposal, but we find that the answer isn't there. It's in the genes of our ancestors. It's like opening a book in the middle and starting to read. The story doesn't make sense. The beginning of the story is written in those missing genes. That's why we need to go backwards."

"You seem to understand it very well," Radic said.

Torver shook his head. "There's a difference between understanding and doing. You're going to need a hell of a biometrician to do the job. Have you got somebody in mind?"

Radic looked up at Gerry. "I'm working on it."

## Chapter Nine

GERRY STOPPED IN THE DOORWAY TO STRINGER'S ROOM, PREVENTING THE DOOR FROM closing. This bit of defiance gave him the illusion he wasn't trapped, even though he knew he wouldn't make it past the stairs if he tried to leave without Stringer's permission. He shivered. The room was freezing, especially in contrast to the street at midday.

"Get inside," Stringer said in a querulous voice. "You're letting the heat in."

Gerry stepped over the threshold. The door swished closed behind him, making him wince. It was the second time that week Stringer had commanded his presence, and he was getting nervous. At least this time he hadn't had to wait at the Lickspittle. He hated that bar—the people, lost in a world of their own chemical choice, scared him. He felt exposed, as if they'd somehow learned he was in part responsible for their drug taking and were going to jump him any minute.

Their choice, wasn't it? He wasn't forcing anything down their noses or into their veins. They wanted the escape, and it was his genius that provided it. If they'd kept a run of exciting projects like he did, they'd never need that kind of outlet.

He thought about his latest. Maybe he should've thought the process through more thoroughly before he'd presented it to Stringer. It had sounded so easy, but he'd hit a snag and didn't know how to fix it. Stringer wanted results, and Gerry was now certain he couldn't deliver. Not by himself, anyway. He was banking on Lockwood, but he couldn't be sure the young scientist would work out. He mentally shrugged. If Lockwood couldn't help him—willingly or not—he'd think of something else.

He surveyed Stringer's office. With its red-on-red tones, the room gave an immediate impression of power. The walls, drapes, furniture—all of it smelled old and expensive. The red color scheme wasn't really to his taste, but he understood why Stringer had chosen it. When you stepped inside, your whole body turned red, as if you'd been drenched in blood at the door.

Then you saw Stringer behind his desk. He reminded Gerry of a porcupine fish he'd seen once at an Asian aquarium—bloated, prickly and poisonous. Masses of fat obliterated his shape; he looked as if he'd inflated himself. His head disappeared into his shoulders, and there within the blubber were his onyx-hard eyes and miniature mouth, accentuating the resemblance to the fish. Like the aquatic animal, Stringer's power was in his sting. It was always wise to stay well away from him, and when you couldn't, you moved slowly and carefully so as not to get him excited.

Maybe because of his size, or for other uncorrected reasons, Stringer sweated constantly. The man had found a way to take advantage of this problem. The red room and the acrid, almost metallic smell of his sweat made it appear as if blood ran in rivulets over his face and arms. The overall effect was frightening.

Stringer's eyes were focused on him. "Sinclair."

"I have to get back to GeneTech soon, Stringer."

"Have a seat. This won't take long."

Gerry heard the door behind him open, and he turned. A small man he didn't know stumbled over the threshold, followed by Argus's giant shape. Stringer's factotum closed the door and planted himself in front of it, arms crossed over his chest, while the smaller man stared uncertainly at Stringer then at Gerry before he shuffled to the center of the room.

"Did you contact all our distributors?" Stringer said to Argus, ignoring the other man.

Argus nodded. "They screamed bloody murder, but everything's off the streets."

"Good. We'll reallocate from the old stock."

Gerry studied the man Argus had brought with him. Away from Argus's height, the man seemed taller and more muscular. His gaze flitted everywhere around the room. He flinched several times, as if what he saw caused him physical pain. A smell of cloves and cinnamon, typical of a whitestar user, wafted over to Gerry.

When the man realized Stringer and Argus had fallen silent and all three were watching him, he passed his palms over his temples and straightened his clothes.

"How've you been, Pill?" Stringer said.

Panic crossed Pill's face. "Can't complain. Been selling more star these days. Folks are scared of the dust."

"You haven't been spreading rumors that dust kills, by any chance, just so you can make more profits?"

"No, no." Pill's voice came out as a squeak. "It's just that, us entrepreneurs, we have to take advantage of a situation. You know."

"Of course. I'm a self-made man myself. Seize the opportunity when it comes and all that." Stringer paused, stared. Pill shuddered and sat down on a chair beside Gerry, as if his legs wouldn't hold him any longer.

"You've shown initiative, Pill," Stringer continued. His puffer mouth pursed. "That's why I want to bring you in on this new project. Dr. Sinclair, here, has fixed the brain dust problem. I'd like you to be the first to distribute the new product for me."

Pill glanced at Gerry, who tried to keep impassive at the blatant lie, then back at Stringer. "I'm not sure, Stringer. I'm kinda used to selling star. I have my regulars. You know."

"Why don't you try the dust first, then let me know what you decide. Argus?"

Argus took out a nasal spray from a drawer concealed in the wall and handed it to Pill, who stared at it.

"Here?"

Gerry leaned towards him. "Stringer," he said, "I don't think—"

Stringer raised a hand. Argus's fell on Gerry's shoulder. He decided to keep his mouth shut.

Stringer nodded at Pill. "Yes, Pill, here. That way, you'll be able to tell us what you think right away."

"Could I keep selling star, too?"

"Certainly."

"Okay." Pill inserted the nozzle in his nostril, pressed the plunger and took a breath at the same time. He removed the nozzle and blinked. "Nothing so far."

The jowls on each side of Stringer's mouth stretched sideways into a smile that made his lips disappear. "You should feel something soon."

Pill's eyes opened wide. He gasped, clutched his shirt and pulled back and forth as if to cool himself. He began to pant.

"Oh, man." His voice had become lower, richer. He squinted, staggered a few steps, and bumped into Gerry's chair. "It's too bright in here. Oh, man.

Look at that." He giggled and pointed at a spot above Stringer's head. "Hey, I got me a double."

He walked around the room, his face a panorama of emotions. He fingered the drapes, caressed the sculpture, spun in a slow circle while staring at the overhead light. He hummed under his breath, mumbled and giggled, totally oblivious of the others.

Then he stumbled. He caught himself on the chair and clutched his chest. His face turned purple, and his breathing rasped in his throat. He staggered, collapsed into the chair. Pink foam bubbled out of his mouth.

Pill looked frantically around then focused on Stringer's face. His mouth opened and closed spasmodically, spewing out more pink foam.

"I'm going to explode." His back arched, he convulsed once then fell back. Dark blood spurted from his ears and nose.

His breath short in his lungs, Gerry pressed two fingers to Pill's throat. "He's…He's dead."

Stringer tsk-tsked in the sudden silence. "As you can see, Dr. Sinclair, your latest formula doesn't work."

"Stringer, I told you it would take time." Gerry stepped away from the dead man. "It's only been two months since I started changing the formula."

"Meanwhile, it's killing off my clients."

"I know that, but chemically changing addiction genes through the dust isn't like perfecting a new flavor of iced tofu. I'm trying to affect the genes that control the reward circuitry in the brain."

"How?"

"If you have a mechanism—in this case a series of genes that impact the feel-good receptors—that quickly mops up the good feelings the drug gives the user, he'll want to repeat the experience sooner. The more efficient the genes, the stronger the addiction. Plus, you have to make it resistant to all the anti-addiction drugs on the market. It's complicated. I have to test the dust somewhere. You agreed we should use dustheads."

"I wasn't expecting you to start thinning out my market base. Word is spreading that dust kills."

Gerry cleared his throat. "I need more time."

"I run a business, not a research facility." Stringer paused. He smiled wistfully, and his eyes took on a dreamy cast when they rested on Pill, still enveloped in the self-molding chair. "The pressure on his brain must have been tremendous. I'll have to keep some of that dust in my personal stash." He refocused on Gerry. "I want results, Dr. Sinclair."

He motioned towards Pill. Argus hauled him up by an arm and carried him to the door, where he handed him to someone outside. Argus smiled slightly when he saw Gerry watching him.

"One of the reasons I've been able to work on the dust formula," Gerry said as he turned back to Stringer, "is that I've been working on a project for my boss at GeneTech in tandem with creating, then altering the dust."

"Let me guess. You're stuck there, too."

Gerry grimaced. "I knew from the start I couldn't help Radic. I just didn't tell him, because it gave me a legitimate excuse to play with illegal genetic material with his blessing. He also omitted to place the project under his Secnet, so I can pretty well do what I want. Unfortunately, he became impatient, so I had to recommend he bring in someone else." He went on to explain about Torver Lockwood.

"I'll borrow what I need from him and apply it to the drug formula," he said finally. "We'll both be working on the compounding effects of several genes. The difference between him and me is that, with his training, he'll get there a lot faster than I ever could. That's why I encouraged Laslo to get this guy." He hesitated, concerned about what he was about to say next. "There's a glitch, though. Radic is transferring the project and the lab I was using to Lockwood. It's a segregated lab from the others, and that's why I was pretty much free to work on my sideline." He pulled at his earlobe. "I'll need a new lab."

Stringer tapped his deskpad a few times and pointed to the right. Bright light, sharp as a laser, split the center of the burgundy wall. The two halves moved sideways to reveal another room.

Gerry squinted against the sharp illumination. When his eyes adapted, he stared in surprise. He walked around the lab, checking equipment, punching datapads, stroking plasmer tables. It was small but well-appointed, perfect for the kind of tests he needed to run on the dust.

"I never liked to rely on GeneTech's facilities," Stringer said. "Too risky. It took considerable maneuvering to get all the equipment together without attracting MGRC's attention, but I believe you'll find everything you need."

"I'm impressed," Gerry said. He rubbed a metal plate. "How did you get the scope?"

"DyneMed owed me. They also advised me on what you'd need."

Gerry raised an eyebrow. "Barton's firm? He's in trouble these days."

"Barton's an ass."

"Maybe. Did you know that Lockwood worked for Barton until the day before his arrest?"

"Lockwood ratted on Barton?"

"There's no way to prove it." Gerry fiddled with the datapad of a microsampling device. The machine flashed red to indicate its tray was empty. "But Lockwood is clever. He's found ways to use the system for his own projects without anyone noticing. Nothing prevented him from gathering dirt on Barton at the same time."

"And now he has MGRC on his tail."

Gerry shrugged. "I doubt they'll find anything."

"Pill was selling for a competitor of mine while he was on my payroll." Stringer's eyes traveled to Pill's chair then back to Gerry. "No one double-crosses me and gets away with it."

"I've no intention of selling the formula elsewhere." He thought fast. Using the lab meant working two jobs and being too close to Stringer for comfort, but it was a lesser evil than having Mungers breathing down his neck or Lockwood finding out about the dust. "I'll need volunteers, since you don't want me to test on dustheads."

"Who said anything about volunteers?" Stringer's eyes shifted to Argus. "We have a perfect pool of test subjects at our disposal."

Gerry sent Argus a questioning glance.

"Termites," Argus said.

"Yes, Termites," Stringer repeated. "I've been informed a group of them have set up a temporary camp in the Gatineau Hills. If we remove two or three from the colony, their friends are not likely to go to the authorities and complain, are they? And if we end up eliminating a few, we'll be performing a public service."

Gerry grinned. Stringer's idea was nothing short of brilliant. Termites were on a shoot-to-kill status with the cops *and* the Mungers. No one in the Greater Ottawa Metropolis wanted a bunch of nonconformists coming to their city and creating chaos by raiding plant genebanks, destroying data, wiping out databanks—destroying months, sometimes years of research. The Termites had taken their protest against genetically modified plants to an extreme and were considered no better than terrorists. All this crap about the dangers of monoculture made them sound like lunatics when it was obvious that, with water resources diminishing rapidly, the only way to keep feeding the planet was to genetically modify crops. They were just a bunch of displaced farmers who had turned their bitterness into violence. The fact there was a rumor their numbers were increasing, and that they were becoming better organized, would quell any protests if a couple of them were found dead.

Stringer was right. If they used Termites, nobody would object, especially not the Termites themselves. That was if Argus could catch any. No one knew how many Termites were around. Very few people had seen them, and no matter how often the authorities organized raids to catch them, the cops always found the Termites gone, as if they'd received advance warning.

"How are you going to find them?" Gerry said. He moved back into Stringer's office.

"Argus will organize the hunt," Stringer said. "Just concentrate on the dust." He tapped his desk, and the walls closed on the lab, making the room appear more bloodied than before. "If this Dr. Lockwood is so smart, maybe I'll steal him and have *him* work for me."

Gerry could hear Stringer's next thought: *Then maybe we could try the dust on you.* He forced himself not to look at Pill's chair.

"Lockwood wants his license back. Radic can offer him something you can't—respectability. Officially, he'll be working on a new synthetic protein."

As soon as he said the words, he regretted them. He'd had a sense of control over the situation because he knew Stringer needed him. Now that there was a potential replacement on the horizon, maybe it wasn't smart to push.

Silence flowed like a bleeding wound. Gerry ignored the trickle of cold sweat on his temple, concentrating on maintaining an indifferent pose. Stringer watched him through narrowed eyes for a few seconds then wheezed. He slapped his hand on the desk and wheezed again.

"Respectability. I like that." He extended his arm to the side, and Argus placed a large glass of water in his hand. "Very well," he said after a few noisy slurps. "Argus will let you know when we have the Termites." He waved Gerry away. "Take him back, Argus,"

Before Argus could touch him, Gerry hurried to the door.

"Dr. Sinclair," Stringer called. Gerry stopped and turned around. "This is another one you've used up. You're running out of lives."

Gerry rushed out of the crimson room, Stringer's wheezy laugh following him down the stairs. Argus accompanied him until they were outside. He stared at the closed door and Argus standing in front of it.

"I take it you're not bringing the car around," he said. When Argus didn't answer, he turned his back on him and started walking.

Several houses down from Stringer's, and hidden from Argus's watchful gaze, Gerry accelerated his pace. Stringer's parting comment resonated in his ears.

He jumped onto a bus, heedless of where it would take him, intent only on getting away from Stringer as fast as possible. It really wasn't fair that he was always running from goons who had half his brain power. He should be the one in the boss's chair, giving the orders, making the decisions. Instead, he invariably ended up on the receiving end, spending all his energy trying to protect himself from the whims of a moron with too much money and power for his own good.

He thought of all the jobs he'd done in his life, the risks he'd taken. He wasn't squeamish about breaking the law; he did what had to be done when the promise of reward was worth it. But, somehow, nothing had paid out as promised. It hadn't been his fault. Every time he was close to his goal, some other asshole messed it up for him. That was because he didn't make the decisions, of course. He had to leave it to those who thought themselves smarter than he was. He chuckled. The poor sods never even realized he was the one who'd put the ideas in their heads in the first place. Hence the failures.

Not this time, he vowed. The modified dust was his ticket to the big time. He closed his eyes and imagined himself in a temperate climate—maybe even Greenland. He'd grow himself a couple of female clones, give parties, become a patron of the arts. People would respect him. He'd choose his projects and control them, from start to finish. Then he'd become even richer. His dream was closer to reality than ever—with his promised cut on the sale profits, he'd finally have enough to live in the manner he deserved.

The bus passed through the poorest section of the metropolis, where people lived in houses that had no climate control. They fried in summer and froze in winter. The concrete crumbled; the white walls were a dingy brown, the air filters clogged with dust.

Gerry's throat contracted. Memories of growing up in a neighborhood much like this one filled and repulsed him. They were more recollections of the senses than images—the choking dust, the grittiness of unclean skin, the fetid smell of defective plumbing mixed with the sounds of screaming and daily misery breathing through the too-thin concrete walls.

He shivered and clenched his eyes shut. He forced himself to concentrate on Greenland, on the airy, pristine house he'd build. His resolve strengthened. He'd get that dust working. It was just a question of opportunity. He'd created the best situation possible—Lockwood would do the work, and he would be there to reap the rewards. Not a bad arrangement, as long as he could keep

Stringer off his back.

That was the problem with goons. They were predictably dangerous. He would wait to see if Lockwood was as good as he said he was. If not, he'd have to think of an escape plan. Fast.

## Chapter Ten

Zelimir sat on his cot in the Smokey Bears cabin and rubbed his big toe. He hadn't had any sensation in it for weeks and he was starting to worry. The skin around the toenail was paper-white up to the joint, where it gradually changed to pink. The toe didn't give when he squeezed it. It was hard and a bit cold, even when the rest were warm.

Maybe he should have mentioned his toe to his dad. He'd thought about it for a long time then imagined how much worse his father would have become if he knew something was wrong. These days, wherever Zelimir went, there appeared his father. His father reminded him of a vid he'd seen once about some ancient African hunters who could track an animal for days before they moved in for the kill. The animal was so unnerved that, in the end, it would stand, trembling, waiting for death. Zel knew how the animal felt. So he'd said nothing and tried to avoid meeting his father's eyes as much as possible, in case his fear would show.

The permission to come to Manitoulin had been a surprise and meant a respite from his father's constant attention. Before his dad had a further change of heart, Zelimir had packed a bag and left. Now, on his third day here, he thought that hiding his toe from his father might have been a mistake. He wasn't feeling very well; his head had been in a fog all yesterday, and today he couldn't remember where he was supposed to go.

Graeme burst into the wooden structure; the screendoor slammed behind him. Zel quickly slipped on his shoe.

"Hey, Zel, let's go. The instructor is waiting for us."

"I'm coming. I can't wait to get into the..." He frowned. "The—what's it called again?"

"A canoe, you fluke." Graeme laughed. "Come on."

Zel stared at his friend. A canoe. It was exactly what he'd wanted to say, but he couldn't find the word. He saw the picture of it in his mind, the shining red color, the two curved pointed ends. He could see himself and Graeme kneeling in it, with a long stick flattened at one end to dip in the water. What was it called?

"Zel? Are you okay?"

"Sure." Zel shook his head quickly. He put his arm around his friend's shoulders and steered him towards the door. "I just had this great idea."

Graeme groaned. "Oh, no. All your great ideas get us in trouble."

"Let me tell you about it, my friend." Zel let the screendoor slam behind them. When he went home from camp, maybe he'd speak to his dad about his toe.

LASLO TOOK A SIP OF COFFEE AND LOOKED VACANTLY AT THE VIEW FROM THE WINDOW OF HIS living room. Even in this upscale neighborhood, all he could see were other houses. Not a hint of green or other color that occurred naturally. It wasn't the lack of desire for gardens that prevented people from growing plants—these days, eco-scientists had developed UV- and drought-resistant hybrids that grew very well. Only most people didn't have the kind of money to buy the minimum of water to grow them.

He'd seen old vids of twentieth-century gardens; some had even had sprinkler systems where the water was programmed to come on by itself. It would fall for several minutes at a time, sometimes for an hour. Today, the waste would create an uproar. Even so, sometimes he longed to see more than the neighbors' bare walls. A bit of ivy would go a long way.

Zelimir shared his passion for plants. Even as a toddler, Zel would sit quietly watching vids as long as they had trees and flowers in them. His favorites had been those of the African and South American jungles. When Zel had learned that most of the green spaces had disappeared in the Thirty-Year Drought, their animal life with them, he'd cried for hours.

He tried to picture his son at camp. There wouldn't be too many trees, but at least he'd have the lake. Laslo told himself he'd done the right thing by allowing his son to go. He *had.*

Last night he'd come in late and reflexively looked into Zelimir's room. Empty. He'd stood there, stunned, terrified, until he remembered Zel was still alive. He'd become dizzy with relief. At that moment, he realized he couldn't hide Zelimir's disease from Jelena anymore. She had a right to know.

The discreet peal of his vidcom distracted him. He got up and answered.

Stan's craggy face appeared on the screen.

"I don't like calling you at home, Radic."

"It's easier here than asking my security chief to set up an untapped line at the plant."

"We could have met at the Lickspittle again."

"Did you call me just to whine?"

Stan showed his teeth. "Laslo. Haven't we been friends for a long time?"

Laslo nodded. Like him, Stanislav Kostevic came from a long line of Croatians who'd fought assimilation with a fierce pride. He remembered his father telling stories about Stan's and Laslo's great-grandfathers who had joined the terrorist groups that harried the Serbs in the hopes of ousting them from Croatia. Fifty years later, their grandfathers had survived ethnic cleansing, fought in the freedom war of 1990 and celebrated the independence of the Republic of Croatia, only to see their country disintegrate, like so many around the world, under the geopolitical influence of Government Mundial.

The ties went deep, and even though their fathers had left the rugged mountains behind, they'd kept the stories alive for their sons. In many ways, especially in their customs, none of them had left the old country. Laslo felt his stomach cramp. It was because of the blind observance of those customs that his son carried that awful disease.

"Get on with it, Stan. My wife is around, and I don't want her to walk in on me."

"The authorization code took a bit more effort to obtain than I thought. It'll cost you extra."

"Christ, Stan, you don't change. Always trying to milk the deal. Even our friendship has limits."

Stan laughed. "I could have got you an unprotected code, but since we have a past together..."

"Go on."

"Even though MGRC keeps a series of authorization codes ready for use, they haven't assigned one in more than twelve years. At least three members of the Committee must sign off on the code before you can use it. If I'd just stolen one, they'd have swarmed down on you the first time you used it. Plus, most codes have heavy-duty restrictions. Every time you access a databank with the code, it sends a signal to the Enforcement Branch at the Committee office so they can monitor whether you're using only the data they authorized you to. If they judge you're not, they can sever the link right then, and that cancels your code. Then they'd have been on you like radiation from a sunspot." Stan showed his teeth. "So, I made an executive decision to improve on your order. I took a bigger risk, and I deserve compensation for it."

"You obtained a code that bypasses Enforcement?"

"Not only Enforcement, but the warning system *and* the data logs. When you use the code, your access won't be recorded anywhere."

"How did you manage that?"

Stan gave him a smug grin. "Tell me, Laslo, who's watching the watchers?"

"Someone's monitoring the Committee members?"

"Not someone, something. Not many people remember that when Government Mundial established MGRC they made sure those in power wouldn't be subverted. They set up a dedicated bionet to monitor the Committee members' use of their own auth codes. They did that by providing the bionet with an all-privileges code."

"I'll be using Government Mundial's own authorization code?"

"Yup. I set up a sentinel on one of the Committee members. As soon as she used her auth code, I waited for GM's bionet to activate then used a new worm one of my guys designed to crawl up its pathways until I got the code. We also found a loophole—the bionet isn't set up to detect the use of its own code. You can therefore use it—alone or with someone else—without fear of discovery."

"Are you sure it'll work?"

"I tried it myself. Never raised an alarm."

Laslo grunted. "I knew I could count on you. How much?"

"Thirty percent over the agreed fee."

Laslo calculated quickly. He'd have to sell some stocks. "Done. You'll have payment after I receive the code. Send it here, will you?"

"Agreed. Now, about that other matter you asked me to look into."

"Sinclair."

"Your chief scientist has been fabricating brain dust."

Laslo's jaw clenched at the same time as his hands. He slowly relaxed them. "For how long?"

Stan shrugged. "Long enough. At least a year."

"He's using GeneTech's labs?"

"Yes."

"Who's he working for?"

"Sinclair's dealing with Val Palmodus, otherwise known as Stringer."

"Damn. You're certain of that."

"I wouldn't drop a name like Stringer's just for the fun of it. They say he's got a death grip on all his employees. The only one who's allowed close to him is his cousin, Argus. He's the big guy who waited by the limo."

"Gerry's swimming in a bigger pond than I thought."

"If I were him, I wouldn't wait for the water to dry up."

"That only concerns me if he leaves me flopping around beside him. I want you to find as much as possible on Stringer's brain dust operation."

"Why don't you ask me to knock on his door and drop in for tea, while you're at it?"

"If that's what it takes, fine." Laslo cut the comm on Stan's shaking head just as he heard Jelena's steps on the marble of the foyer.

She entered the room, unaware of his presence. Every time he saw her, he was struck by how slender and graceful she was. Her blond hair, now marbled with gray, flowed past her shoulders to the middle of her back in the same style she'd worn when he first met her. In profile, her face and his son's almost merged into one.

He made a slight movement, and she turned.

"Laslo. I heard the comm but I thought you'd taken the call in your office. Have you seen my shopping list?"

"No."

"Ah, here it is." She picked up a thin metal card that fit in the palm of her hand. She went back to the hall, hesitated, then turned. "I just made some fresh coffee. Would you like another cup?"

Laslo saw the hesitant warmth in his wife's eyes. He knew he hadn't been easy to live with for a long while. She'd become leery of his dark moods. "Sure." He pushed himself up and followed her into her kitchen.

Jelena had created a world for herself in that room. Scattered amongst every modern appliance needed to create the elaborate meals she favored were little touches that lent an atmosphere of elegance to the room. Sheaves of dried yellow flowers from the GeneTech garden were scattered about; white, blue and yellow antique pottery from Portugal hung on the walls; marble-topped counters, white panels, blue ceramic tiles were arranged into a perfect combination.

He watched her pour two cups of the dark brew. He wondered fleetingly what it was made of, now that real coffee wasn't readily available anymore. Jelena would know—she tracked down details like that.

She handed him the cup with a tentative smile. He nodded and leaned against one of the counters. Talking about the contents in his cup would give him an excuse not to bring up Zelimir. Unfortunately, he'd stalled long enough. As it was, Jelena would probably murder him for keeping her son's condition secret from her.

Jelena pulled a chair away from the kitchen table and sat down, then very carefully placed her cup on the white surface. "Will you be going to work?"

"Why, am I disturbing your plans?"

"Of course not. We don't need to entertain each other."

Laslo pursed his lips. "No, I guess we don't." He studied his wife, so outwardly serene and composed, and saw definite signs of nervousness. She fidgeted with her hair, bit the inside of her lip. His heart beat faster. She'd always seemed tuned to his state of mind. Maybe she sensed what he was about to tell her.

She frowned. "You seem in a strange mood today. Did you receive bad news?"

"Hmm?"

"The comm."

"Oh. Yes." He'd forgotten about Gerry. "One of my scientists is using my plant to make illegal drugs. Someone I trusted."

"That's terrible. What are you going to do?"

"I'm not certain. Nothing for the moment. I sure don't want the police or the Mungers involved. My own affairs wouldn't stand close scrutiny right now." Her eyes widened slightly. "What, do I shock you?"

"In the twenty years we've been married, Laslo Radic, you never felt the need to unburden yourself."

"I know." He set the cup on the countertop, untouched. "Speaking of marriage, do you miss the Community, Jelena?"

She stilled. One hand tightened around the cup until her knuckles became white. "You've never asked me before. Why now?"

"Sometimes you need to look back, reassess your choices. Make sure you've made the right decisions."

She raised her chin and looked directly at him. "Choices? Decisions? We didn't choose each other, our fathers did. We didn't decide it was time to marry, the Community did."

"We could have said no."

"And so? They would have chosen someone else for us." She made a small, helpless gesture. "I didn't expect you to take me out of the Community and I didn't think I'd come to care for you, but both happened, and I'm grateful." She smiled softly, her face full of emotion. "And I feel blessed that we have our son."

Laslo felt his body begin to shake, and his vision dimmed. His chest felt hot, his hands cold. Dimly, he heard Jelena's voice. Two hands appeared in his field of vision and they cradled his face, forced him to follow with his eyes until he saw her face. She pulled on his hands and directed him into a chair.

He slumped, feeling very tired. Jelena bustled away and came back with a bottle of water. Eyes closed, he sipped it slowly until he felt more settled. He could smell the coffee just brewed, and the rich, spicy aroma, so familiar in this room, calmed him. He nodded his thanks.

Jelena sat cater-corner to him and placed a hand over his. "Tell me what's wrong, Laslo."

He pinched the bridge of his nose. "Something's wrong with Zelimir," he said.

She snatched her hand away. "What do you mean?"

"He has this genetic mutation—"

"No. He's a beautiful boy. He's perfect." She pushed away from the table and stood by the window, her back to him.

Laslo stared at her rigid shoulders, astonished. He hadn't counted on denial. Strangely, it gave him the strength to continue.

"Two years ago, I received a comm transmission from a man in Arizona claiming to be my kin. He wanted my permission to use my DNA in a study. Naturally, I went down there to assure myself that everything was legitimate. It turned out to be true. He was a very distant cousin, and we had something in common—we shared a genetic mutation."

"But you're not sick." She spoke to the window.

"Neither are you. But when a carrier of the mutation has children with one who has a compatible one, the result is deadly."

She turned slowly. He saw her swallow.

"Are you saying I'm a carrier, too?"

"Yes. The disease is recessive, which means that you need two carriers to create it. That was one of the reasons that cousin called me. He also married a carrier. Two of his six children were dying of the disease. They're dead now. MGRC turned down his request for a study."

Jelena grasped the back of the chair. "Are the other children affected?"

"In a way. All his children are carriers of the mutation. If they marry a carrier, the chances are one of their kids could have it. As soon as I came back, I paid a lab to have us tested. Zelimir has the disease. It could get triggered at any time."

She stared at him mutely, then: "You've known for two years. How could you hide something like that from me for so long? I had the right to know. Damn you—" Her voice broke. She swallowed. "I had a right."

"I thought I'd have the cure for it by now. I'd tell you and cure our son at the same time." He finished his water in two gulps. "It hasn't happened."

"What's the name of the disease?"

"Barcina's xylopoiesis," he said. This time, the words came out more easily. He explained what it was, and what it would do to their son. Jelena clamped a hand over mouth, but he could hear the little moans she made; tears filled her eyes, but they didn't spill over.

When he was finished, she sat down across from him.

"That's why you asked me about the Community, isn't it?"

"Yes. By refusing to accept new families into it, the elders have facilitated the propagation of the disease. If we'd both married outside, the chances that our son would have Barcina's would have been infinitesimal."

Jelena shuddered. She rubbed her face then straightened her shoulders. "MGRC turned down your cousin. You won't let that happen to Zelimir."

"I'm not going through MGRC. Zel won't be a victim of paper pushers and politics. I told you, I thought I'd have the cure by now. My chief scientist's been at it for more than a year. It's more complex than he originally thought."

"He's the one making the drugs, isn't he?"

"Yeah. I just hired someone else to take over, though. He has a plan, and I think he can do it." It was his turn to grasp his wife's hand. "What I'm doing is illegal, you know that."

"Do you think that scares me? I expect you to do whatever you need to do to save our son." For a moment Laslo thought she would lose control, but instead she got up and walked away from the table. "Now, you go to work. I have shopping to do, plus other errands."

He banged the table with his fist, suddenly very angry. "How can you go on as if everything were normal?"

She stopped but did not turn around. "Believe me, Laslo, I'm far from feeling normal." Her shoulders stiffened. "We need to be strong, to focus on the goal. When I break down, I'll do it in private."

She left him sitting at the table, his hands wrapped around his cup. She was right, he thought. As he had told himself hundreds of time, focus on the goal. He grimaced.

And break down in private.

# Chapter Eleven

"Of course," the building administrator said, "you break anything, you pay for it. The furniture's brand-new."

"What there is of it," Torver muttered.

They stood in the middle of a living room three times the size of his bedroom. It was empty except for a single armchair, which stood between the wall-length window and the dining room table that was flanked by two flimsy-looking chairs.

"You want the place or not?" the man said.

Torver walked to the window. The metropolis rolled away below like an immense carpet, the thousands upon thousands of high-rises, as far as the horizon, making up its pile. "You're certain you have nothing higher?"

"Like the hundred and twenty-sixth floor, maybe?" The man snickered. He came to stand beside Torver and waved at the panorama of the city. "You're standing in the last building erected in the Hills before the area became a protected forest, and this is the only apartment I have. Make up your mind—I have things to do."

"I'll take it." Torver extended his hand. The administrator touched his data reader to Torver's palm and Torver authorized the transfer of his Identic and his financial status.

After checking the small screen of his reader, the man nodded. "The place is yours."

Torver had already turned back to the view before the administrator was gone. Gray clouds had covered the sky all day, but nearing dusk they had dissipated and the sun set fire to the sky. He adjusted the glass to almost-clear and watched the sun lower towards the horizon. Lights below popped on, one here and one there, then faster and in greater numbers, like bunches of spring flowers shooting up in a field. Soon it was dark, except for the lights below. The moon rose while his emotions churned. Finally, he had his own place; and by cosmic force, fate or sheer luck he'd found the apartment of his dreams, high above the rodents scurrying through their mazes, with windows so wide he felt he was hovering, suspended, above the city.

It felt right, as if he were home. Tomorrow he'd bring over his bionet and his mouse and things. He cocked his head and listened to the silence. The walls didn't groan or crack, no vid played in the background, no appliance hummed around him. He shifted his feet and coughed once. The walls resounded the noises, sharp and high against the bareness of the room. His stomach growled, reminding him he hadn't eaten since breakfast when he went in search of an apartment, and that he had no food with him. Yet he was reluctant to leave.

He sat in the armchair, letting its back and the darkness envelop him. He loved the night. At night he couldn't see anyone's eyes.

The hellish year he'd spent as a thirteen-year-old came back to him. He still didn't know if the problems he'd developed with his ability had been a function of puberty or whether they'd been needed to gain full control over it; but he kept falling into the eyes of every person he faced, and had learned more secrets from them than he'd ever wanted to know. Depression, lost hope, self-mutilation, loneliness—they festered in people, spread along their lifepaths, blighted them. Most of their secrets were ugly and mean, and made him feel the same.

Desperate for control, he'd walked the streets at night to avoid staring into people's eyes and crashing into their pasts. Even now, eighteen years later, able to control and to use his ability for his own ends, he still yearned for darkness, comfortable in its anonymity, its possibility of bodies without lives.

Torver thought about the little girl in the pink dress. When he was alone, surrounded by darkness and silence, her childish face often blurred and transformed itself until he was looking at his own. Maybe this happened because he understood her. She, too, had been living among the strangers who were her family.

He never went anywhere without her picture. She was his security blanket, he thought jokingly, a battered reminder of his self-discovery.

The first time he'd stepped into her past had been a fluke. He'd found an old piece of newsprint on the floor in his mother's kitchen that must have escaped the recycler. On it was a vidstill of a girl no older than six or seven. In the still, the vidstealer had cut off the head of the flat-chested woman who stood behind her; the woman's hand gripped the girl's shoulder more in a detaining gesture than one of affection. The picture was yellowed with age and crumbly, probably some old piece his father had kept to wrap one of his precious electronic components. There was no caption, no name, and no indication of where the vidstill came from. He'd almost thrown the piece into the recycler when his eyes fell on the girl's face. It was closed and tense, angry. He looked into her eyes and stepped through.

He'd been so surprised he'd jumped back out immediately. Then the wonder of what he'd just done struck him. He'd entered someone's eyes through their picture rather than having a live person in front of him. If he could do what he'd just done with any vidstill, the scope of his talent was even broader than he'd thought.

For weeks afterwards, he'd pick up vidstills of strangers from vidbooks or the news and gorge on their lives. He was totally indiscriminate, and after a time, their secrets fused one into the other until they became a confused jumble and he grew numb to them. But for all that, he learned much during that frantic time. Dead people had inaccessible lifepaths. As soon as he entered, the thread unraveled and became as insubstantial as sunlight. With the living, he soon discovered that, although he could travel their pasts, he couldn't go beyond the instant in which the picture had been taken. It was as if time had been arrested there.

He had gone back to the girl's picture many times over, watched the same scenes in her life repeatedly, and even though he still didn't know her name, he felt more connected to her than to any other human being. Tonight she seemed to be calling him, to defy him to know her better.

He wanted to cross the place-time barrier of the picture more than anything to see how she'd grown up, what sort of woman she'd become, what unmentionable incidents she'd hoarded in her past.

"Lights on, low," he said. The room glowed from a soft illumination that carved shadows around him. He took the picture from his pocket and looked at the girl, her face cropped and enlarged from the original still. He fixed his gaze on her eyes and plunged in.

The wispy thread behind her eyes gleamed and made it easy to follow down through the darkness, from the moment of the picture to the wrenching of birth and beyond. He grabbed the thread with his left hand, and instead of facing her past and moving along it, he turned to his right, the thread at his back but keeping a hand on it. Its resilience no longer surprised him; it comforted instead. The effect of the void into which he stared—the nothingness of obscurity—was disorienting; his only grasp on reality was the feel of the life thread in his hand.

After a few moments, the darkness began to glow faintly. He peered through the feeble twilight, and as he kept looking, it took on the straggly thread-shapes of lifepaths. There were hundreds of them, maybe more, intricately woven together. His hand still holding the girl's thread, he followed one with his eyes, but he soon became lost in the tangle and gave up.

He turned back to the girl's. For the first time he noticed that, at certain points along her thread, other light ribbons speared through it.

Why had he never noticed that phenomenon before? He focused on the place-time of the girl's birthday and he was there, facing the flat-vid that unfolded when he willed it. Her lifepath ran through the screen-like image; he could see it coming in, but the scene obscured the thread behind it, as if a wall had been erected.

He saw the girl and the mother and the butler. Instead of watching them, he ran his eyes along the border of the flat surface. There they were—two threads coming out. He let the scene collapse. The threads now crossed the girl's lifepath. Her mother's and the butler's.

Torver grinned. Connecting lives, events that linked and affected more than one person, converging through their lifepaths. Every life was touched by so many, some for longer periods than others. Strangers you bumped into on the street, waiters, bus drivers, parents, lovers, colleagues. Every lifepath intersected countless times or wrapped around others. With the girl's path as an anchor, maybe he could explore other people's lives.

Events would unfold from the perspective of the person's thread he held. What would happen if he switched from one lifepath to another? Would events be rewritten? Were the lifepaths a true representation of past events, of its owner's memories?

If he followed someone else's thread, it raised another problem he wasn't certain he wanted to test. His body wasn't physically present in this halfway place, and he needed a pair of eyes to enter, to follow a lifepath and exit back into his body. If he left the girl's and followed another's, whose eyes would he come through? And where would he find himself? Outside his body in another place or back in his new apartment? Or again maybe he would lose the way, unable to find the original lifepath he'd come in on, and walk the threads until his real body gave out or died.

The questions triggered a memory that gave him an idea. Years ago, he'd gone on an outing with his parents in the far north. The flat, shapeless terrain gave no clue as to where they were. To find their way back, his father had planted electronic beacons along their route.

That was what he needed to do. Only he didn't have access to markers. Something to think about. Today, though, he wanted to go forward, through the time the picture had been taken, into the girl's future-past. Future from the vidstill, past for her.

Torver grabbed the thread with both hands and ran his eyes to the left. The distance between the scene with the butler and the time the picture had been taken was short. A couple of years—three at the most. At that point, the thread stopped, truncated. He couldn't see the barrier, but he knew it was there.

He selected a point close to the truncated thread, and he was there. He'd found that if he looked ahead towards the invisible barrier while he moved, he became dizzy and was yanked out, so with his right hand on the thread, he began to walk as if he were in his own body, eyes down. He could see now that he was passing through intersecting threads; they fluttered and swirled like a band of fog, reshaping themselves into shimmering filaments behind him. It appeared that, as long as he had a hand on a lifepath, only that one was substantial.

The darkness on which he walked felt solid, but when he looked more closely, he saw that threads, fainter than those around him, ran under his feet.

The closer he came to the point of entry, the more unsound the surface felt. It wavered every time he took a step, as if he walked in melted plasmer; it began to stick to his soles, to suck at his legs, to make it difficult for him to raise his foot.

He frowned, his mind suddenly foggy. He wanted to raise his head but seemed to recall he shouldn't. His right hand held a wisp of murky brown fog. "It should be white," he said to the darkness. His last word echoed around him.

Another step forward, only to bump against a hard surface. He stared down at his hand. What was it that he was holding?

The thread was the answer. He closed his eyes and tried to chase the confusion from his brain. White. The thread should be white. The white thread was a path to the past. It connected to the present. An entire life. His mind saw the barrier. Or a gate? The face of a young girl flashed in his mind.

He remembered now. The picture. He wanted to know who she'd become.

If he expanded the thread at the juncture of the wall, maybe he could use the opening to push through. He focused exactly on the point where the thread was cut off.

Just as the familiar scene began to enlarge, Torver looked slightly higher, beyond the barrier. He felt the familiar disorientation of his body moving without his conscious help. In front of him ran a length of wispy thread, shinier than what he was used to. He looked behind him. The thread stopped abruptly, as if severed. He was through! He concentrated on the very end of the thread ahead. The lifepath expanded on its own as he arrived there.

At first he saw nothing but black. Then the black moved and he was staring at hair—her hair—still silvery black. She had her back to him. When she walked away, he realized he was watching her in real-time. She pulled her hair back and fastened it with an ornate barrette. Even though she was short—definitely under two meters—she had wide shoulders, and the muscles of her back rippled under her black, clinging one-piece suit.

After a few steps she seemed hesitant, as if she'd forgotten what she was going to do. She tilted her head to the side.

"Come on, turn around, I want to see your face," he muttered.

*Face...*an echo repeated.

As if she'd heard him, or the echo, the woman stiffened then turned her head sharply to the left.

Torver yelled, staggered by the sight. The face had no flesh. The mouth was set in a fixed grimace and in some parts the bone of her jaw showed through. She had no ear. Reflexively, he raised his hand to ward her off.

As soon as he let go of the lifepath, he knew it was a mistake. Something wrenched him from behind and he lost his footing. He was pulled back, very fast, until his spine slammed into a hard surface. He heard a sound like breaking glass. He was still being pulled, but he wasn't moving.

It was the barrier. It held him.

Before he could think of what to do, he felt it shatter, and he was pulled backwards again, faster than before.

He couldn't stop. He tried to catch the lifepath, but his surroundings had become a blur. There was nothing to grab on to. Pressure built in his chest until it was difficult to breathe. In a lucid moment, he wondered if he'd be going back in time until he didn't exist anymore.

"No!"

The scream hadn't come from him. His speed slackened.

"Come back," the voice said again. "Take my hand."

In front of him, a white wispy thread appeared. He grabbed it and lurched to a stop. The thread had a familiar feel, and he knew it was the girl's. Now all he had to do was go back to the point of entry.

His eyes moved along the lifepath, as far as he could see. The slight disturbance that told him where he'd entered her eyes wasn't there. He searched for a well-known scene, but the thread stayed closed. He'd been stopped in his descent, but now he was lost in the void. He tightened his grip on the thread.

Two days after Laslo's offer, Demetria was still angry. It was a righteous anger, she felt, the indignation of the betrayed.

"Vincent's despicable, Dympna," she said. "I never imagined he'd stoop so low as to humiliate me like that."

"Dr. Francis may not be the one who told Mr. Radic about your dermophagia."

"How would you know? You're not the one who had to deal with that slime."

"About which slime would you be talking?"

"Both! Does he think I'll come to him like a puppy for the unique chance of a better prosthesis?"

"It would make your life easier. You should call Mr. Radic back. Tell him you will take the job."

Demetria strode to the window and watched the sun set ablaze the high-rises one hundred and twenty-six floors below. She waited until she could see nothing but a mass of darkness sequined with lights.

"He had no business telling anyone."

"Try to calm down. Look at this situation rationally."

"There is no such thing as rational in this case. I'll kill Vincent."

"Before you eliminate Dr. Francis, consider that there were other ways for Mr. Radic to obtain his information. You have led a quiet life, but not a cloistered one. If he has an EP, or a clever assistant, it would be fairly easy to access medical records."

"It's illegal to do that."

"Yes, but there are always loopholes. Mr. Radic did say he had done research on you. If he told the truth and his company developed a new prosthesis for Brett's dermophagia, GeneTech probably also made the first one. They might have been given the names of all prosthesis users."

"How would he even think to check medical records?"

"You refused to meet him." Demetria almost heard Dympna shrug. "It might have led him to the conclusion you had a medical condition. There are so many genetic mutations and environmental diseases today, it would be a logical place to start, especially since it's your only eccentricity." Dympna paused. "Your only major one, at least."

Demetria flopped into her carved Victorian sofa. "Very funny. You must admit that Vincent is the easiest source of information."

"Yes, but would he jeopardize his friendship with you by doing that? He has profited from it several times in the past. He knows about your desire for secrecy on that subject."

Demetria smiled. "Are you sure you're not a real person hidden in the wall? You make too much sense for a machine."

"You know that I build upon experience. In fact…"

Demetria's neck prickled. She heard the traces of an echo in her ears. Dympna's voice droned on, but she couldn't concentrate on the words. She got up and headed towards the kitchen, but stopped after a few steps in the middle of her living room. It felt as if someone had grabbed the vision line that connected her to reality when she meditated and yanked. The room filled with whispers, the light around her dimmed. Something threatened, she was sure of it, but she didn't know where it came from.

She withdrew the barrette clipped to the front of her suit and fastened her hair with it to get it out of the way. The whispers became louder, and she strained to hear them.

"I want to see your face," someone murmured behind her. *Face…*the whispers around her repeated.

She turned her head to peer over her shoulder.

Someone screamed, and whatever held her let go. She tumbled forward. Instead of the floor stopping her fall, it opened, and she toppled through it. Green grass sped up towards her; she slammed facedown onto it. Breathless, aching from the fall, she pushed herself up on all fours and looked around.

An avalanche of green hit her—leaf-green and moss-green and grass-green all jumbled together, verdant vegetation as far as the eye could see. Amongst all that green, wildflowers sprouted, their bright petals like a patchwork quilt. Stunned by the profusion of color, she got to her feet and studied her surroundings.

Below and to her right, at the bottom of a lichen-covered cliff, a fast-flowing river sparkled in the sun. She lifted her eyes to the sky. The soft warmth of the sun fell on her face, melted on her neck and flowed into her limbs. She could stay here forever, she thought, and dream lazy dreams. If only she could figure out how she came here.

She looked behind to see the vision line attached to her back. Somehow, without the benefit of meditation, she'd fallen through into the dream world.

Movement on the left caught her eye. A man ran in parallel to where she stood, and it wasn't a controlled run. His arms windmilled as if they worked to keep his balance or to stop his legs, which seemed to have a life of their own. He was headed straight for the cliff, and his unbridled gallop would throw him off the rock and into the river below. He'd certainly die.

She started running while her brain automatically calculated an intercept course. The probability that he'd drop off the cliff before she reached him was high. Closer now, she recognized him—he was the grownup version of the boy in her last vision. Surprise made her slow down. Her hesitation cost her—the man was now in front of her. She ran harder. In a few seconds, he'd be over the edge.

"No!" she screamed. He seemed to hear her and slowed. Now he stood on the brink of the cliff. "Come back!" were all the words she could yell while running. She pulled up just behind him, and when he half-turned, still running, she extended her hand. "Take my hand."

He grabbed it. His foot slipped off the cliff and he fell. Demetria crashed to the ground, her hand tight around his. Quickly, she grasped his wrist with her other hand. The weight of his body dragged her shoulders over the edge of the cliff.

"I have you," she gritted out. She was still out of breath from her run. Her shoulder muscles burned. "Push yourself up. I won't be able to hold you much longer."

The man hung limp like a rag doll.

"Can you hear me?" Her breasts cleared the cliff. She dug the toes of one foot, then the other, in the soft ground.

Time slowed. The river sparkled below, and the gush of its rapids matched the sound of the blood rushing in her ears. The sun beat hot on her back, and the sweet smell of crushed grass made her dizzy. He was a dead weight at the end of her arms. Some force pulled him in the opposite direction, in the same way earlier his legs did not seem to obey him.

Demetria searched around for something to grab on to, but she was lying on smooth grass. The closest tree was several yards away.

Then she remembered her thread. Quickly, she let go of his wrist with one hand, reached behind her back and tugged gently. The thread stretched tight. When she tugged again, this time more forcefully, it wrenched her backwards, dragging the man along with her until they were both lying at the door of the dim no-man's land of her vocal scanning.

She shook him, and suddenly, he looked straight at her.

"It's you," he said. His voice was raspy and weak.

"Do you know where we are?" she said. "What we're doing here?"

Slowly, he rose to his feet. "No." He took her hand and pulled her up. "I'm not supposed to be here."

She pointed to the door. "I usually cross the threshold to get home." She opened it and felt her vision line pull at her to take her through. "Maybe it'll work for you, too."

He smiled, and his blue eyes bored into hers. "You're as beautiful as I thought you would be."

With the line pulling at her, she felt her consciousness shift outwards and sideways. Just before she left the vision, she grabbed his sleeve and pulled him through the door with her.

WHEN DEMETRIA OPENED HER EYES, SHE WAS LYING FACEDOWN ON THE FLOOR OF HER living room.

Alone.

TORVER SLAMMED BACK INTO HIS BODY. HIS ARM JERKED OUT, AND SOMETHING FLEW OUT of his hand. He heard it shatter somewhere to his right. He didn't recognize where he was; maybe he'd crossed into another halfway place.

Then myriad lights, pinpricks through a dark cloth, winked in the night far below, and he remembered his new apartment.

He tried to get up but couldn't. His muscles felt slack, as if they'd been stretched taut for a long time and now had loosened up in reaction. Both his legs and arms shook. He flopped back into the chair.

Maybe it was only relief that made him loose-limbed. Or fear. He would have died out there if it hadn't been for her. How could she have known he was in trouble? How could he have heard her, talked to her, been with her? Where was that place he'd gone to and how did he get there? How did she manage to send him back into his own body?

Too many questions leading to other confusing questions. "Increase lights," he said.

The living room, as empty as it was before he'd gone into her lifepath, nevertheless seemed less unlived-in. Torver looked to his right and saw that the shattering sound he'd heard had been her picture crashing to the floor. Even from where he sat, the crack that speared through the eyes horizontally, splitting them in two, made a statement, telling him that getting to know the woman through that picture was now disallowed, improper.

She'd brought him back. Whatever he thought, he told himself, the truth remained. Without her, he'd still be lost in that half-reality, falling, maybe forever. Whether she knew it or not, they were somehow connected, and it didn't matter whether he never traveled her lifepath again. They would find each other.

He shuddered, awed by what he'd experienced. More than ever he needed to know what he was, whether this ability, this talent, this curse, was a gift or a nasty mutation.

He knew what he and his mother would have been called five hundred years ago—witch, sorcerer, warlock. Today, as in times past, they were still in hiding.

But now he had a job where he could begin to research his origins and legitimize his ability.

Yes, he thought, things are looking up.

DEMETRIA WONDERED IF SHE SHOULD GO SEE HER DOCTOR THEN REJECTED THE IDEA. ALL he'd advise would be to talk to her scanning guide. He'd definitely reject her idea that her out-of-control visions were a side development of her dermophagia.

She'd never wondered before why the vocal scanning had been so easy for her, even at the very beginning. Now she suspected the scanning had acted like a key to unlock a dormant ability in her.

Then there was the utter certainty that the last two visions had not come from her subconscious. In olden times, shamans dreamed; spirits visited them in the night and instructed them about the future through symbols. Did her visions predict the future? If so, whose?

She felt as if events still unknown to her were moving towards a concordance, and they would involve her. The boy in her mother's living room had challenged her to find him. *Pay attention to the double helix,* he'd also said. Then Laslo Radic had called her to work on a genetics project.

The man who looked like the boy grown up had needed her help. What did it mean? How had she come to be there when he'd needed her?

She sighed. One thing was certain. She was the first one of her family ever to have premonitory visions. The logical hypothesis would then be that this ability was related to her disease. Somehow, her genetic mutation had induced a change in her psyche.

One way to confirm this would be through comparative analysis of all documented cases of dermophagia. Unfortunately, the only way she could do the research was with an authorization code.

"Dympna, how many codes did the Genetics Review Committee give out in the past, say, ten years?"

"Apart for those issued in the medical environment, none."

Except, now, Laslo Radic could supply one.

Demetria took a shaky breath and let it out slowly.

It would be unethical and dishonest to use the code for herself.

She couldn't do it.

But it would be the only chance she had.

Her honor against knowledge.

She bit her lip. Maybe she didn't have to decide now. She could accept Radic's offer, take time to sort out her feelings without burning her bridges.

"Dympna, contact GeneTech in the morning. Let Mr. Radic know that I'd like to speak to him about that project of his."

# Chapter Twelve

Even after having made her decision to accept Laslo Radic's job offer, Demetria couldn't settle down.

"Out," she muttered. "I need to get out of here." She knew that if she stayed in she'd dissect every detail of the vision, she'd rehash her motives for taking Radic's job after she'd told herself she wouldn't let him manipulate her, she'd mull over her genetic defect, and still she'd have no answers, only more questions. She needed to run, get the stress and anxiety of the past few days out of her system. It was the perfect time to do it, after sundown, when she had a better chance of being alone on the paths.

She looked out the window. The darkness of the woods beckoned. Even though she couldn't see the treetops from these heights, she imagined them moving in the breeze, whispering secrets to each other.

She quickly changed into shorts and a loose top and put her prosthesis back on. On her way out she grabbed her kali stick from the closet. She felt more secure running with the meter-long stun stick in her hand, especially since she'd heard that Termites were rumored to roam the woods. It was said Termites didn't take well to strangers; if she met one in the dark, she wanted to have something with which to defend herself. The kali stick wasn't good against a firearm, but Termites weren't known to carry guns.

Once outside, she strolled at first, not to warm up but to get used to the heat on her skin, cloying like thick honey. Darkness was full now, and the lights from the city formed a dome over the metropolis, obscuring whatever stars were out. It would be enough to see by, even in the woods. After a few minutes, she broke into a loping run.

All Demetria could hear was her syncopated breathing and the pounding of her feet on the gravel trail, and both had a calming effect on her brain and her emotions. The trees loomed dark around her, giants bending at the waist to obscure the city lights. It didn't matter. She knew the path by heart, had run this way hundreds of times.

Every time she entered this last piece of the Gatineau Woods, she was deeply thankful to the topographic anomaly that had saved the forest from the Thirty-Year Drought. She loved the trees, the last bit of forest for kilometers around, mostly white oak, and fir—they were old, soaring and majestic—although she preferred them when they wore the deep emerald of spring or the fiery reds and yellows of fall, not like now when their leaves had taken on the dried-out green of summer.

It was really too hot to run, even in this green space. Her hair was wet, and sweat dripped into her eyes, but every time she slowed images of her last vision flashed in her mind and mixed with the previous one.

The visions themselves were disturbing, but it was the loss of control that scared her the most. Twice now she'd slipped into one without warning or preparation. Each time she'd felt more of a spectator than an actor; even when she'd found herself at the familiar door, she hadn't been in control. The vision had dissolved, and she was back. It frightened her. Was the dermophagia getting worse, causing hallucinations, or was *he* the one who, somehow, had succeeded in controlling her visions? Was he sending her a message, or was she going mad?

She ran harder.

When her breath came out in gasps, she stopped in the middle of the path and bent at the waist, hands on her knees. She needed to slow down, pace herself.

She straightened and walked in circles, breathing deeply. The blood pounding in her ears subsided. As her respiration slowed to normal, she began to notice the night noises around her again. Rustles in the grass. The song of cicadas, forecasting even more heat. The hoot of an owl.

Demetria blinked at the impossible sound. Owls had been extinct for at least thirty years. The owl hooted again. It came from off the path, ahead and to her right.

She squinted and peered through the trees. The woods were thick, and light barely pierced the treetops, but there, about two hundred meters off the path, she saw a shadow move. A light flickered. Not Termites, then. They'd never use a torch at night.

A shape stepped through a patch of moonlight. From its size and breadth, she decided it must be a man, and he was carrying a large sack over his shoulder. The package wriggled slightly. The man was followed by another with a similar bag. They were coming towards her.

The owl sounded again, this time on her left and down the road. She whipped around. She saw a light bob up and down, then it was gone.

This isn't good, she thought. Whatever these men were doing, it didn't feel or look legal. They wouldn't welcome an eyewitness.

She tightened her grip reflexively on her kali stick. She'd use it if she needed to, but she'd much prefer to leave unnoticed. No kali stick could compete with a plasma gun.

The shorter way back to her apartment lay to the right. She hesitated another few seconds, straining to make out where the men would end up, praying they wouldn't see her in the near-darkness. She was equally handicapped—they'd turned their lights off, and she couldn't see them. Better to go to the left, even though it would take longer. There was a ravine in that direction, close by. She'd slide into it and slip by them.

She turned and came face-to-face with a dark, misshapen figure. A light shone in her eyes, blinding her. She raised her hand to protect what was left of her night vision.

"Well, what have we here?" a man's voice said. "Hey, guys," he said to a spot above her shoulder, "found another one."

He lowered the light to shine it along her body. In those few seconds, she realized the hump was a man he held on his shoulders in a rough fireman's carry. He dumped his load and reached for her.

She didn't hesitate. She sidestepped, rushed in close when he would expect her to run and with two stiffened fingers jabbed him in the eyes. He howled, dropped his torch. She half-turned, slammed her shoulders into his chest and, while he was stumbling, rammed her kali stick into his crotch. The man grunted and fell to his knees with a moan.

Knowing she'd soon run out of time, she flipped the stick and slammed it on the base of his neck. He fell flat on his face.

"What the fuck's going on?"

Demetria raised her head, readied her stick. Two men dressed in black faced her, balaclavas hiding their features. She glanced over her shoulder and saw another coming up behind her. All three dumped their burdens on the ground. Even in the weak light she could see they were bodies. One of them looked to be a woman.

When in doubt, she told herself, scream your head off.

She centered, found her balance, tightened her grip on her stick and ripped the night with a piercing cry.

TORVER TURNED AWAY FROM HIS BIONET AND RUBBED AT THE SORE SPOT ON HIS SHOULDER. The tracking chip Ashar Mahoud had implanted in his collarbone was bothering him tonight.

He heard a little scratching patter just before his mouse appeared at the edge of the table.

"Hey, you," he said, "what are you doing here?" His eyes traveled to the near-empty plate on the table. "Ah, I see. Trying to find out if I left any crumbs for you." He picked up the mouse and placed it in the middle of the plate. It instantly set to eating.

Torver stretched. After he'd come back from his excursion into the woman's lifepath—he couldn't think of her as a girl anymore—he'd splurged on a cab to go back to his parents' house. He'd given them the good news, packed his bionet and his mouse and gone back to his apartment. He'd ordered a meal at the small deli downstairs, and just before it closed, too, then set to work.

He'd sunk into genetic modeling for a while, and he'd made some important decisions he'd implement when he started at GeneTech on Monday; but as he became more tired, the woman's face kept intruding in his work. After a while, he gave up.

"Time," he said to his bionet.

"Two-thirty-five."

"I thought I told you to stop me at midnight."

"Affirmative. Message delivered as requested."

"Damn." He must have been so deep in thought he hadn't heard the warning.

Torver surveyed his apartment, as empty as it had been a few hours ago. Got to get some furniture, he reminded himself. The first piece would be a vid, so he could unwind by stagnating in front of it. Since he currently didn't own one, the only alternative was to go for a walk.

He picked up his cardkey and left the mouse to its own devices. As soon as he stepped outside, he greeted the night like an old friend, even though the heat pressed on him. He hesitated, balancing on the curb, glancing right, then left. Right was the city with its concrete towers and endlessly paved road and a bar or a synth-caf bistro on every corner. Left was the park, with cooler air and solitude.

Torver pursed his lips, contemplating the murky patch the forest made against the city sky. It would be dark in there. Before he had time to reconsider, his feet turned him to the left.

He'd been walking for a half-hour and thinking of turning back when he heard the scream. Only one, but piercing and very close. He ran towards the sound. As he got closer, he heard grunts and mutters and swearing.

"Come on, Witty, stun her."

"I can't. I'm outta juice."

"Fuck. Grab the stick."

"I'm trying. Ow! Fuckin' bitch."

Torver stopped and took stock. Three men kept darting forward then retreating as a woman kept them at bay with a long stick. She'd soon be in trouble, though. The ground seemed to disappear a few steps behind her, and the men would wise up any time now and gang up on her.

The woman moved sideways and light from the torch on the ground fell on her face. He gasped. It was her.

He looked around, picked up a rock bigger than his fist. "Hey!" he yelled. Four heads turned towards him.

The woman took advantage of the distraction. She used her stick like a sword and thrust it at one of the men's solar plexus. As he folded over, she whipped the stick backhanded and hit the side of his head. The man fell to his knees, stunned. She turned slightly and readied her stick again. The strike had taken no more than two or three seconds. Damn, she was good.

The two other men backed off, wary now that Torver was moving towards them. They both eyed the rock he was holding.

"Hey, man," one of them said, "it's rad, okay? We got nothing against you."

The man she'd downed was back on his feet but didn't seem inclined to fight anymore. The men loped to where they'd dropped the bodies, heaved them over their shoulders and ran up the path. After a moment, all Torver could hear were the moans of someone in pain not far off.

"Are you all right?" he said to the woman.

"Yeah. You got a comm unit on you?"

"Yeah."

"Call the cops, will you? I'll check on the guy I dropped."

Torver keyed in 911 while he followed her. She picked up the torch beside the groaning man and illuminated him. He was still unconscious. Blood flowed from his nose. She ignored him and walked a few steps to the other form on the ground and crouched. Her light revealed the face of a man, eyes closed. He couldn't see if he was breathing.

Just as she was about to feel for a pulse, the man's arm darted out and he grabbed her wrist. An eyeblink later he let go, rolled away and jumped to his feet. For a second he teetered, then turned away and ran into the trees.

"What was that all about?" she said.

"Looks like he didn't want to make a complaint to the cops." He glanced back at the man on the ground. "This guy looks like a thug. You sure did a good job on him."

"A fallout among thieves, do you think?"

"There's a price on Termites' heads, didn't you know that?"

"No. That's disgusting." She straightened at the sound of gliders approaching. "Let's hope it's the police."

---

DEMETRIA GAVE HER STATEMENT, HER HAND STILL CLASPED TIGHTLY AROUND HER KALI stick. Adrenaline zinged through her body, and she felt elated. She never thought she'd use what she'd learned in Kali classes. She'd taken them more as an added exercise in concentration than as a self-defense tool, but in a real situation the moves, endlessly repeated until they'd become second nature, had saved her life.

No, she thought, they almost did. If not for the man also talking to the police, she would have come to serious bodily harm. She also felt confused and relieved.

While he was talking about the Termites, before the police had arrived, all she could think was *That voice, I've heard it before.* It made her shiver, suddenly cold. Then he'd approached her, the light from the torch had illuminated his face, and she'd recognized him.

"You," she whispered. "I've seen you before."

"You have?"

"Yes." She hesitated, unsure what to say next. Any way she tried to explain the visions, she'd sound like a nut. "Never mind."

Now the police were dropping them off at her building. She turned to her rescuer. Strange, she still didn't know his name. The officers had talked to them separately.

"I haven't thanked you for your help."

"Didn't do much. You seemed to have things pretty much in hand. What kind of fighting was that?"

She laughed. "Desperate. I just went with my instincts."

"And your stick." He pointed at her hand.

She balanced it on the palm of her hand and shrugged. "I was lucky they didn't have stunners. Thanks again."

"Wait." He stopped her with a hand on her arm. She lifted her eyes to his. Suddenly, something was crawling inside her head. Angry, she resisted, pushed back. The feeling stopped.

"I do know you," she said. She pulled away from him. "You're the one I saw."

"You saw me where?"

She shook her head. "Don't play games with me. Besides, didn't I save your life?"

He jumped at her words and flushed deeply.

"I guess I repaid the debt, then."

"What did you just try to do a moment ago?"

He looked around, clearly uncomfortable. "This isn't a good place to discuss it. And you said it—it's late. Maybe we can meet later, when we're both more rested."

"Give me your address. I'll contact you."

He pointed to the building. "I live right here. Apartment 8014." They walked through the entrance to the elevator. Demetria turned to him.

"What's your name?"

"Torver Lockwood. And you?"

"Demetria Greyson."

The elevator doors swished open, and he followed her inside. Demetria pushed number one hundred and twenty-six. She saw Torver smile.

"So, you're the one with the great view."

She watched him punch eighty. "Listen, Mr. Lockwood—"

"Torver."

"You'll think this is strange or stupid, but somehow we're connected, I'm sure of it."

He eyed the seam separating her face then lifted a hand to touch her left cheek. She recoiled.

"I saw you without this, but afterwards your skin was flawless. I thought I'd been mistaken." The elevator pinged and swished open. He stepped out then held his hand against the door to keep it from closing. "You're right, Demetria Greyson. You and I aren't finished with each other." He gave her a brilliant smile and let the door close after him.

"Hey, wait!" she yelled, but it was too late. She slapped her hand on the closed door. A few seconds later, it re-opened on her floor. Her finger hovered over the eightieth-floor button, then she shrugged and left the car. He was right. They should talk with a clear head.

The sun had just begun to peek over the horizon when she entered her apartment. She passed her hand over a metal disc, and the outer east wall became transparent. She stood facing the sun, eyes closed, humming under her breath. For ten minutes she stayed unmoving and imagined the heat of the sun on her face. In her vision it had felt like liquid gold, flowing through her every pore, forcing her body to melt from the inside out. It wasn't supposed to be a real sun, but she wasn't so sure anymore.

Torver Lockwood wasn't a crazy firing of neurons or a sick twisting of DNA. He was real, he existed. At least that relieved her mind. So, how had he ended up in her vision?

She stopped humming and opened her eyes. As the sun grew stronger, the translucent wall had darkened to filter the deadly rays. It had cooled in the last hours of the night, enough to lift the quasi-permanent smog. Her building being at the top of a hill, and her apartment being at the top of the building, she could see almost all the way to Montreal. The dome of the Casselman Mosque gleamed a burnished copper. Farther to the east, smokestacks rose, dormant now, like a forest of black toothpicks.

She smiled at her comparison. Not many people today would know what a toothpick was. Last year, she'd been lucky to find a box of the little wooden sticks used to clean the teeth after a meal. She'd paid a hefty price for them, but they were worth it.

Her thoughts shifted back to Torver Lockwood and how he was connected to her. How, in a few short days, her orderly, quiet life had been turned upside down. Images of her visions jumbled with the attack and battered her brain in gruesome, half-lit vid images.

All at once, her brain turned off, leaving a blank place inside her head.

With the sun rising fast on the horizon, Demetria walked to her bedroom. She flopped facedown on her bed and never knew when she fell asleep.

DEMETRIA GREYSON. TORVER'S BRAIN WAS ON FIRE. AFTER ALL THIS TIME OF WONDERING who and where she was, he'd learned both in a matter of a couple of hours. A greater surprise was that she had Brett's dermophagia. He should have recognized the gruesome sight from her lifepath for what it was, but he'd thought he'd been mistaken when she appeared in that strange place and saved his life. There, her face was unmarred and beautiful.

How did she know she'd saved his life? He had thought the scene had simply been another expression of the vid-like scenes he usually witnessed. He had never thought she had been an active participant. Then, a few minutes ago, he could have sworn she'd sensed that he'd tried to enter her eyes and that she'd pushed him back.

He stared outside his window. It was barely five in the morning, but already the sun was rising. He was too strung out to sleep. He'd head for GeneTech. To hell with the early hour. He had a feeling he'd accomplish a lot today.

# Chapter Thirteen

"...IS THAT?"

Torver sat up, instantly awake. Radic stood in front of him across from his desk, but his attention was riveted on the spinning hologram.

Torver rubbed his face, surprised to find more than stubble there. "What time is it?"

"Nine-thirty," Radic said. "Now, for the second time. What's that?"

Torver looked where indicated and immediately felt a rush. He changed his cot back to a chair.

"This," he said with a smile, "is what you hired me for."

Radic raised an eyebrow.

Torver laughed. He got up to stretch cramped muscles. "I have it. Well, not all of it, but this is certainly more than the beginning. Translating theory into practice proved more difficult than I'd thought. I've tracked down some of the defects, removed them one by one. The fossilized DNA I worked with was often damaged, so I tried to repair the sequences. But each time the strand collapsed. Finally, I used several samples, spliced together the chunks I wanted, then engrafted all the parts together. The procedure paid off.

"I'm going to start studies on mice today. Do you realize how long it took me to develop the theoretical concepts, working in secret, stealing time here and there from various bionets? Here, with the right tools and no need for stealth, it took me two weeks to realize those ideas. Two weeks!"

"Hold on a minute," Radic said during Torver's pause for breath. "What are you saying exactly?"

"Didn't you listen to me? I've worked out the technique to build what I call a retrogene. Not exact terminology, but it has a nice ring to it." He rubbed his hands together. "Now what I need to do is interchange it with its equivalent in a live biotype. I'll use mice. Once I can do that, I'll be ready to engineer it into stem cells. If that works, then we go to gene therapy."

"So, you're close."

"Yeah. That biometrician you hired has had two weeks to extract genome combinations for me, and I've used them as they came. I'll continue tomorrow—ask him to give me more."

Radic stared at the revolving DNA section. "Tomorrow's Sunday. Most people take a break on the weekends."

Torver sat on the edge of his desk and crossed his arms. "I'm used to a team that works with me on-site. I don't work regular hours. I need someone who's available when I need the data."

"Has that been a problem?"

"Not so far. Why is it, though, that I can't even communicate one-on-one with him? I'll need to discuss some specifics soon, and I don't want to have to go through his Perceptron every time."

"Dympna's pretty unusual, I'll grant you that."

"Who?"

"Your statistician's EP."

"He named his Perceptron?"

"She. Your colleague is somewhat eccentric." Radic crossed his arms over his chest. "I'm dead serious about this, Lockwood. No direct contact between you and her. This is for her and your own protection. You'll just have to make it work."

Torver was puzzled. Given the risks they were taking, if he were Radic, he'd want to keep all the people involved together. Then it hit him.

"She thinks the project is legitimate?"

"It *is* legitimate, just not legal. All you need to do is give her clear instructions and keep your mouth shut about why you need that data. The last thing we want to do is arouse her suspicions." Radic's gaze turned back to the DNA image. "Two Mungers came to see me on Friday. Alim and Martin. They wanted to make sure I was aware you didn't have a license."

"Really." Torver mulled over the new information. Then he smiled slightly at Laslo's unsubtle but effective reminder that he was also taking a risk. "I guess I can work it out with the EP." He rubbed his jaw then yawned. He was still tired, even though he'd slept. His brain felt mushy and he had a headache. "I think I'll hit the decont before I get back to work." He pushed away from the desk, tapped a key, and the DNA holo disappeared.

Radic nodded and strode to the door of the lab. "Keep me posted."

Torver yawned again and followed him out. "Sure."

He turned in the opposite direction from Radic. As he made his way to the public decont units, he had the uneasy feeling he'd forgotten something.

DEMETRIA LAUGHED OUT LOUD. SHE WAS DELIGHTED AT THE SIGHT OF THE FOUR-SIDED matrix that floated in front of her like a dangling piñata, leisurely spinning with the small push she had given it. She only needed to hit it the right way, to crack a small hole in the right place, and it would reveal its secrets. Then, a poke here, a tap there, a few nudges, and the trickle would become a shower of gifts.

She tipped the matrix down, making it roll on itself. She hadn't realized, when Laslo Radic had offered her the job, how huge the project would be. She'd started with macro information—number of genebanks, their location by country, their types and coded groups. She'd had to sort the data, reject the irrelevant until she kept only what she wanted. Then came the hard part—making sense of it all. The challenge would have been daunting for anyone else. For her, it made her want to float right beside the matrix.

There had been very few occasions in her life when she'd felt this exhilaration. She still remembered the first time, as vivid in her mind as if it had happened the day before.

She'd been seven years old when her mother, reportedly the greatest pianist in the Mundial States, had been given permission to play a special concert on one of the last acoustic grand pianos in existence, housed inside the Music Room of the Twentieth Century Museum. In one of her unexplained whims, her mother had brought Demetria with her. She hated going anywhere with her mother, who usually ended up criticizing her in that oh-so-reasonable voice in front of as many people as she could find.

Her mother had dragged her, sullen and uncooperative, into the stone building, an imposing structure built like a castle with crenellated towers and iron-spiked doors. They'd opened the museum just for them, she said, so let's show our appreciation by not letting them wait for us, shall we?

When Demetria crossed the threshold, she felt a little flutter at the top of her stomach, just under her heart. The sounds of their feet on the marble floor flew before them in the huge entrance hall and disappeared in the dim corners, as if the building had decided to add them to its permanent collection. She looked up. The ceiling, held up by massive columns, soared high above them. When she squinted, it seemed to recede and shrink, as if, by staring at it, she was making the walls grow.

Her mother yanked her hand, breaking the trance, and dragged her into the music room. Soon Demetria grew bored watching her mother play the shining black instrument. She sneaked out and wandered away to other rooms, strolling past strange electric implements, walls filled with books made of paper, and improbable pieces of clothing that men and women wore in the first part of that century.

She contemplated her own face in a myriad of polished kitchen appliances, marveled at a mid-twentieth-century bathroom—she could even flush the toilet with real water—meandered through a forest of metal boxes that showed images or played music. Everything seemed impossible, alien and clumsy.

The jumble of articles and the church-like silence that surrounded her left her numb and disoriented. Then, coming out of the exhibit, she noticed the smell. Rich and spicy, it invaded her, coursed through her veins, made her fingers and toes tingle. She tiptoed into the room from which it came.

It was filled with pieces of furniture, but they were made of a strange material. She looked around to see if there were any guards and, when she saw none, placed her hand flat on the surface of a small table and let it glide. It was like satin under her fingers, but warmer. She brought her nose near the surface and breathed in. The intoxicating scent she'd first noticed came from it.

Next, she walked to a larger piece—an *armoire*, she read on the tag. She looked up, taking in the diamond-point panels of the doors, the cornice—so high above it hovered in the dark—the wooden latch. She lifted the latch and pulled. The door opened with a creak that tore through the silence. She stopped, certain someone would come running, but no one did.

She stuck her nose inside, then her torso, then her legs. Unable to resist the musty smell, she closed the door and sat in the bottom. The darkness intensified the wonderful perfume, and she laughed, delighted with her discovery.

It was the same feeling she had now, this feeling of magical discovery, of potential, of owning something private that gave her joy. Of course, Demetria recalled, that feeling had been cut short when her mother had found her.

This time, though, her mother wasn't there to berate and pinch. Demetria could do what she wanted.

GeneTech's geneticist had sent her a list of what he needed, but it had taken a few days to get organized. She'd been surprised to find that the information was not centralized, but that each state within Government Mundial kept its own genebanks. The Northern States had twelve; the Central and Southern States had more than seventy; the European Communities close to two hundred. Some banks had closed operations, and their data were dormant, while others had just started or were long-running.

Data collection procedures differed from one state to the next, and so did the ID codings that identified each DNA entry. She had had to devise a program, with Dympna's help, that normalized all data points to compare them. Then she began to extract only those she needed.

The geneticist wanted her to group every ID code with a certain DNA signature then analyze the differences among them in a chronological, geographical and hierarchical order. A complex, intricate, multi-layered problem that would give nightmares to any statistician.

She smiled and rubbed her hands together. This was fun. She touched one side of the matrix and plunged in.

THE DECONT HAD BEEN A GOOD IDEA, BUT AS IF IT SERVED AS A SECRET SIGNAL, TORVER WAS now ravenous. He walked along the empty hallways, trying to remember the last time he'd eaten, except for the couple of nutribars and the countless cups of cold coffee he'd swallowed to keep going. It seemed like days since he'd had a full meal. Now might be a good time to go home. He'd reached a milestone in his research; he could take a break and plan his next steps. Besides, he needed to check on the mouse, make sure it hadn't got into trouble while he was away.

He halted in the entrance to his lab. Gerry Sinclair was bent over his bionet, tapping the keypad and staring at the vidscreen. He strode in, and Gerry jumped away from the desk.

"What are you doing?" Torver said.

Gerry smiled nervously and pulled on his ear, but his gaze remained on the screen. "I heard Laslo had to pry you out of deep sleep."

"I worked late. What were you looking for in there?"

"When people are tired, they make mistakes. I was checking on your security. Anyone could have walked in here." Gerry approached the desk and tapped a last key. The regression model popped up over the holo plate. Torver swore silently. He'd forgotten to passlock his bionet.

"That looks interesting," Gerry said.

Torver shrugged, trying to appear nonchalant. "Something I'm testing. It's not ready yet."

"Hmm." Gerry turned off the holo. "Regardless, you left it unprotected. Not smart, considering this doesn't look at all like a synthetic protein."

"It won't happen again," Torver said through clenched teeth.

"Good. I guess I'll go back to my office and finish a couple of reports. Go home and get some rest, will you?"

He watched him leave the room. The scientist's lab coat had pockets, and it looked like one of them held something. Was Gerry hiding a datadisc in there? Would he have had time to dump data onto one while he was alone in the lab?

Torver called up his files. Gerry had been busy. He'd accessed all of them, although it didn't appear he'd copied anything.

"Damn." He passlocked his system, closed off his lab. Even though it rankled that Gerry had caught his lapse in security, he admitted he'd pushed himself too far, and that had made him careless. Gerry might have been earnest and told the truth, but he knew what the man was capable of. He'd had only one glimpse into Gerry's lifepath and it had been enough.

He thought about Nevik's secret. Compared to Gerry's activities, his father's past actions seemed like peccadilloes.

Yes, Radic's chief scientist deserved a close watch.

## Chapter Fourteen

"WHO PAGED ME?" VINCENT YELLED AS HE STOPPED IN THE ENTRANCE TO THE emergency room.

"Right here, Dr. Francis."

One of the interns waved him over to the side of a bed at the end of the long, narrow room. Vincent rushed past a number of cubicles filled with patients.

"What have you got?"

The intern pointed to the writhing figure on the white sheets. "Dusthead. He's still conscious, but barely. There's nothing we can do." The young doctor lifted deadened eyes to Vincent's face. "You wanted to see one that was still alive."

"Thanks."

The man on the bed was thin to the point of emaciation. His eyes, opened wide, showed a fully distended pupil. Vincent held the man's chin with a hand and shone a light in his eyes. The pupils did not contract.

"How long has he been like this?" he asked the intern.

"Ever since he was brought in, ten minutes ago." They both listened to the fast, raspy breathing. "He'll go into respiratory failure soon," the intern said.

The man's arms and legs jerked. Vincent grabbed his arm.

"Can you hear me?"

The dusthead groaned. He turned his face towards Vincent's voice.

"Who sold you the stuff?"

The man shook his head.

"Tell me, damn it," Vincent yelled over the groans.

The man's mouth worked open as if he meant to say something. Vincent and the intern leaned closer. He croaked the beginnings of a word.

"What?" Vincent glanced at the intern who shrugged and shook his head.

The dusthead stopped thrashing. His eyes, pupils tight as the head of a pin now, bored into Vincent's, pleading. He tried to speak again. His back arched like a bow. He convulsed then lay still. Dark blood streamed from his ears and nose.

"Damn." Vincent straightened and turned to the intern. "Did you get what he said?"

"Not really. I thought I heard 'stree,' but I could be mistaken. He might have wanted to say he got the dust on the street."

"That's pretty much useless to me."

The intern stiffened. "I sent for you right away."

"I know." Vincent slapped his shoulder. "Ship him over to the lab will you? I want to do an autopsy. And call me if you have any other live ones."

"Will do." The intern turned his head at a commotion two beds down. "Gotta go."

With a nod, Vincent left him to deal with the emergency. He dug into his pocket for his portable comm and punched in his team's code.

"I want to see everyone in the path lab's meeting room in an hour. Please bring all the data you have on your brain dust cases."

An hour later, he surveyed the group clustered around the conference room table. They were a diverse bunch, considered strange and even anti-social by the rest of the Health Center staff, but they were hard-working, motivated, and they loved a challenge.

"Okay," he said. "I want us to exchange ideas on the brain dust problem. We had another fatality today. Su-Li, I'm assigning the autopsy to you—you haven't done one of the new cases yet. Maybe you'll find something we've overlooked."

The diminutive woman at the end of the table nodded.

"Let's start with a review of the facts we have. Sara?"

All heads turned to his deputy, Sara Bélanger. She cleared her throat, pushed her frizzy hair behind her ears, rubbed the spot between her eyebrows. "Vincent, if you don't mind, I'd like to run a vid." Her red-rimmed eyes rested on each person around the table. "I want to make sure everyone here knows that figuring out who's putting tainted dust on the market isn't an intellectual exercise."

She picked up the remote in front of her and pointed it at the center of the table. The lights dimmed, and the 3D face of a boy, maybe sixteen or seventeen, appeared. The family resemblance to Sara was unmistakable. The boy had inherited the same kinky hair and green eyes.

"Macki, my brother," Sara said. "Also an ex-dusthead."

"How long since he stopped using the drug?" Su-Li said.

"Two weeks ago." She shot a look at Vincent. "I did the autopsy myself."

The stunned silence was palpable. Then everybody spoke at once, words of sympathy and questions, until Vincent slapped the table three times quickly.

"People, Sara's dealing with her brother's death the best way she knows how—by trying to find clues that will lead us to the culprits. I suggest we help her do that." He nodded to her. "Let's play your vid."

Sara cleared her throat. "The only reason Macki talked to me is that, towards the end, he got scared. One of his friends died in front of him." Her mouth twisted. "That didn't prevent him from using it one last time." She pointed the remote at brother's image.

Macki suddenly smiled and rubbed the spot between his eyebrows, so similar to his sister's habit of doing the same thing. "A lot of guys bang dust, now, instead of whitestar, 'cause you don't have to go to detox regularly." His voice was high and soft, as if it hadn't caught up with his man's body. He had the red irises and black tongue of a regular user. "You can find it pretty much everywhere, and the cops don't hassle you when you buy it. I guess they don't care 'cause it's not addictive."

"Who's your supplier?"

Macki shrugged. "As I said, it's out there. Sometimes I just buy it from a friend, other times I get it over the counter at some of the bars I go to."

Sara pointed the remote at the vid image, and her brother's face disappeared. "The dust is as readily available as oxygen. The users like it because it doesn't create identity confusion—they know who they are at all times.

"There *is* a derivative effect to the dust, and it's permanent and cumulative; so after a few uses, there is a radical change in personality. Even if Macki had stopped using, the person I knew didn't exist anymore. But—and this is why the authorities aren't reacting quickly to the dust—dustheads can stop using any time. Many do, but there are always more kids like my brother who want to try it out."

Silence stretched in the conference room as the people around the table digested the information.

Someone at the end of the table coughed. Everyone turned towards Peter Farnsworth. "But the dust has changed now. People are dying from it. Why would they mess with something that works so well?"

"Exactly," Vincent said, pointing at the gangly, bug-eyed tech-head. "Since it appeared on the market, the death count from the dust itself—including Macki and the man up in the ER—is now fifteen. Still not enough for the police to make it a priority, but if we find what's being done to the chemical structure, they'll have to start paying attention. Peter, have you introduced the modifications I requested into the neuronet?"

Peter shifted his bony shoulders. "Sure. It took me a while to set it up, but you should've been able to use the modified protocol yesterday."

"I have," Purvis Black said. He pushed his chin forward and stroked the mangy beard on its underside. "You were right, Vincent. I did a blood residual analysis on the dust victims, concentrating on molecular structure. They've added a biological element to the chemical composition."

Vincent leaned forward in his chair. "Interesting. What else?"

"I haven't had time to analyze the data in detail yet," Peter said. "Here's what I have so far." He tapped a key on the table, and a series of chemical analyses appeared on a flat vid screen in front of each team member. They studied the data in silence for a minute.

"Okay," Vincent said, "here's how I want to do this. I want everybody to have access to everyone else's data, so all new information will be downloaded immediately on the neuronet. I'll do the compilation and prelim analyses, draw some conclusions. We'll have a weekly meeting to discuss developments."

"You want to place a copy of the data on the Health Center net as well?" Peter asked.

Vincent grimaced. "No. Until the Health Center cuts down on the security locks we have to go through every time we have to use their net, we'll stick to ours and continue to dump archival results only. Anyone have a problem with that?"

"As long as we input the genetic information from the deceased directly into the genebanks," Su-Li Truong said, "I don't."

Vincent looked up and down the table. They all shook their heads. "Fine. Thank you, people. Sara, please stay a moment."

While his assistants filed out of the room, he sat back and contemplated his second-in-command. "Are you going to be okay?" he said as soon as the door closed on the last tech.

She nodded once. "Dustheads are still dying out there, Vincent."

"We'll figure it out."

"You should hassle MGRC or the police. Get them to listen."

"To what? I don't have solid evidence of anything yet. And so far, whoever is producing the brain dust doesn't know we're tracking down how the drug has been modified. You know that as soon as we tell the authorities we might as well have broadcast what we've learned on the six o'clock news. The dust makers will go to ground."

"You're right." She sighed. "One more thing. Could you do something about Peter? His attitude's getting worse. He drags his feet on everything."

"I noticed he seems more nervous than usual these days. I'll talk to him."

Sara raised a hand in farewell and left. Vincent's thoughts immediately turned back to the brain dust question. Surely, it was only a matter of time before they figured out how the drug had changed.

Su-Li burst into the room. "We have another brain dust DOA, Vincent. Female, adult, possibly a Termite."

"What? Impossible." He rose and followed her to the lab. A body draped with a sheet lay on the plasmer table in the center of the room. He checked the med tablet data then uncovered the woman.

Her heavily muscled body had very little fat, as if she'd undergone extensive physical training or even some reshaping. With her straight nose, high cheekbones and full mouth, she had an attractive face, if he discounted that the skin was tanned and lined from too much sun.

"Her name was Looyse Platt," Su-Li said, "twenty-five years old, born in Warren, Michigan. Her medical history stopped when she was eighteen, and there's a missing persons report still active on her. That's why I think she joined the Termites when she disappeared."

"You may be right. Carry on with the ER casualty. I'll do this one."

Five hours later, the anomaly of the corpse still puzzled Vincent. The body in front of him, even after so many hours of poking and prodding, remained an impossibility. The med data indicated she'd been found at the edge of the road, in a culvert. In all his years as a pathologist, he'd never received a Termite. Out of curiosity, he'd done some research and found that very few centers in the world had. He'd begun to dig deeper, eager to learn more. If he had a hobby, it was chasing Termite facts and lore.

Leaving one of their dead on the side of the road—and a female one at that—was inconceivable. The community followed the ancient custom of burial.

Male Termites rarely came out of their hiding places unless they were raiding genebanks, which occurred less often these days. The females never did. The community had reverted to a matriarchal structure in which the females held the positions of authority and owned the family's possessions. They never ventured very far from their homes, the locations of which Government Mundial had never been able to discover.

Initial diagnosis indicated a heart attack and traces of whitestar and brain dust, which made no sense, either. Termites were violently opposed to drugs, or any mood-altering substance. A Termite using a hallucinogenic drug was difficult to accept. A female Termite using two drugs at the same time was unthinkable.

Yet, the dead woman in front of him definitely had both drugs in her bloodstream.

He sighed. It was late, he was bone-tired, and his pathologists had left hours before, so he couldn't confer with any of them about his findings. He would go home after that one final test—determine if the biological element Peter had mentioned earlier was also present.

He brought up Purvis's data, then Looyse's for comparison.

"Warning." The voice of his neuronet made him jump. "DNA composition of deceased does not match Identichip map."

"The chip is defective?"

"Negative. DNA composition does not match."

"I know, you said that already. How does it not match?"

"Identichip map indicates female Caucasian with minor genetic defects as follows—"

"Skip the details. Compare Identichip data to sample DNA taken from cadaver."

"DNA composition does not match."

Vincent took a deep breath. He pinched the bridge of his nose and rubbed. "Okay. Indicate areas of difference between two maps."

"DNA map from tissue sample indicates that point zero one percent of genetic material does not belong to basal genetic data on deceased."

"What?" The neuronet began again. "No, don't repeat that, I got it the first time. Match areas of anomalies with those on Identichip map, block both, then compare remaining map areas."

Vincent contemplated the dead body in front of him. In the heavy silence of the room, all he could hear was the faint buzz in his ears.

"Comparison complete."

"Report."

"Match one hundred percent."

"Someone tampered with her DNA. That's what killed her, not the drugs."

He shivered, suddenly conscious that he'd come across very dangerous information. Whoever was playing with the most sacred temple of humankind would not want to get caught.

"Maybe I'll make two sets of notes," he muttered.

As state-of-the-art as Stringer's lab was, Gerry thought, it came with one major disadvantage—Argus. The man latched on to him every time he set foot in Stringer's complex.

"Don't you have something to do?" he said, without turning from his bionet.

"I'm doing it."

"As if you understood anything." He continued to review the data from the first Termite.

"Where are those figures coming from?"

"You dump the Termites, I pick up the data."

"You're tapping into the Health Center's neuronet."

Gerry nodded. "All dusthead cases are sent to Metropolis Health Center. The dead ones end up in the pathology lab for autopsy. Dr. Francis, the Chief of Pathology, refuses to use the Health Center neuronet. He says it's too cumbersome. He and his team have their own, separate from the rest of the Health Center.

"One of the net-techs maintaining the path lab neuronet has a fondness for whitestar. He set up an outside line for me directly into the path lab neuronet in exchange for a continuous supply of 'star. I had the lab at GeneTech, and have the lab here, but not the analytic power of the path lab neuronet. Every time they do an autopsy on a dusthead, I get the results and I don't even have to do the work. And I know exactly what I'm looking for, as opposed to Francis."

"Someone will end up noticing if you keep doing it long enough."

"If I were tapping into the Health Center neuronet, maybe. But the Path neuronet is totally segregated."

"And that net-tech makes sure it stays that way."

"Exactly. He restructured the shadow sets so that all the brain dust records are contained in one set. If things get too hot, he can wipe all traces of the analyses. No one will be the wiser. Just a glitch in the system. So sad. I hope you're impressed."

When Argus grunted, Gerry shrugged and went back to the data on his screen.

"I'll want to meet your net-tech."

"I don't think it's a good idea. The fewer people involved—"

"If something happened to you, we'd have to cover our tracks."

Gerry swallowed convulsively. Argus might look like a big lug, but he *was* Stringer's second-in-command.

"I'll set up the meeting." He frowned at the vid. "Let's see," he muttered. "My, you've been busy, Dr. Francis. Let's get the genetic data. Ah, yes..." He hit his fist against the table. "Damn. I'm close, real close. If I had more time...As it is, I'll have to use Lockwood's data, modify it to use in a pharmaceutical environment, use the stripped down genetic material, add the chemicals that target the addiction genes, and test." He got up but couldn't move back. "Do you mind?"

Argus remained silent but moved aside.

"Tell Stringer I'll be ready for another test soon."

He turned back to the sequencer. Taking Lockwood's retrogene model out of GeneTech using that fancy—and very illegal—protocol his Health Center associate had designed for him had been worth every gram of whitestar he'd forked over. A copy without a trace was a precious thing.

"This Dr. Francis," Argus said, interrupting his thoughts. "Why doesn't he go to the authorities?"

"He wants to build a case first." Gerry sighed in annoyance. He faced the man. "I need him for another trial, two at the most. Then you can do whatever you want with him."

Argus didn't smile, but his eyes became slightly more brilliant.

# Chapter Fifteen

DEMETRIA PUSHED AWAY FROM HER DESK AND STRETCHED. WORK SEEMED THE BEST cure for her strange visions—she hadn't had a disturbing one since the day, two weeks before, she'd plunged into the construction and analysis of the DNA matrix. She hadn't heard from Trevor Lockwood, either, which suited her fine. She didn't want to know whether her visions were linked to him.

She stretched again, stared at the screen with its data display. Her hard work, the sleepless nights, the missed meals had paid off. She'd made an amazing discovery.

Based on the five DNA maps GeneTech had provided her, she had tracked down several coded IDs that closely matched those maps. They were few, and most had, beside their ID, a black square with a slash across it. Deceased. When she correlated the black squares with gender and age, she found that all were males who hadn't lived past twenty-one.

Next, she tried to match the ID codes, rather than the DNA maps, to the rest of the genebanks using the protocol she'd designed to standardize data entries. For each, she found IDs that significantly matched. After several iterations, she retrieved date of birth for each ID and sorted the data. The pieces arranged themselves into a linked hierarchy.

She then took the ID codes in the hierarchy, extracted their DNA maps and compared them to each other. There, in front of her, was the astounding result—they were all related by blood.

The hierarchy had rearranged itself into a circle with concentric rings. Some places were sketchy and the circle looked more like a set of gears with missing teeth, but there was no doubt—every match was blood kin taken from the hierarchy.

She wondered how far she'd be able to go to find out how many people were at the incept of the DNA combination from which all the others came. The further down she went, the murkier the data. There were virtually no ID codes after one hundred years. She'd have to dig through historical archives, birth and medical records, if they still existed, and correlate on the basis of genealogy. For that, though, she would need names. Somewhere in those hundreds of databanks was the connection between ID code and name.

"Demetria," Dympna said, "Dr. Francis is here."

"Already?" She glanced at the clock then turned off her holograph viewer and her screen. "Let him in, will you? I'll go freshen up."

When she returned to the living area, Vincent stood holding a bottle, looking lost. His features were drawn with fatigue and something else she couldn't identify.

"Looks like you need a stronger drink than wine," she said.

Vincent jumped. "Oh. You startled me." He gave her the bottle. "Vosges-Romanee. Thought you might like it."

"Thanks. It'll go well with the pasta. I splurged and bought two tomatoes."

"Hmm."

She waited for him to say more. He didn't, obviously distracted. She went to the liquor cabinet. When she came back with two glasses of brandy, he still stood in the same spot. She placed the brandy under his nose. He blinked and focused on her.

"I thought that might do the trick," she said, smiling. She grabbed his arm and pulled him to the sofa. "Now, tell me what's bugging you."

"We received another DOA dust case yesterday."

"Another kid?"

"No. Twenty-five. It's not what's unusual. She was a Termite."

"Really? I thought they didn't take drugs."

"Exactly. Remember, maybe a month ago, I told you that I thought someone was experimenting with new brain dust on street users? She was full of dust, too. But there's an added element—someone tampered with her DNA. There's no bacteria or virus included in the dust, so we can probably rule out terrorists, and it's her own DNA that's changed."

"Why would they use a Termite?"

"Maybe too many dustheads were dying. It scares off the clientele."

"That's true, but Termites aren't thick on the ground. How would they have got to her?"

"Probably kidnapped her. If that's the case, they probably got more than one."

The image of two men carrying sacks flashed across her mind.

"I wonder..." She bit her lip.

"What?"

"I went running in the park a couple of weeks ago. Some guys attacked me."

*"What?"*

"They were carrying people. I thought at the time some thugs had brought someone out to the woods to kill them, but then they took them along when they left. One woke up and escaped before the police arrived. Maybe they were Termites."

"Back up a minute. When was that?"

"I told you. Two weeks ago."

"Did you call the police?"

"I did. They recorded my statement and everything. They took the guy I'd knocked out with them."

"Why didn't you call me?"

"What for? I wasn't hurt. They ran off. There's nothing you could have done." Demetria mentally crossed her fingers. She'd thought about that night every day since it happened, about Torver Lockwood, who hadn't contacted her yet, about her runaway visions, about what she'd seen in the park. For some reason she'd left Torver's involvement out of her story. It was too early to tell Vincent about him.

Vincent narrowed his eyes. "I can't believe you didn't call me." He finished his brandy in a gulp and got up. "I don't know why I keep thinking that one day you'll need me."

"We're not going to get into that again, are we?"

He walked to the window, looked out. After a moment he sighed then turned. "No. How's that contract with Laslo Radic working out?"

"It's a fascinating project." She grimaced. "I can almost forgive you for giving him my name. Did you tell him I had Brett's?"

"Of course not." He frowned. "Radic knew about it?"

"Yes."

"He might have found out through his contacts. Don't look at me that way. Do you want me to swear I didn't tell him?"

Demetria studied his face for a moment then shook her head. "I believe you."

"So, what's your project?"

"Contract confidentiality. I have an MGRC auth code, though."

Vincent whistled. "You've become a high flyer."

"You have one."

"Yeah, but I can only use it in my job. You don't know how long it took me to get one. I'm surprised you didn't have to go through a rigorous security screening."

Demetria frowned. "That's something I wondered, too. Although Mr. Radic said the project had a certain urgency to it. Maybe MGRC waived some of the requirements."

"It's more likely they got the information without asking you."

"No way. I can't believe—"

"Demetria." The urgency in Dympna's voice broke through her annoyance.

"What."

"Comm for you."

"Take a message."

"It's your father."

"You interrupted us for him? You need an overhaul, Dympna."

Dympna didn't answer. Demetria hesitated. She hadn't spoken to her father in months. The last time they had they'd parted with angry words. She shook her head and grimaced. She couldn't remember a time when she *hadn't* fought with him.

"Demetria?" Dympna said. "He says it's important."

"Fine, fine, put him on."

She strode to her office. A holo of her father's head and chest appeared in front of her, startling her—Dympna hadn't put him through the regular comm channel but sent his image through her tactile holograph.

Her father's eyes immediately ran along the seam of her prosthesis and she suddenly wished she wasn't wearing it. It would serve him right. As the foremost evolutionary psychologist in the Americas, he had advanced the groundbreaking theory that mutations were a result of an unconscious choice of the human race towards evolution. She wondered what her dermophagia meant to him in terms of evolution and what it said about him and her mother.

She studied his features, even more gaunt than usual. She'd always thought of his expression as a study in punctuation—a thin mouth bracketed by two long dimples, like a dash between parentheses; a straight, thin nose like a slash between the two periods that were his small black eyes.

"Hello, Charles," she said. "You look tired."

He shook his head briefly. "Never mind me. I'm calling about your mother."

"What about her?"

"She's dead."

Demetria blinked.

"Carlotta died yesterday on the way to her concert. She was driving and her car went off the road." His mouth compressed further. "She was drunk, of course."

The words felt unreal, as if she'd stepped into another vision. "She'd never drink when she was playing."

He laughed harshly. "You haven't bothered to see her for years. How would you know? Apparently, the tour wasn't going well. This was her third and last venue."

"I'd heard on the arts news she was supposed to play in fifteen cities."

"They cancelled the rest of the trip."

"Where did she die?"

"Some highway between Paris and Dijon. The road cop who read her Identichip recognized her name. He called me right away. He couldn't hide her death, of course, but he kept quiet about her condition."

"What difference does that make?"

"Your mother was a virtuoso. We'd like to keep that reputation intact."

"What's this 'we,' Charles?"

Her father closed his eyes briefly. When he opened them again, they were hard. "Your mother named you executor of her estate."

"Me?" she said, her voice squeaky.

He gave her a bitter smile. "Obviously, your mother trusted you more than she did me."

"It must have been quite annoying to stop in the middle of writing another of your brilliant articles to call me with the news of your wife's death. I'm surprised you didn't ask one of your assistants to call me."

He smiled slightly. "I thought about it. But then I decided that, considering how she died, I should minimize the number of people involved."

"I can't believe Mother's drinking problem would affect your research funding."

"There are conservative elements on the board who might think her drinking was caused by neglect."

"Fancy that." Demetria's jaws ached. "I'll contact Mother's lawyer." She took a deep breath then muttered, "Dympna, if you don't cut him off right now, I swear I'll delete you."

Her father's face winked out.

She should be feeling something other than anger. She should hurt somewhere, or at least want to cry. Instead, she remembered her mother's face, half-furious, half-mortified, when she'd found Demetria in that museum armoire, and her mother's hand, like a claw on her shoulder, propelling her outside. Another image, even more vivid, of her mother's disgust when she'd first seen her daughter with her prosthesis.

A hand landed on her shoulder. She started, then remembered Vincent.

"Sorry, I forgot you were still here."

"I'm the one who's sorry, Demi. Why don't you come back into the living room? I'll fix you some tea."

"I hate tea. It's a waste of perfectly good water. What I need is another drink." She pushed past him and strode to the kitchen counter. She busied herself opening the Vosge-Romanee. "At least you're not telling me what a loss she is to the world."

Vincent smiled slightly. "I imagine you'll hear that phrase quite often in the next few days."

She handed him a glass of wine. Her hand shook. She picked up her own wine and took a large swallow. Vincent never gulped wine. He twirled, sniffed, sipped, swished and swallowed. It was a ritual she knew as well as her own face, and it was a comfort to her now, as if despite the harshness of the world outside some habits, some small gestures, remained the same inside the protective enclave of her home.

Vincent cleared his throat. "I'll take care of the arrangements to repatriate your mother's body if you want."

"Would you? I don't think it's sunk in yet that she's dead. Maybe when I see her..." She swallowed more wine. "I have to call Mother's lawyer."

"I'll stay. See if there are any special requirements I should know about your mother's remains."

"Okay."

"Demetria," Dympna said, her voice more subdued than usual, "your mother's lawyer wishes to speak with you."

"He didn't waste any time."

"The lawyer's name is Longhini," Dympna said. "He is waiting on the comm. He is calling from Florence, Italy."

"Put him through the intercom. I want Vincent to hear this as well." She flopped on her sofa and patted the seat beside her. He grimaced and sat down.

A moment later, a smooth, liquid voice surrounded them.

"Signorina Greyson. *Le mie condoglianze.* Let me offer my condolences for the passing of your mother."

"Grazie, Signor Longhini."

"Carlotta—I mean, Signora Danterini—was an exceptional woman. The world has lost an invaluable treasure."

She rolled her eyes at Vincent, who smiled ruefully.

"Signor Longhini," Demetria said, "I have just learned of my mother's death. I'd like to expedite this call, if at all possible. You have my mother's last instructions?"

"Forgive me, Signorina Greyson. Of course. You are grieving. I am sorry that I cannot travel at this time to speak with you in person, but the exigencies of my practice…you understand."

"Certainly."

"You are aware that you are the executor? Your dear mother's will is very straightforward. Her piano goes to the Music School at Ottawa-Carleton University. A few paintings go to friends. The rest is to be sold, with thirty percent of the proceeds going towards an appropriate mausoleum dedicated to the remembrance of her genius and her art. The rest goes to you."

"And my father?"

"Your father?" The lawyer couldn't hide the contempt in his voice. "Carlotta instigated divorce proceedings six months ago. Dottore Greyson will receive more than his due from it. In her opinion, of course."

"Of course. By the way, Dr. Francis, who is chief pathologist at Ottawa General, will arrange the return of my mother's body. I will send you his coordinates. You may contact him directly."

"Ah…scusi, signorina, I should have mentioned right away. Your mother wished to be cremated and for her ashes to remain in Firenze, the city of her birth."

Demetria frowned. Her feeling of remoteness increased. To her knowledge, Carlotta had never gone back to Florence, let alone uttered the wish to see it again.

"I can't travel overseas at this time, signor," she said.

"No need, signorina. Your dear mother mentioned your reluctance to leave your lodgings. Therefore, I took it upon myself to have a small ceremony for her on your behalf."

Another shock. Demetria wondered how many her mother had in store for her. Vincent took her hand and patted it. She was suddenly very grateful he was there with her.

"Are you saying my mother has already been cremated?"

"Should I have waited?" Longhini's voice became oily. "I only abided by the conditions of your dear mother's will."

Demetria clenched her teeth and wished he would stop referring to Carlotta as her "dear mother."

"Nevertheless, signore, you should have consulted me. I might have wished to pay my respects, even from a distance."

"Of course. Although I understood that you were not close."

"You seem to know an awful lot about our family situation, Signor Longhini."

Longhini cleared his throat. "As I mentioned before, I was a great admirer."

"Much more than that, I think," she muttered. "Anything else?" she continued more loudly.

"One last thing, signorina. Carlotta instructed me to send you some personal papers upon her death. My assistant will dispatch them presently."

"Very well, Signor Longhini. I'll contact you if I need more information. I'll also want a copy of the will if you haven't included it in the package already. Off."

"That was a bit abrupt," Vincent said.

"I was getting sick of his smarmy attitude."

"It seems I won't be needed after all."

"Not for that. But I'm glad you're here." Demetria plucked the glass from his hand. "We need another drink."

"I take it from your mumbling that your mother had more than a professional relationship with her lawyer."

"Her lawyer, her doctor, several orchestra conductors, her manager—anybody except my father."

"Is that why they separated?"

"No. They split up because of me. Or rather, my dermophagia. They couldn't take the shame of having a daughter who turned out to be a freak." She placed the refilled glass in his hand.

"You're kidding." He looked so stunned and offended she chuckled.

"Thanks, Vincent. I needed that."

"Demetria," Dympna piped up, "the documents from Longhini have arrived."

She put her glass down and went to her office. She scanned the information on the vidscreen, did a double-take and scrolled back to the beginning.

"Vincent," she called out, "come and have a look."

He came to stand behind her.

"Maybe you can make sense of all this." She scrolled to another page and frowned. "This can't be right. Do you know anything about an organization called AMAD International?"

"No. Why?"

"Dympna?"

"It was an adoption agency, Demetria. It was dismantled twenty-five years ago, under accusations of mismanagement and dubious adoption practices."

"Vincent, look at this." She felt him peer over her shoulder at the screen. It was obviously a copy of a sheaf of papers, and it retained the original yellow tinge of age. The letters in the creases were faded, as if the sheet had been folded and unfolded several times. At the top, in bold letters, was printed AMAD INTERNATIONAL—HAPPINESS IS A CHILD. Below the letterhead were only a few entries:

>Child's ID number—1069
>Gender—F
>Birth date—9/28/2065
>Race—Caucasian
>Eye color—Black
>Hair color—Black
>Health condition—No known pathologies.
>
>Note—Donor parents to remain anonymous under article 207(d)(ii) of Government Mundial Adoption Act.

"That's my birthdate," Demetria said. She looked up at Vincent, then went back to the screen. She shook her head. "I was adopted."

He squeezed her shoulder and sat beside her.

"They never told me." She reread the scant information on the sheet. "All this time I agonized because I never could get their love, never could come up to their standard, never could do anything right, and they never told me."

"What difference would that have made?"

She laughed, and heard the beginnings of hysteria in the sound. "I could have hated them without guilt. Then I could have tried to find out who my real parents were."

"Even if you had known," Dympna interrupted, "you would not have been permitted to seek them out. The Government Mundial Adoption Act precludes providing information on birth parents, under any circumstances, then and now."

Vincent nodded. "It's an offshoot of the genetic privacy law. Anyway, it's been thirty years, and AMAD doesn't exist anymore. That would make it extremely difficult to find out who were your natural parents."

Demetria smiled slightly. You're wrong, Vincent, she thought. I have the perfect tool to track them down.

She thought of the DNA matrix she'd built in the past two weeks. She imagined it still turning, waiting patiently for her to come back to it. With it, she could access all the genebanks and their peripheral databanks in the world. That matrix contained the secret of her parents' identity.

## Chapter Sixteen

"I NEED FIVE MORE GENE MAPS," TORVER SAID TO DYMPNA. "I'M SENDING YOU THE details now." He activated the datacom line.

"One moment, please."

He drummed his fingers on the tabletop. He hated working with a go-between, especially a machine.

"Prepare to receive," Dympna said.

"It would be more efficient if I talked directly to your boss."

"Unfortunately, you cannot."

"Tell her I'm impressed by the speed and quality of her work. It would facilitate my research if we coordinated our activities."

"Sorry. A clause in the contract prevents it."

"Only she and I need to know we're bending the rules. I'm certainly not going to tell anyone."

"Since you are so impressed with the work, maybe you should let her do it instead of wasting her time. Of course, as her assistant, I am only relaying this message. Comm off."

"Damn." He slapped the comm switch off. "What a tight-ass. And that goes for both of you."

A loud ping brought him up short. He turned to the cage where he'd placed his mice. The gene fragments should be in place by now. Programming nanoprobes to snip portions of the genome and replace it with the ones he'd cloned from the fossilized DNA had been a good way to test the technique he'd need to use on a fully developed human.

He opened the cage door and inserted his hand carefully to pick up one of the mice. Instead of cowering in a corner, all three rushed him. Torver pulled back his hand in reflex, but not quickly enough. One of the mice sank its teeth into his hand.

"Ow!" He yanked his hand out of the cage, the mouse dangling from the fleshy side of his palm. Before he could grab it with his other hand, the rodent let go and fell on the floor. He watched in astonishment as its legs and tail shook with palsy. A few moments later, it was dead.

He checked the cage; the other two mice were also dead, their posture as rigid as the one on the floor.

This was not good. Quickly, he used immuno-healing cream on the bite on his hand. The wound was fairly deep, but when he made a fist it didn't bother him much. He gave himself a rabies shot, just in case.

He picked up the mouse from the floor and set it on the counter, extracted some blood and placed it into the sequencer. It unraveled the chromosomes and spliced them into DNA strands. He inserted the uncoiled DNA into the tunneling microscope, punched in the coordinates and watched the machine zero in on the DNA segment he'd replaced in the mouse.

The genetic material came into focus. The section of ancient DNA fitted perfectly into the strand, in the spot he'd designated for it.

"Compare current genetic structure to previous one and extrapolate effects on human body," he said to his neuronet. "Give me a prelim analysis now."

"Preliminary analysis indicates DNA successfully spliced into correct chromosome site. Technique compatible for use on human genetic structure with ninety-eight percent probability of success."

Torver frowned. What had gone wrong, then? "Bring up the amino acid chain from the new genetic structure." A series of chemical symbols filled the screen, a holo of the sequence floating beside it. Something was wrong with the protein structure.

Two hours and three autopsies later, he slapped off his neuronet. His technique worked—and it didn't. There were no changes to the morphology of the mice, but the introduction of the gene fragments into the mouse DNA had started an irrevocable cascade effect. Every mouse had died from rapid degeneration of the nervous system. Something had turned the process on and prevented it from turning off.

He was so close. The problem had to be in the fossilized gene fragments, not in his technique.

"Time," the net said, very loudly. "Twenty-three hundred hours."

Torver stretched his neck in an attempt to get rid of the tension. He shut down his instruments and passlocked everything. Time to go home and rest.

Back in his apartment, he couldn't settle down. It had taken him two hours to get home from GeneTech—the buses had been filled to capacity; he'd been jostled and pushed and spewed out three times before he'd made it home. He'd wanted to scream, but when he'd raised his eyes to the faces around him, red and sweaty from the swelter of the city, he'd resigned himself to the pace and fought against his exhaustion. At least high above in his apartment, with its bank of windows, he had the luxury of being alone.

He thought about Demetria, higher still in the building, and wanted to hear her voice. He shook his head. One o'clock in the morning didn't even stretch the acceptable.

He retrieved his green mouse from its cage and turned on the new vidscreen he'd had delivered while he was at the lab. Instead of setting it against the wall, the delivery guys had installed the huge horizontal surface in the middle of the living room, halfway between his chair and the window.

He slumped into his chair. It automatically corrected his posture. He grimaced.

"News," he said. "MBC."

A middle-aged anchorwoman, dressed in the plain blue-and-white MBC uniform, appeared on the screen. Torver was briefly tempted by her tired eyes but couldn't be bothered. The point of watching the vid was to unwind. He closed his eyes and let her professionally modulated voice wash over him.

"The court is expected to rule today on whether the head of the Hongfeng, Bala Myiko, will stand trial alone or with the rest of his confederates. The Hongfeng, a politico-paramilitary terrorist organization accused of planning a biogenetic attack on Government Mundial, remain under heavy police guard in the Swiss Frauenfeld stronghold. The MGRC are petitioning for a maximum sentence for Myiko, arguing that public security and human rights have been violated..."

Torver's attention wavered while he let his moss-backed friend scurry up his arm and nibble his neck, his mind turning over the glitch in his genetic sequence. On the screen, a face he recognized mobilized his attention.

"Hold," he said. "Back up to the beginning of the story."

The anchorwoman spoke again. "In other news," she said, "the world is mourning the death of one of the world's greatest pianists, Carlotta Danterini. Miz Danterini made her debut..."

"Forward," Torver said. "Stop. Play."

"Miz Danterini leaves behind her estranged husband, evolutionary psychologist Charles Greyson, and a daughter, Demetria." Pictures of father and daughter appeared on the screen. "Neither was available for comment."

"Hold." He picked up a vid frame from the stack that came with his screen and inserted it in the console beside his chair. "Download picture of Demetria Greyson."

When he withdrew the frame, Demetria's face was inside it, staring at him.

"What do you think, mouse? The picture dates from before her dermophagia, so her face is smooth." He picked up the mouse from his shoulder and put it back in its cage. His fatigue had been replaced by a thrumming excitement. If he couldn't talk to Demetria, he could do the next best thing—visit her lifepath and learn more about her.

DEMETRIA'S EYEPIECE CHAFED AT THE CONNECTION ON HER TEMPLE, A SIGN THAT SHE'D been using it too long. For the past five hours since she'd finally got rid of Vincent—claiming mental exhaustion, which had been true—she'd done nothing but watch the matrix revolve upon itself, and wrestle with her conscience.

Her adoption papers had given her a second motive to use the GeneTech authorization code for herself. One reason was possible to resist, but two threatened to trample her principles and leave them for dead.

When she'd come to the conclusion she could search through the genebanks for cases similar to hers, she'd been tempted but had talked herself out of it. Now she knew that using the code would be her only chance to discover who her family was.

*Family.* The word seemed more inscrutable to her than the histories of the antiques she collected. She'd always felt out of step with her parents, out of kilter with their ambitions and their dreams. She wondered why they'd even bothered to adopt a child. Once they had her, they'd had no idea what to do with her.

She bit her lip, torn between wanting to know and preserving her integrity. Over the years she'd forged her own set of rules. Do no harm. Be truthful. Be trustworthy. Then her dermophagia had reinforced her need to be certain of who she was and what she stood for, and she'd stuck to those rules.

Someone else would have no compunction about digging into the genebanks. In bowing to the impulse, she'd betray everything she'd ever believed in.

But, oh, she was tempted.

She turned off her tactile holograph and threw the eyepiece on her desk in disgust. She couldn't work. Dympna had fielded questions from the press and messages from a surprising number of well-wishers who called about the death of her mother. She had talked only to Radic, assuring him that her loss wouldn't affect the project.

An uneasy feeling crept between her shoulder blades. Like something crawling under her skin. Like someone watching her. Torver Lockwood's face flashed in her mind.

She shrugged off the sensation, and her thoughts turned back to her mother. She'd have to begin the inventory of the house soon. She'd be glad to get rid of it. Maybe she didn't have to set foot in it, really. She could hire someone to catalogue and sell everything.

"Dympna, get me my lawyer."

"Demetria, it's two o'clock in the morning."

"Oh. Forget it, then." She couldn't shake that strange feeling. She stepped out of her office and crossed the living room to the bay window. Dympna lowered the illumination in the room to a dim glow so Demetria could see through the glass. The night was deeper here, far from the ground and the lighted houses. The line between earth and sky blurred and the stars mixed with the lights below; the earth glowed, as if surrounded by a globe of plasma-charged particles.

She was tired. Too tired to think, too weary to sleep. The death of her mother, the news of her adoption, and the possibilities for the use of the auth code circled endlessly in her mind. She looked down, longing for the peace of the night-shrouded city even though she knew it for an illusion. As if she could reach out and touch the sweltering darkness, she laid her hand on the pane.

It sank through the glass.

She cried out, pulled, but her hand was stuck. Despite her panic, she registered that she couldn't see it. Impossibly, she felt cool, motionless air on her fingers, as if her hand had disappeared into another world. A passenger jet descended towards the airport, and she followed it past the spot where her hand should be. She yanked again.

Instead of coming free, she was pulled forward, into the glass then through. She staggered and lurched and found solid floor under her feet.

She stood in amazement. Around her, plasmer counters, their surface crammed with equipment, hugged pristine white walls. A body covered with a sheet lay on a center steel table under the bright lights of an operating theatre. Chemical smells floated in the air. A laboratory, she decided—small, cluttered and quiet.

The silence was oppressive. She stared at the shrouded body. She could make out the tips of the big toes, a vague outline of legs and breasts and the oval shape of the head. When she approached the table, she detected another smell, one she knew well—spicy vanilla, her own perfume. Her heart beat faster.

She extended a hand towards the head then wiped her sweaty palm on her pants. She looked over her shoulder at where she'd come from. The wall was solid and opaque. Her heart skipped a beat. She couldn't see the thread that usually connected her to reality.

"This is just a dream," she said to the body on the table.

She whipped the sheet off and wasn't surprised to see who lay there. It was her, down to the red star-shaped mole on the side of her breast and the mangled left side of her face and neck. Something was moving, just under the surface of the skin—her skin—like the ripples of maggots moving under the hide of an animal several days dead.

Slowly, the skin on the right side of the face shifted, stretched. New tissue crept from the edge of the lesion on her neck and quickly covered her chin, then her ear. Next came a new cheek, an eyelid complete with lashes then a forehead, the connection between old skin and new seamless.

Pain shifted under her ribs. This is how she saw herself in her mind, how she thought of herself, until she looked in a mirror and saw the truth.

She had lifted a hand to touch the smooth, unbroken skin when it undulated again. She followed the ripple to the feet, which slowly spread out. Subtly at first, then more rapidly, the legs shortened and thickened. Her pelvis stretched down and the thighs shifted sideways.

Demetria watched as the arms lengthened, the fingers of the hands curving inward. The bones of the face—her face—rearranged themselves. The jaw thrust forward and down, the nose flattened out, and the eye sockets sank into the head. She looked back at the body and realized it was now covered with a fine duvet of dark hair.

She backed away. The body on the table wasn't hers anymore, yet it retained her features. Distant school memories resurfaced, and she shuddered. This is what she would have looked like hundreds of thousands of years ago. Primitive, like a Neanderthal.

The body began to convulse with something like an epileptic seizure. She heard a whistling sound and realized it was her breath coming in gasps.

"No," she said aloud. "I've seen enough." But she couldn't take her eyes off the body that was now shaking uncontrollably. Its eyes were open wide, and she could only see the whites. The hands were cramped into claws that scratched at its torso. Blood spurted from deep gouges, splattering the stainless steel table and the floor.

As suddenly as they started, the seizures stopped. The body flopped back on the table. Without checking, Demetria knew it was dead. She retreated, horrified, until she was stopped by the wall against her back. The contact broke her trance; and she wheeled about, to come face-to-face with a grinning Torver Lockwood.

"You!"

Her fear switched to anger. Without thinking, she reached out to grab his shirtfront. Her arm passed through the wall. She blinked and was back in her apartment, her hand on the window. The old-fashioned clock on her writing table rang the quarter-hour. Two-fifteen. Less than fifteen minutes had passed since she'd crossed over.

"This time you won't get away with it, Torver Lockwood. I don't care if it's the bloody middle of the night."

Before she let herself listen to reason, she rushed out of her apartment and headed towards the eightieth floor.

EASIER THAN DRINKING WATER, TORVER THOUGHT WHEN HE ENTERED DEMETRIA'S EYES. He'd half-expected to be blocked, the way she'd done it that night in the park, but it had worked even more smoothly than usual. Amazing that she'd been able to block him at all. Demetria and Laslo. They were the only ones who'd ever done it

Demetria. Her name had floated in and out of his consciousness ever since he'd learned it. It had cropped up at unexpected times, startling him from even the deepest concentration. Suddenly, there it was, and once her name had invaded his mind her divided face soon followed, hovering at the back of his eyes until he paid it full attention and reviewed its features. The mangled face always superimposed itself on the unbroken one, and yet, he still found her beautiful.

He looked up and down Demetria's lifepath. Which way should he choose? To the right, he'd go from the time her picture was taken to the childhood he knew intimately. To the left, beyond the timeline of the picture, lay her dermophagia and the death of her mother.

The disease would have crept up on her face, slowly disfiguring her, threatening to move on and nibble at her entire body. He shuddered.

The ribbon of her lifepath fluttered. He turned to the left, towards her present. Eyes downcast, he stepped forward. Soon he passed his point of entry. There was no resistance—the barrier between past and present was gone.

At a point not far from him, one lifepath joined Demetria's thread, paralleled it for a distance, wound tightly around it for another space, moved away then crossed her path over and over again in a narrow zigzag until it passed through the place-time of the picture.

Someone close to her, he thought, someone who had touched her life over and over again. Not her parents, since the connection started later in her life. A boyfriend?

He focused on a point where the two paths crossed and he was brought there. Demetria stood beside a tall man with silvery blond hair in a room full of very old furniture. She looked excited, he looked sullen. Torver shifted his eyes left—forward in time—to another junction of the two paths. Demetria and the same man. He held her hand across a table in a restaurant. This time, their emotions were reversed. Her face was taut with something like disapproval, his flushed with enthusiasm. *Vincent,* he heard Demetria say. Definitely a boyfriend.

What if he could piggyback onto Vincent's lifepath? The more Torver studied the pattern of their entwined lifepaths, the more attractive the idea. The only difficulty would arise if he couldn't find his way back to Demetria's lifepath and his point of entry. On the other hand, their paths were intertwined so tightly he was bound to come across hers again and could jump back onto her thread.

He needed a marker, something that pointed the way, told him when and where he'd entered. He grabbed a fistful of Demetria's thread and it stayed solid in his hand, like a rope. If he tied a knot as a marker, a point several days ahead would be tightly wound around a point several days in the past. Would he create a time paradox for her? He looked down towards the place-time of the picture of Demetria as a young girl. It shone like a beacon. He moved down towards it, stopped, turned around. The place of Demetria as an adult shone in the same way. The entrances to her lifepath were his markers.

He took hold of Vincent's path. The ground shifted under his feet, and when it stopped, Vincent's lifepath had straightened and others twisted around or crossed it. Torver searched for his markers. After a few seconds he spotted one, like a flare at a cross-point in Vincent's life thread. Satisfied, he turned his back on it. The present beckoned.

His focus moved ahead, and a point on the thread opened. Vincent stood beside an emergency gurney. The old man on it was clearly dying. Torver let the image collapse and moved on. A series of images flashed past him— Vincent in front of the rubble of what looked like a house, Vincent sweating at an interview, Vincent dissecting dead bodies, Vincent having sex with someone who wasn't Demetria.

Torver stopped at that image. Where was Demetria in all that? He hadn't seen her in any of the last few scenes. He turned around and searched for the marker. There, far in the distance. Even though it still shone like a guiding light, it was difficult to sort out her path from among all the others around. Then, halfway between him and the marker, he saw her path deviate away from Vincent's. He selected the last intersecting point before that and, after a short dizzy moment, stood in front of the expanded image.

Demetria and Vincent sat across from each other at a dining room table. The left half of Demetria's face was covered by a mask.

"It doesn't bother me, Demi," Vincent said. He took her hand in his. "I'm a doctor, after all. Besides, with the proper prosthesis..."

She shook her head. "Everything has changed. The way I see myself, who I am."

"You're still beautiful."

"What the hell does that mean?" Demetria disentangled her hand and got up. "I can't give you what you want, Vincent."

The image winked out.

"What the—" Torver said, startled. His concentration had not wavered, he hadn't moved his focus to another point on the path. He tried to reopen the image, but it didn't work. Memories of his headlong fall through the void made him nervous. *I'd better get out of here.*

His fingers brushed Demetria's lifepath. His head pounded with an insistent thrum. The ground heaved. He reeled from the sudden motion and gripped Demetria's thread to prevent himself from falling. He shot forward towards his marker like the beam from a plasma gun. Just before he slammed into it, he squeezed his eyes shut and ducked.

When he opened them, he was back in his apartment, Demetria's picture still in his hand. He shook his head. The pounding continued but from outside his head, not inside. Someone was banging on the door.

He set aside Demetria's picture and made his way towards the noise.

"Yeah, yeah," he muttered. "Can't you use the doorbell like a civilized person?"

He punched the door open. Demetria stood there, her fist still raised.

"You will explain yourself right now," she said, her tone tight and furious. She planted a hand on his chest, pushed him out of the way and marched to the middle of the living room.

## Chapter Seventeen

Torver keyed the door closed and followed her. Demetria turned to face him, crossed her arms over her breasts. "Well?"

He rubbed his eyes with his knuckles and yawned. "Kind of late for a visit, isn't it?"

"It's obvious I didn't drag you out of bed. What were you doing out there?"

"Out where?"

She uncrossed her arms and advanced on him. Her eyes glittered, and the seam of her face flared purple. He hesitated just long enough for her to slap a hand on his chest; it sent him bumping against the window.

"I am not in a good mood."

He swallowed and nodded, remembering that she'd taken on three men with only a stick. He looked straight into her eyes, and could go no further.

"I can see that. I have no idea what you're mad about."

She walked over beside him; after a moment's hesitation, she flattened her hand on the glass.

Torver turned sideways and watched her. The sky had begun to lighten, making it feel darker inside. "What did you mean by 'out there?'"

"I'm not going crazy."

"Okay."

"You're involved."

"In what? I haven't talked to you in two weeks."

She turned her head and stared at him. Her eyes were so intense he felt she was the one who would enter into him and walk his lifepath.

"But you've seen me, haven't you?" she said after a moment.

He wanted to deny it. "Look, you want some coffee?"

Demetria shook her head. She returned to the center of the living area, scanning the empty room like someone searching for a way to broach a difficult subject. She stopped when she got to his chair. Her eyes widened. She snatched up the still of her face. "What are you doing with this?"

Torver shrugged.

"What are you doing with my picture?"

"Something to eat, maybe? Breakfast is the most important meal of the day."

She stared at him, incredulous for a moment, then angry again. Her face was moved by her emotions the way the surface of the earth was jostled by plate tectonics, with as much force but with more speed.

Torver raised his hands, palms out.

"I got it from the news. I'm curious about you."

"When did you move here?"

"About two weeks ago. A bit more."

"Last time in the park, I said that I thought we were connected."

"I remember."

"Maybe you were curious about me before that."

Torver blinked at her perception and wondered how she'd come to that conclusion. Then he understood her real meaning and was outraged.

"I am *not* a stalker."

She motioned towards him with the vidstill. "Then explain this. While you're at it, explain why you suddenly appeared in the park."

He thought how, a few minutes ago, his visit to her lifepath had been cut short. "What happened tonight to bring you here?"

She bit her lip. "I saw you. You were laughing at me."

"Where?"

She didn't answer. As if her anger had exhausted her, she went to the dining room table and slumped down on a chair, setting the vidstill in front of her. Torver followed and pulled out the chair opposite her. He waited.

From up close, she seemed to overflow with intensity, an emotion he didn't think he'd ever experienced, except maybe when he was working. He watched her as she seemed to come to a decision.

"Do you have visions?"

"Visions? No."

She looked straight at him, a direct gaze that held no fear of him, no hesitation or loathing, just defiance.

"I've used vocal scanning techniques since the onset of the dermophagia," she said. "They lead me to a state in which I have visions. They help me deal with the disease, and other issues as well."

"Like why your mother hated you?"

Demetria narrowed her eyes and studied him for a moment, but didn't respond to the question.

"Since about a month ago, I've been losing control of them. One second I could be walking to the kitchen, the next I'm somewhere else."

"Without warning?"

"Yes. And in every one of them, I wasn't certain how I'd get out. I don't know why the visions changed, but I know one thing—you appeared in every one of them. That makes you involved."

Torver broke eye contact and gazed over her shoulder. He'd never discussed his ability with anyone before, and he wasn't sure he wanted to do so now. It was a private thing; it belonged to him. He focused back on her face.

"I met you for the first time two weeks ago."

She raised an eyebrow. "Physically, maybe. But you've trampled through my mind. You admitted I saved your life. You also said you'd seen me without my prosthesis." She leaned forward, her body tense, her palms flat on the table surface. "Maybe you're not an ordinary stalker, Torver Lockwood, but you've been plaguing me. I'd get dumped into a vision and there you'd be."

Breathlessly, she summarized the first two visions in which he'd appeared. For some reason she didn't want to examine yet, she was reluctant to tell him about the one that had led her to this confrontation.

She hit the table with her fist. "That night, in the park, you looked into my eyes, and for a moment I felt invaded. It's like you were there, inside my head, walking around. I *felt* you."

"I can't help you."

"How did you know I didn't get along with my mother?"

"The news said you were estranged."

"They said my *parents* were. They didn't say she hated me. How did you know?" She picked up the picture of herself. "You need to see a person to read her mind, right? That's why you need my picture."

She was getting dangerously close to the truth.

"Take the picture, then," he said. "You'll have to leave. I have to go to work in a few hours."

She said nothing. He refused to lower his eyes, but it was hard. Anger he could deal with, even reproach. But her silence was like her face without the prosthesis—harsh, loathsome.

Her clothing rustled when she got up from the table and started towards the door. She'd left the vidstill on the table. Without a word, she'd given him a clear message—stay out of my life. She could sense him and would kick him out. Her lifepath was closed to him forever.

"Tell me one thing," he called out. "How do you block me?"

She stopped but didn't turn back. "I don't know. I just push back."

"Really."

Her back stiffened. "You don't believe me."

"Oh, I do."

When he didn't say more, she raised her hand to the door plaque.

"I can see people's pasts." He rushed the words, as if in a few more seconds he wouldn't have been able to say them. He waited, breathless, her reaction.

Demetria faced him. She looked disconcerted rather than horrified. "I don't understand."

He approached her carefully and stopped half a meter away from her. He tried to enter her eyes. He felt the resistance, not like a wall but rather like a jellied mass that made the half-world he traveled hazy and indistinct. She blinked, then flushed.

"You're doing it again," she said.

He smiled slightly. "You're the only person I know who is conscious of it. Most people don't even notice, some look a bit uncomfortable." He shrugged. "At least, that's what I think. I've never asked anyone how it feels."

"How does it work?"

He took her hand. She stiffened and tried to pull away, but he didn't let go.

"Let's sit down again."

She let him lead her back to the dining room.

"The people we are today, what we've become," he said after they sat down at the table, "are shaped by the events in our past, by what we choose to remember, by the decisions we make. I call it a lifepath."

"You can see all that behind a person's eyes?"

He nodded. "It's more than that. My mind enters this world where all pasts exist. The person's lifepath isn't really substantial, although when I'm there, I can touch it. It looks like—"

"A thread. Like mist, but also solid." She smiled at his astonishment. "I also use a thread in my visions. It anchors me, helps me to return to the physical plane."

"You've seen only your own. I've traveled along the paths of hundreds, maybe thousands of people. I search their pasts. Find out who they are by the events that made them."

"That's..." She blinked and shook her head. "Why?"

"What do you mean, why?"

"Isn't it kind of useless? What do you get out of it?"

Torver snickered. "Secrets, Demetria. Incidents people want to keep buried forever. I collect them. It's been useful."

She turned her head away from him. When she looked back, her eyes were sad. "Useful but lonely."

Something clenched in his chest. He leaned towards her, suddenly angry.

"I've done fine for myself," he said. "See, I know a lot about you. I saw you slash your mother's hand with that blade, Demetria. She never could play as well after that, could she?" She paled. He continued. "I laughed when you were five and you jumped on your cake. I would have done the same. And good riddance to Vincent. He would have bored you to tears." He took a deep breath and let it out in a loud whoosh.

Demetria held her midsection, her eyes wide and wounded. Torver stared at her, appalled at what he'd done. He raised a hand towards her. She flinched, the same way she'd done that first time in the elevator, and lifted her own to stay him. Her smile was bitter.

"Do you see only the bad things in people's lives, or are they the ones you want to remember?"

The question perplexed him. "There are places I can't open on any path," he said after thinking about it, "but I've always thought it was because nothing important happened there. How many times do I need to watch someone in the decont unit or taking the bus?" He raked his fingers through his hair. "Did you have a happy childhood, Demetria?"

"Not really, but in amongst the sadness there were glorious times, too." She smiled. "I was just thinking about one the other day."

"Tell me."

She shook her head briefly. "I collect nineteenth and twentieth century antiques, did you know that? I fell in love with them when I was seven. I also had a dog, called Lennon. Every time I was sad, I used to play with him. He made me laugh."

"I saw you bury him. You cried for a long time."

"Did you ever see me play with him?"

"No."

"You must have very few friends."

He laughed, but it came out strangled. "What would I want with friends when not even the people closest to me can be trusted?"

"Your perspective is skewed."

"Maybe I see what's real."

"I don't envy you." She rubbed the frame of the vidstill with a finger. "A year ago I found a picture of your mother with you as a child. You were standing in a garden."

"I remember that picture. It was part of a publicity shoot. You know, the down-to-earth virtuoso. I think it was the only picture in which my mother and I were together."

"I tried to enter your eyes in the picture. It worked."

"I was only—what, seven?"

"Just about." He didn't dare tell her how obsessed he'd become with her life. "I've been restricted to the period going back from the time the picture was taken." He hesitated. "Until recently."

He got up and went to the window. The dawn light had increased, the cloud-laden sky taking on an apricot hue.

"You tried something new tonight, didn't you?"

"Yes. Before you kicked me out of your head, I stepped onto Vincent's lifepath."

She didn't say anything to that. After a few seconds, she cleared her throat. "Maybe the closer you are to my present, the more I can sense you."

"Hmm."

They fell silent. Torver contemplated Demetria, who'd come to join him at the window. She stood tall beside him, and he noticed she was the same height as he was. He liked that. He liked her, even though she had a bit of a righteous streak. All the same, it felt good to talk to her.

She broke into his thoughts. "Torver? Why do you suppose you've appeared in my visions?"

"I don't know. I don't understand how you could sense me, either."

"When I began to have visions outside my scanning, I concluded they may have developed out of the genetic mutation that caused my dermophagia."

"Funny, I've also thought that my ability was some form of genetic mutation."

"But how could we be connected?"

He shrugged. "Maybe our mutations are compatible, or it's the same mutation that expresses itself differently. We're tuning in to each other." The germ of an idea made him smile. "Wait a minute. We could compare our DNA maps to look for similarities. It might give us a clue."

"How are we going to do that?"

"Don't worry," he said, his smile broadening to a grin, "I know this brilliant statistician. She can help us."

## Chapter Eighteen

"Jesus, you didn't have to pump gallons of the stuff into them." Gerry peered through the bars of the cage where two Termites lay on the floor, dazed. Their unwashed bodies and dirty clothes, coupled with the lack of sanitation facilities in the enclave, produced a foul smell that made his nose twitch. "At least you could clean them up a little. I won't be able to work if they stink like that."

It was Argus who answered. "Amazingly fierce creatures, those Termites."

"They may be rejects of society," Gerry said, "but I don't have to put up with that smell. Look, they're lying in their own waste. It's disgusting." He turned to one of the guards sitting on a bench in the corner. "You gave them too much."

The guard shifted uncomfortably on his seat. "It took a lot of whitestar to calm them down after we took the female away," he finally said.

"Well, clean them up," Gerry said. "And while you're at it, get rid of their clothes."

The guard glanced at Argus, who gave him a short nod. Satisfied, Gerry left the enclave, followed by a smiling Argus.

Gerry was worried by that smile. When Argus was happy, you could find yourself in a mess. He was probably imagining what he'd do to Gerry if that next experiment didn't work.

Stringer had been escalating the threats, taking advantage of his proximity to the lab. Gerry knew that some of those threats were empty, that Stringer needed him, but in his nightmares he was the one collapsed on that chair in front of Stringer, his brain oozing out of his ears.

Within the next two hours, he'd know whether Lockwood was as good as he appeared. When he thought about it, the idea was so simple. Lockwood had created a chunk of DNA that was much simpler, pared down, so that he could insert new genetic code into that strand if needed. Gerry could use the research to target the addiction genes as they were in the ancient DNA, a "pure sample" of genetic code and watch for results. While Lockwood tested it on mice, he himself would be working on live people.

He was worried, though, that he couldn't wait until Lockwood completed his tests. He didn't even want to think about the possibility that the procedure didn't work. He wished he'd had more time.

He'd spent a week studying the new genetic structure, in awe at Lockwood's inventiveness. The ultimate test would be whether the dust had the desired effect on the genes. His latest attempt at using his own formula had been another failure. He just couldn't afford to fiddle with the dust indefinitely.

Someone had cleaned up the Termite and found him a shirt, although the man was so big it barely covered him from shoulders to crotch. He lay on the black plasmer table, still spaced on whitestar, wrists and ankles tightly secured with cuffs. Gerry donned surgical gloves, his eyes averted from the spectators who cramped the small laboratory. He inserted a needle attached to a tube to the side of the Termite's neck and fastened it with a piece of tape.

"He looks ridiculous in that shirt," Gerry said.

"If your little experiment succeeds," Stringer said, "we'll put more clothes on him."

Gerry nodded to the man, who levitated beside him in his maglev chair. Away from his desk, floating above the floor, Stringer reminded him even more of a deadly fish, the live conductive strips on the floor behind his chair extending like a lethal tail.

"If this works," Stringer said, "I'll keep him. He'll be my living proof. Nothing like showing concrete results for boosting sales." He chuckled, then sobered abruptly. "That is, if you can pull this off. This is your second chance, Gerry. I got you three Termites, but that's it. The community has disappeared. Get on with your experiment. If it's like the last one, he'll give us a pretty good show. Argus, make sure his restraints hold."

Holding a vial of brain dust, Gerry inserted his hands in a clear thermoplastic box where he'd already placed the rest of the equipment he needed. "At this point the dust is volatile," he explained as he removed the stopper from the vial, extracted a small quantity, mixed it with a liquid compound and inserted it in a syringe. "I wouldn't want us to breathe it in and find ourselves in the same predicament as that guy."

The man on the table moaned.

"He's metabolizing the whitestar at a rapid rate," Gerry said. "That's good. I'll give him the counteragent to wash the drug from his system before I inject the dust. I don't want the two to interact and skew the results." He flipped a switch, and blue liquid moved up the tube into the needle on the Termite's neck. They waited in silence until the cleaning machine beeped. Gerry removed the tube.

The Termite opened his eyes then closed them tight. "My head," he croaked.

"Don't worry, you'll feel better in a minute." Gerry sprayed antiseptic in the crook of the man's arm, placed the tip of the syringe that contained the brain dust on the skin and let the needle home in on a vein. He watched the gray liquid leach out of the transparent vial.

"How will you know the gene is activated?" Stringer said.

"When he wants more dust. When he gets sick or nuts because he can't have some."

The Termite smiled and began to hum. His skin flushed pink, and his penis poked up through the shirttails.

"It's taking effect," Stringer said. He moved his bulk closer.

"Once he's crashed, I'll take a cell sample and check that the genes were modified. Then we wait to see if the effect is the one you wanted." Gerry turned back to his monitors to follow changes in the body.

The Termite stretched, pushing against his restraints. He tossed his head violently from left to right, forced it up and let it fall hard with a thud.

"His vitals have speeded up," Gerry muttered. "Too fast." He was unsure if the body's reaction was a natural result of the procedure or if something was going wrong. The initial reaction to the dust had seemed normal, the vital signs similar to those during the delta waves of sleep. Now brain activity was irregular, heartbeat jumped, respiration was uneven. He threw a glance at his subject. The man strained against an invisible force, his body arced above the table.

Gerry backed up a few steps. "You're sure the restraints will hold, Argus?"

"I'm sure."

He checked the monitors again. The heart was racing. Brain patterns were changing radically. There was no activity at all in some areas of the cortex, as if the neurons had been burnt out.

He frowned at the man on the table. The Termite's extremities were purple; his panting sounded loud in the small lab.

The man twisted and stared directly at him. His eyes had the feral, savage look of a wild animal. His lips curled up in a snarl then he uttered a deep, prolonged howl and tried to hurl himself at Gerry. Teeth bared, screaming, he lunged forward again. And again.

"What the hell is going on?" Stringer yelled above the noise.

"I don't know!" Gerry said. He turned to his monitoring equipment. "His heart's beating too fast. I'll give him a tranq." He turned to prepare the syringe. He heard something rip behind him, then "Watch out!" Before he could turn, he was pulled backwards by his lab coat. He slammed against the Termite's hard body. A snarl nearly busted his eardrum. He squealed.

Gerry's feet came off the floor. His lab coat popped open. He slid out of it and sprinted to the end of the lab where Stringer and Argus had backed away and stood, transfixed. The wild man ripped the empty coat in his hand.

"You said the restraints would hold," Gerry screamed.

"They should have," Argus said. He pointed to the Termite, who was now crouched near the floor, sniffing the air around him. "That ain't normal."

"Fascinating," Stringer said. "He gets wilder by the minute."

The Termite jumped towards them. Argus whipped out his weapon and aimed; but before he could fire, the man stopped in his tracks, a grimace of pain on his face. He clutched at his chest, slashing the shirt with his nails, gouging his own flesh. He uttered a sound, half-groan, half-whimper, then collapsed on the floor. His body shook as with palsy, his hands cramped into claws, his knees locked. The man uttered a long, mournful cry then lay still.

The three of them waited for a long minute to see if he would move again.

Stringer said in a calm voice, "I believe your patient has expired, Dr. Sinclair. Better have a look."

Gerry hesitated until Argus pushed him forward. Cautiously, he leaned down and felt for a pulse. "He's dead."

"Get rid of him, Argus," Stringer said.

"Tests on the next one should work," Gerry said, more to reassure himself than to convince Stringer.

"I hope for your sake third times' the charm," Stringer said. He pursed his lips. Gerry shivered under his scrutiny. Stringer glided out of the lab without a backward glance.

Gerry looked down at the dead hulk at his feet. He had no idea what had gone wrong. Could it have been an interaction between the dust and the gene?

Because of Stringer's insistence on quick results, he'd abandoned the first principle of experimentation—test one variable at a time. What he should have done was to try to modify one addiction gene at a time. If that worked, he'd have introduced another change with the dust, thus compounding the addiction for the product for which it was intended. He'd been in too much of a rush, too afraid it wouldn't work, too sure of Lockwood's genius.

Maybe Lockwood hadn't announced his success with the new DNA strand because there was a glitch in it. Something that caused what he had just witnessed in the Termite. He needed access to Lockwood's work again. If he knew what the problem was—if there was one—maybe he could adapt the formula easily enough that it would work for him. He'd have to burrow into Lockwood's system again and check out his tests on animals.

He turned to Argus. "Make sure you dump the body in a place where he's found quickly. I need the results of the autopsy, and fast."

Argus gestured to two men who had been waiting in the shadow of the doorway. Gerry wondered what they had thought of the experiment; they appeared fairly stoic about the whole episode. As for him, he was still shaken, more with the thought he'd failed again than with the fact he had almost lost his life.

When you worked for Stringer, the fear of dying soon lost its edge. It was the fear of failure that was scarier.

## Chapter Nineteen

DEMETRIA TRIED TO CONTACT VINCENT AGAIN. SHE COULDN'T COUNT THE TIMES SHE'D called but she still couldn't reach him. After several futile attempts to focus on work, she resorted to roaming her apartment.

She was tempted to sink into her vocal scanning exercises, to center back, to remind herself of who she was, but she was more afraid now of what she'd find in the visions than she'd been upon learning to scan, when she'd discovered she could shift her consciousness and move into another world. That world had its own rules, and it had never transposed them into the real one. Everything that had happened to her, especially in the past twenty-four hours, had the surreal quality of a nightmare that wouldn't release her.

It had started with the news of her mother's death and the vision of herself in the laboratory, regressing towards the beginning of evolution. Then she'd seen Torver and stepped out of the vision and into his revelation that he, too, lived with a shift of reality. It had ended with another terrifying vision that had left her weak and desperate to reach Vincent.

When Torver suggested they might have a similar genetic mutation, it had intrigued her. When he mentioned who he was going to ask someone to map their genetic code, his words were like a slap in the face.

She had forced herself not to gape. "Why a statistician?"

"She's working on a genetics-related project with me right now. I'm a geneticist. She has this auth code that gives her access to the gene banks. She can use it to access our DNA maps. I'll ask her to compare yours and mine and give me the results. It would take her only a few minutes. She's good."

Goose bumps ran from the crown of her head to her fingers and down to her feet. She turned to face the window and stared out at the dawn. "Do you believe in coincidences, Torver?"

"In a kind of luck, maybe."

"I don't believe in either." She turned back to him, looked him straight in the eyes. "I've always thought I could direct my life, that I had control over the choices I made, not that events have been pre-determined for me. I'm beginning to change my mind about that."

He looked confused. "Okay. So?"

She smiled, amused by his obtuseness. "Don't bother asking that statistician to analyze our DNA for you. If it's not part of the project, she won't do it."

"How do you know that? Besides, she doesn't need to know—" His eyes widened with understanding. "You're her."

She nodded. "Now do you see what I mean about coincidences?"

"I don't believe this," he said in an injured tone. "Are you always so tight-assed and self-righteous, or is it just with me?"

Demetria crossed her arms under her breasts. "I'm getting really sick of your cheap shots."

"Well, it's true," Torver said. "Who would it have hurt if we'd talked face-to-face?"

"I have a contract that stipulates I can't talk to you. It also specifies that I can't use my auth code for anything other than the research I've been contracted to do."

"So, I'll send you the request through Dympna, and you can say it's part of your contract."

"No."

"Don't tell me you haven't been tempted to compare other dermophagia cases with yours."

"Oh, I have. And on top of it, I learned today that I was adopted."

He digested that piece of news for a few seconds. "All the more reason to compare our DNA. What if we're related somehow? You could find out who you are."

"I know who I am." The bitterness of the past three years swooped down on her. "You described me perfectly. Only you left out that I have half a face."

"Hey, I was angry when I said those things."

She shook her head. "I won't break my contract."

"You already have."

Demetria shrugged. "We didn't meet through work. I haven't violated the letter of it."

"Fuck." Torver raked his hand through his hair, walked away then circled back, standing opposite his vid. "You know what? I need a drink. Let's go out."

"The only bars open at this time of night are on the East Side. We don't want to go there."

"Damn. I have nothing more than soy milk here, and I definitely need something stronger."

She hesitated, contemplating him from her position near the window. He'd put distance between them, as if he were aware she needed the space. Or maybe he was the one who needed it.

She found his ability to pry into people's pasts repulsive but also fascinating. She hated it that he'd invaded her life. On the other hand, because of his ability, he didn't find her visions surprising or impossible; and, she admitted to herself, he made her feel less alone.

She made a decision. "I have some wine in my apartment if you like."

"You mean the real stuff?" At her nod, he grinned. "You're on."

As they entered her place, she watched his face. Few people had seen her apartment, but of those who had, their reactions had been extreme—they either hated or loved it. He glanced around him curiously then toured her living room in silence. He peered through the glass case at her bibelots, examined her paintings, caressed her gleaming commode.

"You do like antiques. You have some weird stuff in here." He spotted her Victorian sofa. "Is that the real thing?" He sat on it and waited for the back to mould itself to his shape. When it stayed rigid, he slouched backward and leaned his head on the back. "Ah, heaven. I'm sick of good posture. The closest I've come to this position is when I lean against a wall." He smiled. "I like your apartment. It suits you."

She smiled back, pleased by his verdict. "I'll get the wine."

When she came back with the bottle and two glasses, he took a glass from her. He sipped, rolled his eyes, and grinned.

"Yum." He took another sip. "About what you said at my place. Those coincidences."

She sat beside him and sipped but said nothing.

"It's uncanny, isn't it?"

Demetria nodded. "First you find my picture as a young girl and it fascinates you. You try to learn as much about me as you can. Then I start having visions. In the first one, you appear and point out a double helix to me. Next I get hired on a genetics project in which you're the principal player."

"The onset of your visions dovetailed with your joining the project."

"Hmmm. I have a vision in which I save your life. You rent an apartment in the building where I live, and on the night when I'm in trouble, you arrive on the scene."

"I needed some fresh air."

"I've run in that park hundreds of times. I've never had a problem, except for the time you showed up."

He gulped the last of the wine and gave her back the glass with a pleading look. "When you came barging into my place earlier, had you just come out of another vision?"

"Yes." She refilled his glass, handed it back to him. "I was in this lab, and there was a body under a sheet on a table. When I lifted it, I saw the body was me. Something started to happen." She swallowed, waited until she could speak without a quaver. "Skin grew over the left side of my face, and I was whole again. But it didn't stop there. I started to...de-evolve, that's the only way I can describe it."

He was staring at her, a stunned look on his face.

"What?" she said. "Does that mean something to you?"

He continued staring at her. She touched his arm.

"Torver?"

He started.

"An old twentieth-century theory," he said with surprise in his voice, "advanced that people are attracted to each other according to their genetic similarities."

"You don't really believe that."

"It's a better explanation than the Hand of God."

"Not much, if you ask me. Care to enlighten me about what just happened?"

He shook his head. "We have to do that genetic comparison."

"I told you, I am not using that auth code."

"Fine. Give me a sample of your DNA and I'll compare it to mine in the lab. It won't take much longer than searching through the databases."

Demetria was surprised he'd asked. Tired as she was, it would've been easy for him to distract her and steal her glass. It had her saliva on it with all the DNA he needed.

"You can't do that. That's not part of your project, either."

"They gave me my own lab. I can do what I want in there." He smiled. "I can run the comparison while I work on something else."

"I don't know."

The wall behind his right shoulder shifted. Demetria blinked, clenched her eyes together and opened them again. She felt dizzy, and Torver's face receded into a foggy distance. She tried to get up, staggered, and fell back. Her fingers did not seem to work; she dropped her glass.

"Torver," she yelled, her voice faint to her own ears, "I'm sliding away."

FLIES. THEY WERE THE FIRST THING SHE SAW—AND HEARD. SHE STOOD AT THE ENTRANCE to a room where hundreds—thousands—of plump, iridescent bluebottles obscured the windowpanes, buzzed around the light fixture, walked the walls and ceiling. Their collective drone vibrated in the empty room, like an amplified echo of her own vocal scanning.

Next she noticed the stench. A sweet, sickly rotting smell, like the one she'd encountered once on a scorching summer night in the woods. She'd stepped on a decomposing animal, and the same foul stink had assaulted her. She'd heard the flies then, too.

She moved three steps into the room, compelled to find out why she'd been brought here. She looked down. Dried-up flies littered the hardwood floor and lay scattered around her feet. She squinted in the low light that filtered through the dirty windows and shifted incessantly with the movement of the insects. She surveyed the room methodically, beginning at the nearest left corner.

There was nothing much to see. Just an empty room, its walls yellowed and in need of paint, the floor scuffed and scratched. Three high latticed windows had been cut through one side of the wall and were the only source of light.

Something fell on her head with a slight plop and started moving frantically. She cried out and rubbed at her hair. Something squished; she felt a gooey wetness in her hand. She looked at it—pieces of wings stuck to a whitish mass. She shuddered. Her lips pressed tightly together, she took a deep breath to settle her stomach. The stench went in deep and made her gag.

Suddenly, she was frightened. She turned to the doorway, but a movement on her right made her stop. There, in the darkest corner, the one farthest from the windows, she saw a teeming mass of the big bluebottles. Their droning increased as she watched.

Compelled, even through her fear, she walked over to the corner. In the dark, she could make out the shape of a body that wriggled and rippled with the bustle of the flies. The reek was almost overpowering now, but she couldn't take her eyes off the shape. Despite the gruesome blanket, she could make out feet, and legs, and a torso. A human body.

For a second, the flies stopped their busy dance, then moved off the head.

It turned slightly towards her. The eyes were gone, but she recognized the face. Her hand flew to her mouth and she moaned.

Something jarred her. She tried to turn, but things became fuzzy around her. Then all was dark.

DEMETRIA OPENED HER EYES. SHE WAS BACK IN HER APARTMENT, STILL SITTING ON THE couch facing Torver. She rolled away from him and whimpered. He turned her back, pulled her to him and took her in his arms. She let him cradle her and pat her back until the hysteria subsided and she could speak again. She pushed away from him. He looked relieved.

"Why don't you go," she said between clenched teeth.

"That was nasty."

"What?"

"Your vision."

"You saw it?"

"I followed you in. I guess you were too busy with the vision to block me." He squeezed her shoulder. "Are you all right?"

She felt curiously detached, incapable of getting angry with him.

"No."

She pushed to her feet then noticed the pieces of glass on the floor. She bent down and picked them up one by one. Her hand shook, and glass cut into her finger. Torver took her hand and pressed on the cut to stop the bleeding.

She looked up at him. "You took advantage."

"You did say your visions connected us. After you said you were sliding into one, you just sat there, your eyes wide open. I decided to follow your lifepath and try to see what you saw."

She bit her lip. "Did you see the body?"

He looked directly into her eyes. "Yes."

"It was Vincent." She shoved her fist in her mouth to prevent herself from screaming. When she was back in control, she said, "He's going to die."

"You don't know that." He took the pieces of glass from her hand, deposited them in a plate on the side table, then pulled her back to the sofa.

"I have to warn him," Demetria said.

"You can't. What are you going to say to him? That you saw his eyeless, putrefying body in a vision and that he should be careful? He won't believe you."

"You saw him, too. You can tell him that what I say is true."

"He doesn't know me. Besides, I'm not telling him I can travel lifepaths."

"You saw what I saw."

"It could mean all sorts of things."

She let her head loll on the back of the sofa, weary beyond belief. "I hate it that I can't control these visions, and I hate it that I don't understand what they mean."

"The only way to stop them is to learn more about them. The first step is to look at the genetic angle."

"No." She felt a slight tremor throughout her body. "I–I couldn't stop it," she croaked. "Oh, God." She hid her face in her hands.

"It's okay." She felt him pat her shoulders. "You're fine, now. Do you have any brandy or cognac?"

At her nod, he rose from the sofa and went in search of the bottle. He came back with two snifters half-filled with amber liquid. She took a hefty sip and breathed out the alcohol. The warmth spread quickly from her chest to her extremities.

"Torver," Demetria said after a moment of silence, "something brought me back."

"Ah." She heard the satisfaction in his voice. "So it does work. Remember when I said I'd seen you step on your cake when you were a little girl?"

The question startled her. She frowned and tried to recall their conversation. Instead, she saw herself as a five-year-old and remembered the feel of that cake sticking to her body through her dress. "I had this compulsion to destroy that stupid cake," she murmured. "It felt great."

"I witnessed that scene not long ago," Torver said. "At the time, I thought you did exactly what I would have done. In fact, I'd been thinking about squashing that cake when you suddenly jumped on it."

"Are you saying you influenced my actions?"

He shrugged. "Either that or we think very much alike."

"But that's impossible. I was five years old when that happened."

"I know. Anyway, when I saw Vincent, I knew I had to try to help you. I could see the thread attached to your back, so I thought, 'Yank on it.' Then you did."

"I don't remember doing it." She stared at him for a long moment. "I'm exhausted, I can't think anymore."

"I can stay here while you sleep, if you want."

She shook her head. "Go, please."

"You'll call Vincent, won't you? Even though it's not a good idea."

"I'd rather he think I'm crazy then have something happen to him because

I said nothing."

"I thought so."

She watched him make his way to her front door.

"Torver?"

He stopped and turned. She ran a finger along the seam of her prosthesis.

"Doesn't my face bother you?"

"I don't see it."

"Funny. When I'm with you, I don't think about it, either."

"We're quite a pair, Demetria. Let me know if you want me to do that DNA test."

She glanced at the broken pieces of glass in the plate. Traces of blood were drying slowly. "I was certain you would do it anyway."

He shrugged. "Somehow, when it comes to you, I've acquired a conscience." He grinned. "At least a mild form of it. See you."

She watched him leave with a smile of her own. Then she got up and went through her nightly routine mindlessly, fighting not to give in to the overwhelming fatigue or the hysteria that hovered just at the edge of her gathered calm. She'd sleep for a couple of hours, then call Vincent.

Just before she drifted off, she realized she'd made her decision; despite her promises to herself, she would let Torver do the comparison testing of their DNA.

## Chapter Twenty

VINCENT RESTED HIS HEAD AGAINST THE BACK OF THE CHAIR AND SWIVELED TO FACE HIS Cluny. The swirling motions of the colored holo didn't do their usual job of relaxing him.

In the last two days, while he'd been busy with budget meetings, forecast meetings, work review meetings and, it seemed to him, meetings about meetings, all he could think about was what he now called "the brain dust mystery."

He'd reviewed the data from the dust victims of the past three months, including the Termite, and found plenty of clues that someone was performing genetic engineering experiments; but he didn't have enough to convince the Health Center Board. He needed solid evidence; otherwise, the Board would refuse to let the police investigate. No one wanted to create a panic in the population or have the Health Center patrons lose confidence. After all, the Health Center was a DNA repository. To state that some unknown was experimenting with genetic material could give rise to a major credibility problem if it turned out false.

In all the DOA dust cases he had re-examined, about half contained evidence of some sort of genetic tampering—something the Protocol had not picked up, simply because he had been concentrating on the effects on the body rather than the genetic code. This meant that whoever was responsible for modifying the brain dust had to be a chemist with a background in genetics, and some familiarity with human molecular biology.

As to why they were trying to change the drug, he could hazard a guess. If they could make a chemical that changed the user's DNA and made it impervious to every anti-addiction compound, they'd have clients for life, just like the heroin and coke addicts of the twentieth century. Drug makers were experts in human nature. They knew that, regardless of the danger of being hooked, there would always be people who'd resort to drugs. If they could create a foolproof one by modifying the genetic structure of the user, their profits would increase, especially if they flooded the market with the new drug before it was widely known detox didn't work for that particular substance.

The reason he and his team had not picked up the pattern of change was that there was no pattern. Vincent had used his neuronet to try to find a logical sequence to the different formulae but had come up with nothing concrete.

Until that Termite. With her, the geneticist's strategy had changed, become more aggressive, more transparent. Enough, anyway, that the genetic tampering could be detected. He expelled a frustrated sigh. His knowledge of molecular biology was too limited to be able to speculate how her genetic code had been changed.

He clamped his hand on the back of his neck and stretched. His last meeting had been with his team. They hadn't been able to give him anything more. With the heat of July, crime was rising in the Metropolis, and they'd had to deal with a dozen cases while he was upstairs listening to the drone of voice after voice in the string of endless meetings.

He turned back to his desk. The list of cases for review beckoned, but there was only one that kept interfering with his concentration. He planted his elbows on the desk and rested his chin in his hands.

"Bring up brain dust records."

"Brain dust dossier is currently in use. Do you wish to make a copy?"

Vincent frowned. "Who from the team is using it?"

"Ident does not match current users list."

"What's the username?"

"No user name attached to Ident."

"From where are the records being accessed?"

"Dossier accessed via comm channel."

"That's impossible. Our net isn't connected to an outside channel." He paused. "Or is it? Trace channel to originator."

"Access terminated."

Vincent tapped a key to connect to his tech's office one floor below. Peter Farnsworth stood at a counter performing holo diagnostics. Vincent stared at the jumble of connections and rushing light that slowly rotated in front of the man. The inside of the bionet reminded him of his Cluny.

Peter raised his head at Vincent's appearance on his vid and started.

"Vincent. What can I do for you?"

"Our neuronet just told me that someone from the outside was accessing the Path Lab's records."

Peter stiffened. "Impossible."

Vincent nodded. "That's what I thought. I don't want to go to the sec chief with another false alarm. The last one made me look ridiculous."

"I had a right to restructure the shadow net. It was strictly maintenance."

"I know. I told you, I thought someone was playing with our data."

"Just me."

"Yes, well. I want you to look into this one, make sure it's not a glitch."

Peter nodded once. Vincent contemplated his rigid posture for a moment.

"Everything all right, Peter?"

"Yes, why?"

"You seem edgy these days."

"I'm fine." He turned off the diagnostics protocol he was working on. "I'll check on the net problem right away."

"Give me more details on it as soon as you can, okay? If we have an intruder, security should know it sooner rather than later."

"Yeah."

Vincent turned off the vid, puzzled by Peter's terse manner. He'd always been uncommunicative, but lately he was becoming almost antisocial.

He was about to call up the brain dust records again when his comm beeped him. He punched in the number for the lab. Su-Li's face appeared.

"Vincent, we have another DOA Termite here. I think you'd better come and take a look at him."

"Is he in the same condition as the female?"

"If you mean naked and pumped full of drugs, yes."

"I'm on my way."

Moments later he dashed into the lab. Su-Li stood beside a covered body.

"Tell me what you have," he said while he suited up.

She pulled the sheet off the corpse to reveal the massive bulk of a man. His tanned skin almost looked like leather in the harsh light. Deep purple gouges striated his chest. Vincent pinched one of the arms. Rigor mortis was still present.

"He's been dead less than three days."

"Yes. The Forensic Pathology Protocol estimates thirty-two hours. He's definitely a Termite. No Identichip. I'd say he was born in the community."

"Where was he found?"

"On the edge of the road between here and Montreal. The police think he may have been dumped there. The coroner says he was already dead when they dropped him off."

"Preliminary diagnosis of death?"

"Undetermined. Possible heart attack."

"Any diseases?"

"No. In fact, his heart is well proportioned for his body and has no pathophysiological defects. He had elevated levels of brain dust in his blood plus traces of whitestar. That's why I called you. I thought you'd want to take him over since you did the first one."

Two Termites in four days with the exact same cause of death was an improbability. He hoped he'd find the same genetic anomalies in this man as in the woman. That would certainly give him enough evidence to bring in the authorities.

He pressed his palm over the metal plaque of the neuronet.

"Identic verified. Forensic Pathology Protocol active."

"Analyze DNA composition of current subject."

While the FPP did its job, he began to perform the regular autopsy. Midway through it, he stopped. Tissue from under the deceased's nails was his own, and the shape of the gouges on his chest matched the shape of the nails. He had dug into his own chest. Musculature, organs, skeletal structure, dentition—everything was normal for a man of his age. Even the heart was fine. Vincent couldn't determine the cause of death.

Next step was to examine the brain and the spinal chord. The FPP interrupted his speculation.

"Analysis completed. Genotype shows genetic discrepancies with basal human DNA."

"Expand."

"DNA composition is ninety-nine point nine-eight-two percent similar to current human genetic structure."

Vincent's heart skipped a beat. He looked up the code for the female Termite.

"Compare DNA from sample TE108764-X with current subject." He thought quickly. "Wait. Remove anomalies in both and compare remaining DNA."

"DNA match one hundred percent once differences in chromosome 21 accounted for."

"Okay. Now compare DNA anomalies of both subjects."

"Match impossible."

"Damn." It would have been too easy. He had another idea. "Analyze blood sample for differential genetic material."

"Amino acid sequence found. Polygenic combination found for following genes—CHRNA4, AGS3, LGN, A118G."

"What are those genes?"

"Four alleles tied to modification of mu-opioid receptors."

Addiction genes.

"What does the amino acid do?"

"Amino acid sequence may be related to neural functions."

Vincent picked up a syringe and performed a spinal tap. He passed it through his analyzer.

"Identify genetic material in sample," he said to his FPP.

"Same amino acid sequence present in necrotized cells."

"The cells I provided you were dead?"

"Affirmative."

Vincent performed a similar operation with brain cells. The FPP gave him the same results. "Provide diagnosis of death," he demanded.

"Irreversible accelerated apoptosis."

Vincent blinked in surprise. Unstoppable death of nerve cells. He shuddered. The man must have been in excruciating pain. No wonder he'd tried to open his chest with his fingers.

He shook his head. So maybe he was right, and they were trying to create detox-resistant addiction genes. On the other hand, what were those amino acids doing there? Was it someone targeting drug takers, trying to eliminate them? There were plenty of fire-and-brimstone zealots with money to throw away. Yes, because all this research would take money.

He needed to consult a geneticist or a molecular biologist, and quickly.

One person could help him, and the way he looked at it, Laslo Radic owed him a favor. Without Vincent's contacts, Radic would still be looking for a statistician.

He checked the time—eighteen hundred. Peter should have got back to him by now.

"Connect me to Peter Farnsworth."

"No response."

Vincent frowned. Everyone on his staff had to be available twenty-four/seven. He wondered what Peter was doing. The latest data from the Termite still flashed on the vidscreen, and suddenly, he felt uneasy. Even if nothing was wrong with the neuronet, he wouldn't take any chances. He'd make a copy of the brain dust records and hide it in a secure place. That way, he'd be certain that no one would tinker with the data.

PETER FARNSWORTH STOOD HUNCHED OVER THE PUBLIC COMM SEVERAL KILOMETERS AWAY from the Health Center, where he was certain no one would recognize him and wonder why he needed to use an outside comm. Crowds walked by him, oblivious, but the anonymity didn't make him feel more secure.

After Vincent talked to him, he'd agonized for hours about what he should do. The easiest solution would be to tell Vincent the outside comm into the neuronet had been a glitch. But what if it happened again? Besides, Vincent was intensely curious and wasn't satisfied with easy answers. Peter would have to invent a specific reason, and that could trip him up later on.

Finally, he'd decided that since he wasn't the one who had created the problem he wouldn't be the one to find a solution. He hesitated another moment then tapped a channel number. Gerry Sinclair's face appeared on the screen.

"I know I'm not supposed to call," Peter stammered, "but Dr. Francis caught an outside tap of his neuronet. He's suspicious."

"Have they brought in a male Termite?"

"Yes. Francis was almost finished with him when I left to talk to you."

Sinclair cocked his head for a moment, his eyes speculative. "I'll meet you in your office tonight at one."

"What are you going to do?"

"One o'clock." The vidscreen blanked out.

Peter leaned on the edge of the booth, exhausted. For the millionth time he cursed his friend—ex-friend—Nale for introducing him to the delights of whitestar.

LASLO HAD BEEN READY TO LEAVE FOR HOME, EARLY FOR ONCE, WHEN HE'D RECEIVED Vincent Francis's urgent comm. He had seen the tension, the barely suppressed excitement in Vincent's features and had been intrigued. Then Vincent had said worrisome words.

*Brain dust. Pharmacogenomics. Possible genetic tampering.*

Laslo had hidden his surprise with difficulty. His first reaction was to think that Francis had discovered Gerry was making brain dust and that he, Laslo, was sponsoring illegal genetic experiments. If that were the case, he reasoned quickly, Francis would have gone to the authorities directly. But Francis's involvement had to be more than coincidence, so maybe he wanted something from him. It wouldn't be the first time someone had tried coercion or blackmail on him.

An hour later Satah, his assistant, came in. "A Dr. Francis is here to see you."

Laslo braced himself when Vincent walked in. He searched for accusation or cunning in the pathologist's eyes, but all he could see was anxiety.

"Vincent," he said, going around his desk to shake his hand. "You must have urgent business to come all the way to GeneTech."

"I appreciate your seeing me, Laslo. I need help, and you may be the only one who can safely provide it."

Laslo raised his eyebrows. "Really."

"I didn't want to say much on the comm because I may be watched."

"Monitoring comm transmissions is a tricky business these days."

Vincent shook his head. "I know how it sounds, but if you could hear me out..."

Laslo waved to one of the armchairs. "Why don't we sit down first." He went back behind his desk, rested his elbows on the arms of his chair and tapped his fingertips together. "You mentioned something about brain dust and genetic tampering. It sounds pretty serious. Have you gone to the authorities?"

"Not yet. Three months ago, we started to receive dustheads with increasing regularity. Death from brain dust is quite rare, overdose is impossible, and it isn't addictive, even though it does have side effects. That's what makes the drug so popular. But then dust casualties began coming in. What our Forensics Pathology Protocol found is that the brain dust formula was being modified and that a biological element was being added to it. This element was not readily identifiable."

"So the chemists were playing with the formula."

"That's what I thought at first. They were experimenting with other mixes and using the streets as their test lab. With those different blends, it was now very easy to die from the dust. A week ago the pattern changed again."

"How so?"

"In the last week we received two dead Termites. Their systems contained brain dust."

"Termites? Unusual."

"Yes. But there was something more. Both bodies held clear indication of genetic tampering. With the last one, it was as if someone tried to chemically modify a series of genes that control addiction potential, but it didn't work."

Laslo blinked once, unsure he'd heard correctly.

"I believe someone is trying to turn on what I can only call an addiction switch," Vincent continued. "but, so far, it hasn't been successful. The last victim died of rapid deterioration of his neural cells. It's as if what was inserted with the dust triggered cell death of the nervous system."

Holy shit, Laslo thought. Francis's story bore too much resemblance to Lockwood's work to be a coincidence. Two days ago, Lockwood had explained to him that something in the DNA strand he'd put together was turning the brain into mush. He wondered if Gerry had recruited Lockwood. No, he decided with sudden insight, Gerry must have somehow got his hands on Lockwood's data. Lockwood was too focused on his research to have time for brain dust.

Vincent continued and explained his theories. Laslo liked the zealot one, but he knew he shouldn't count on it.

"I'm not a geneticist," Vincent concluded. "I was hoping you could help me."

"You have a genetics lab at the Health Center. Why not use them?"

"The brain dust records have been accessed from the outside."

"You mean that whoever is producing the dust is monitoring your analyses?"

"Possibly. And they might want to stop me from going to the authorities." Vincent rubbed his neck. "Of course, I may be totally paranoid."

"I would be if I were you."

He seemed to relax slightly. "Thank you."

Laslo rubbed his chin. "An addiction switch. That's pretty sophisticated genetics." He chuckled. "If I had such a scientist working for me, I'd make a fortune."

Vincent flushed. "I agree that it's farfetched, but I have to make sure. You have a son, Laslo. How would you feel if he were addicted to dust for the rest of his life?"

Laslo grimaced. "Believe me, Vincent, I'd do anything to protect my son." He turned towards his garden and stared unseeingly at the riot of yellow flourishing under his window. Unless another crew was trying to encroach on Stringer's territory by modifying the dust, it sounded as if Gerry was in even deeper than he had first thought. Vincent said the pattern of changes in the dust had occurred a week ago. Two weeks ago Lockwood had told him about the problem with the retrogene. It fit.

He needed to keep Vincent as far away from this discovery as possible for as long as possible. He had to give Lockwood the time to refine his technique.

He turned back. "You realize what you're asking me to do is illegal."

Vincent cleared his throat. "It's not. As chief pathologist, I'm entitled to request the help of consultants."

Laslo contemplated him for a few seconds. "All right, Vincent. I can't promise anything, though. GeneTech is into pharmacogenomics, not genetic engineering. We may not be able to tell you much more than what you found."

Vincent smiled for the first time since he'd entered the office. "A confirmation of what I found would be a good start. Anything else will be a bonus."

Laslo grinned. "You mean a corroboration by a member of the Health Center Board that you're not crazy would be a plus?"

"Yes."

"Maybe you should avoid accessing those records until I send word to you."

"One of my staff might want to work on them. They're interested in this problem, too."

Laslo sighed. "Vincent, I don't think you understand. I'm not a security expert, but if an outside comm was set up, someone from the inside had to do it. Or certainly help."

"Impossible. My staff is a dedicated, professional team. No one would do such a thing."

"It may not be one of yours. It may be someone from security, or from maintenance. At this point, though, you don't know. That's why you have to be careful." He thought about his own illegal activities and the motivations that drove him. "Someone may have paid him, or he may be a discontented employee who wants to do some damage. What's important is that you keep the lid tight on this information. We don't want whoever is monitoring your data to know you realize he had help."

Vincent looked stricken. Then something like recognition fleeted in his eyes. "It may be too late for that. I just didn't think…" He nodded. "I'll keep a low profile for the next few days."

Laslo placed his hands flat on the desk and pushed himself up. "Well, Vincent, I appreciate your confidence."

Vincent jumped from his chair. "Thanks again. When will I hear from you?"

"I can't promise you a time frame, Vincent. I'll have to decide who I can trust with your data then discuss a strategy. We want to make sure what we'll bring to the Board and the police is solid evidence. I already have someone in mind, but I have to talk to him first. I'll let you know as quickly as I can."

Laslo breathed a sigh of relief as the door closed behind Vincent. He sat back in his chair and turned again to his garden. His son was like one of those flowers, he thought. With the proper genetic fix, he would survive.

Damn Gerry Sinclair. He could string Francis along for a couple of days, but then he'd have to provide the promised help. Those few days might give him the time he needed to decide what to do about Gerry. He only hoped Francis would not become a snag he would need to take care of.

## Chapter Twenty-one

Peter placed his hand on the passlock. The door glided open to reveal Gerry Sinclair, a huge man lurking behind him. Peter swallowed convulsively.

"I thought you'd be alone."

"The streets aren't safe, these days. This is Argus. Don't worry, he'll keep his mouth shut."

"I don't like sneaking you in here," Peter said.

"It will be the last time," Sinclair assured.

Argus raised his hand in a signal, and three men barged through the door in front of him.

"Hey, who are those guys?" Peter said.

"They won't touch anything. Let's go to your office."

Peter closed and locked the door then rushed after Gerry, who was following Argus and his men.

"I tell you, it scared the living crap out of me when Vincent told me he'd intercepted a record transfer. He wanted to go to security but came to me first. I made him look like an ass three months ago when he blew the whistle on us. Of course, he didn't know it was us. I convinced security I was reorganizing the shadow sets, which was true, but not for the reasons I gave them. Dr. Francis—"

"I want you to sever the connection," Gerry said.

Peter nodded. "That's a relief. You have everything you need, then?"

"Almost."

Peter sat at his console and brought up the neuronet structure. He traveled deep into the neuroconnections until he highlighted a faint corner where the outlet for a comm channel was coded in. He picked up tiny digital scissors and snipped the code in two. "There. In a few minutes the code fragments will be absorbed by the neuronet. There won't be any trace of the connection to the outside."

"You'll give me the shadow set and erase the brain dust records on the Path neuronet."

Peter frowned. "But...won't that make Dr. Francis more suspicious? I mean, if all the records are deleted?"

"Do it."

The three men who had come with Argus advanced and loomed over Peter. He turned back to his console.

"I hope you know what you're doing. You'll have to give me a plausible explanation for Dr. Francis."

"Does anyone else have access to those records?"

"Pretty much the entire team. They've all been working on the dust cases. Su-Li especially. There's the activity log." He pointed to several places. "See? Here's Su-Li, then Sara, Su-Li again, then Purvis Black. Oh-oh."

"What?"

"Dr. Francis copied all the brain dust records before he left."

"Where?"

Peter threw a glance at Argus. "Into an MGRC neuronet."

"You'll delete those as well."

"I can't. First, he encrypted the records before he copied them. The encryption process scatters the data throughout the neuronet. I wouldn't be able to find them without using his encryption key to reassemble them."

"So, he didn't leave with the records."

"No, but he probably downloaded the code into a key generator that he keeps with him. The key has to match the one generated simultaneously at the other end. Plus, unless someone else has an auth code, he's the only person who can access the records. You need the code to get on an MGRC neuronet." He extracted the small disc that rose from his console. "I've deleted the files. Here's the shadow set."

"Call the Path Lab Team. Tell them Dr. Francis asked you to contact them and that he wants them all here. Tell them it's urgent. But don't call Francis."

"Why would I want to do that?"

Argus looked down at him. Peter swallowed.

"Fine." He activated the emergency channel and called up the team. Each acknowledged within two minutes. "They're on their way. They'll all go to the conference room once they get here."

Argus nodded. "I'll wait for them there." He glanced at one of his men.

"Kill him."

VINCENT ALWAYS FELT ENERGIZED BUT CALMER WHEN HE ENTERED HIS HOME. ITS STRAIGHT, angular lines, bare walls and gleaming floors reminded him of possibilities, of forward motion. The modern style also reminded him that he'd wiped out the old house. That he'd chosen his own destiny.

Tonight the house seemed too big for one person. His talk with Radic had shaken him—why hadn't he seen that someone from his team might be working for the dust producers? It would certainly explain Peter's change in behavior, for instance. As the information manager, he'd be in a perfect position to set up a commlink with the outside.

On the other hand, anyone could have used the confusion of three months ago to plug in a comm line. Maybe the confusion had been created as a smokescreen to do just that. If so, then Peter was the prime suspect once again.

Any way he turned the problem in his mind, he knew he had no choice. He had to go to the authorities.

He lifted the disc containing the encryption key to eye level. The key generator's size and shape had given him the idea for the perfect hiding place. Scrambling the brain dust data onto an MGRC neuronet might have felt a bit paranoid at the time but now he was glad he'd followed his instincts. If anything happened to him, Radic would be able to point the police in the right direction. He shifted the disc slightly. Its surface reflected the light in a rainbow of colors. Just in case Radic decided he didn't want to get involved, Vincent would make sure at least one other person knew what he suspected.

He walked to his vidcom and brought up Demetria's comm number. "Record following message to be released if stasis code not provided within forty-eight hours."

Yes, tomorrow he'd go to the authorities. If for some reason he was prevented from doing so, Demetria could go for him. He smiled at the vid and began his message.

VINCENT WAS STARTLED AWAKE. HE STARED AROUND HIM, CONVINCED HE WAS HAVING A nightmare. He sat in a red chair in a room drenched in red. Facing him behind a desk sat layers upon layers of fat.

The gelatinous mass lifted a hand in greeting. "Nice to finally meet you, Dr. Francis."

Vincent straightened in the chair. His tongue was thick in his mouth, and it took him several tries before he could speak. "Who are you? How did I get here?"

"My name is Stringer. You should have paid more for your home security." Stringer gestured at a spot behind Vincent. "Argus here fed a bit of sleeping gas into your air recycler then bypassed your system."

Vincent twisted in his chair. A massive man stood in front of a door.

"He brought you here because I need some information. I hope you don't mind." Stringer opened a jar on his desk. "Tea?"

The aroma of bergamot and cloves wafted over to Vincent. He blinked. "What sort of information?"

"You don't get the chance to work on Termites very often, do you, Dr. Francis?"

For a moment, Vincent failed to register the question. When he did, sweat broke out over his entire body. "You're the one manipulating the brain dust."

"Let's say I'm the instigator of the project." Stringer slurped his tea. "Many count me as a power in the Americas' entertainment trade, but it's become a limited market.

"Have you ever thought about water, Dr. Francis? If one controls water resources...one can control the world. The new drug formula will provide me with the down payment on my investment to buy the world. Imagine, permanent consumers for an endless supply of dust. To them, it'll be worth the price I'll ask. It's a difficult proposition to resist, for them as well as me."

Vincent realized he was a dead man. His hands began to shake. He grasped the arms of the chair. "Why did you bring me here?"

Stringer slurped more tea. "Are you sure you wouldn't like a cup? I import the leaves directly from the China States."

He shook his head.

"Very well. You've been a busy man, Dr. Francis. Clever, too. Unfortunately, I must put a halt to your research. Sooner or later you would have involved the police." Stringer seemed to read something in his face. "Ah, so I was right. My timing was perfect, then."

He wished the man would just stop babbling and come to the point. He swallowed and found his voice.

"Other people know about your experiments, Stringer."

"If you refer to your team, I wouldn't worry. They won't be in a position to say a thing." Stringer set down his cup. "What I want is the encryption key, Dr. Francis."

Vincent thought about the message he'd left for Demetria. He almost groaned aloud. If Stringer found out about that, her life would be worth as much as his was right now.

He plastered an innocent look on his face. "For what?"

"Please, don't play that game. Give me the encryption key and you'll save yourself a lot of pain."

"I still don't know what you mean."

Stringer smiled and took out a laser scalpel from somewhere in his desk. "Argus."

Argus grabbed Vincent's hands and flattened them in the center of the desktop.

"We'll start with one finger. Which one do you prefer I cut off first, Dr. Francis?"

Vincent stared at him with dawning horror. "Are you crazy?"

Stringer smiled. "There are all sorts of ways to obtain information. This one will be more fun. For me, at least."

Vincent blinked away the sweat trickling into his eyes. "I told you, I don't have an encryption key."

Stringer shook his head. "I have information that tells me otherwise. You know, on further thought, we won't go for the fingers. You're a big fish in that Health Center pond. You'd have access to limb replacement. No. We'll go for the eyes. The trick with a laser scalpel, though, is to be precise enough to get the eye without nicking into the brain." Stringer giggled. "Don't worry, doctor, I've had quite a bit of practice. And just think, your wounds will be cauterized immediately."

Argus held Vincent's head steady. Stringer raised the scalpel. Vincent started screaming.

## Chapter Twenty-two

As he strode towards Torver's lab, Laslo told himself he'd always listened to his instincts and today they were howling. Ever since Torver had told him the retrogene didn't work, he had grappled with a sense of imminent disaster. It was like standing on the edge of a cliff and waiting for someone to push him over.

His sense of unease had been reinforced that morning when he'd watched his son leave for school. To his eyes, the boy looked tired, listless. When Zelimir had returned from camp a week ago, he had expected exuberance. Instead, Zel had smiled and said he'd enjoyed himself. When Laslo asked him what he'd done at camp, a wave of panic fleeted through his son's eyes. Then Zel gave him a vague answer—"You know, Dad, camp stuff."

He'd mentioned Zelimir's answer to Jelena, but she'd dismissed it. Children were typically close-mouthed about their activities, she'd said. But to Laslo, who'd been observing his son closely for the past two years, Zelimir seemed more subdued than usual.

He entered the darkened interior of Torver's lab. The lack of light annoyed him. He slapped the light plate.

"Hey," Torver yelled from the back, "turn that off."

"Why don't you answer your comm?"

"Simple." Torver's back stayed firmly turned. "I don't want to talk to anyone."

"You'll talk to me." Laslo strode to the end of the room, where Torver sat hunched over a vidscreen, and waited.

Torver sighed and turned his head to look at him. "I don't have anything for you, Mr. Radic."

"You said you were close."

"I did. I am. But I'm not there yet."

"What's the problem? Two weeks ago you could barely contain yourself."

Torver turned the screen off. "I guess you have a right to know what's going on."

Laslo smiled thinly. "How big of you." He tapped his wrist unit to call up a privacy bubble. "Go ahead, and try to use English words."

"Sure." Torver frowned in concentration. "Remember I told you that, for some reason, the retrogene I put together triggers programmed cell death of the nervous system? It's as if some dormant developmental genetic material in the host responds to the gene."

"You can fix it, right?"

Torver shrugged. "In time, yes. I have a feeling the problem lies with the introns. That's what I'm testing now."

"Introns."

"In humans, about twenty-seven percent of the DNA is not actively involved in coding for proteins. I assume you know that the proteins are responsible for shaping our body? You know, muscles, bones, organs—"

"I'm not a complete idiot."

"Sorry. Well, some of the non-coding DNA is made up of introns. You can find them between codons, which are the portions of DNA that signal the beginning and end of a gene. The codons may have been mini-genes that coded for special functions during evolution. Once the organism became more complex, the codons got tacked together to form genes. It's always been thought that the introns were the packing material that was used to patch the codons together. My theory is, since the introns have been around unchanged from the beginning, they're the ones affected by the retrogene."

"What's the solution?"

"I'm working on neutralizing the introns. I'm going to check kindreds to see if there are any differences in their introns. Maybe they're part of the polygenic effect. I wouldn't think so, but I've got to check everything."

"That statistician's still working out, then?"

Torver grimaced then chuckled. "She's...quite capable."

Laslo didn't understand Torver's meaning, but he didn't care so long as Torver kept working and getting results. His attention shifted to the blinking light on his wrist unit. He froze. Only one person used that link, and only for emergencies.

"I have to get back to my office." He collapsed the privacy bubble. "Keep me apprised of your progress," he said while making his way to the door, "every day, more often if you get positive results. Is that clear?"

"Gerry said he was keeping you up to date."

Laslo stopped short and wheeled around. "Gerry asked you for progress reports?"

"Yeah. I stalled him."

"Why?"

Torver shrugged. "I don't trust him. I caught him snooping around my bionet right after I nailed the retrogene. He said he was only checking my security, but I didn't like it."

Damn. It was Gerry who'd stolen the data and was manipulating the dust. Laslo swore silently. If Sinclair got caught, the whole retrogene project—and his son—would be dead.

"I'll deal with Gerry. From now on, you talk directly to me." He checked his wrist unit. "I have to go."

He rushed to his office, his sense of premonition stronger than ever. He didn't bother to close the door behind him, just sat at his desk and entered the number to his private channel. Jelena's worried face appeared immediately.

"Laslo," she said without preamble, "we have to go to Zelimir's school."

"What happened?"

"Apparently, he fell at recess and tore open his knee. They brought him to the nurse's station, but he refused treatment. He also refuses to talk."

Laslo shivered. "Did they say he *refused* to talk...or is he unable to?"

Jelena gasped and pressed her fingers to her mouth. Perversely, Laslo was relieved that she had difficulty keeping her composure. "I don't know," she said. "I didn't dare ask. I want to get there as soon as possible."

"I'll send a message to Met Traffic Management that we're taking the car. I haven't used all my permits for this year. I'll pick you up in twenty minutes." He saw the relief on her face. "We'll decide if we need to take him to the Health Center when we see him. We may be worrying for nothing."

Her smile was wobbly. "Hurry."

Laslo stared unseeing at the blank vidscreen. He had to hurry, get to the car, go to his son, but he seemed unable to budge. He'd anticipated this moment, dreamt it countless nights, seen it during many hours of imaginings. In all cases, he'd underestimated the anguish he'd feel.

This was it, he was certain. Barcina's had been triggered, at least two years too early. He didn't have any illusions. He wished he'd find his son healthy but sullen, like any other boy hovering on the edge of adolescence, but he knew in his bones that his son's disease had begun its slow destructive crawl.

He wondered how long Zelimir had known that something was wrong with him. He hoped and prayed his son hadn't procrastinated too long.

The drive to the school took place in tense silence. Jelena had entered the car with the words "I'll let you concentrate on driving" then promptly turned her face to the side window and lapsed into silence.

Traffic consisted mainly of the long articulated buses that raced through the streets on their balloon-like wheels and official vehicles. Laslo hated the buses, although like everyone else he had no choice but to tolerate them. The snakelike conveyances crisscrossed the city in all directions, but they were slow and always crammed with people. He couldn't imagine taking his son to the Health Center in one of those. He was lucky his status and money allowed him to have a car, although he was limited in the number of times he could use it.

Despite the need to concentrate on traffic, his mind wandered to his son. Zelimir had blossomed in the community school in which he had placed him, and even if his learning curve would have been better at home, he saw Zel as more well-rounded than he himself had ever been. Zelimir was a gregarious child with lots of friends. Girls had always been crazy about him, even in toddler school, even though it didn't please his son in the least. The thought made him smile. All grown up, women would swarm around Zel. And Laslo had long made the decision that Zelimir would choose his own bride, not have that choice dictated by the elders.

If he made it that far. The helpless feeling washed over him again. He became conscious of a dull pain in his hands and realized the steering bar had bitten into his clenched fists.

"Pull in at the back of the building," Jelena said. "When I called the nurse to tell her we were on our way, she told me there should be space there."

Laslo blinked. He forced himself to relax while he parked the car. Jelena hurried out and was already standing at the door of the school before he had time to step out.

He rushed to her side. "You know the way?"

She nodded once and waved her hand over the metal plate in the wall. The door swished open, and they hurried inside.

"I didn't realize security was so lousy here," he said.

"They must have left it unlocked for us."

"Any nut could have come in. I'm going to speak to the principal about it. This is totally unacceptable."

Jelena stopped so quickly he nearly rammed into her. She turned and looked up at him.

"Both of us are under stress, Laslo. I would appreciate it if you kept your grumbling to a minimum. If Zelimir really is sick, we'll have to present a united, positive front. I don't want you to scare or embarrass him by threatening school officials or bullying the nurse. If you can't do that, you can go back to the car. Do you hear me?"

"He's my son."

"Yes, he is, and I know you're very angry, but think of him, how frightened he must be. He doesn't need your temper at this point."

"We're wasting time, Jelena."

She peered into his face for a long moment. He worked at tamping down the anxiety and the anger. He darted forward his hand and took Jelena's. He squeezed it, and it seemed the answer she needed. With an abrupt gesture of her head, she motioned him forward. He nodded and marched down to the nurse's office.

The first person he saw when they entered the room was his son. Zel sat on an examination table, motionless, expressionless, his legs dangling over the edge, his arms at his side like borrowed appendages. As if he could sense the presence of his parents, Zelimir's eyes flew to the door.

A woman blocked Laslo's field of vision. She was scrawny with a hooked nose and small black eyes that seemed to move constantly. Her hair was glossy black and flowed down her back.

"Mr. and Mrs. Radic? I'd like to speak with you before you see your son."

"I don't think so, Miss…" He read the name sitting high on her chest. "…Lancaster. I'll see my son, then we can talk."

"But—"

"Get out of my way, please."

Her eyes widened, and she moved aside. Laslo approached Zelimir, who hadn't budged from the table.

"Hey, Zel," he said very softly. He could feel Jelena's hand on the small of his back, her breathing on his bare arm, but she said nothing. Swiftly, she approached Zelimir, kissed him on the cheek. When she saw that her son's eyes were still on Laslo, he heard her sigh slightly before she backed away to let him deal with their son.

Zelimir opened his mouth then closed it quickly. His eyes filled with tears. Pain twisted in Laslo's chest. He smiled.

"That nurse is something, isn't she?" he continued in the same tone. "Remember the crows we saw at the zoo last year? It's a good thing she doesn't wear black, too."

That made Zelimir smile. It was small and tentative, but still a smile.

"The nurse called to say you hurt your knee."

"That's what I wanted to speak to you about, Mr. Radic," Nurse Lancaster said, as she came up beside him. "There's something peculiar about his injury. You see, it hardly bled."

Laslo kept his eyes fixed on Zelimir. "Didn't you understand me the first time, Miss Lancaster? I want to speak with my son. You'll get your turn."

"Well, good luck to you. He hasn't uttered a sound since they brought him here."

Laslo straightened. "Did you get the job because of your insensitivity, Miss Lancaster, or are you just plain stupid?"

Jelena squeezed his arm in warning then moved between him and the nurse.

"Why don't we go into your office," she said. "You can tell me what your concerns are." She turned the nurse around and gently steered her away.

Laslo turned back to the boy, rubbed his son's cheek with the back of his hand. "I know why you won't talk, Zel. It's because you can't, right?"

Zelimir frowned in concentration. "Can. Losing worts."

Laslo felt chilled. He reviewed the initial symptoms of Barcina's in his mind—incoordination of voluntary movements and loss of the ability to articulate ideas or comprehend spoken language. "I know," he said to Zelimir. "Can you understand what I say, though?"

Zelimir nodded.

"Good. Now listen to me, son. Do your feet hurt?"

"No." Zelimir frowned. "But like inside the really big plants in the forest."

"You mean the trees? The inside of trees. You mean wood."

Zelimir nodded.

"Should I have a look?"

At Zelimir's nod, Laslo unfastened a shoe and pulled it off slowly. Two of the toes and part of the side of the foot were white and hard, but thankfully there was no gangrene yet. He looked up at his son. "You know we're going to have to go to the Health Center, don't you?" At his son's grimace, he shook his head. "That's why you didn't tell me about your toes, isn't it? You knew I'd take you to the Health Center."

"Don't like school."

Laslo was confused until he realized Zel had substituted the word "school" for "Health Center." "I know, but we have to go now." He smiled. "You know what? You get to ride in the car."

Zelimir's face lit up. He put his son's shoe back on his foot.

"Can you walk?"

Zelimir nodded then lifted his arms to his father. Laslo laughed. He took his son in his arms.

"Jelena," he yelled, "we're leaving."

Nurse in tow, Jelena appeared. She looked at him questioningly. He shook his head once. She bit her lip as she approached them.

"We're going, sweetie," she said to Zelimir. She caressed his head. "Your dad and I will take care of you, don't worry." Zelimir didn't resist the caress. "Is it okay if I ride with you in the back of the car?" Jelena asked. She smiled when her son nodded.

"You can't just leave!" the nurse squawked.

Jelena turned, her face tight. "Zelimir needs to see a doctor. Thank you for calling us promptly." She marched out of the room ahead of Laslo, who rushed to follow her.

"Like a crow," Zelimir piped up.

Jelena punched the car door open. "I hope you're talking about that nurse and not me, sweetie," she said with a smile. "In you go."

As much as they had kept silent during the drive to the school, they rode to the Health Center amid Jelena's constant chatter. She talked about what she was going to fix for dinner, about Zelimir taking a holiday from school—he didn't need it anyway, since it was only summer school not the regular classes—how she'd let him watch his favorite vid when they got home.

Laslo understood what she was doing and was grateful for it. Her avalanche of noise prevented Zelimir from uttering a single word. His son gradually relaxed until he lost the watchful pose he'd adopted in the nurse's office then leaned his head on his mother's shoulder. There was an additional benefit to Jelena's jabber; it kept them from thinking too much about where they were going and what came next.

"MR. RADIC, THE INFORMATION YOU GAVE US ABOUT INCIDENCES OF BARCINA'S XYLOPOIESIS in your family may help us arrive at a diagnosis. But first we must address the major symptom, which is your son's aphasia. We'll begin by eliminating the obvious, such as a stroke."

Laslo stared at the emergency intern incredulously. "Are you deaf? I just told you that my son has the disease. I want him properly treated."

The intern, whose plate bore the name CARSON, consulted his diagnostic vidscreen. Laslo and Jelena sat across Carson's desk while Zelimir waited in a treatment cubicle with a nurse.

"Nothing in your son's Identichip indicates his DNA was screened for Barcina's xylopoiesis. It's a very rare disease, you know, sir."

"Yeah. Don't think I didn't see you look it up."

Two red spots appeared on Dr. Carson's cheeks. "As I said, Mr. Radic, it's not the first pathology I'd be testing for. I've also checked your medical history and Mrs. Radic's, and there is no indication that either of you have been screened for that genetic defect. As you know, it is a recessive disease, so both of you would have to be carriers for your son to have Barcina's. The odds that both of you are carriers, given the extreme rarity of the disease, are astronomical."

"How do you explain his foot?"

"I confess I haven't seen that type of tissue decrepitude before. That's why we need to do more tests."

Laslo felt Jelena's hand on his arm. "Take care," she said under her breath.

He snapped his mouth shut. She'd guessed he was about to tell the doctor about the tests for Barcina's he'd carried out on his own. If he said anything about that, Dr. Carson would be obliged to call the authorities.

At this point, regardless of what he said or did, the doctors wouldn't be able to control the disease, let alone find a cure. That was the reason Lockwood was working in secret, right now, in a lab at GeneTech.

"Are you at least going to test for Barcina's?" Jelena said to Dr. Carson.

The intern hesitated for a few seconds, then nodded. "I suppose I could do that, if it would relieve your minds."

Laslo took a deep breath. He was going to strangle the little squirt. Jelena squeezed his forearm.

"In the meantime, what can you do for Zelimir?" she said.

"Your son demonstrates the initial symptoms of primary progressive aphasia." The doctor seemed relieved to go back to more familiar territory. "He talks around a word, switches one word for another, makes mistakes in pronunciation. Unfortunately, we won't be able to determine proper treatment until we've identified the cause. We'll check the apolipoprotein gene for anomalies. If it is a genetic defect, we'll be able to correct it if you get the proper permissions. In the meantime, we can try EmaseFour to prevent further damage to the left hemisphere."

"Will you need to keep him here?" Jelena said.

"No. We'll fit him with a health chip that will monitor his condition and warn us if he worsens. It will also give us the possibility to extract more medical data if we need it." The doctor checked his watch and got up. "Now if you'll excuse me, I have other patients to see. You'll be able to take your son home in about a half-hour."

Laslo stood up also. "You will test for Barcina's."

"Yes, Mr. Radic."

"When?"

"As soon as we have time. The test is quite involved."

"That's not good enough."

"Mr. Radic—"

"Listen, I've had enough of your feeble answers. We're talking about my son's life. I want to know when you'll do the test."

"Radic, I thought it was your voice I heard."

Laslo whipped around to face the newcomer. A tall woman with steel-gray hair and sharp blue eyes stood in the entrance.

"Leila," he muttered.

"What are you doing here?"

"My son is sick. He's in the other room getting whatever treatment your doctor here chooses to administer. I'm trying to convince him that he should run more tests."

"Didn't you tell him who you were?"

"I was getting to that. I didn't know you had to pull strings to get proper treatment in this place."

"Come on, Radic, that's not fair. I'm sure Doctor..." She peered at the intern's name plate. "Carson was going to get to those tests, weren't you, Doctor?"

"Uh, yes, of course, Dr. Pratt. Of course."

Jelena cleared her throat. Laslo and Leila turned towards her.

"I'm sorry, Jelena," Laslo said. "Leila, this is my wife, Jelena. Jelena, meet Dr. Leila Pratt."

Jelena nodded in acknowledgement. "You seem to have some influence, Dr. Pratt," she said. "We'd appreciate any help you could give us."

Leila smiled. "Being CEO of the Health Center does have a few perks." She turned to the intern. "Why don't you give priority to those tests, doctor. Mr. Radic is a valuable member of the Health Center Board. Surely, we can accommodate his request."

"Right away, ma'am."

"Good." She smiled at Laslo. "I hope your son feels better soon. Get in touch when you have a chance, Radic. I want to discuss a couple of budget items before the quarterly meeting."

"I will." He and Jelena stayed silent while Leila and the intern left.

"Good thing you know people in high places," Jelena said, her tone cold. "You could have used your influence instead of browbeating that intern."

"You know I'm not the type to ask for favors."

"This isn't the time for false pride."

Laslo closed his eyes and nodded. "You're right. To tell you the truth, I didn't think about pulling strings. I was too focused on Zel's condition."

Jelena said nothing for a moment. "I know."

"Let's go check on Zel."

"Yes. This place..." She shuddered. "It's making me crazy."

The door to the examining room where they'd left Zelimir swished open before Laslo. The bed seemed to engulf the small shape of his son lying in its center.

"Hey, Zel. Ready to go home?"

Zelimir nodded vigorously. "Home."

"That's good, because your mother here is starting to act funny." He twirled his index finger near his temple. Zelimir giggled. "I think we should take her out of here soon," he continued in a confidential tone.

Jelena grimaced. "Very funny, you two. Let's see if we can get permission to leave."

"He's ready to go, Mrs. Radic," Dr. Carson said from the doorway. "We'll contact you as soon as we have the test results."

"Fine." There was no doubt in Laslo's mind as to what the diagnosis would be—Barcina's xylopoiesis.

"Come on, buddy," Laslo said to his son. "You can walk to the car this time."

## Chapter Twenty-three

Torver couldn't wait to see Demetria. He'd finally compared their DNA, and now he couldn't wait to discuss the results with her. Then, on the heels of that one revelation had come a shattering insight on the consequences of his own research. What he'd found out was almost too much for him to accept, and for the second time in a week, he'd suffered from a twinge of conscience.

Fortunately, he thought as he punched the bell for her apartment, he did have someone he could talk to, even if she had a tendency to nag. By a turn of fate she was involved, but he had to be careful. He needed her. She had no idea that the Barcina's project was illegal; and from what he'd learned of her, if she knew she'd probably rat on them.

The door opened, and Demetria faced him.

"Whoa, what happened here?" he said. "You look a mess." The right side of her face was blotchy and swollen, her nose was runny, and her eyes were red and puffy from too much crying. Her left side, devoid of its prosthesis, was rusty brown and pulsed slightly.

"I should have called him right away," she said between hiccups. "I was too tired. I needed a nap."

"What are you talking about?"

"The news. Haven't you heard?"

"No. The only things I've done in the past two days are eat, sleep and work."

"Vincent's dead. They all are."

"Who else?"

She shook her head.

"What happened?"

"What do you care?" she said, and turned back into her apartment. He followed her inside and closed the door, trailed her to the kitchen. She opened the cooling unit and took out a bottle of water. She stared at it, as if she'd forgotten why she had it in her hand, then her face crumpled.

"Oh, God."

Torver grabbed the bottle when it dropped from her hand, placed it on the counter. "Why don't I make coffee while you clean up?" He pushed her out of the kitchen. "Get into the decont, freshen up, put on clean clothes."

She stood, unmoving, looking lost.

"Demi," Torver said loudly, "did you hear what I said?"

She looked at him with stricken eyes. "Vincent used to call me Demi. He was the only one who did."

"I won't call you that, then."

"That's not what I meant."

"Would you just go?" He turned her around and pushed her towards the decont room. "I'll be right here when you come back."

As soon as she was gone, he turned on the vid in the kitchen and called up the news of Vincent's death while he quickly made coffee.

"A grisly and incomprehensible series of murders have rocked the foundations of the Greater Ottawa Metropolis Health Center. Early this morning, the entire team of the pathology department was found dead in the autopsy laboratory. Five pathologists, three lab technicians and two net techs were eviscerated with what the police think was a plasma gun. Later in the day, Dr. Vincent Francis, Chief Pathologist at the Health Center, was found dead in his home. Although he also died from a plasma gun wound, in addition both of Dr. Francis's eyes had been surgically removed. At this point, the authorities are baffled. Milo Carr, a spokesperson for the Center, stated that the staff is in shock and several post-trauma teams have been called in for counseling. Carr said that they did not know what exactly Dr. Francis's team was currently working on and whether the killings were related..."

Torver heard a sound behind him and turned around to see Demetria standing in the middle of the room, staring at the vid. She looked marginally better in clean clothes with her hair combed and her face scrubbed. She'd put on her prosthesis. It gave her a mildly psychotic look, one side of her face red and swollen from crying, the other smooth and untouched, the seam bisecting her face darker than usual.

"I foresaw his death, Torver. I might have prevented it."

He stood up to face her. "You can't think that way. You can't know that if you'd talked to him he'd be alive today. He's not the only one who died. Maybe you'd be dead now, too."

"It doesn't make it easier to take." Her face crumpled for a moment. "Who would do something like that?"

"Do you know what Vincent was working on?"

"No." She bit her lip and frowned in concentration. "Wait. He mentioned something a few weeks ago about dustheads. Someone was changing the formula and was using the users on the street as test subjects. Maybe he stumbled onto something that got him killed."

"The way Vincent was killed…I read somewhere that's how the drug cartels send messages. He might have found damaging evidence, and he shared it with his staff. It would explain why his whole team was killed."

"I have to go to the police. Tell them what I know."

Torver held her in place. "Take it easy. They probably have that information already. There must have been records."

"You heard it on the vid. They said they didn't know what he was working on. What if the records have been wiped out, just like his team? I won't take that chance."

"Do you know what it takes to erase records that aren't yours, especially in that Health Center?"

"Demetria," Dympna piped up.

"Yes?"

"I have a message for you. From Vincent."

"What!"

"He coded it so that you would receive it if he didn't disable it before a certain number of hours. It's on vid."

"I don't understand. Are you saying Vincent sent me a message before he was killed?"

"Let's hear it, okay?" Torver said. He steered her towards the sofa and pulled her down beside him.

Vincent's face appeared on the vidscreen, larger than life. Demetria groaned and pressed her fists hard against her mouth. Torver stared at her for a moment then wrapped his arm around her shoulder. She burrowed against him. It felt good to comfort her. With the newfound knowledge of what she was to him, he understood why he'd been so fascinated by her. On a cellular level, he'd recognized her. His gut twisted. He wasn't sure he liked this feeling of caring for someone else.

"Hello, Demi," Vincent said on the vid. "If Dympna passed on this message it's because I haven't been able to disable the stasis code I put on it, which means I'm in trouble somehow. I loaded some encrypted records on an MGRC neuronet. You can access them with your auth code and de-scramble them with the two-key encryption disc I hid in my house. I won't tell you where it is in case this message is intercepted, but hopefully you'll be able to find it quickly." He frowned slightly then shrugged. "Don't be too horrified when you get to the house. I never had the heart to tell you. Give the records to Su-Li or Sara at the lab. They'll know what to do with them. Thanks, Demi. That's another one I owe you." He smiled, then his face disappeared.

Demetria buried her face in Torver's shoulder and cried, great wracking sobs that pushed him back farther into the sofa. After a few minutes she hiccupped, dug a handkerchief from her pocket and blew her nose. Torver said nothing as she composed herself, but his mind was racing.

He had to prevent her from going to the authorities. If she did, they might become curious as to why she had an authorization code, and which research she used it for. Since Demetria was unaware that his was not an MGRC-sanctioned project, she would detail all she knew about it, including who she was working for and with. Then Alim and Martin would fall on them like vultures.

"I have to go to his house," she said, her voice hoarse from the crying.

"Now? It's probably still a crime scene. The police won't let you in."

"I'll give them Vincent's message."

Torver shook his head. "If you do, they'll take over. Aren't you curious to know what he left in there for you?"

"I'm more concerned with bringing whoever did this to justice."

"I agree, but Vincent sent the message to you. He could have sent it directly to the police or the Mungers. Obviously, he thought that he didn't have enough evidence. Who are Su-Li and Sara?"

"Two of his pathologists."

"And they're also dead. The way I see it, as long as no one knows that Vincent contacted you, you're safe. Besides, the police will surely come talk to you." At her startled glance, he shrugged. "You were close to Vincent. They'll want to ask you if you have any idea why he was killed. Right now, you have only a vague notion, but if you were to retrieve the encryption key, you'd be in a better position to give them an informed opinion. Maybe even proof."

She bit her lip. "I suppose."

Torver realized she was wavering. "We'll wait until tomorrow or the next day, then we'll slip into the house. You retrieve the key, we have a look at the records, then you decide if you should talk to the police."

"You don't have to get involved in this."

"I know. But I want to, anyway."

"Why?"

He smiled ruefully. "I admit helping people is a new concept for me." He sobered suddenly. "I came here to tell you something. Two somethings, in fact. I got sidetracked when I came in and saw you looking like a half-drowned cat."

Demetria rubbed her eyes with her fingers. "I'm not up to any more surprises, Torver."

"You're the one who asked why I decided to help you." He walked to the kitchen and poured two cups of coffee. He offered her one before he slouched back onto the sofa. He saw a glimmer of resentment in her eyes.

"Has it occurred to you that you're making yourself quite at home in my apartment?" she said.

"I told you, I like your place."

Demetria took a sip and grimaced.

"You know, I have an idea. Vincent wanted you to give some records to one of his colleagues first. If it has to do with the changes in the brain dust formula he mentioned to you before, maybe I can help."

"How?"

"Maybe he needed someone to interpret the data. I can do that for you, help make a report. That way you'll have a more solid case when you go to the police."

"Okay. Spill it."

"What?"

"The reason you want to help me."

Torver cleared his throat, suddenly nervous. "I compared our DNA."

"And?"

"You're my sister."

Demetria's mouth fell open. She stared at him with huge, rounded eyes for a few breathless moments. Then she snapped her mouth shut, rose and walked to the window. Torver straightened on the sofa, unsure of his next move.

"You're certain," she said.

"One hundred percent."

"That changes everything for you?"

"It explains a few things."

"The reason we feel connected."

"You're not afraid of me. My parents were."

She turned to him. "Did they have such horrible secrets?"

"My mother's a DNA reader. For some reason, her ability evolved after she was tested for it. She's terrified MGRC will find out and lobotomize her."

"Poor woman." Demetria turned back to stare at the city. "How can we be brother and sister?"

"That has to do with my father's secret."

Demetria shook her head. "I don't want to know about it."

"You have a right to." He knew his smile was bitter. "My father is sterile, but they badly wanted a child, a perfect child, so they used a sperm bank. The bank they chose did in vitro fertilization then DNA testing to select the embryo they'd implant. It's a very expensive process, and my father didn't make that much money, and he wanted a new house to go along with the new baby. He kept one embryo—me—and sold the additional fertilized eggs to the clinic director, who in turn sold them to other hopeful parents. He and my father told my mother that only one egg took. I saw the whole transaction on his lifepath. It's a highly illegal procedure. Even today, he could go to prison for that."

"No wonder your father's afraid of you. And now that you found me, you can prove he did it. Is that what you want? You'll help me so you can punish your father?"

"I don't care what my father did thirty years ago. Not anymore." He let the silence build for a minute, then cleared his throat. "There's no doubt that we have the same DNA."

Demetria walked back across the room and sat beside him. "So we might have other brothers and sisters out there."

"It's possible. It's also possible only the two of us survived."

"What do you mean?"

"Regardless of my folks' ambitions, we're not genetically perfect, are we?"

She looked startled by the comment then shook her head. "We sure aren't, brother."

Torver smiled. "You were right, you know. Our mutations are similar. We have corresponding anomalies in the alleles of chromosome thirteen. Just a couple of reversed base pairs here and there throughout the entire gene sequence." He let his gaze roam Demetria's apartment. Strange how he felt more at home here than in his parents' house.

"Torver," Demetria said, her voice hesitant, "could you follow Vincent's lifepath?"

"I thought you didn't approve."

"If it means finding out who killed him…"

"I can't. For some reason, the path becomes unstable when someone dies."

"So you'll come with me to Vincent's house simply because we're related genetically?"

"I said I would."

She contemplated him, her mouth pursed, for so long he was certain she didn't believe him. He was scrambling for a better reason when she brushed her prosthesis with her fingers then nodded.

"I'm going now."

"I thought you didn't like going out during the day."

"This is more important than what time of the day it is." She raised a hand to stop his protests. "I know a way to get inside without being seen."

He sighed. "Okay, we'll go. On one condition—if we find the key, we don't give it to the police without first having a look at the records."

"I confess I'm curious, too."

Torver jumped up. "Let's go, then."

As Demetria walked to the door, she seemed to remember something. "You said you wanted to tell me two things. What was the other one?"

"Later. I'll need your full attention for that one."

She said nothing more. In the bus, she seemed oblivious to his presence, lost in her own thoughts, all the way to Vincent's house.

They got off at Elgin and walked the rest of the way. He saw the bright yellow electronic police barrier from a long way away.

"That must be Vincent's house," he said.

She looked up then froze in her tracks. She was staring at the house, her face registering complete disbelief.

"Oh, my God," she said in a choked voice.

"What is it?"

She pelted down the street until she faced the ultramodern structure sandwiched between two three-storied, gabled red-brick houses and blocked with police barriers. Torver ran to catch up with her.

"How could he do that?" she cried. "The jerk! Look at that house!"

"What's wrong with it? It's incredible. Must have cost him a fortune to build."

"You don't understand. There was a heritage house on this site. His family lived in it for more than a century and a half. It was very similar to the ones beside it, but in much better condition. He tore it down. It's gone. Obliterated." She shook her head. "Now wonder he said he didn't have the heart to tell me."

Torver raised an eyebrow. "Obviously, you didn't know the guy as well as you thought you did."

"Obviously." She huffed an impatient breath. "I'd have never forgiven him if he'd told me. I can't believe this."

Torver touched her shoulder. "Let's get out of here, Demi. There's bound to be police around somewhere."

"I have to get inside."

"But you don't know this house."

"Hopefully, Vincent didn't change everything. The old house shared a cellar with the neighbors. You could get in from either basement."

"You can't go in through a neighbor's house."

"When I started dating Vincent, his father took to me. We shared a...a reverence for the past. I loved that house. You should have seen it."

"Maybe it's the house you loved, not Vincent."

"Mmmh. Vincent's father hated technology with a passion. He convinced the neighbors to keep the underground cellars and the original mid-twentieth century security system."

While they were talking, Demetria had made her way onto a path that led to a yard between Vincent's house and the neighbor's. At the back of what might have been a common garden in ancient times, behind the brick house, rose a stone structure that imitated its style but was probably a storage shed. She pointed to the front of it. "That's an old fashioned door. To open it, you have to twist the knob and pull. It swivels on the hinges you see on the right side."

"Really." Torver leaned over and squinted. "What are these buttons with numbers above the knob?"

Demetria smiled. "You press the buttons in a specified order and the door unlocks."

"You mean this lock is mechanical?"

"Yes." He watched her punch buttons then twist the knob and pull. The door moved with a groan. "Vincent's dad gave me the combination. Fortunately, that's one thing Vincent didn't change. He probably forgot about it." She slipped through the opening before Torver could ask any more questions.

"Wait." He hurried after her. The door clanked shut behind him, and they found themselves in the dark. "Why don't the lights come on?"

"There's a switch somewhere." He heard her fumble for a few seconds. "Ah, here we are." He blinked in the glare of a pear-shaped bulb in the ceiling. "It's a little bright," Demetria said, "but it's an old electric bulb. You'll get used to it." She took his hand and pulled. "Come on."

They stood on a wide landing that led to a set of stairs encased between smooth stone walls. As Demetria pulled him downward, the stone lost its manufactured look.

"It's almost as if they hacked through the rock to dig these stairs," he said. His voice sounded hollow.

"They did. When this vault was built, they didn't have lasers or nanotechnology."

"Amazing."

At the foot of the stairs, they landed in a room that was empty except for metal shelves and cobwebs. Here and there, massive pillars jutted out of the ground like stone fountains. "This place is huge," he said.

Demetria strode to a door similar to the one through which they had entered. "Let's see if Vincent kept this avenue open." She punched in another series of numbers, twisted the knob and pulled. The door glided open without a sound. She looked inside then back to where Torver stood. Her smile was resigned.

"Maybe I didn't know Vincent very well," she said, "but there was one thing I was sure of. He would never have got rid of these."

With a grand gesture, she waved him inside. Torver stared through the entrance in amazement. Inside the equally huge room lay hundreds upon hundreds of wine bottles, most of them wrapped in dust and cobwebs. He heard Demetria's slow chuckle behind him. She pushed past him and skimmed several rows of dark bottoms with her fingers.

"Some are more than fifty years old." She glanced at him. "Maybe it was the wine I fell in love with, not the house."

Torver shook his head. "And it all goes to you, now. Lucky."

"Why do you say that?"

He shrugged. "I just bet he left you everything."

She swallowed visibly. "Let's go upstairs. We came here to find that key."

She was already up the stairs. He followed in her wake. This time, the door was modern. Demetria placed her hand on the plate. The door swished open.

He had expected another dead garden. Instead, they stepped inside Vincent's living room.

## Chapter Twenty-four

Torver knew instantly that Demetria would hate the house. It was the most modern, the most powerfully stark, coldly beautiful house he'd ever seen. The walls and floor were made of translucent plasmer and showed, in random areas, the framework of the house. Light was absorbed by the material, as if they'd entered a high-tech, angular womb. The sparse furniture and the art were cutting edge, both figuratively and literally. Torver thought he'd probably open a vein if he sat in one of the living room chairs or brain himself if he came too close to the sculpture in the far corner.

The room was a shambles. Paintings hung crooked on the walls, furniture was overturned, and the contents of the desk near the window were strewn on the floor. He searched for Demetria amid the clutter. She stood at the far wall in front of a framed picture.

"Let's find that key and get out of here, Demetria," he said. "Whoever wrecked the place may come back." She said nothing. "What's wrong?"

"I gave him this sampler for his birthday a year ago." Her voice was very soft. "Of all the antiques he had, it's the only thing he kept."

Torver came to stand beside her. He peered at the contents of a thick wooden frame and frowned, confused. All he could see was row after row of small, flat, circular objects with a design and a date embossed on them. "What are they?"

"Quarters."

"Huh?"

"Silver tokens that were used as money up to eighty years ago. Four of them equaled a dollar. I gave him forty for his fortieth birthday." She smiled sadly. "He laughed when I gave them to him and said they would really stand out in his house. I thought he meant it was a unique gift. Now I understand what he really meant. They're the only old pieces in here."

Torver agreed with Vincent. The series of quarters was a pretty boring gift. Typical of Demetria, though, he thought with a smile. He was about to turn away to check other parts of the house when something shiny tucked halfway inside the bottom of the frame caught his attention. "One of them fell off." He pointed to the shiny circle.

"No, they're all there," she said. She peered at it more closely. "Wait. That looks like a key generator."

"Let me." Torver pushed her gently aside and unhooked the frame from the wall. He staggered from the weight. "Whoa."

He was about to turn the frame over when he heard a noise. Demetria raised her head.

"That sounds like the front door."

Voices, indistinct as yet, came from the other side of the house.

"Come on," Torver said. "Let's get out of here." He set the frame down.

Demetria stopped him. "No. We bring it with us."

"It's too heavy."

"Give it to me, then."

Torver gave her an unbelieving look, picked up the sampler and started for the cellar. The cumbersome load blocked most of his field of vision. His foot connected with an overturned chair, making it screech across the plasmer floor. They froze.

"Someone's here," Torver heard distinctly.

"Go, go, go, go," he whispered to Demetria.

She ran to the door and slapped her hand on the door plate. The door stayed close.

"It worked coming in."

"Do it more slowly. Those plates can be finicky."

"There they are," he heard behind them. "Hold it! Metro Police!"

The door swished open, and Demetria slipped inside after Torver. He heard the door close behind them. She picked up a corner of the frame and they scrambled downstairs and through the wine cellar. A few minutes later the door on the neighbor's side slammed behind them.

"Wait," he said, already out of breath. "This thing weighs a ton. Let's take the disc and leave the rest here."

"We can't wait, they'll find us."

"I doubt it. Not unless they can break through Vincent's door. Besides, we'll be much more conspicuous if we leave here with that big frame in our hands."

"What if they have the code to the door of Vincent's living room?"

Torver waited for a few seconds, his ear cocked towards the door. "No one's coming. I think we have some time."

Demetria paced away from him and came back. She threw her arms in the air. "What are we doing? They were the police. I don't want to run away, I want to help them. We should have stopped and explained to them what we were doing there. We should go back and do just that." She started for the door to Vincent's cellar.

Torver blocked her path. "Wait a minute. Think about this. What if they weren't cops?"

"What do you mean?"

"What do most people do when the police yell stop?"

"They stop," she said.

"Right."

"What makes you think the men up there weren't who they said they were?"

"They might be exactly what they claimed, but you have to remember a few things. Every one who worked for Vincent is dead. He was found here. His house was trashed. Someone was searching for something, and I bet you they wanted that disc. Obviously, they didn't find it. What's to prevent them from coming back to look for it again?"

"The fact that the house is a crime scene?"

"Sure. That really stopped you."

Demetria glared at him for a moment then seized the frame from him. "Here, let get that disc. I don't want you to damage the frame. It's an antique."

Torver watched as she laid it face down on the stone floor and began to remove small, pointed pieces of metal from the back. "How come you could open Vincent's door?"

"We decided two years ago that we'd exchange Identicodes for our houses. Just in case something happened to one of us. I never thought..." Her voice broke on the last words. Torver said nothing, just watched the top of her head as she bent to peel off the back of the frame. "The nails were loose," Demetria said. "He must have taken them out then put them back by hand. Here, take the disc while I hold the display."

Torver crouched beside her. As soon as she lifted the thick board on which the quarters were mounted, he saw the disc and picked it up. He jumped to his feet. "Okay, let's go."

"Just a minute, I want to fix this."

"Demi, we don't have time."

"You go ahead, it won't take a minute."

"Suit yourself." When he reached the stairs, he turned around. Demetria was pushing the nails back into the frame, pressing each with her thumb. When she was finished, she righted the frame and leaned it against the wall. Slowly, she caressed the wood, her eyes fixed on the contents.

"Demi."

She started and turned. "I'm coming." She threw him an annoyed glance as she passed him. "I told you to go ahead."

"Not much point, is it? I don't know the code to go out."

"Didn't you notice? The lock is only on the outside. You just had to twist the knob and push."

He grasped her wrist to prevent her from opening the door. The data disc cut into the flesh of his other hand, making him realize how tense he was. He slipped it into his chest pocket and sealed it.

"Careful. We don't know if someone's waiting on the other side."

Demetria nodded and turned the knob slowly, opened the door a crack,and peeked into the courtyard. She opened the door wider and gestured with her head for him to follow. They were halfway through the old garden when Torver heard the cry.

"There they are!"

He turned his head towards Vincent's house and saw two men, one pointing in their direction. He snatched Demetria's hand and broke into a run.

"Come on."

"Stop!" he heard behind him. The voice sounded closer this time.

Torver kept running until the neighbor's house provided them with cover. He flattened himself against the wall. "There were two of them. Definitely not in uniform. If it were me, I'd send my buddy to the front while I covered the back." He eyed the fence that blocked the next lot. Too high for him to jump. He ran to the wall, leaned against it and made a step with his hands. "Come on, over the wall. You pull me up."

Without a word, she sprinted towards him, stepped into his hands and leaped on top of the wall. She turned and extended an arm. He gripped her hand and walked up the vertical surface. Demetria didn't flinch or falter, just pulled. He was almost at the top when he heard a noise. He turned his head, saw a huge man come around the corner of the house. The man saw them just as Torver vaulted over the wall. He felt a sharp pain in his right calf. The three-meter drop jarred his body.

"Are you okay?" Demetria asked.

"Yes. Let's go. It won't take them long to follow us." He got up, but his leg gave way under him.

"What's wrong?"

"I think I hurt my leg on the wall." He twisted around to peer at his leg. Demetria scrambled over to his injured side.

"Oh, my." He heard the sudden alarm in her voice. "It looks like a gun wound. We have to get out of here. Right now."

Torver pushed himself up and away from the wall. His calf throbbed. Teeth clenched against the pain, he grasped her hand and started running towards the other end of the courtyard. "I was right, then. Those guys aren't police."

"Maybe the police don't use stun guns when they're at a crime scene."

"They haven't used guns for ten years," he said between pants. "Don't you remember that big inquest? Government Mundial banned the use of plasma guns after that." Torver pulled her behind a storage shed. He eyed the next wall. "I can't jump this."

"This is an old wall." Her eyes roamed the stone structure. She pointed to a door at the far end of the yard. "There."

"Let's go." He hobbled to the door, Demetria ahead of him. She pulled the panel open. Stone exploded beside her head. She screamed and scrambled through. Torver followed and slammed the door. He moved aside and a plasma beam punched through the metal. They started running again.

"There should be doors like that one right up to the canal," she said. She pulled another metal door open.

"Then what?"

"There are buses on the QE Driveway every minute or so. We'll hop on one of them."

They burst through the last door onto the road that hugged the Rideau Canal. Torver was panting heavily. He noticed that Demetria was barely breathing hard. He blamed his breathlessness on his injury but knew he wouldn't be able to go much farther. He looked up and down the road. "There," he pointed, "there's one coming."

"The stop is on the other side. Hurry."

They'd crossed the road when Torver saw the man who had fired on him emerge from the same door he and Demetria had used. The man lifted his gun and pointed in their direction.

"Watch out!" He shoved Demetria to the ground and dropped beside her.

He heard the ground sizzle where his feet had been. He was about to roll down to the edge of the canal when he heard a pneumatic whoosh.

"Are you folks all right? Do you need help?"

Demetria scrambled to her feet and jumped on board.

"I slipped," she told the driver.

Torver followed quickly, wincing when he put weight on his injured leg. "Stay low," he murmured.

The bus driver shook his head, a perplexed look on his face. He shut the door and continued his route.

"I can't see them, now," Demetria said. She sat in the back behind several empty seats. "How's the leg? You want to go to the Health Center?"

"No." He shifted uncomfortably in the seat. "We'll have a look at it first. I think it's just a graze. Boy, do I need a drink."

"You'll have to wait a little longer for that. You said you'd look at Vincent's data, remember?"

Torver slanted her a disgusted glance. "I was right all along. You are a tight-assed drag." He leaned his head on the headrest and closed his eyes. "Even if you are my sister."

"Ow!"

"Stop being a baby. I need to pull the edges of the wound together before I apply the skin plaster."

"You could at least use some anesthetic."

"Why? I'm finished."

"You loved that, didn't you?"

"Yes." Demetria bit her lip. "Do you think they know who we are?"

"Nah. They didn't see our faces." Torver hoped she'd accept his reassurance for the moment. He freely admitted to himself that it was flimsy at best. Demetria was brilliant. Soon she'd figure out that if the guys who had shot at them were resourceful enough to get into a house protected by a police lock, they'd have little difficulty in finding out who she was. He frowned. They might have more of a problem figuring him out. He was an unknown quantity, totally unrelated to Vincent, and as far as he could tell, no one knew of his association with Demetria.

"I knew this excursion was a bad idea from the start," he said.

"You offered to come with me." She got up from the floor where she'd been sitting to bandage his calf. "Just give me the disc. You've done more than enough. Even if those thugs find me, they won't know who you are."

Torver smirked and shook his head. He should have known she wouldn't buy his explanation. He pushed himself up and took a few experimental steps around the room. "Not bad. I can barely feel the cut."

"It was only superficial," she said, her tone distracted. "Torver, you still have the disc, don't you?"

"Right here." He patted his chest pocket. "But if you think I'm leaving now without knowing what's on it, after all I've been through, you're mistaken, sister."

Demetria made a face. "Don't remind me."

He unsealed his pocket and extracted the disc. "Let's go to your office." Once there, he sat at her desk and inserted it in the slot of her bionet. "Identic required," the bionet voice said. He pointed to the reader plaque. Demetria placed her hand on it. "Identity confirmed. Enter authorization code." Demetria keyed in the starter string that would trigger the code sequence. "Authorization confirmed."

A complex table appeared on the vidscreen. Torver frowned.

"What are those?" Demetria said.

"Chemical analysis results."

"Of what?"

"I don't know yet. Look, why don't you leave me with this for a while. It's going to take time to wade through all the data."

"Is it related to the dustheads?"

"As I said," he articulated very slowly, "I need time." He turned back to the data. "Go away."

As soon as she was gone, he called up the starter string Demetria had used for her auth code then copied it into his Identichip, just in case he'd need to use it later. Then he sank into the information in front of him, in the same way he did with his own research.

Vincent had kept detailed notes, accompanied with data and comments from his colleagues. Torver saw almost right away what Vincent had suspected but couldn't prove—someone was trying to add a compound to the dust that altered the genetic code.

He followed the progress, or rather the lack of it, of the experiments. Each mortality bore witness to genetic tinkering.

His heart beat faster when he imagined what it would be like to have an unlimited supply of human beings to test his theories. Pick them up from the street, dump them when you're finished. Direct feedback from the designated target. He could do so many things.

He toyed with the idea for a moment then rejected it. As gripping as the concept might be, he knew he'd never go that far, even for the advancement of science. The wretched lives he'd traveled, the people he'd known and would meet, didn't belong to him. He applied himself again to Vincent's notes, this time with a cooler head.

The data on the first Termite gave him pause. Something in the change of design made him uncomfortable. When he reviewed the data on the second Termite, he knew what he was looking at—his own research, somehow distorted.

Had Laslo used him? Or was it Gerry, who popped up in his lab at odd moments? Regardless, the leak came from there. Another link between him and Demetria.

As if thinking of her had acted as a call, she appeared beside him. She had a plate in her hand. "Thought you'd be hungry by now."

He continued to stare at the vidscreen for a moment longer. "What time is it?"

"Past seven. You've been at it for four hours." She placed her hand on his shoulder. "You found something, didn't you?"

"Yes."

"Well, I did, too."

His stomach growled. "I guess I'm hungry after all." He took the plate from her and made his way to the dining room table. He took a bite of his sandwich. "What did you find? Hmm. Good. What's in it?"

"Avocado and tomato-flavored soybeans with sprouts and real mayo." She came to sit by him and put two glasses and a bottle of Chardonnay on the table. She poured slowly, all her concentration on the simple act.

Torver recognized the gesture from the countless times he'd watched her on her lifepath. Demetria was trying to avoid thinking of something important.

"Is there any more?" he said, after swallowing the last of his sandwich. She pushed her own meal towards him. "Okay," he said around another bite, "what's bothering you?"

"You go first."

"Oh, no. It's going to take me a while to go through the whole story. Remember when I came here this morning? I told you that I had two things to tell you." She nodded. "Well, somehow, Vincent's findings are tied to what I wanted to discuss. So we'll wait until you've cleared your mind of whatever is bothering you."

"This afternoon I looked over your shoulder for a while, but you were engrossed and I didn't understand any of the data. So I decided to continue a bit of work I was doing for your project using my hand-held remote." She swished the wine around her glass then took a sip. "I pulled up the gencode matrix and searched for variants of the five genetic combinations GeneTech provided me. I found quite a few. I tried to arrange them geographically. They were from everywhere, but there was a slight pattern. When I added a chronology, it began to take shape. Then I matched them by ID number instead of codes. They started pairing off."

"What do you mean, pair off?"

"Pairs, as in couples."

"You mean they're all married to each other?"

"Married, or cohabiting, producing offspring. I know one thing for certain—they're all related."

Torver pushed his plate away. "Brothers and sisters."

"Uncles and aunts, cousins and grandparents. Sometimes the link is remote, but it's there."

"That's what you found?"

"I knew that from before. Today I wanted to see how far down the genealogy these links went."

"Great idea. If you could find the first instance of the disease, it would help me pinpoint the ... ah ... I'll explain later. Go on."

"I reached over one hundred years back." Demetria absently rubbed the seam on her chin. "The farther back I go, the sketchier the data is."

"The genetic combination you're using wasn't identified until thirty-five years ago. You won't find anything in the old records."

"But I did."

"What do you mean?"

"Well, you see, a hundred years ago they couldn't read the genetic map, but a lot of the medical procedures required that doctors withdraw blood from a person to analyze it and determine the disease. They still have those on file."

"Sure, I remember now. The Gene Banks scandal. Even before the Human Genome Project, hospitals would send blood samples to gene banks for safekeeping."

"Exactly. The only problem is that they were classified under name and social insurance number. The records never got converted to Identicodes. There was no need since most of the patients were dead by the time the new system came into effect."

"I sense a 'but' there."

"Of course." Demetria grinned. "There's a way to track down families. All I had to do was match a name for the gencodes I had in my genetic family, then follow the genealogy."

"What did you find?"

She sobered instantly. She contemplated the golden color of the wine for a few seconds then met his eyes. "I was able to trace the gencodes to four people who lived in what used to be called Yugoslavia. Two married couples. One was named Kostevic."

Torver felt as if the room was shrinking. "What was the other?"

"Radic."

## Chapter Twenty-five

Torver banged the table with his fist. "I knew it. I suspected from the start that Radic had a personal stake in this project."

"There's more. I also found out that the five genetic samples Laslo Radic gave me came from his family—a cousin, a nephew, himself, his wife and his son."

"His wife. She's related to Laslo?"

"She's a very distant cousin. It's so remote they wouldn't be able to track it unless they did it the way I did. How come you didn't know that Radic had given me his family's DNA?"

"He didn't tell me, and I can't get onto Laslo's lifepath. He blocks me."

"There're two of us?" She sounded amused.

"No, with him I can't even get in. Although I didn't try it with a vidstill of him. Hmmm...maybe..."

"Not while you're with me."

"Somehow, I knew you'd say that."

"What had Laslo Radic asked you to do?"

"I'm doing research on a genetic disease called Barcina's xylopoiesis. From what you just said, it means Laslo's son has it, and Radic and his wife are carriers."

"So that's why he hired us. I was beginning to wonder how these biometrics data pertained to pharmacogenomics."

Torver was amused again by life's irony. He'd come to Demetria this morning to sound her out before telling her everything. Several hours later, he had no choice but to tell her everything. He gulped the last of his wine.

"If Radic's son has Barcina's, it could be a matter of months before it triggers." He remembered the urgent comm Laslo had received in the lab the day before. "Maybe it started already."

A really nasty idea came to his mind, and it scared him. If he was right, both he and Demetria were in bigger trouble than he'd thought. He jumped up from the table and strode back to Demetria's office. He turned off the vidscreen and extracted the encryption key.

"Do you have somewhere secure to put this? Somewhere that doesn't need your Identic?"

"Wait a minute. I thought we'd agreed that once you deciphered the records Vincent had left on MGRC net we'd go to the police."

"Plans change. Where can you put this?"

Demetria planted herself across the doorway and crossed her arms. "I'm not doing anything with that disc until you tell me what you found."

Torver pondered what he'd say next. "How did you get the contract with GeneTech?"

"Mr. Radic approached Vincent…" She stared at him. "You think Radic had Vincent killed? Why would he do that?"

Torver's sense of urgency increased. "Listen, this situation is getting really complicated, not to mention dangerous, and it's tied to what I wanted to talk to you about this morning."

"Vincent's data, too?"

"In a way. Let's say, for the sake of argument, that Radic had Vincent killed and that he knows Vincent left the key to his records somewhere in his house. The killers trash the house but can't find the disc. Maybe they're interrupted, so they come back while we're in there. They don't know who we are, but they report to Laslo, who makes the connection between Vincent and you. What Vincent found is tied to my research. Laslo has us working together, so he'll connect me to you. After that, it won't take him very long to come for a visit."

"We're safe here. Dympna won't let them in."

"I wouldn't count on it. Vincent said in his notes that they tapped into his bionet files at the Health Center. They also got back into his house without alerting the police. Those guys are pretty sophisticated. We can't take the chance."

"I need to know what's happening, Torver."

"I promise I'll tell you everything I know or suspect once we're in a safe place."

She thought about that for a moment then nodded. "I can put the disc in my wall safe. It's an antique, just like the doors at Vincent's." She walked over to a picture frame in her bedroom and pulled the left side towards her. It swiveled and revealed a square gray door with a black knob in its center. Torver watched with interest as she turned the knob clockwise, then counter-clockwise, then back again and pulled on the handle. The inside revealed a few papers and small boxes.

"You keep paper in this safe?"

"Not just any kind." She withdrew a single sheet covered by a thin clear plasmer coating. "This is a rough drawing Alex Colville made before he painted 'A Small Picnic,' his last work before he died."

"Oh. Art."

She threw him an ironic glance and replaced the drawing. "Yes, art. Just place the disc in there."

"Can't a plasma gun pierce this thing?"

"Maybe, but they'd have to find it first. They wouldn't be able to use electronic detection, and to open it without damaging the contents, they need the combination. It's a safe that was used during Prohibition—don't ask—designed to resist explosions and fires." She slammed the door closed, spun the dial and replaced the picture frame over it. "Of course, today's lasers would cut through, but who would think of looking for an antique wall safe? The only person who might have guessed about it was Vincent. It's the only place I have that's really secure."

"Demetria." Dympna's voice made Torver jump.

"What is it, Dympna?"

"Someone in the lobby is trying to override the access to the lobby door. I estimate he will be able to do it in the next thirty seconds."

Torver grabbed her arm. "Let's go."

"Where?"

"I don't know yet, but we have to get out of here."

"We should call the police."

Torver lifted his eyes to the ceiling. "Dympna, who's trying to get in?"

"I do not know. I suspect he must have access to a sophisticated bionet. As soon as I fragment the code, it defrags. I estimate no more than ten seconds before breach. I am sorry, Demetria. I can block your apartment door, but not for long. Maybe another thirty seconds."

Torver glanced at Demetria. "Now do you believe me?"

Demetria avoided his gaze and walked to the living room. She stood, her back rigid, her hands clasped around her upper arms. "They'll destroy everything here, won't they?"

"Maybe, but isn't your life more important than a few pieces of old junk?"

She gave him a withering look. She took a deep breath and let it go slowly, walked to the apartment door plate and slapped it. The door opened silently. "Dympna, try to delay opening the door as long as possible, but don't burn yourself out, okay? Let's go."

They trotted toward the elevator.

"Demetria," Dympna said from the wrist unit Demetria wore, "they are in the elevator. Two men."

Torver grabbed her hand and pulled her towards the end of the corridor. "Come on. The stairs."

"We can't," she said. "They're lock-coded. Only the administrator can open them."

Torver looked down the hallway. The elevator was now between them and Demetria's apartment. "We can't go back, not enough time. As soon as they're out, they'll see us. Damn." He searched for a recess or a small place where they could hide, but the doors of the other apartments were all flush with the wall. He looked up and had an idea.

"Dympna!" The Perceptron didn't answer. He shook Demetria's hand.

"Dympna," Demetria said.

"Yes, Demetria?"

"Dympna," Torver interrupted, "can you fool the fire alarm system into thinking there's a fire on this floor?"

"Of course."

"Do it, Dympna," Demetria said, instant understanding in her eyes.

The doors to the elevators opened, and Torver recognized the man who'd shot him. The giant looked to the left, then to the right. His eyes widened when he saw them at the end of the hall. He raised his gun.

A sharp, shrill sound exploded in the hall, and somewhere above them, a disembodied voice began its announcement: "Warning. This is not a drill. You have five minutes to evacuate. Follow the emergency stairs down. Warning..."

From the ceiling a shower of foam flooded the corridor. The two men at the elevator lifted their hands above their heads to protect their eyes from the fire retardant. At the same time, Torver pushed Demetria in front of him and slapped the door plate of the emergency exit. They burst through the fire door into the stairwell.

"Run," he shouted. "They won't be far behind."

He clattered down the stairs after her. They had descended two floors when the door to the stairwell opened. Demetria jumped aside and flattened herself against the wall as a stream of tenants poured into the small space and rushed down. Torver stopped on the stairs above. She pointed to the open door.

"Through here," she yelled above the babble.

Torver squeezed past the throng into the corridor. "What now?"

"We'll take the other set of stairs," she said while running to the far end of the corridor. There was no foam here, but the sirens were strident. They squeezed in just before the fire door closed. "If they come after us, they're likely to use the same escape well we took and that comes out into the street. These stairs give onto the back of the building." She continued through the open door and down.

"We'll end up in the woods."

"Yes. It's perfect."

Torver stopped on a landing and bent at the waist. "No," he said between gulps of air, "we should go towards the city. There's safety in numbers."

She pulled him forward. "A plasma gun doesn't make any noise. They could shoot both of us and no one around would realize it until too late. I know these woods. We can use them as cover until we cross them. We'll go to my mother's house. It's a fortress."

After that, Torver concentrated on not tripping on the stairs and taking deep breaths to ease the stitch in his side. Then they were outside punching through a throng of people milling about waiting for the fire department. Someone detained him, asked him if he knew where the fire was. By the time he'd answered the man, he'd lost Demetria. His chest tightened until he saw her at the edge of the woods, waving for him to join her. He pressed his hand to his side and ran. Something crackled beside him, then again.

"Quickly," Demetria shouted. She crouched in a gully. "They're behind you."

He gestured for her to continue on and picked up speed he didn't know he had. Demetria entered a thicker part of the brush instead of taking the open path. He followed as quickly as he could.

"I warn you," he puffed, "I won't be able to go much longer without rest."

"Just a little farther."

The crash of branches behind them gave him the incentive to go on. Demetria had slowed down to a quick walk and was now weaving around trees in a seemingly haphazard direction. After a few minutes, he noticed the crash of branches behind them came more to their right. She slipped behind a huge boulder and motioned him to be quiet.

Now that they'd stopped, his breathing sounded very loud in his ears under the quiet dome of the trees.

"Breathe through your mouth," Demetria whispered. "Less noisy." He obeyed, still convinced his gasps would give them away, but after a few more minutes of waiting, it seemed they'd lost their pursuers.

"When I was young, I used to get lost in this forest on purpose," Demetria whispered. "I know it by heart." She pushed away from the rock. "Come on, we still have a ways to go." She brought them back to the path two minutes later. "Stay on the grassy side of the path," she whispered. "It'll dampen our steps."

"Won't they see us?"

She smiled slightly. "They'd have to find their way first."

She began a loping run. He found he could follow if he didn't speak, and if he counted his breaths and focused on the rhythm of her feet.

He must have fallen into a trance, he thought later when he was inside the house. He flopped on one of the white leather couches, exhausted, thirsty, footsore. In total, they'd run more than twelve kilometers.

Demetria was puttering around in the kitchen, reconstituting something or other for them to eat. When he cracked his eyelids open, she was watching him with an amused smile on her face.

"Here," she said, presenting him with a glass full of a murky orange liquid. "Drink this."

"What is it?"

"Water, salt, sugar and other things you don't want to know about. It will help with dehydration."

"Sounds revolting."

"Yep." She smiled again. "You deserve it."

He took the glass with a trembling hand, careful not to spill a drop, and tasted it. "Just what I thought. It's disgusting."

"Drink up." She went back to the kitchen. "It'll stabilize your electrolytes.'

Torver braced himself and downed the whole concoction. After a few minutes, he began to feel better. When Demetria brought plates of food for them, he ate ravenously.

"Aren't you tired?" he said between bites.

"A bit. I think I'm running on adrenaline and shock."

"You've certainly had a few surprises this past week."

She finished her food in silence. When she pushed her plate away, he knew the time for answers had come.

"We don't have anyone shooting at us now," she said. "Start with Vincent's research."

The food had made him lethargic. He nodded and got up, walked to the grand piano, lifted the cover and poked an ivory key. The sound reverberated into the room like a gong.

"I was right, wasn't I?" she said. "You, me, Laslo, Vincent—we're all connected."

"More than you know." Torver sat on the piano bench and leaned his elbows on his knees. "Vincent found out that someone was manipulating the brain dust and testing it on homeless dustheads. He discovered a biological component inside the dust but couldn't pinpoint what it was."

"Yes, I remember him telling me about it." She frowned. "He also mentioned a Termite, if I recall."

"Yes. He actually received two of them during a one-week interval. Everything changed with those two autopsies. He began to suspect that someone was genetically manipulating the users, and that whoever was doing it wanted to create a detox-resistant addiction gene."

"Was he right?"

"His data show incontrovertible proof."

"Vincent wasn't a geneticist. He must have wanted to confirm his suspicions before he gave his records to the police." She paused. "Waiting cost him his life. Can you tell exactly what's been done to the samples Vincent collected?"

"Sure." He got up and faced the window. "The method they used on the Termites was extrapolated from my own research."

Demetria said nothing for a moment. "You're working on addiction genes?"

He shook his head and turned towards her. "How much do you know about Barcina's xylopoiesis?"

"Nothing. I didn't even know it was a disease until you mentioned it earlier today. *Xylo-*, that's Greek for wood, isn't it? I can't make out the rest, though."

"Still, that's very good. Few people would get that far. *Poiesis* means *make* or *create*. Among other signs of the disease, the person's muscles, tendons, ligaments and skin change into a woodlike tissue. Blood circulation stops, and the regions affected have to be amputated. The disease creeps slowly from the extremities to the center of the body. Once it reaches the major organs, the person dies. It's very rare and, at least until now, incurable."

She shivered. "And I thought my dermophagia was pretty awful. Radic's son has the disease."

"I'd say that's a given."

"Yes." Demetria rubbed her arms. "The guilt Laslo must be feeling."

"Guilt? It's not his fault. He couldn't know."

"What does that matter? To pass on a genetic disease to your child, it would be unendurable."

He thought about his own mother. Could it be that the distance she'd put between them was due more to guilt than fear?

"How come Laslo knew his son had the disease?"

Torver shrugged. "I don't know how he suspected—probably from those other codes we were given—but I doubt he got permission from MGRC for DNA analysis."

"He tested his family himself?"

He let the silence stretch between them, watched her face as she worked out the logic.

"This research you're doing," she said finally, "it hasn't been sanctioned by MGRC, has it?"

"No."

"And the authorization code I have, it's a fake?"

"I don't think so, but I don't think Radic obtained it legally."

"Why us?"

"I'm sort of in trouble with MGRC right now." He explained about his license. "As for you, I don't know. I only said I needed a biometrician. Radic found you."

"With Vincent's help. That's why you think Radic had Vincent killed. He knew too much."

Torver shrugged.

"Still," she said, "it's strange that Radic took the risk to ask you to do this kind of research. Maybe he put one of his own scientists on the problem first. When he didn't get results, he went in search of you."

He thought about Gerry Sinclair. "That geneticist had to know what he was doing was illegal."

"It didn't stop you, did it?" Demetria got up and came to stand in front of him. He straightened and faced her. "I know you well enough by now," she said, her voice tight with anger, "to understand that you didn't accept this project out of a need to save a few innocent children from a horrible death. You just wanted to do it for the sake of figuring it out, didn't you?"

"And what's wrong with that?"

"How could you drag me into this?"

"*I* didn't hire you."

"But you accepted the job. Without you, there wouldn't be research."

"Oh, no, you're not pinning that one on me. You took on that contract, all on your own. You could've said no. You could've checked with MGRC to see if the project was legitimate. But you didn't do it, did you? You wanted something out of that project, the same way I did."

He saw in her eyes that he'd hit on the truth. She backed up two paces and hugged herself. "What are you getting out of this, Torver?"

He shrugged. "All my life I've seen people wish they could turn back the clock, relive part of their lives, change something or other. I guess I just wanted to do it for real."

"I don't understand."

"The gencodes you provided me were all from farther back in the past than the ones we originally started from."

"Yes."

"I've used these codes to design a gene that will repair the defect that causes Barcina's. I call it a retrogene, and I'm very close to perfecting it."

"Tracking down the defective genes then repairing them?"

"That's the theory." He paced to the couch, turned back. "There's one problem."

"Somehow, I suspected that."

"Once it works, if it fell in the wrong hands, the retrogene could be turned into a weapon of mass destruction."

## Chapter Twenty-six

"S IR, THAT MAN WHO WAS HERE TWO DAYS AGO...?"

Laslo raised his head to frown at Satah, his mind half on the brief in front of him, half on his son. "What man?"

"Dr. Francis."

"What about him?"

"He was murdered."

The words separated themselves from Satah's gossipy tone and registered. "Vincent's dead? When?"

"They found him in his house yesterday morning."

He touched a pad on his desk to bring up the MBC news channel. "Give me all news related to Dr. Vincent Francis's death."

The face of a news announcer appeared.

"A grisly and incomprehensible series of murders have rocked the foundations of the Greater Ottawa Metropolis Health Center. Early this morning, all the members of the Pathology Department were found dead..."

"Police are baffled..."

"Still no news in the horrible murders perpetrated at the Greater Ottawa Metropolis Health Center. The families of the victims have gathered at the Alta Vista United Church to pray..."

"Meanwhile, no clues have been uncovered as to a motive for the slaughter. Sgt. Patterson of the Greater Ottawa Police Bureau stated that they are pursuing links to the drug underworld, although the members of the Pathology Department were tightly screened by Health Center's Security. Police are attempting to retrace the steps of each member of the department..."

Laslo turned off the news and coded in Leila Pratt's number at the Health Center.

"I just heard about Vincent and his team," he said after the usual preamble. "I'm so sorry. Anything I can do?"

Dr. Pratt shook her head. She had livid circles under red puffy eyes and her skin was ashen, as if she hadn't slept in a month. "Nothing, Laslo, but thanks. We're trying to regroup here."

"Have the police found any leads?"

"That's what's so baffling. There's absolutely nothing to indicate a motive." She bit her lower lip. "Although there is something slightly off..."

"What do you mean?"

"That department is always so busy they can't keep up. Well, I checked the cold storage right after they found the team and..." She shrugged and rubbed her eyes with her knuckles. "I'm probably just hoping to make sense of it, like everyone else."

"Leila, what did you see?"

"Seven of the compartments were empty."

"What's so unusual about that?"

"Admission told me that one of the pathology technicians rerouted three bodies the day before our people were killed, saying they were full up."

"Did you mention it to the police?"

"Yes, they're checking into it. As I said, maybe I'm grasping shadows."

Or maybe you're too close for comfort, Laslo thought. He wanted to ask about Vincent's lab records but didn't—Leila might realize he knew more than he'd let on.

"Do you know another thing that's strange?" she continued. "Vincent used to say he liked to keep his hands dirty, so he always had at least a couple of cases open. I checked to see what he was working on before he was killed and he had no new records in his bionet. None that were dated more recently than two weeks ago."

"How about his staff?"

"His pathologists had their normal workload, as well as the lab techs. We have nothing on the net operators, except for the routine file maintenance."

Laslo let out a guilty sigh of relief. Whoever killed Vincent and his staff had done a relatively good job of getting rid of the evidence. Almost every possible trace linking him to Vincent had been eliminated. The link to Admissions worried him, though. Whoever had wiped out the records may not have thought of cleaning up the list of bodies sent to the path lab.

Leila coughed then sniffed, bringing his attention back to her. "How's your son, by the way? I meant to call, but with what happened here I completely forgot."

Laslo swallowed. "He has Barcina's xylopoiesis."

She stared at him, stunned for a moment; then her face reshaped itself, softened, melted. "Oh, Laslo, I'm so sorry."

"Yes. That's what happens when you have restrictions on genetic testing."

He could see that he'd shocked her. He knew she'd expected him to absorb her pity, to swallow it, to return it with despair that his son had an incurable genetic disease. Instead, he was criticizing the system. At that moment, Laslo hated her compassion, hated what she stood for, her blind acceptance of the rules. He took a deep breath and grasped the edge of his desk to calm his hands.

"You'll let me know if I can do anything, won't you?" he said, surprised that his voice sounded even. "I can interview a few people for you, maybe help rush their security clearances with MGRC."

He said his goodbyes abruptly, eager to get away from Leila's baffled expression.

Laslo turned to his garden and concentrated on the yellow blooms, for the moment pushing away thoughts of his son. He knew who'd killed Vincent—Stringer or Gerry, although he'd put his money on Stringer. Nevertheless, the stakes were high for both of them. If they succeeded in modifying the addiction genes, Stringer would be a very rich man, and Gerry wouldn't need GeneTech anymore. The newsperson stated they'd tortured Vincent. Had Vincent told them he'd visited GeneTech? If so, they might think Laslo was the only one who could incriminate them, and that put him in danger. Unless...

Unless Vincent had also spoken to a good friend before he died and told her everything he'd told Laslo.

He called up Demetria Greyson's number. An impersonal voice came on the comm.

"The comm number is temporarily out of service due to a fire emergency. Please call again."

Strange, he thought. Had Stringer's men gone after her and somehow disabled her comm? She'd told him she rarely left her apartment. Maybe she was already dead. Laslo felt a fleeting regret for the woman he'd never seen, which was quickly replaced by urgency. She was still crucial to the research. Lockwood had assured him he needed her.

"Satah, get me Mahoud. I want him in my office, right now."

While he waited for his chief of security, Laslo pondered how much to tell him. He'd barely made his decision when Mahoud sauntered through the door and sat in the chair on the other side of the desk.

"I have a problem," Laslo said.

"You mean GeneTech has a problem."

Laslo raised an eyebrow.

"I thought you called me here because you had decided to do something about Dr. Sinclair."

"What about him?"

"I learned he was making brain dust at just about the same time you did. I was about to tell you when I realized you already knew."

Laslo placed his hands flat on his desk. "You're monitoring me?"

Mahoud's face remained impassive. "Sometimes people need to be protected from themselves."

"Aren't you taking your dedication a bit too far?"

"Not when it's your ass I'm protecting. Along with mine." Mahoud broke into a smile. Laslo grunted, feeling like he'd just been strip-searched and told it was for his own good.

"What do you know, exactly?"

"Sinclair's associated with Stringer. I'm reasonably sure that Gerry stole GeneTech research, which was begun before, shall we say, the proper authorizations were received from a certain government body."

Laslo nodded. "Impressive. But disturbing. After this is over, we might have to rethink our relationship." Mahoud only smiled. "You've heard about the Health Center killings?" Laslo continued.

"When I reviewed the building activity logs, I noticed Dr. Francis came to visit you a few hours before he died."

Laslo nodded. "Vincent came to ask me if I could have one of my geneticists help him find proof of genetic tampering caused by the brain dust." He paused. "Now he and his staff are dead, his records have been erased and the bodies he was using as evidence have disappeared."

Mahoud whistled. "Does Dr. Lockwood know about Gerry stealing his research?"

"No, and I want you to keep it that way."

"So, you think Stringer will come after you."

"He might. Who knows what Vincent told him."

"I'll arrange protection for you."

"And for my family. Stringer might go after them to get to me."

"Done." Mahoud pushed himself out of the chair. "How about the woman you had me investigate, Ms. Greyson? Dr. Francis was a friend."

"I tried to contact her. Apparently, her building is on fire."

Mahoud shrugged. "It's possible."

"It's also a hell of a coincidence. Try to determine if that fire is real and find out if she's all right. She's ornery enough to fake that message just so she doesn't get bothered."

"She has her EP to run interference."

"Yeah. When you find her, if she's still alive, tell her she might be in danger. With as few explanations as possible, of course."

"Mr. Radic?" Satah stood in the doorway to the office. He was using the tone of voice he reserved for occasions he knew would upset his boss.

"I'm busy, Satah."

Satah cleared his throat. "Two people from MGRC are here to see you, sir."

"Do they have an appointment?"

"Ah, no, sir. These people don't need an appointment. They're entitled to see you at any time." He lowered his voice to a whisper. "They're those genaudit officers, Mr. Radic."

Laslo took a deep breath and swore inwardly at MGRC's rotten sense of timing. About to dismiss Mahoud, he changed his mind and gestured for him to stay.

"Bring them in, Satah."

Officer Martin, dressed in her usual black-and-white MGRC uniform, preceded Inspector Alim, his white suit shining in the copper room. He moved past the woman and extended long, graceful fingers towards Laslo.

"Hello again, Mr. Radic," the man said in his soft, contained voice.

Laslo nodded a greeting and shook Alim's hand, who then placed it on the metal plaque on Laslo's desk. A holo of his identification number and MGRC authorization floated in front of Laslo's eyes.

"We're here to perform an audit of your organization to ensure that all your projects respect MGRC authorized practices."

"Is this because of Dr. Lockwood? I thought everything had been cleared up with you guys."

Alim smiled. "You were only next on our list, Mr. Radic."

"Sure." Or maybe hiring a geneticist under investigation so quickly after he'd had his license yanked had piqued their interest. He motioned to Ashar Mahoud. "This is my chief of security. You'll need to be cleared to enter certain areas of the plant. As you know, we have our share of theft and espionage. We have to protect ourselves."

Alim's smile disappeared. "I hope we'll get your full co-operation, Mr.

Radic."

"Of course, but you'll have to be patient as well. Our system is not set up to accommodate external auditors. Did you bring protocols with you?"

A look of annoyance crossed Martin's face. "Yes. They've been confiscated by your security system."

"It's set up that way," Mahoud said, "so as to avoid corruption of our own files and sabotage. I'll make sure your documents are cleared right away."

He smiled, and Officer Martin blinked. Mahoud then turned to Laslo and winked lightly. Laslo had to repress a smile. By the time their protocols were released to MGRC officers, Mahoud would know exactly what they had brought and could act accordingly.

"I'm sorry to interrupt again, Mr. Radic," Satah said.

"Now what?"

"Your wife on the comm. She says it's urgent."

"Excuse me, please."

Laslo sat at his desk and raised a privacy bubble before he took the comm. When she came on line, Jelena's face was harrowed.

"What is it?"

"I'm at the Health Center. The surgery department. I need you here. Now."

"I'm on my way."

Laslo lowered the bubble and got up. "I'm sorry, officers, I have to leave right now. Family emergency. Mr. Mahoud will take care of your needs until I come back."

Alim placed a hand on Laslo's arm to stop him. "Your priority should be this audit, Mr. Radic. It will look very bad if you leave at this point."

Laslo stared down at the dark hand on his sleeve then at the cool ebony features. "It'll look even worse if I bash your face in."

"Are you making threats?" Officer Martin squeaked.

Jethro Alim let his hand fall. Laslo turned to the woman. "What do you think?"

Mahoud cleared his throat. "Ah, why don't you go, Mr. Radic. I'll take care of these officers until your return."

Laslo nodded and rushed to the door. "See to that other matter we discussed as well," he said. "Satah, medical emergency. Call and say I'm taking the car. I'll pay the fine."

The drive to the hospital was infuriatingly slow. He wasted more precious time trying to locate the surgery section in the Health Center complex. Once he found it, he left the car parked in front of the building and rushed inside.

Jelena sat at the entrance, waiting. She got up slowly when she saw him.

"I refused to let them perform any surgery on Zelimir until they talked to you," she said, her voice faint.

"Where's Zel?"

"In a room upstairs." She lifted a hand. "No, he's not alone. His friend Graeme is with him. I must say I'm impressed with that child. He's been very supportive of our son." She grasped Laslo's sleeve as if caught by a wave of dizziness. "Laslo, they want to…" She shook her head. "I think it's better if you talk to the surgeon yourself."

She led him to the third floor and the surgeon's office. The man sitting behind the desk was short and round, with the blinking gaze of someone who needed lenses replacement. He frowned when he saw Laslo with Jelena.

"Laslo, this is Dr. Canute. Doctor, my husband."

The surgeon got up and motioned Laslo and Jelena to a group of chairs in the corner.

"I came as fast as I could," Laslo said.

"Yes, yes, I know." Dr. Canute sank into the chair across from them. "Did your wife say what we want to do?" Laslo shook his head. Dr. Canute pursed his lips and threw a resentful glance at Jelena. "Your son has an unfortunate disease, Mr. Radic. All we can do at the moment is try to slow the advance of it as much as we can. His aphasia is in remission due to the drug we're giving him, but I can't say the same thing for the xylopoiesis itself. We'll have to amputate both feet."

Laslo gasped. His mind blanked out. He sat straight in the chair, unable to move or say anything. Something shifted below his heart. He coughed once, then felt the bile rise like lava from his gut. He jumped up and rushed out to a decont room he'd seen in passing, barely making it before his stomach heaved.

Over the past two years, he'd imagined scenes in which he told his son that the doctors would hack him to pieces, but he knew now they were meant to strengthen his own resolve to find a cure, not to prepare him for the real thing. Deep down, he'd always clutched at the hope that he might be able to avoid telling Zel about his disease, that at the last minute the boy would be spared.

He came out of the decont to find his wife standing beside the door with a bottle of water from the vending machine. She smiled sadly.

"If it helps, I had the exact same reaction."

He nodded, took the bottle and went back into the decont. There he rinsed his mouth with a small quantity of the water, drank the rest then went out again.

He stared at her, still unable to speak. She stared back and then, with a small moan, threw herself into his arms. They closed convulsively around her. He leaned his cheek on the top of her head, feeling the tremors in Jelena's body.

"I don't want to lose him, Laslo," she said, her voice muffled.

"We won't. I promise." He kissed her forehead, knowing it was a foolish promise and that she would never forgive him if he didn't keep it. It wouldn't really matter, though, because he would not forgive himself.

After a minute they broke apart and returned to the surgeon's office in silence. Dr. Canute was sitting in the same chair in the corner, his elbows on the armrests, the fingers of his hands making a steeple above which he blinked at them. He didn't comment on Laslo's reaction.

"What exactly are you going to do?"

"As I said, we need to amputate both feet. So far the hands haven't been affected, so we can be thankful for that."

"What about bioprostheses?"

The doctor shook his head. "We won't be able to attach them until we have stabilized him. So far, we have no means of doing that."

Laslo was grateful for the surgeon's abrupt manner. It helped him keep his emotions in check in a situation that seemed hopeless. Nearly hopeless, he thought.

"I want to talk to my son, explain to him. Then you can do your surgery."

The doctor nodded. "Your wife can lead you to him. I have the op room ready." He rushed out of the office.

Zelimir's room was not far. When the door opened, his son turned towards him. Laslo never saw who else was in the room. His eyes were fixed on his child, more precious than his own life. For a moment he faltered, unable to move. Then Zel extended his arms and whispered, "Daddy."

The word propelled Laslo into the room. He took his son into his arms and hugged him carefully then set him away and sat on the edge of the bed. Truly, he thought as he suddenly filled with rage, no parent should have to tell a child such a harsh truth. He took a deep breath and prepared to kill his son's childhood forever.

Laslo's anger sustained him. He fueled it constantly. Otherwise, he'd have to give in to despair, and he refused to do that. In despair lay madness.

He left Jelena to wait with Zelimir for the surgery while he went back to GeneTech. She'd understood his need. He wanted to talk to Torver, impress upon him that this wasn't a theoretical exercise anymore, that time was running out on Zelimir.

The problem was no one knew Lockwood's whereabouts. The building traffic log indicated he'd left GeneTech before midnight the night before. It was now late afternoon, and he hadn't shown up yet. There was no answer at his apartment.

Laslo made his way to Mahoud's office, careful to avoid the auditors.

"You have the records for Lockwood?"

"From his tracking chip? Of course."

"I want to know where he is."

Mahoud brought up a holo map of the area and inserted the code for Torver's chip. His 3D likeness popped up on the other side of the Gatineau Woods.

"Well, he's not around here, that's for sure."

Laslo had a sudden idea. "Do you have the address for his apartment?"

"Sure." A point of light appeared on the map. "It's about twelve kilometers from where he is now."

"Now give me Demetria Greyson's address."

"Well, well," Mahoud said a moment later. "Same address as Lockwood."

"Damn. Backtrack and see where he was about five hours ago. That's when I called Greyson and was told the building was on fire."

They watched as Torver's holo moved from his apartment building and entered the woods.

"He's running," Mahoud said. "As if someone's after him."

"If he made contact with the Greyson woman and she's the one who's being pursued, they may be running together."

"He ran to that spot," Mahoud said, pointing to the place on the other side of the woods. "He's been there for three hours, at least."

"Can you find out where that is?"

"Sure." After a few seconds, Mahoud looked up. "It's Carlotta Danterini's house. Ms. Greyson's late mother."

"Damn." Laslo knew he'd been right to be worried. His son was being eaten alive, and now he might be in danger of losing the only person who could save him.

## Chapter Twenty-seven

GERRY CAME INTO STRINGER'S OFFICE FROM HIS NEW LAB TO FIND ARGUS ALREADY there. His usually impeccable gray jacket was stained with dark patches and torn, his hair was stuck to his scalp and his face and hands were scratched.

"What's that smell?" Stringer waved a hand to waft away the stink.

"Fire retardant," Argus said.

"No, I recognize that. It's the other one. Like something rotting." Stringer peered at Argus's shoes. "What did you step in, man?"

"Some dead animal. We chased the woman through the woods behind her building."

"You haven't brought her with you?" Argus shook his head. Stringer rested his entwined fingers on his belly. "And you don't have the encryption key."

Gerry examined Argus's closed face and thought he saw a flicker of unease. Argus shifted his feet; the scraping sound on the hardwood floor broke the pin-drop silence.

"The woman had help," he said.

"She was expecting you?"

Argus nodded. "The guy who was in Francis's house with her was at her apartment, too. Her EP triggered a fire alarm and they escaped with the tenants evacuating the building. We lost them through the woods."

"And the disc?"

Argus shook his head. "We went back to her apartment. It took us longer than anticipated to go through her things." He paused. "She collects antiques."

"Valuable?"

Argus shrugged.

"You took care not to break anything?"

Argus nodded. Stringer rubbed his hands together.

"When things calm down again, you'll go back there. I've just become Ms. Greyson's closest heir."

"We didn't find the disc. She must have it with her, or she hid it somewhere."

Stringer grunted. "And the man?"

"We don't know who he is."

"Doesn't matter. Once you catch up with them, get rid of him. I still want the woman, though."

"You could just kill her," Gerry said.

Stringer glanced at him. "I want to make sure she didn't arrange for someone to access the genebanks and retrieve Francis's data."

Gerry permitted himself a small smile. "It must be hard to be taken in by amateurs, Argus."

Stringer swiveled his chair to face him. "Have a seat, Dr. Sinclair. Let's chat."

Gerry swallowed his smile. "Designing a new drug is not exactly like catching a pair of fugitives, Stringer."

"I said, have a seat."

Argus moved in Gerry's direction. Gerry, deciding he'd rather get there on his own, sidestepped him and plunked himself in front of Stringer, who was contemplating him with a frown.

"I sincerely hope you're not going to tell me that you need more time," Stringer said.

Gerry hated it when Stringer's voice became all soft. It usually meant he was getting volatile.

"It's this gene structure," he said, his voice deliberately calm, "I need to adapt it, that's all."

"That's all." Stringer's eyes traveled around the room then returned to Gerry's face, as if he were following a fly. "Tell me about the gene."

Gerry shifted in his chair when he realized Argus had moved behind him. "The data we collected from Dr. Francis's records confirm that, somehow, the compound I added to the dust acts the way it should, but it also forces the cells from the brain and spinal chord to commit suicide. I'm convinced that, once what causes that reaction is found and removed or neutralized, the drug will work. There's something wrong in the research I borrowed from Lockwood. His retrogene should've worked."

Stringer was staring at him without blinking. "That gene. The one that doesn't work. It would kill anybody?"

"Yes."

"But, theoretically, could you pick a specific gene, say from a racial feature, and selectively have that new gene bind to it? Make it harmless for those who didn't have that gene?"

"If you mean that the gene would attack the brain of everyone who has, let's say, a particular Asian gene, theoretically, I suppose it's feasible. To do that, you still need to know what causes the cell death. It's a long shot, though."

Stringer jerked his head to the side. Argus clutched a handful of Gerry's collar and propelled him over the desk towards Stringer. Stringer seized Gerry's neck and squeezed. Gerry gasped, barely able to get air into his lungs. He pulled frantically at Stringer's wrists. It was like trying to move concrete. Just before he thought he'd pass out, Stringer eased the pressure on his neck.

"Dr. Sinclair, you are the stupidest man I've ever been privileged to know," Stringer murmured.

"Wh..." he coughed. "What do you mean?"

"Can you make the killer gene selective?"

Gerry tried to shake his head. Stringer squeezed.

"No," Gerry croaked. Stringer let go, and Gerry fell flat on the desk. He stayed there for a few seconds until he realized Argus wasn't pushing him down anymore. He crawled off the desk and sat back in the chair, massaging his neck.

Stringer threw him a disgusted glance then shook his head at Argus. "It's the ultimate weapon. You launch it over the population of an entire city, or you slip it into the food reserves. Everyone ingests it, but only those you've targeted with your killer gene are affected. Untraceable genocide on a grand scale in a clean, efficient fashion." He leaned forward, his sunken eyes boring into Gerry, his face taut with tension. "Now answer this question—why *can't* you make it selective?"

Gerry shook his head, berating himself for being twenty kinds of moron. He should have seen it, he thought, should have realized the potential of Torver Lockwood's discovery. Instead, he'd presented it to Stringer on a platter.

"It's beyond my abilities. There's only one person who may be able to do it for you."

"The scientist you stole the process from."

"Yes. Torver Lockwood."

"Can you access the GeneTech staff databank from here?"

"Sure."

"I want to know what this Lockwood looks like."

Argus fished in his pocket and took out a handheld, which he handed to Gerry. After tapping a few keys, Torver's still appeared on the screen. He could feel Argus's breath on top of his head.

"That's the man who was with Greyson," Argus said.

Gerry scooted forward in his chair and passed the handheld over to Stringer. "That's not good. If Lockwood's had a chance to study Francis's records, he knows I stole his research and what I've been trying to do with it. He won't go to the authorities, though. He's as good as dead if MGRC catches him."

"So are you," Stringer said. He sat back with a sigh then looked up at Argus. "Get him for me."

"I'll find them," Argus said.

"Radic fitted Lockwood with a tracking chip," Gerry said. "If you could somehow tap into the device frequency…"

"Forget it. Too difficult for what it's worth," Stringer said. "I've just rewritten your job description. You'll help us locate Dr. Lockwood."

"I don't know anything about searching for people."

"What are the odds that Radic suspects your activities?"

"Laslo?" Gerry snickered. "I'd say negligible. He's so concentrated on that project of his he doesn't see anything else. It's become an obsession."

"Wouldn't Dr. Lockwood share his suspicions about you with Radic once he knew you'd stolen his data?"

"I doubt he's had the opportunity. From what I heard, Argus and his men kept Lockwood and Greyson pretty busy."

"Good." Stringer said. "You'll go back to GeneTech and find out where Dr. Lockwood is through his tracking chip."

"You want me to get into security? I can't do that."

"It's either that," Argus said, "or you can join the last Termite in his cage."

"Now, Argus, no need to threaten Dr. Sinclair. He knows what I need."

"But…" Gerry exhaled loudly. "Security at GeneTech is extremely tight. I won't be able to find out anything without alerting the chief of security."

"Dr. Sinclair."

Gerry shivered.

"If Radic doesn't suspect you, why should his chief of security find it strange that you're inquiring after one of your staff? You're Dr. Lockwood's supervisor. He's not in his lab. It's quite natural for you to want to track him down, make sure he's where he should be."

"Yes, but I don't want the chief to go after Lockwood himself. What do I do then?"

"Just say you'll take care of it. Surely, they trust you." Stringer smiled.

Gerry swallowed. The grin made him imagine a plasma beam taking one of his eyes, or gutting him, or worse. He rose on shaky legs. "I'll let you know as soon as I find out where Lockwood is."

"Do that. In the meantime, Argus, you'll find out all you can about Ms. Greyson. If they left together, they must be hiding together. We'll approach the problem from two different directions."

Gerry aimed for the door. "Oh, and Dr. Sinclair." He turned to face Stringer. "I want Lockwood. I can be generous when I get what I want."

Gerry jerked his head in assent and left quickly. Underlined in Stringer's parting phrase was that there was also a price for failure. What would be his reward? he wondered. The plasma beam he'd felt but didn't get? A lifetime addiction to dust, once he'd created it for Stringer?

He shook his head. Once Lockwood was found, Stringer wouldn't need him anymore. It was time to make plans to disappear, get a new identity. First, he'd have to erase all traces of his activities at GeneTech. He was good at that—he'd done it before, in a different place.

The bus arrived almost immediately. Gerry found a cramped seat at the back near the window. He let his gaze roam over the rows of houses stacked on each side of the riverbed. Nothing but rocks had grown here for almost half a century. He tried to imagine the river the way it had once run, full of water, moving swiftly, grass and trees growing along its banks, birds flying overhead, fish jumping in quiet pools along the banks. The picture couldn't take shape in his mind. That was his main problem in life, he reflected. He was plagued with a complete lack of imagination.

The woman sitting beside him turned to look at him, and he realized he must have been mumbling aloud. He frowned, and she faced forward again. In the distance, the first bridge spanned the dried-out river. He was like this riverbed they were riding on—open to the elements, surrounded on every side, used for a purpose other than what had been first intended.

He shook himself. It wasn't like him to turn philosophical. He ought to concentrate on the practical. He cursed Lockwood. The woman beside him started then got up, leaving her place empty. He ignored her. Because of Lockwood, he'd have to shelve his own plans yet again.

Stringer was no better. Maybe he should have approached someone less greedy, or more malleable. What did it matter? He had to recoup whatever was left of the situation. Turn matters so he could at least get a minimum of reward out of the entire fiasco.

*Reward.*

The word brought back Stringer's promise to him and reinforced his resolution to disappear as soon as feasible. He looked down at his right hand. That would mean removing his Identichip and replacing it with another. He hated pain. Even so, it would have to be done. He wondered if he'd get to choose his name this time.

Gerry worried the problem through two bus transfers and the short walk that led him to GeneTech. He entered the lobby with affected nonchalance and stepped inside the narrow, opaque plasmer security booth. The door behind him sealed as soon as he stood in the center. He wouldn't be able to get out of one door or the other until his identity was confirmed by GeneTech's security protocol. He placed his hand on the plaque beside the door in front of him and triggered his Identic.

A green light appeared above his hand, and the door slid open. Gerry stepped out and came face-to-face with Ashar Mahoud, who was holding a stun stick. Two guards stood behind him.

"Good afternoon, Dr. Sinclair," Mahoud said, his teeth uncovered in a grin. "We were hoping you would join us sooner or later."

"What's this all about?"

Mahoud tapped the stun stick against his leg. "Well, for starters, Mr. Radic would like to speak with you about certain production issues. Then there's the problem of your supervisory duties." He stepped aside and pointed down the hallway with his weapon. "After you, please."

GERRY SAT ACROSS FROM LASLO, IN THE CHAIR WHERE HE'D SAT COUNTLESS TIMES TO discuss one point or another with his boss. Mahoud stood behind him, once in a while tapping his stun stick in his open palm. Gerry thought ruefully that he seemed to be destined to have a muscle man hover behind his head.

Strangely, the only emotion he'd felt at seeing Mahoud waiting for him was relief. Despite his unenviable situation, he was now shielded from Stringer, at least for a while. The magnitude of his new problems would depend on how much Laslo and Mahoud knew about his activities.

He had been shocked when he'd come into Laslo's office and faced the man behind the desk. Laslo seemed to have shrunk. The skin of his face was gray and taut, and there was a tremor to his hands.

"Why the security, Laslo?" he said.

"Our objectives seemed to have deviated in the past two years, Gerry."

"What do you mean?"

Laslo got up from his chair, walked around his desk and sat on the edge of it, his hands gripping each side. "I only have myself to blame, I suppose," he continued. "You turned out to be a boon and a curse. You brought Torver Lockwood to me, and he's very close to a solution. So, I must admit you've had your uses."

"I was more than that, Laslo. Who did you turn to when you wanted corners cut?"

"True. I'm not usually naive about people, but in your case, maybe because I saw you as a partner, so to speak, I didn't worry too much about your outside activities. I should have paid more attention."

Gerry looked up at Mahoud and smirked. "I didn't realize you were in on our illicit activities, Mahoud."

"Contrary to some, I don't bite the hand that feeds me."

"Ouch. A bit melodramatic, aren't we?" He turned back to Laslo. "Do you realize that your chief of security is in a perfect position for a bit of blackmail?"

"I choose to keep quiet for reasons of my own, Dr. Sinclair. Mr. Radic and I understand each other."

Gerry chuckled. "You're too cheap to be had," he said. "If I were you, Mahoud, I'd hold out for more."

Laslo stared at him for a moment then walked to the window. He turned off the sunshield and let the glare of the sun flood the room. Gerry's eyes watered from the sudden intensity.

"Do you know," Laslo said, his voice holding a reflective, almost faraway tone, "if it hadn't been for my own illegal activities I wouldn't have learned about yours. Unfortunately for you, I saw you get into a limousine one night. That got me curious."

"Nothing wrong with that, Laslo. I paid the guy for a ride. Always wanted to see what it felt like to ride in a car."

"Enough," Mahoud said. Gerry started when he poked him with the stun stick. "Why did you use GeneTech to fiddle with brain dust?"

Gerry thought about denying it, then gave up. He snickered.

"Because it was easy. You said it, Laslo—you never thought of checking up on me." He lifted a hand to stop the next question. "If you're going to ask me why I made the dust in the first place, don't. I have no intention of telling you." He let his arm fall, examined his open hand then closed it in a tight fist.

"Let's just say that I made choices long ago that led me here."

"Cut the crap, Gerry. I know you created brain dust for Stringer, that you tried to manipulate it to make it detox-resistant, and that to do so you stole Lockwood's research. You're also the cause of Dr. Francis's death. I wouldn't be surprised if you killed him yourself. I know all of it."

Gerry chuckled then laughed outright. "You think you do, don't you? Well, let me enlighten you some more. What your boy wonder is developing is not a cure but one of the most powerful biogenic weapons that will exist today. It'll be a virus with a genetic homing device that can destroy only the specific bearers of that gene target. You deliver it as a gas or a spray, or put it into the food supply, and there you have it—some fall off like flies, and others are untouched. What do you think of that?"

Laslo turned around slowly. Gerry smiled.

"And there's something else you don't know," he continued. "Right now, Stringer is searching for Torver Lockwood, and when he finds him, he'll force him to create this perfect weapon. What will you do, Laslo? Intimidate Stringer with a stun stick?"

He sensed that Mahoud had moved to the door.

"I'll get them right now," the man said.

"Ah, you know where they are," Gerry deduced.

Laslo turned to him. "You said 'they.' Is Stringer looking for Ms. Greyson, too?"

"Of course. Dr. Francis left her his data. Stringer wants it back." Gerry smiled. He was beginning to enjoy himself.

"I'm going with you," Laslo said to Mahoud.

"Stay here. I know what to do."

Laslo shrugged. "Assemble your team right away. I'll meet you in the stables in fifteen minutes." He nodded at Gerry. "You've made your point, Gerry. But I have my own reasons for finding Torver Lockwood before Stringer sets his fat paws on him." He looked up at the guards who had come into his office. "Take him away and lock him up until I decide what to do with him. And stay clear of those Mungers."

# Chapter Twenty-eight

ASHAR CHOSE TO TAKE FIVE OF HIS ASSISTANTS WITH HIM AND FOUR HOVER-RIGS, ENOUGH to surround Carlotta Danterini's house if it became necessary and to bring back Lockwood and Greyson. He and his people each wore padded protective clothing and a plasma gun on their hip. He had just finished giving his instructions when Laslo came into the stables.

He waited for Laslo to reach him, saw the determination in his face and sighed. "You're not coming with us, Laslo."

Laslo pointed to the plasma gun on Ashar's hip. "You're expecting trouble?"

"Ten to one Stringer's men will make it there, too. Stringer had ample time to figure out Demetria Greyson would head to her mother's house."

"It's a compound, not a house," Laslo said.

"Yeah. When Carlotta Danterini surrounded her residence with the latest security grid, it was state-of-the-art. Unfortunately, that was ten years ago, and the grid is seriously outdated. I called up its protocol and had a point of entry in two minutes. I only hope we'll get there before Stringer's men do." Ashar signaled his people. They hopped on their rigs. He turned to Laslo. "You don't want to get caught between Stringer's men and the cops."

"Same goes for you."

Ashar pointed to the waiting team. "I trained these men and women. I trust them to do exactly what I tell them. I can't say that about you." He smiled. "Besides, I need someone at the comm who can take charge." He saw Laslo's hands close into fists. "Don't even think about it, Laslo."

Laslo's gaze shifted to the security guards then back to Ashar. He grunted. His hands opened.

"I'll be in your office." He turned around and left.

Ashar breathed a small sigh of relief and gestured his people out of the hover stable. They activated the magnetic field under the air cushions, turned on the microjets and filed out the door, each hover-rig raising a small cloud of dust before it stabilized into cruise mode.

He winked to trigger his comm piece.

"Okay, people, it's thirty-five kilometers to our destination. I want you to spread out and meet me at the designated spot in...half an hour." He switched channels and called up Laslo.

"I'm here," Laslo said. "I need Lockwood, Ashar. Don't screw up."

"Do you believe what Gerry said about the retrogene being a weapon?"

"I don't know. But if it's true, that gives us another incentive for bringing Lockwood back in one piece."

"WE'RE AGREED, THEN?" DEMETRIA CALLED OUT FROM THE KITCHEN.

Torver nodded with a resigned sigh. "Yes, as long as I get to finish the research. I can't believe you'd rat on me."

He heard her plunk down a glass. "I told you. I'd rather go to prison for the rest of my life, or worse, than risk unleashing that horror."

"It works for both sides, you know. What do you think MGRC would do with a weapon like that? You don't think they'd want to experiment with it? Maybe use it on a few terrorists to see what it does?"

"MGRC was created to prevent these kinds of things from happening. Surely..."

"Surely nothing. You should see what that guy Alim does for a living. It's not pretty."

Demetria slammed a drawer shut and came to stand in the doorway. "You've been on his lifepath."

"Only briefly. I was upset at the time. But I guarantee you, sister, that the only thing that differentiates him from others of his kind is the outfit he works for."

Her face took on a mutinous look. "All the more reason why you can't hide your research anywhere. You can't leave it out there for just anyone to use it if they happen on it."

"They'd have to know exactly what and where to look for. But, hey, that's not the point. This research could also save lives. Think of Laslo's son." She always managed to twist things around for him. "I didn't set out to create a doomsday weapon."

"That's just it, isn't it? You never stopped to think of the consequences."

"Ha. You'd sing a different tune if I'd found a way to reverse your dermophagia."

Demetria winced and hugged herself, turning away from him.

"Damn," he said. "You always bring out the worst in me."

"You gave me your word," she croaked. "Can I count on it?"

"Yes." She was annoying him again. Every time he felt guilty about something he said to her, she managed to turn it to her advantage. "I said so, didn't I?"

"Those people who are after us—I don't want any more killing. The Termites, Vincent…it's too much already."

"You'd rather they kill you?"

"Find a way to deliver them to MGRC or the police."

"I'm not going to the authorities."

"I'm not asking you to."

"Not now, maybe. But with you, who knows?"

"What if this Dr. Sinclair comes to the same conclusion you did? Do you think the man he works for, whether it's Radic or someone else, won't be interested in a gene-specific weapon?"

"As long as I have access to a lab, I can take care of myself."

"I know you're not the type to pick up a plasma gun and start shooting, but I don't want you to use your genetics knowledge to kill, either."

"It's us against them."

"It doesn't have to be that way."

"I'm not staying holed up here forever."

"Promise you won't try to kill anyone."

"What, no threats, this time?"

Demetria stood there, arms crossed, eyes boring into his. He felt the pull of her lifepath, the connection he had with her.

"Fine. I promise. As long as my life isn't directly threatened. Happy, now?"

"I think I'll go lie down. I'm tired all of a sudden." She moved down a corridor off the kitchen doorway.

Torver felt a rush of anger at her lack of appreciation for the concessions he'd just made. "What about me?"

She turned her head and looked at him over her shoulder. "You can do whatever you want. There are a number of bedrooms if you want to rest. We can decide what to do later."

Torver watched her disappear down the hall. "Bossy, that's what you are," he muttered. "You were much more interesting when you were a little girl." He surveyed the white-on-white living room. He'd seen Demetria often in this room, sitting there at the piano trying to please her mother, who never seemed to find satisfaction in her dark-haired daughter.

Her memories crowded the room. He needed to get out of the house, to breathe non-filtered air, to feel the searing July sun on his skin.

Earlier, he'd noted with surprise that the grounds still had the well-kept gardens of Demetria's youth. She'd smiled.

"Fakes. Good fakes, mind you, but that's always what they've been. Appearances were everything to Carlotta."

Now he wanted to examine the false greenery. He glimpsed a small gazebo, way at the back, that beckoned him. He hesitated for a second, thinking he should tell Demetria where he was going then shrugged. Let her worry for a while if she realized he was gone. She deserved it.

He turned off the security protocol the way Demetria had shown him, slipped outside through the glass door of the living room, made sure the protocol was back on then ambled along the verdant path. He touched one of the leaves, then a tree trunk. All the plants, shrubs and trees were made of some substance he'd never seen before, maybe a version of plasmer.

Nevertheless, they provided shade and produced a noise similar to the stirring of leaves. The late-afternoon sun was hot enough to burn his skin, but the air seemed cooler here than in the city.

When he stepped into the gazebo, a trilling sound warbled around him. He moved farther in and it began again, but with other sounds, too, things cracking and rubbing and scraping. Then came a sweet smell that reminded him of the grass he'd crushed under his feet in the woods, and a mix of flowery scents. He recognized roses, from the perfume his mother wore, but the others eluded him.

Torver was charmed. In the center of this gazebo, Carlotta Danterini had put together the sounds and smells of a pre-drought garden.

The gazebo was larger than it appeared. On seven of the eight sides, shades were drawn to protect from the harshness of the sun and the unrelenting heat. To the left stood a table and four chairs, and in a corner at the back a chaise longue waited to cradle his body. He lay down in it with a sigh of contentment, and before he could think again of the promise he'd made Demetria he was fast asleep.

ASHAR STOOD AT THE EDGE OF THE WOODS AND SURVEYED THE AREA SURROUNDING Carlotta Danterini's estate. The house and grounds were protected by a three-meter stone wall topped with motion-sensitive high voltage wire. Climb one meter up that wall and you got zapped.

On the east side, a twenty-meter cliff, above what probably used to be a lake, protected the house. One could scale it, but it was a difficult and treacherous climb, so he had ruled it out as a possible approach.

The entrance to the drive and the house faced northwards. The grounds inside the wall were arranged in the old-fashioned way, with a long strip of bare lawn in front of the house that provided no cover at all, something Stringer's men would avoid. The route Ashar had taken with his people, from the south side through the woods, was also difficult. They'd had to leave their hover-rigs half a kilometer away because the forest close to the house was too thick to accommodate their transport. They'd ended up strung along the garden wall behind the residence.

The most probable access for Stringer's men would be the west side, which gave onto the neighbor's grounds and was also the shortest distance to the house.

"What do you think, Ashar?" Tomas said. "Let's just ring the bell and see if someone answers the door."

Ashar smiled and fished a small box from his pocket. "We don't need to ring the bell. I can bypass the security protocol with this baby." He switched to a general comm channel. "Okay, people, let's get this over with. Bibi and Ricardo, you take the west side. Let me know if anything moves. Souko and Taps, I want you to watch the main entrance. Tomas and I will breach the perimeter."

Once his team was in place, he sneaked out of the woods, Tomas right behind him, and crouched close to the wall. He tapped a few times on his box then frowned.

"There's no current from the wall," he said. "That can mean one of three things. One, this doesn't work."

"Unlikely," Tomás said. "Two, Ms. Greyson didn't turn on the secsys."

"Even more improbable," Ashar said. He drummed his fingers on the box.

"Someone's already inside," they said together.

Ashar fished a roving cam from his pocket, activated it and let it float to the top of the wall. It scanned left and right then hovered in position, waiting for further instruction. All his hand-held vid gave him was the sea of green with the path that led to the house.

"Ashar," Souko's voice came on the comm. "Do you want us inside with you?"

"Negative. Stay where you are. If anyone comes out, shoot them, unless it's the man or the woman we came to get. Set your guns on short bursts." He took out his own gun and set it to burst, kept it in his hand. "I don't want anyone killed, just disabled. Dead people usually attract the attention of the police. Understood?"

All four acknowledged.

He recalled his cam and turned to Tomás. "The cam didn't show sign of people outside the house, but it's a large garden. Jump as close as you can to the edge of the wall. The plants will give us some cover."

He examined the wall for toeholds. He fit one foot into a crevice between two stones, stretched as far as possible, grasped the edge of another crack in the wall and pulled himself up until his body lay over the top. He dropped to the ground. Tomás landed beside him a few seconds later. He touched a shrub.

"Nice fakes."

Ashar was about to comment when he heard a noise to the left and ahead of his position. He unsnapped his plasma gun from its holster and waited. Ten meters away, two men emerged from the greenery, following a path that led to the house. Their backs were to him. He aimed, but a red light flashed on top of the gunsight.

"Damn. They're out of range," he whispered. He waited until the two men disappeared. "Come on." He stepped out of the brush and hurried in the direction the others had gone.

Once on the edge of the path, he stopped to survey the area. The garden was crisscrossed with gravel paths amid lush foliage. To his right, in one corner, stood a pavilion.

"Ashar," Souko said, "I can see movement outside the front door."

"I see them," Taps said. "Two men. One of them's big. And I mean huge."

"Ashar, Bibi here. Ricardo's still at the neighbor's wall, but I went to check the front of their house. There's a delivery van parked in front, but no one's in it."

"Keep alert," Ashar said. "We're going to try to get closer. I want a shot at the two guys we just saw."

He gestured to Tomás and inched along the grass edge of the path towards the door. Suddenly, he heard a voice.

"Argus, we're in position."

Ashar crouched low behind a hedge and gestured Tomás down. Between them and the house was a series of flowerbeds ending about a meter before the glassed-in corner of the house. The two men they'd been following were flattened against the wall at the side of a door, facing away from the house. The hedge itself afforded little protection. One wrong move and the men would see them.

He felt Tomás touch his sleeve and motion to his right. Ashar nodded. Tomás silently backed away and disappeared into the greenery.

Ashar waited, all his attention on the two thugs at the door. From the corner of his eye, he saw a dark shadow move then crawl to the hedge.

"I'm in position," came Tomás's voice in his ear. "I'll take the one on the right."

"Go!"

Ashar jumped the hedge, shooting as he ran. He hit the man directly in the chest. He saw the burst from Tomás's gun. The second man fell. It was finished in ten seconds.

Tomás leaned over and felt the men's pulses. "They're alive, but they'll hurt when they wake up."

Ashar fished out his security box and tapped a code. "The security protocol for the house is off as well. The tracking chip places Lockwood in the compound but doesn't pinpoint his location. This is a big place. Maybe we can find him before Stringer's men do."

"What about the woman?"

"If we can get only one, we get Lockwood." Ashar aimed the box at the door and pressed the pad. The panel opened silently. They crouched low and slipped inside. The door swished closed behind them.

The entrance was just off the kitchen. Through the kitchen's far doorway, he could see part of the living room. To the right, a small hallway led to the opposite end of the house. All areas were empty. Ashar pocketed his black box and took out the hand-held bionet that contained the plans to the house. He motioned Tomás to the end of the corridor.

"The hallway leads to the bedrooms," he whispered. "See if anyone's there."

Tomás nodded and moved off. His plasmer soles made no noise on the marble floor. Ashar entered the kitchen then proceeded to the living room. No one. He whistled silently at the sight of the white furniture and the grand piano.

He approached an archway to his right and looked through. Front entrance hall, empty. Facing him, a dark corridor. He was about to slide into the hall when he heard a scream.

"Let me go, you big ape," a woman's voice yelled. Ashar heard a grunt then a curse.

He saw movement. They were coming out of a room into the darkened hallway. He retreated behind the living room wall.

"Argus," he heard a man say. "Lockwood isn't here."

"Where's Lockwood?" The voice was low and gruff.

"Who?" the woman said.

"The man you escaped with."

The voices were approaching. Ashar sneaked a look around the corner. Two men, the larger holding the Greyson woman; the other had fallen behind. He flattened himself against the wall. In a few seconds, they would enter the living room and discover him.

They weren't finished here—they were also looking for Lockwood. The good news was they hadn't found him yet. It was either retreat or attack. Ashar heard another curse. He whipped through the archway to face the trio.

The man holding the woman saw him and fired. Ashar threw himself to the side. He heard the wall behind him melt. The second man screamed and fell.

"Got him," Tomás murmured in his comm. Ashar stretched his neck around the doorjamb just in time to see the man who held Greyson turn and fire. Tomas recoiled with a grunt and backed away into the gloom. Ashar retreated behind the living room wall, gun at the ready.

"Don't move," the man called, "or I'll kill the woman." Ashar heard a grunt of pain. "Stop that, you bitch," he heard.

He peered around the corner. The man stood flat against the wall. Obviously, out of patience with the struggling Greyson, he raised his gun and hit her on the back of the head. She fell limp in his arms. He kept her upright, his gun at her temple, then looked straight at Ashar.

"She dies before I do."

"Leave us the woman," Ashar said, "we'll let you go." He saw the man's gun shift slightly. He jumped back. The plasma beam took out a chunk of the corner of the archway. He risked another look through the doorway. "Cover my back," the man said into the air.

"Ashar," Souko said, her tone urgent, "the delivery van. It's moving towards the entrance."

"He has a remote. Shit. Souko, Taps," Ashar whispered, "one man coming out with a woman. See if you can get a clear shot at him."

"We'd have to get in closer," Taps countered. "No time."

"Hit the tires, immobilize the van." He heard the zing of a plasma gun, then another.

"No go on the tires," Taps said. "Sidewalls look reinforced. So's the windshield."

"The van is at the bottom of the stairs," Souko said.

Ashar moved forward and peered around the doorjamb. The cargo door opened. Another man stood in its entrance holding a plasma rifle and started to shoot in a series of short bursts. Brick exploded, wood charred. The man turned around, using the woman as a shield, and fired a shot. Ashar rolled against the wall. The window beside him exploded. Another shot, and he knew that Tomás had to retreat.

He heard the snap of plasma beam on metal. The guy with the rifle continued to fire, making it impossible to come out and aim properly to hit the kidnapper without risking the woman.

"Fuck!" Souko's voice. Either she'd missed or she was hit. Ashar came through the front door of the house just as the door of the van slid shut. The engine roared, gravel spit under the tires. The van was gone in the space of a few seconds.

He fired a shot at the retreating vehicle, but it was too far to even hit it. He got up from his position at the front door and swore. "Everybody all right?"

"We're fine," Taps said. "You want us to go after the van?"

"No. Come and join us. We still have to find Dr. Lockwood."

He turned back to the hallway. Tomás was coming towards him, holding his left arm in his right.

"Are you okay?" Ashar said.

"Sure. He just nicked my upper arm. Nothing to worry about."

Ashar nodded. He and Tomás had seen worse during their clone farming days. They had the scars to prove it. Then they'd acquired a few more during the rebellion. He wasn't worried about a small plasma wound.

"Let's bring in those guys, see if they can tell us anything."

Two minutes later, Tomás was back. "They're dead."

"You killed them."

"No. They're just dead. No trace of a wound."

"We have to get out of here. I bet the cops won't be far behind." Ashar switched channels. "Laslo, I'm afraid we lost the woman. One of Stringer's men took her. Lockwood isn't in the house."

There were a few seconds of silence, then Laslo's voice came on. "His tracking chip indicates that he's still there. Check the entire house."

"There are plenty of places a guy could hide in here," Tomás said.

Ashar recalled his people and organized a fast, systematic search of the house. In the process, they discovered several hidden closets, a cellar with a top-to-ceiling safe, a soundproof music room, a library full of paper books, and a white marble room with an empty whirlpool bath. But no Lockwood.

Ashar sat on one of the white couches in the living room and tried to puzzle it out. Where would someone be able to hide in a house like this? He stared outside, his mind vaguely taking in the greenery. He straightened as he saw the roof of the gazebo.

"Tomás," he said, "you're with me."

He rushed to the pavilion at the back of the garden. As soon as he stepped inside, he saw Lockwood lying on a chaise, unmoving. He approached slowly. After a few seconds, it registered that the man he was watching was sound asleep.

"Laslo," he whispered, "we have him."

"Well done, Ashar. And thanks." He could hear the relief in Laslo's voice.

At that moment, Torver opened his eyes, saw Ashar hovering over him and straightened up quickly. "What?" he said. "What's going on?"

"Hello, Dr. Lockwood," Ashar said. "We've been looking for you."

"Mahoud? What are you doing here?" Torver got up and rubbed his eyes.

"Mr. Radic sent me to fetch you." He pointed to Torver's neck. "Tracking chip, remember?"

He noticed wariness in Torver's eyes.

"What does Radic want?"

"Oh, just his money's worth. Come along, please."

"Wait. We have to get Demetria. I mean Ms. Greyson. She can't stay here alone."

Ashar hesitated then shook his head. "I'm afraid someone already got to her, Dr. Lockwood."

Torver paled. "Who?"

"Let's get out of here first, shall we? I'll see you safe at GeneTech then Mr. Radic can explain."

Torver nodded and stepped out of the gazebo. He turned and gazed straight into Ashar's eyes. For a moment, Ashar felt disoriented, a bit dizzy. Then Torver broke eye contact and the feeling passed.

Lockwood grabbed Ashar's shirt. "You asshole, you let them take her."

He chopped down on Lockwood's wrists. The geneticist let go then turned away from him.

"There are only so many promises a man can keep," Lockwood said, his tone bitter. "I wonder if she'll want to hold me to all of them, now?"

## Chapter Twenty-nine

It took Torver the entire trip back to GeneTech to gather a semblance of calm. Every time he thought of Demetria in her abductor's hands, his head thundered and his vision blurred.

Anger was a new emotion for him. Before he'd met Demetria, his feelings had barely oscillated between indifference and amusement. All his emotions had been channeled into his work. In the whole of his life, he couldn't remember one instance when he'd felt this urge to break something, preferably someone's face. Demetria did this to me, he thought. I never wanted it.

But for some inexplicable reason, even though they'd known each other for only a few weeks, he shied away from imagining his future without her. As different as they were, as exasperating, straight-laced, bossy as she was, she was a part of him, of his life. That was why her being in danger made him mad.

There was nothing he could have done, Mahoud said. He most likely would have been taken as well. Torver knew that, of the two of them, it was Demetria who was better equipped to fight. He's seen her in action. Even so, when he'd walked Mahoud's lifepath he'd seen how they'd taken her. He couldn't wipe the image of her, unconscious, being stuffed into the van.

He swore, but it was carried by the wind. He grasped the sidebars of the hover-rig, willing Mahoud to go faster, and swore again. He had plans to put into action and for that he needed to be at GeneTech. He had to rescue Demetria. If the roles were reversed, she'd do anything to free him.

"Let's get to Laslo's office," Mahoud said. He gestured for Torver to follow him.

Torver blinked. They'd arrived in a square, low-ceilinged hangar. Mahoud and his team had parked their hover-rigs in line with half a dozen others.

"I didn't know about this place," Torver said. "What do you use these for, anyway?"

"You've only been in the laboratories portion of the company. GeneTech has over ten square kilometers of workshops and cybernated factories. The rigs come in handy for security patrols."

He said nothing more as they wended through the maze of corridors and buildings to Laslo's office. He wondered what time it was. The sun had set midway through their return, he remembered. That would make it around ten or eleven at night. Ironically, he wasn't tired. His sleep in the gazebo had been one of the most refreshing he'd had in years.

His face muscles cramped from the constant grinding of his teeth. He forced himself to open his mouth and rotate his lower jaw.

Laslo waited for them, ensconced behind his desk. Torver plunked in the chair in front of it. Immediately, it corrected his posture. He cursed it, jumped up and paced to the end of the room.

"I see our moods match," Laslo said.

Torver threw a glance at him on his way back. The man's features were bleak. He looked old. Torver stopped and stared into his eyes. For a moment, he felt the resistance, then he stumbled inside.

Laslo's lifepath twisted and coiled as far as he could see. Having expected to bounce back, he was at a loss as to what he was looking for; then, the answer came to him. He concentrated, and flipped quickly through one scene after another, subconsciously registering what he saw until he came back to the point where he'd entered. Then he stepped out. He saw Laslo blink and shudder.

"What the hell was that about?"

"I don't know," Torver said. "What?"

Laslo hesitated for a second then shrugged. "Forget it." He looked away to the far wall. "I'm sorry about Ms. Greyson."

"From what I saw," Torver said, glancing at Mahoud, "your people didn't make too much of an effort to get to her. You could have tried to disable the van, slow him down."

"How did you know they had a van?" Mahoud said. "You were sleeping when we found you." The sec chief raised his eyebrows. "Unless you faked the whole thing."

"I was asleep. I just know things. For instance, Demetria would be here with us and the guy would be dead if you'd given the order to shoot to kill earlier."

Mahoud narrowed his eyes. "We couldn't afford to attract the attention of the police."

"Right. You came for me so you weren't going to take any chances to save her." He felt the rage surge up again. "Don't you remember what they did to Vincent Francis, you fleecehead?"

"They may not be the same people who killed Dr. Francis," Mahoud said.

"What do you take me for, Mahoud?"

"You must have met Ms. Greyson only a few days ago," Laslo said. "I didn't realize she'd become that important to you."

"Apart from having the basic human decency to be concerned, you mean?" Torver took a deep breath and let it out slowly. "So, what are you going to do to get her back?"

"Do?" Laslo threw a glance at Mahoud. "As much as I feel for Ms. Greyson, there's not much we *can* do at this point except contact the authorities and say we believe she's disappeared."

Time to change tactics, Torver thought. From his quick trip through Laslo's lifepath, he already knew most of what Laslo was going to tell him. Nonetheless, he wanted the president of GeneTech to admit a few things voluntarily before they began negotiating for Demetria's life. The most important piece of information he'd gathered was that Laslo wasn't associated with Demetria's abductor in any way. That, at least, was a relief.

He let himself down slowly in the chair. "I suppose I must thank you for coming to get me."

Laslo turned towards his garden, even though it was completely dark outside. "How far along are you with the retrogene?"

"Still haven't found the solution, although I'm close. I've thought about a couple more things I should try before I review my theoretical concept."

"You think your theory is unsound?"

Torver heard the panic in his voice. "Everything's possible. In research like this, it's normal to go down the wrong path every so often. You just have to backtrack and start at the point you knew was correct then try another avenue."

"Barcina's xylopoiesis is a horrible disease, Torver."

"You know," he said as if he hadn't heard the comment or the break in Laslo's voice, "when you hired Demetria Greyson, you definitely lucked in. She was right there with the answers I needed when I needed them. That's why I could work so fast. She's a perfectionist."

Laslo turned back to him. He frowned, obviously confused by the change of topic. "So? I'd think that would be a good thing."

"Well, see, from your perspective, maybe it shouldn't be. I asked her to do hierarchies so I could backtrack the development of the disease. She was very thorough. Went so far as to check medical files before people were given Identicodes, and surprise, surprise, you know what she found? Somehow, all genetic material related to Barcina's xylopoiesis came from two families. It was very enlightening,"

Laslo straightened. "I've heard enough."

"Sure, but maybe Mahoud wants to know this. I'm sure he's already guessed that one of those families bears your name, Mr. Radic. But do you know what else she found out? She discovered that your son is next in line to develop the disease, probably in the next few years. That's why you've been so anxious about this research, and why you wanted me back here. If you hadn't had a personal stake in this, I'd probably be sharing a cell with Demetria right now."

Laslo seemed to deflate like a plasmer balloon. "It's already started."

"Yeah, I thought as much," Torver said.

"The disease. They..." Laslo visibly swallowed then hid his face in his hand for a few seconds. When he raised his head, his features were stark with anguish. "The surgeon amputated both of his feet yesterday."

Torver heard Mahoud swear softly behind him and felt a twinge of guilt at what he was about to do. Laslo turned his back to them and stared out at the night.

"So you see," he said, his voice cool once more, "I need you here. You have to find the solution to the retrogene, and soon. Otherwise, my son will die."

"I can understand your hurry, Laslo. But there's more to this little charade, isn't there?"

"Isn't that enough?"

"Not when you send six armed personnel to get me. You knew someone was after us, and you know why."

"I don't care about any of that. All I care about is my son."

"You'll have to start to care. I made a promise, but I didn't say how I was going to carry it out."

Laslo turned and stared at him. "A promise."

"Yeah." Torver chuckled, but there was no humor in it. "Now that I think of it, Demetria has another fault besides being a perfectionist. She's unbending as a steel rod."

"We're back to Ms. Greyson again," Mahoud said. He skirted around Torver's chair, walked around Laslo's desk to stand beside him, and crossed his arms. "You want to make a deal."

Laslo turned back to the two of them.

"You got it right the first time." Torver drummed his fingers on the arm of the chair. "We haven't discussed yet who kidnapped Demetria and why. In a sense, it's connected to me, and it's connected to you, Laslo. And that connection is Gerry Sinclair." When Laslo blinked but said nothing, Torver continued. "Vincent Francis left Demetria incriminating data that someone wants back. I had a look, and they bear an uncanny resemblance to my own retrogene process. There were only two people who were aware of what I was doing in GeneTech. You, Laslo—but stealing my research would be counterproductive; you have a vested interest in my success. Then there's Dr. Sinclair, who's willing to perform illegal activities for you, no doubt for reasons of his own. Gerry steals my technique, tries to adapt it for one of the drug lords of the Three States. While he's busy bastardizing my research, his boss—the other one, not you—realizes that my retrogene has more than curative potential." He stopped and cleared his throat. "How am I doing so far?"

Mahoud nodded. "Not bad, although you seem to know a lot for someone who wasn't here."

Torver grinned. "If I told you how I managed that you wouldn't believe me. How did you come to the same conclusions I did?"

Laslo's grin was feral. "We have Gerry Sinclair. He was quite cooperative."

"Ah. I'm glad we don't need to discuss the alternative potential for my research. I've had enough lectures as it is. Who's holding Demetria?"

"His name is Stringer," Mahoud said. "And you're right, he's a drug lord. Very nasty."

"Hmmm. I take it that he wants Demetria because of Dr. Francis's data."

Mahoud nodded. "And he wants you to complete your research for him—with a twist. Stringer wants to sell your findings to the highest bidder."

"But the retrogene doesn't work yet, and Gerry can't fix it."

"Right."

"This is all moot," Laslo said. "Unless Stringer launches an attack against the buildings here, he can't get at you."

"How about your son?"

"We've taken precautions," Mahoud said. He shot a glance at Laslo over his shoulder. "You don't have to worry about him."

"So." Torver got up from the chair and walked around Laslo's desk to face him. "You want me to finish the research."

"Are you saying you won't?"

"It all depends."

"How about you slowly back away?" Mahoud suggested to him, his tone neutral. "I think we all need some space."

Torver stared at Laslo. He felt the pull to enter Laslo's eyes again but resisted. Slowly, he took one step back, then another.

"As Mahoud said earlier, you'll have to deal for your son's life."

"He's innocent in all this."

"So is Demetria."

Laslo glared at him for a moment then gave him a quick nod. "What do you want?"

"I'll work on the retrogene and fix the glitches as fast as I can. While I'm doing that, you'll find out where they took Demetria and you'll work out a way to get her back."

"The retrogene for the woman, is that it?"

"Not quite," Torver said with a faint smile. "You'll have to bring your son here."

"Come on, Lockwood," Mahoud said, for the first time showing irritation, "the kid has gone through a traumatic experience. He needs to stay in the Health Center."

"Just a minute, Ashar," Laslo said. "I'm curious to know why Torver wants me to bring Zelimir here."

"Simple." Torver shrugged. "All of us here are aware of the potential for destruction from my research. To tell you the truth, a week ago I wouldn't have cared. I never believed a scientist should worry about ethical issues or the way his research is used by others. That way of thinking stifles creativity and paralyses to the point of nonproductivity.

"Today, however, I feel different. Taking the results of my research out of here is too great a risk. Once I've solved the problem, I'll make the retrogene for your son and implant it myself. Besides, if something goes wrong, I'll need to act quickly and that means I'll need my lab equipment. Considering the illegal nature of the endeavor, I can't very well ask to use the Health Center's facilities. The best solution is to bring your son here."

"He'll need medical staff to oversee his condition."

"That's not my concern, Laslo. You can find a doctor who's willing to turn a blind eye to the method we'll use to cure your son." Torver's smile broadened. "Unless you want me to simplify matters and have a chat with the two Mungers snooping around here."

"How did you—" Mahoud stopped when Laslo lifted a hand. He pursed his lips. "I was told you were strange."

"I hate to disappoint," Torver said. "Are we agreed, then?"

"What if we're too late to bring back Ms. Greyson?"

"You won't be, now, will you?"

Silence fell in the room. Torver could hear the others' breathing—Mahoud's slow and deep, Laslo's quick and shallow.

"Why the hell is Ms. Greyson so important to you?" Laslo said.

Torver looked into the night. For the first time he realized that the glass did not reflect the light from the room but absorbed it. He could make out the vague shapes of buildings outside. He thought about his sister, and the one thing they had in common—they both felt comfortable surrounded by the dark. Come to think of it, they were also two solitary people who mistrusted the world. Maybe they did have more in common than he'd first believed. He turned back to Laslo. "Let's just say that she's the only one who can stare me down."

Laslo grunted, obviously dissatisfied by the answer. Torver didn't care, as long as the man agreed with his plan. Of course, he thought, if Laslo knew all of that plan, it would take longer to convince him.

"There's only one problem," Mahoud said. "We have no idea where Stringer's headquarters are. And Gerry certainly won't talk."

"If you let me speak to him, I'll get it out of him."

"What can you do that I can't?"

Torver nearly lost his patience. They were wasting time. He moved beside Mahoud and whispered two words in his ear.

"Clone Revolt."

Mahoud flinched as if Torver had hit him, then his eyes narrowed. Whiplike, he grabbed a fistful of Torver's shirt and yanked.

"You're playing a dangerous game, my friend," he hissed in Torver's face.

"Ashar," Laslo hollered, "what the hell are you doing?"

Ashar threw Laslo a glance. "He knows about me."

Laslo blinked in surprise. "There's a difference between knowledge and proof. I thought you'd covered your tracks, anyway."

"I thought I had, too. I'm interested to know how he found out."

"Now's not the time, Ashar. I need him."

Ashar shook Torver. "Tell me."

Torver sneered. "I found out the same way I did that you didn't lift a finger to help Demetria. If you can figure how I did it, you'll have your answer."

"Take your hands off him," Laslo said. "That's an order, Ashar."

Ashar hesitated, then pushed Torver away. Laslo came to stand beside his chief of security.

"You ought to be careful who you threaten, Lockwood," Laslo said.

Torver smoothed his shirt front then shrugged. "We're wasting time. I want to see Gerry." When Laslo didn't move, he stared into his eyes. "It won't take me two minutes to get an answer from him."

Mahoud's troubled gaze shifted to Laslo. Laslo nodded once, and he strode to the office door without another word. Torver followed, Laslo behind him.

They marched down to the security offices in silence. Mahoud opened a door and motioned Torver to enter. As he did, Gerry rose from a bed molded into the wall. He smiled slightly when he saw his three visitors but said nothing. Torver looked around. The room contained a small decont unit, the bed, a table and two chairs secured to the floor. He sat down in one of the chairs and motioned Gerry to sit in the chair across from him.

Gerry grinned but remained standing. "Those two couldn't resist telling you about me, could they."

"I knew before I got here. I had a chance to study Vincent Francis's data."

"Ah." Gerry crossed his arms. "Tell me, could you do what I did and succeed?"

"Yes. You approached it from the wrong angle."

"I see. So, why the party?"

"Your boss kidnapped my statistician," Laslo said. "I want to know where they're holding her."

"That would be Ms. Greyson. She should be more careful when choosing her friends and acquaintances. They seem to bring her bad luck."

"The way I see it," Mahoud said from behind Torver, "you're the one with the bad luck."

"Stringer's priorities are different now," Laslo said. "I bet he won't bother with a lightweight geneticist who can't deliver."

"So what are you going to do? If you hand me over to MGRC, I can tell them a lot about your operation and this little project of yours. And they'll probably offer me immunity in exchange for information that would stop Stringer's operation. You'd be ruined, and I'd walk free. The way I see it, we're at a standstill."

"So, you're the one who called the Mungers," Laslo said.

"I've always believed in hedging my bets."

"Why don't you sit down for a while, Gerry," Torver said. "Maybe we could negotiate."

"Negotiate what? You surprise me, Lockwood. I took you for the cold-fish type."

"I strive to be. This kidnapping is playing havoc with my schedule. I need my statistician back."

"Then wait. Stringer will contact you." He slanted a glance at Laslo. "One boss or the other, what's the difference?"

"You fucking little weasel," Laslo said as he advanced towards Gerry. "I'll break your neck."

Torver bit back his impatience. If he wanted to find out where they held Demetria, he needed Gerry's co-operation. He lifted a hand to stop Laslo.

"I do have some negotiating strength," Torver said, his voice just soft enough to bring Gerry's attention back to him. "MGRC would be very interested in your past activities. Especially those from ten years ago?"

Gerry stopped smiling and shifted his stance. "You're bluffing."

"Maybe. Or maybe I have proof that you had a nice set-up where you genetically manipulated fertilized human cells on demand. Except you weren't making the babies more intelligent or prettier. You were creating babies with low intelligence or with the criminal gene, then you accelerated their growth so they'd be adults in half the time. You made a bundle with a couple of slave traders who sold to mercenary camps, until they got caught. The authorities never captured the scientist responsible. Maybe I have proof that scientist was you."

Gerry had gone pale and sunk down on the edge of the bed. "Impossible," he whispered. "No one knew about that."

"I found out, didn't I? If I give MGRC the proof to convict you, you know what will happen, don't you? They'll go for maximum sentence—partial lobotomy. They'll leave your memories, your knowledge intact, but you won't be able to do anything. They'll use you to perform menial work while you remember what you once were. You'll be poor, Gerry. Poor and a nobody." He saw Gerry shudder. "Now, why don't you tell us where Stringer's headquarters are? In exchange, I won't give you to the Mungers."

Gerry rose slowly. He gazed at the three of them in turn. Mahoud's face was impassive, but Laslo's registered profound disgust. Torver stared back at Gerry, a slight smile on his lips.

In the face of their common will, Gerry finally nodded and sat down at the table. "I'll need a map of the metropolis," he said.

Mahoud glanced at Torver speculatively then called up a map on his handheld and passed it to Gerry.

"I'll leave you to your planning, gentlemen," Torver said. "I have work to do."

He left the room while Gerry, flanked by Laslo and Mahoud, pointed out Stringer's headquarters and explained its access in a dead monotone.

## Chapter Thirty

Persistent throbbing at the back of her head brought Demetria back to consciousness. She opened her eyes and shifted her head. Instantly, the world started to spin. She groaned and worked on pushing back the nausea. A deep breath made her head pound harder, but it helped her swallow the sour taste that rose up her throat.

Through the pounding in her head a low hum intruded, then the sour oily smells of metal and grease. Her cheek was stuck to the cheap elastomer of a seat. A vehicle, then. She rolled a shoulder; her hands were cuffed behind her. A rustle of clothing told her there was someone beside her.

Then she remembered—the struggle, people shooting, being dragged out of her mother's house. Bile rose again.

The people who had killed Vincent had taken her.

The metallic taste in her mouth almost choked her, until she realized it was blood. She must have bitten her tongue in the struggle. If she was still bleeding, it meant she hadn't been out for very long. She pushed the panic down. The trick was to control her breathing, exhaling on a very low hum through half-open lips. She was good at that—she'd done it countless times through her vocal scanning.

After a moment she felt calmer. The wild pulse at the back of her head receded to a dull ache. She opened her eyes slowly again. When the nausea didn't return, she pushed herself up. The seat moved with her. The seatbelt held her fast, and with her hands tied behind her, she had limited movement.

She was in the back, and a guy beside her cradled a rifle in his arms. She looked up front and met the eyes of her abductor in the mirror. It was the man who'd hit her. Demetria twisted and looked in the back.

Torver wasn't there. Maybe he got away, or they hadn't had time to grab him. They'd been interrupted by some other people, also shooting guns. Or maybe they'd simply killed him. She searched her feelings frantically, sure that somehow she'd know if Torver were dead. She felt nothing one way or the other. So much for her visions and her connection to him.

Where had he been, anyway? The last time she'd seen him, he was standing in the middle of the living room.

"Where are you taking me?" she said.

The driver's gaze did not waver from the road in front of him.

"What is it you want from me?"

He stayed mute.

As if I didn't know, she thought. She leaned into the seat and closed her eyes. She'd learn soon enough who this man worked for. In the meantime, she'd try to regain as much strength as possible. She resumed her humming.

Just before she sank deep into a trance, she wondered if Torver knew where she was and, if he did, whether he would try to rescue her.

Her guard startled her awake with a push of his gun and propelled her outside before she was fully alert, then half-dragged, half-pushed her into a dingy house. Still, she had time to glance around. The van had stopped in an area of town she didn't know. All she saw were old dirty facades with grimy windows and littered sidewalks.

The front of the house was two stories high, a solid surface with small barred windows and an undersized door. She stopped short in the hall, amazed at the contrast between the seedy exterior and the lavish interior.

A crystal chandelier at least two meters long dripped from the ceiling; fully lighted, it hung over a pond in which trickled a fountain of bubbling clear water. Koi the size of her upper arm swam lazily around, their golden-red scales shining under the illumination. The air was humid and smelled of damp earth and flowers. Around the room, plants of all descriptions were arrayed in terra cotta planters set on a ceramic tile floor of the same color. She had the surreal impression of having stepped into Henri Rousseau's *Rêve*—all that was missing was a naked woman lying on a couch—but she knew what she was seeing was dangerous. Everything living in this room had to have been acquired illegally.

Her abductor removed her handcuffs then grasped her wrist and pulled her up a set of gleaming wooden stairs through a brightly lit corridor to a door near the end. The panel glided open soundlessly. A blast of frigid air hit her head-on and instantly chilled the sweat on her body. She clamped her teeth together to prevent them from chattering and squinted to see inside, but the room was in almost total darkness.

"Ah, Argus," a soft male voice said from the back of the room, "You brought Ms. Greyson with you, I see. Dr. Lockwood?"

Demetria glanced at the man called Argus and saw an imperceptible shake of his head.

"Someone was there at the same time we were. I got three men down."

"Dead, I hope?"

Argus nodded. "I detonated their pacemakers."

"Good. Who was there?"

"My guess is Radic's people."

"They were after Dr. Lockwood."

"They sure didn't make much of an effort to free *her*." Argus pushed Demetria across the threshold. She stumbled a little but caught herself. "When they saw I didn't have Lockwood, they didn't chase after me."

"Hmmm. Find out where he is."

Almost immediately, Demetria heard the soft hiss of the door closing. She backed up against it, trying to see in the near-dark. A pale ray of light indicated a heavily curtained window to her right. As her eyes became accustomed to the semidarkness, she began to see shapes. Two chairs close to her. A wide, flat surface that would be a desk, and someone very large sitting behind it.

"As clichéd as it sounds," the voice from behind the desk said, "it's true that good help is hard to find. Too bad he's my cousin. It's so difficult to get rid of relatives, don't you think?" She heard the man sigh. "I wish MGRC hadn't banned biodroid research. I could have a perfect extension of my own body. No more mistakes. Once I have Dr. Lockwood's co-operation, maybe I'll get him to design one for me."

The longer she stayed in the dark, the more her imagination ran wild. She decided to go on the attack.

"What's with the dark room? If you're trying to intimidate me, it's not working."

Sharp light blinded her. She raised her arm in front of her eyes to reduce the glare and tried to see who was at the back of the room.

"I congratulate you, Ms. Greyson. Most women would be hysterical at this point."

"You don't have a very good opinion of my sex, Mister...?"

"Just Stringer, please. I don't have a good opinion of most people. No backbone."

He had turned on the room's overhead light. As her eyes adjusted to the new level of illumination, she gaped at the man behind the desk then at her surroundings.

"You do like red, don't you?" she said.

The fat man behind the desk chuckled. "All original materials, of course. I'm especially proud of the velvet." He swept with his arm to encompass the room. "You're probably one of the few who can appreciate the items here, Ms. Greyson."

Demetria forced herself to come away from the door and cross to the drapes. She stroked the soft material. It felt like sandpaper in her hand.

"Very nice." She skimmed the gleaming top of a Hepplewhite secretary desk and caressed one of the two early Adams open chairs flanking it. "Although somewhat mixed in periods," she added.

Stringer smiled genially. "Bravo. You do know your antiques. I'm told you're quite the collector yourself."

She turned to face him. "You've been in my apartment."

"Don't worry, Argus was very careful not to break anything—he knows I value antiques. I was delighted to know we had that much in common."

"I doubt that will ever make us bosom buddies."

"You know what they say—'Know thine enemy.'"

"I'm not your enemy. In fact, until now, I didn't even know you existed."

"Anyone who prevents me from achieving my goals is an enemy. You have something I want, yes?"

Demetria suppressed a shudder. Calm, she thought, stay calm. "I don't know. What?" She went to one of the chairs across from Stringer's desk and held on to its back.

"You have interesting friends, Ms. Greyson. Of course..." His voice softened even more. "...one of them is dead. Unfortunate, especially since Dr. Francis had a glowing future ahead of him."

Demetria forced herself to stay silent. A rivulet of sweat, cooled by the room temperature, trickled between her breasts. She shivered.

"It's a small world, Ms. Greyson. By some strange turn of fate, you're also involved with Dr. Lockwood. I've been trying to get hold of him. I want to make him a job offer."

"I have no idea where he is." That much was true.

"No matter. Argus will locate him. That was very clever, the way you slipped through his fingers."

"Thank you."

"And your mother was Carlotta Danterini."

Demetria couldn't help the faint smile that came to her lips. Stringer's tone had become reverent.

"Incontestably the most talented artist of this century," he continued. "I have every piece of music she ever recorded. Do you know I saw her once in concert—what was it, twenty years ago? It was in Bonn. To learn that she is not with us anymore..." His eyes glistened with tears. He sniffled once, patted them with the back of his hand then gestured to one of the chairs.

"Please, have a seat, Ms. Greyson. Argus will return in an hour or so, I suspect. While we're waiting, I'll order some tea—I have a very nice Lapsang you'll like—and you can tell me about your mother. Maybe you'll give me some little known detail I can boast about later, hmmm?"

Demetria bit her lip and regarded Stringer for a moment. His changes of mood scared her more than the threat of violence. She should keep him talking, to give Torver time to find her. She'd know if he tried—he'd enter her lifepath and she'd feel him. She took a deep breath and repeated her mantra—keep calm. Other people knew she'd been taken. If he didn't know already, Torver would be told.

She sat in the red tapestry chair.

He would come for her.

She hoped.

MAHOUD WATCHED ARGUS ENTER THE HOUSE. THE INFRARED BINOCULARS HAD EASILY picked up the signal and the few seconds' wait before the big man approached the front door. That meant he needed to turn off some kind of security system before he entered the house and the code was included in his Identichip.

The roof of the building was also well protected with motion sensors that picked up anything bigger than a football. Plasma rifles complemented the sensors. The equipment was barely visible in the feeble streetlight, left weak on purpose, he was sure, but he knew what to look for. His survival had often depended on detecting the traps others had laid for him.

He'd fought his way from east to west, across the Pacific and the European States, until he'd met up with a young Laslo Radic, who didn't care that Mahoud was an escaped clone. He'd made Mahoud his chief of security and in the process had given him and his friends a new life. That was the only reason he'd refrained from damaging Lockwood. He owed Radic.

Now Laslo wanted him to get the woman who would ensure Lockwood's co-operation and save his son, and he would do his best to get her.

He surveyed the houses on each side of Stringer's and those across the street from it. Slowly, he pieced together the security measures. He shook his head. Even with a whole squadron of shock troops, a direct attack would be nearly impossible.

He backed away from his hiding spot, ran to his hover-rig and aimed it in the direction of GeneTech.

STRINGER'S CUP STOPPED MIDWAY TO HIS LIPS. THE DAINTY CHINA LOOKED EVEN MORE delicate in his ringed, pudgy hand. At any moment, Demetria thought, the cup would be crushed.

She'd been surprised that Stringer really wanted to talk about her mother. At first, she'd been angry at the game he was obviously playing; then she'd fed on that anger, because it was more manageable than fear.

"Argus," Stringer said as he put the cup back into the saucer. Demetria turned around to see her abductor standing in the doorway. "What news?"

"Lockwood is at GeneTech. So is Sinclair."

Stringer looked back at Demetria. "Your Mr. Radic is mounting quite a collection."

"Mr. Radic is only a client."

"So he is. Unfortunate for you, since his willingness to help you might be limited. So. We'll start with Dr. Francis's data. Where are they?"

"I don't know what you mean."

Stringer glanced at Argus and nodded. Argus moved behind her, yanked back her hair. She gasped.

"What have you done with the data?" Stringer asked again.

She shook her head. Her eyes watered from the pain.

"Very well. We'll deal with that later. Right now you'll call Dr. Lockwood for me and ask him to join my team." He tapped a few times on his desk and pointed to the far wall, which split in two to reveal a gleaming laboratory. "As you can see, he'll have the latest facilities at his disposal. I still have one Termite left, if he wants to experiment. If it's not enough, we could pick up a few dustheads. You could tell him that."

Demetria swallowed convulsively and shook her head again. Stringer smiled. She shivered.

"Look at it from my point of view, Ms. Greyson. Dr. Lockwood might just be waiting for the right sponsor. I don't think it's fair that you decide for him."

The wall slid back and shut away the lab. The red room darkened.

Stringer stared at her without speaking, his plump fingers crossed over his midriff.

"I wasn't aware that you'd contracted Brett's dermophagia until I saw you. Your prosthesis is well done, although far from perfect. It's the left side, isn't it? I can barely see the seam in this light. Isn't that true, Argus?"

Whatever passed between the two, Demetria did not see. Her heart jumped against her ribs.

"I heard that the connections between your own skin and the prosthesis are quite fragile. Once damaged, they are extremely difficult to repair, if not impossible." Stringer paused, a look of concern pasted on his face. "It would be a shame if that happened, wouldn't it? You have such a pretty face."

Demetria found it difficult to breathe. She understood the threat, feared the pain. She had no illusion she was dead, regardless, but she wasn't prepared for torture.

Then the image of Vincent's body, crawling with flies, appeared in her mind. She lifted her chin in defiance.

"How sad." Stringer nodded at the man behind her.

Argus released her hair. His hand landed on her right shoulder and squeezed. She felt the bones move under his grip and groaned. Before she could react, he pinched her left cheek and yanked.

Pain exploded in a shower of red stars. She slipped into oblivion.

TORVER JUMPED, NEARLY FALLING OFF HIS SEAT. SOMETHING HAD JERKED HIM FROM HIS concentration. He listened carefully. He was still alone in his lab and silence surrounded him, but he felt uneasy, sluggish, as if someone had awakened him in the middle of a dream.

Despite his discomfort, he went back to his scope. He'd decided to refine the plan he'd worked out with Demetria, and for that, he'd used the authorization code he'd stolen from her. She'd probably kill him if she found out, but at this point he didn't care. All that counted was to make sure those who had taken her paid for it.

He was realistic enough to accept the strong possibility she wouldn't come out of Stringer's headquarters alive. His anger was focused now. He'd devised a small addition to their plan that would neutralize Stringer forever. Maybe he'd include Gerry in it, too. The man was nasty enough in his own right.

Vincent's data and Mahoud's secret had given him the idea. If he saw Demetria again—not if, he corrected himself, when—she might be pleased to learn that Vincent's last efforts had led to what he'd wanted.

So, this plan had better work.

He got up and checked the results of his retrogene research on the holonet.

He rotated the gene combination, studied it for a moment then grimaced. No luck. Have to backtrack again, he thought.

The noise of the door gliding open made him turn. Laslo and Mahoud came in then locked the door behind them.

"My son will be here in two hours," he said. "We'll install him in the room beside your lab."

"How about the Mungers?"

"They've been through this section already," Mahoud said. "There's no reason for them to come by here again."

"Lockwood's right," Laslo said. "We don't want them snooping around here. Why don't you ask Taps or Souko to give them a tour of the cybernated plants tomorrow? It should keep them busy for a while."

"No problem."

"Did you find Stringer's place?" Torver frowned. The uneasy feeling increased. "Something's going on out there."

Mahoud shook his head. "It's a fortress. There's no way we can get in. Not with the equipment we have."

"Then it's up to me."

"Not a good idea."

"He's going to ask for me. Vincent's data are important to Stringer, but he'd be able to cover his tracks, eventually. What he can't do is build a retrovirus, the counterpart of my retrogene."

"You're not going anywhere," Laslo said.

Torver studied Laslo for a minute. "I still haven't found the solution." He turned to Mahoud. "If I can get you inside, will you be able to get Demetria out?"

"You'd have to breach their security. We can keep them busy while you do that." He paused. "If you can do it."

Torver lifted a hand when he saw that Laslo was about to protest. "I'll take care of your son first. But I want your guarantee that you'll honor your side of the bargain."

Laslo's eyes narrowed. Then he turned to Mahoud. "You're the one who will put your life on the line."

Mahoud shrugged.

Laslo nodded. He turned to Torver and said, "We still have a deal."

"Fine. Then get out of my lab. I have work to do."

As soon as they were gone, Torver sat on his bench and took out Demetria's picture. She'd know when he entered her lifepath. Hopefully, it would tell her that he was trying to help—he needed a way to communicate with her.

He held the picture firmly in his hand and stared into her eyes. He was inside without encountering the resistance he'd felt the last few times. He frowned. He remembered the sense of uneasiness he'd felt a few minutes ago. What could have caused it. Was it related to her?

He knew she was alive, because her lifepath was still accessible. Only one thing to do, he told himself. Go see what she's doing.

The other side of the picture was a mass of confusion. Two lifepaths were tightly wound around Demetria's, nearly choking it. He touched one and focused. The image of the man who'd shot him while they were fleeing Vincent's house appeared. He touched the other, and a grossly obese man appeared in front of him. He decided that must be Stringer.

Torver forced himself to concentrate on Demetria's lifepath. He peered at a relatively calm area beyond the coils and an image sprang into view. Right away he was in front of it, but the scene didn't make sense.

Then he understood—Demetria had entered another one of her visions.

## Chapter Thirty-one

THE BUILDINGS WERE BLEEDING.

Those were the only words Demetria could fit to the image in front of her. It seemed that all the skyscrapers in the world had been plucked by a giant hand and dropped together like sticks in a jar. Their tops angled outward in a circle, their bodies crisscrossed each other at the base or midpoint. Some stood planted straight in the center.

And they were all bleeding.

At first, she thought it was a trick of the light, maybe the sunrise or sunset reflecting on metal and glass. Then, she realized it was midday. On the structure closest to her, a rust-colored trail trickled down the side like a tear along a cheek. Dark red liquid gushed from the top of another building and ran down the windows on two sides, so fast it created ripples against the frames. Rosy bubbles and pink foam frothed at the edges of the flow.

Demetria went to the brink of the glassed-in platform on which she stood and craned her neck to look down at the ground. A dark-red stain had begun to pool around the base.

She heard a small gliding sound behind her that brought on its heels a sickly sweet smell that made her gag. She turned. On the floor, off-center of the platform, a trapdoor had opened. She looked through it.

The hole opened directly to the bottom of the building, hundreds of meters down. On all sides, the landscape below seemed deformed, as if giant concave mirrors distorted the view. She swayed towards the opening, suddenly dizzy, and caught herself just before she fell. She peered at the buildings. If anything, the flow of blood—if it was blood—had increased.

She sat on the floor and frowned. Why am I here? she wondered. She remembered what blood in a vision meant—loss of energy, a warning that your life was out of balance. But she wasn't the one who was bleeding. Rather, she was protected in an enclave; it seemed that the rest of the world was suffering while she watched. Why high-rises? What was the message? She frowned. What was creating those wounds?

Demetria considered the trapdoor for a few moments then crawled to its edge. The smell of blood was stronger now and made her gag. She forced herself to look down. The platform was held, off-center, by a long pole that rose from the ground. A dozen meters down, she noticed a flash of yellow. Those were flowers, she realized, a garden full of them on a ledge extending from the building opposite her platform. Along one side of the garden a long and narrow footbridge jutted out from a window and stopped at the pole. It hadn't yet been covered with blood and glinted in the sun.

If she could slide down the pole, she might be able to cross that bridge to the building with the yellow garden.

Then what? She would only be closer to drowning in blood. Yet she was certain the footbridge and its garden were important.

She searched for another means of leaving the platform. The footbridge was the only path that connected her to any of the other buildings.

There was only one problem. To reach the pole, she'd have to hang off the edge of the trapdoor and throw herself out into empty space for a couple of meters. If she missed, she'd freefall into a lake of blood.

Demetria rose, scanned her surroundings. Most of the buildings were now covered with rust-colored or bright-red liquid. Soon every window, cement block and supporting beam would be concealed under the stuff. She'd be stuck on the platform.

She walked to the trapdoor and knelt facing the pole. Slowly, careful not to look down, she bent over the hole and placed her hands on opposing sides, then leaned her weight on her forearms. In as smooth a movement as possible, she swung her legs into the hole. She waited, half-in, half-out. Fortunately, she realized suddenly, there was no wind up here.

*Now comes the tricky part.* She pushed up, let go of the sides and grabbed the edge in front of her. The weight of her body forced a groan out of her, but her grip held. She hung there, eyes fixed on the pole. Gently at first, then with more force, she rocked her feet back and forth. With every swing, she could feel her grasp on the edge slip a little. The muscles in her arms and shoulders ached. Her fingers started cramping. *Almost there.*

Her hands slipped off the edge. She yelled and lunged forward. The pole seemed too far away. She wouldn't make it. She stretched as far as she could.

One hand wrapped around the pole. She jerked to a stop and slammed into it.

Reflexively, her legs closed around the pole, but it didn't stop her from sliding down. The windows of the building facing her flew by. Too fast. She squeezed her legs, tightened her arms. She slowed but not enough. Her arms burned from the descent.

She crash-landed onto the bridge. Dazed, she lay on her back.

It was the stench that revived her. Her stomach heaved, and she sat up to vomit over the edge of the decking. Exhausted, she pushed herself up on all fours and raised her head towards the building with the yellow garden. It had also begun to bleed, and the stronger smell emanated from it. She had to enter it before it was completely covered with the blood.

She trod across the footbridge, resolutely keeping her eyes on the yellow flowers. When she arrived at the end, the window was sealed shut.

She heard a gurgle and looked up. A drop of blood the size of a truck was hurtling towards her. She jumped back. The liquid plopped on the bridge, splattering her. Everywhere it fell, it bubbled and hissed and smoked. The droplets singed her skin. She rubbed them off and they fell away like embers.

There was now a gaping hole between her and her goal, but the splatters of blood had also melted the window. Demetria backed up a couple of meters, took a deep breath and let it out slowly. This is where all her running would pay off, she assured herself.

She skipped once and began a loping run. The gap in the bridge came before she was ready. It was either stop or jump. She pushed away, raised her arms in front of her and dove at the melted window. Behind her, she heard the hiss of blood falling on the bridge, then a crack, then she was inside. As soon as she hit the floor, she folded and rolled until something sharp stopped her. She looked up. Above her head loomed a DNA double helix.

She stood and inventoried her condition. Her lower back hurt. Her arms were raw, her skin burnt in places, her hands blistered. She was so tired she could barely walk, and one of her ankles ached. She must have twisted it when she dove in.

She hobbled to the window. The bridge and garden were gone and so was the platform. If she'd stayed up there, she'd have been incinerated and very dead.

She turned back to the room and stopped in surprise. It was filled with parts of the double helix, as if it had been cut up in pieces. Upon closer examination, she found there was some organization to it. The pieces, although tightly packed, stood in pairs. She realized she was inside a cell's nucleus and the organized pairs must be DNA strands segregated into chromosomes.

Then she thought it wasn't quite true. Maybe it was only a representation of a cell nucleus. Instead of tightly packed molecules, the DNA ladder had flat, four-sided rungs separated in the center, but each cylindrical helix had a compact appearance, as if they'd grown out of the floor in one solid piece.

It's almost like strolling in my forest, she thought, looking at the upright ladders that twisted towards the ceiling like the trunks of majestic trees.

The thought was barely out of her head when the DNA strands changed into trees. The room in which she'd landed disappeared. The blood-encrusted buildings faded, and the blinding light changed into the soft muted luminosity of twilight. In front of her, through a clearing, she could make out her own building. The trees were larger than the ones she knew, only there were no birch or pines—just maple trees. She squinted in the fading light. Someone had drilled a hole in each of the trees, and sap leaked out, the rivulets taking on shades of red from the sunset.

When she stepped towards one of the trees, she tripped. At her feet, now scattered by her stumble, were conic pieces of wood. She picked up one, studied it, then looked at the tree closest to her. A plug, she decided. She marched to the tree and inserted it in the hole. It fit perfectly.

The scene wavered, and she was back in the DNA room. Her hand held a piece that fitted perfectly over a sequence of one of the strands. When she withdrew her hand, the sequence at the right of the plug began to glow. She backed away, uncertain of what would happen.

What would Torver say about that, she wondered.

At the thought of her brother, she suddenly knew he was there in her head, observing. Out of sheer reflex, she pushed him away.

She heard the mental gasp, then felt a wrenching that pierced her chest and slashed at her breath. She lost consciousness again.

Stupid, you needed him, she thought just before black night overtook her.

TORVER SLAMMED BACK INTO HIS CHAIR AS IF SOMEONE HAD SLUGGED HIM.

"I wish you'd stop doing that," he said to Demetria's picture. He rubbed his temples at the headache coming on. "Damn." He hadn't learned anything significant. He still didn't know where she was held in Stringer's compound, or what Stringer had done to her.

"That was some weird vision, sister," he muttered. "At least now you know I'm looking for you."

He shoved the picture in his pocket and turned back to his work. He'd been gone for less than ten minutes, although it had appeared to last much longer. He tried to concentrate on the new results but parts of Demetria's vision kept intruding.

"Okay," he said to the air in front of him, "if I assume Demi's right and her visions have something to do with me, I might as well try to make sense of it. Let's start with the obvious. She's been working with DNA data, so that's how the helixes got in there. The yellow flowers were obviously Laslo's garden. But how did she know he had a garden? She's never been here." He shrugged. "The buildings that bled—that, I can't figure. And the DNA that became trees, and the stopper that plugs the leak that changes into a block of base pairs—" He stopped in mid-sentence, his mouth hanging open. He closed it with a snap. "Impossible." He chuckled, then laughed.

"What's so funny, Lockwood?"

He turned to find Laslo standing in the doorway. He laughed harder. "Trees. I got the solution from trees in a crazy vision."

"Are you going nuts on me?"

"Nope. I just have to find the right plug, that's all. It shouldn't take long with the holonet's Probability Modeling Protocol."

Laslo advanced inside the lab. "You have the solution?"

"I'll tell you one thing, Laslo. You owe this solution to Demetria. She's the one who gave me the key I needed."

Laslo's fists tightened. "You've been in contact with her."

Torver smiled. "I haven't talked to her, if that's what you mean. Let's say I sort of read her mind, although she usually objects to that form of communication." He raised his hand at Laslo's confused frown. "Never mind. Remember I told you about how I thought the introns were affected by the ancient DNA? Well, all I have to do is design a type of plug, a repressor. It's so simple I never saw it. The repressor will impede the operation of the introns and will let the retrogene do its job. Simple and elegant." He laughed again.

He saw Laslo hesitate then nod. "I'll leave you to it." Just before he left the lab, he turned. "My son is here. He's not doing well, Lockwood. The amputations have depressed him, and he refuses to talk. We're not certain if it's because he's lost his speech or because of the depression. For his sake, hurry."

"I'm doing the best I can, Laslo. I hope you're doing the same for Demetria."

"I'm sorry," Argus said to Stringer, "we can't seem to bring her back."

"Your treatment of her was too rough."

"No. She's not unconscious, she's just...not there."

"Show me."

A bare room with a single cot against the wall appeared on the vidscreen on Stringer's desk. Demetria sat on it, her eyes fixed in front of her. He zoomed in on her face.

He could barely recognize the woman who'd been brought to him. The left side was swollen and purple; crusted blood rusted in places. Her jaw and neck looked thick and raw. Her left eye was swollen shut. She should be groaning in pain or unconscious. Instead, her good eye was open but had no expression, like a glass marble.

"Her body doesn't respond to any type of stimulation," Argus said. "Look at her arms. I'm not responsible for those welts. They appeared as I watched."

The insides of the woman's arms were red and puffy. "Maybe she's in a trance from the pain."

Argus's face reappeared on the desk screen. "I've assumed that you wanted to keep her alive and in relatively good shape."

Stringer sighed. "We'll wait for a while. Give her the night. She'll look worse tomorrow anyway. That should motivate Dr. Lockwood and Laslo Radic." He sat back and yawned. "A whole night to let them plan how to spring Carlotta Danterini's daughter. I can't wait to see what they come up with." He rubbed his hands together. "In the meantime, you call up Hong Feng and the SSLA. I'll take the Sun Shinri-Kyo and the Sino-Pakistanese movement. We'll start a little advance bidding auction."

# Chapter Thirty-two

THE ROOM WAS COMPLETELY DARK EXCEPT FOR A SMALL NIGHTLIGHT THAT GAVE MORE reassurance than illumination. Torver turned on the overhead beam just enough to see where he was going.

The nurse sat in a chair, fast asleep. He'd checked that the mother was out of the room, resting. The doctor had gone to the small cafeteria for a cup of coffee and some food. He had chosen this time of night carefully. He pressed a small patch on the back of the nurse's hand and waited a few seconds. She snorted once, then her chin fell forward on her chest.

He looked up and saw that the boy in the bed was watching him.

"You're supposed to be asleep," he whispered as he moved closer to the bed. He gestured to the nurse with his thumb. "Don't worry, she'll just sleep a little longer. I gave her a sedative."

The boy said nothing, just kept watching him. Torver glanced at the middle of the bed where an arc placed over the child's legs prevented the covers from touching the edge of his amputated limbs.

"Too bad about your feet," he said. "Your dad will get you some good bioprostheses, though. You won't even know the difference."

"Who...?" the boy whispered.

"Oh, sorry. I'm Torver. Your dad hired me to find a cure for your disease. And I did." He patted his shirt pocket where he'd placed the syringe with the retrogene. "Except that it's also a dangerous weapon some bad guy wants. He's holding my sister, and soon he'll want me to give him the formula in exchange for her. I don't have time to test it really well, so I thought I'd ask you what you want me to do. I could test it on you now and it could work or not. Or I could wait until after I get my sister back."

"But if you go save your sister, you won't come back, maybe?"

"Right. I'm glad you understand the problem."

"What happens...?"

"If the retrogene doesn't work? You're pretty much gone. As in dead."

"Fast?"

Torver nodded. "Very fast. It may be painful, though. I don't know."

Zelimir stared at him for a long time then at his feet. "I want..." He pointed to Torver's pocket.

"Okay. After I administer the retrogene, I'll stay with you a while, just to make sure everything's okay. Then I want you to call your doctor. He's the one who'll monitor your progress. I have to finish my plans to get my sister from the bad guys, and then I gotta get some rest. I have a feeling I'm going to need to be sharp to beat those guys."

Zelimir nodded. Torver took out the syringe and applied it to the child's arm. It homed in on a vein and pierced the skin after sending a spray of antiseptic.

"Ow!" Zelimir yelped.

Torver smiled. "It won't take a second."

He watched the liquid containing the batch of DNA-charged nanoprobes disappear slowly into Zelimir's arm. When he was finished, he put the syringe back into his pocket and ruffled the boy's hair.

"Now we wait."

He sat beside the boy and looked at the sleeping nurse. "You won't tell her I put her to sleep, will you? She was sleeping anyway."

Zelimir, his eyes closed but a small smile on his face, shook his head. He looked so small in the bed, a little patch of rosy skin against the white sheets. Torver closed his own eyes and relaxed. If anything was to happen, it would likely be within the first half-hour, when the body rejected the treatment.

The room was quiet, with only the nurse's snuffles and Zelimir's slight breathing—Laslo had had all the monitoring equipment installed in the next room so the usual beeps and swooshes were absent. It was restful, and Torver felt he needed to think of nothing for a while, just float.

Zelimir stirred, taking him out of his light trance. He checked his wrist unit, surprised to find he'd been in the room for forty-five minutes. He got up, took the child's pulse. It seemed steady. Zelimir opened his eyes.

"How are you doing, kid?"

The boy shrugged.

"Don't feel anything, do you? That's good. Well, I hope that's good." Torver grinned. "I'd better get out of here before someone catches me. Good luck, kid. You know, if I wasn't so certain it would work, I wouldn't have tried it on you. Don't worry about a thing."

Zelimir nodded then picked up the call button. "Don't let the bad guys win," he said.

"Not a chance."

Torver left the room without looking back. It was only when he was down the hall that he realized Zelimir had spoken a full sentence. Damn if the treatment didn't work!

THE HOVER STABLES WERE DARK EXCEPT FOR A FEW SECURITY LIGHTS, WHICH CREATED more shadows than illumination. Torver sat on one of the hover-rigs that faced the door. The spot provided him with enough tangible darkness to hide his presence until he knew who would cross the threshold into the stables. He hoped Alim would get there soon—someone was bound to notice he was gone from his lab and start searching for him. The task was too simple with the tracking chip he wore. If Alim didn't show up within five minutes he'd head back and devise Plan B.

The hint from Demetria's vision had solved his problem. He'd adjusted his retrogene by adding the repressor, and just like that, his mice thrived. If he had more time, he'd do more tests, more analyses. He'd perfect the technique, just for the elegance of it. But time he didn't have.

A shuffling sound intruded into his thoughts. Alim stood in the doorway, peering into the dark room, obviously hesitant to go in.

"I was about to leave," Torver said from his post. "You barely made it."

Alim turned towards the sound and wove his way around the rigs until he found him.

"Mahoud is reluctant to let us wander alone through the buildings. He was surprised that I'd show up so late to do some work."

"How did you lose him?"

Alim's teeth flashed in his dark face. "I don't exert MGRC clout often, but this time I did. I'm sure he's lurking around somewhere, trying to figure out where I've gone and why. So, I suggest you get to the point of this meeting, Dr. Lockwood."

"It's been over two months since you took away my license. The fact that I'm here talking to you leads me to believe you haven't found anything to pin on me."

"Officer Martin is very dedicated to her job. If there's something to find, she'll find it."

"You've sounded less eager than she from the first."

Alim moved under a security lamp. His white suit appeared even brighter than in daylight.

"Don't mistake my more casual approach for a lack of fervor, Dr. Lockwood." He hesitated. "I've always found that lobotomizing our most promising scientists was counterproductive."

"There are plenty of rumors floating around that MGRC is involved in what would otherwise be called prohibited research."

"You don't expect me to admit to that, do you?"

Torver jumped onto Alim's lifepath and shuffled quickly through the memories.

"Not at this point." He moved into the light so Alim could see his grin. "But you just confirmed the rumors anyway."

"I haven't said a thing."

Torver grunted. "I have a deal for you."

"I suspected as much. And I suppose that in exchange you'll want immunity?"

"And a job."

Alim raised an eyebrow. "I don't have that kind of power."

Torver pointed to the vicinity of Alim's suit pockets. "Maybe you should clarify that detail right away with your superiors, since they're eavesdropping."

Alim gave him a rueful look and pulled out a comm piece from his pocket. He inserted it in his ear and listened for a few seconds then nodded.

"What have you got?"

"The formula for a compound that renders addiction genes detox-proof."

"Really."

"Yes. If you're willing to help, I'll deliver the formula and the people responsible for its development."

"That kind of genomic manipulation sounds more like something *you'd* be doing."

Torver shook his head. "I could. If I had, though, would I be stupid enough to give you the proof you need to put me away?"

"Who's responsible, then?"

"You'll know when you agree to my plan. I'll give you the research and the proof to put those guys away." He smiled. "I'll even throw in a way to neutralize them."

"This is MGRC business."

"Without me, you don't have anything."

"I'd have thought you'd be happy not to be involved."

"You know that carnage at the Metropolis Health Center? Dr. Francis stumbled upon secret research while performing a series of autopsies. They killed him and his team because of it. Before he died, he left the data with a friend of mine, Demetria Greyson. She didn't know what to make of the information, so she called me. I saw right away what it was."

"You should have handed everything over to us."

"Before I could talk to you, they kidnapped her. The information is encrypted, and she's the only one who has the key," he lied. "Without it, you have nothing. If they force it from her, they'll walk free with a dangerous weapon in their hands. I want my friend back. I'm sure you want the research. What do you say?"

Alim narrowed his eyes. "I say you're too smart for your own good. I have enough to bring you in."

Torver shrugged. "From what I saw of the data, the process doesn't quite work. That was confirmed when I received a job offer from the guy who owns it. You can bring me in right now, but I guarantee you that he'll find someone, somewhere, who's willing to fix it. Then you'll have a bigger problem on your hands, like trying to find someone who can undo the damage."

Alim considered him for a long moment then seemed to come to a decision. He leaned on a hover-rig and crossed his arms. "Maybe we can help each other. A sort of mutual back-scratching, if you like."

"What do you mean?"

"We've heard that a scientist has developed what someone is calling a retrovirus. It can be programmed to degrade the DNA of a group of people with a specified gene combination. It's perfect bio-terrorism—by the time you figure out who the targets are they're already dead."

Torver's heart beat so hard, he felt his ribs move. "Are you sure it's not just a rumor?"

"GommNet picked up an offer of sale two days ago. That kind of thing is not advertised without backing." Alim pushed away from the rig and closed in on Torver. The whites of his eyes shone in the dark, making him look like a blind man. "If the Sino-Pakistanese movement or the Southern States Liberation Army get hold of this retrovirus, can you imagine the chaos? It would incite world-wide panic. Government Mundial is not prepared to accept this eventuality. They've given MGRC full power to recover this weapon. We want the retrovirus, Dr. Lockwood."

"What will you do with it once you have it?"

Alim backed away slightly. His voice was very soft when he answered. "That shouldn't be your concern."

Torver thought about Demetria. She'd be really annoyed when she learned he'd been right. He could just imagine what MGRC would do with his retrogene. "All right, I'll help, but I don't see how I can."

"We need someone to buy the retrovirus. Someone with credibility, and with the knowledge to back it up."

"In other words, you need someone who knows enough to determine if what you're getting is the real thing."

"That's it."

The offer definitely complicated matters. Obviously, Alim wasn't aware that Stringer was negotiating for Demi's life with the retrogene. Torver had to keep it that way.

"Who would I buy it from?"

"We can't take the risk that the retrovirus might change hands. We'll buy it directly from the seller."

"You know who he is?"

"His name is Stringer. He's a small drug lord who happened on something big. I guess he was too excited about it to take the usual precautions about advertising the sale. That's how we picked up on it."

Torver raised his eyebrows and opened his eyes wide, trying to look stunned.

"Well." He cleared his throat. "That guy's certainly busy all of a sudden."

"What do you mean?"

"Unless there are two Stringers, he's the one with the compound formula." He grinned. "I guess that back-scratching won't be too difficult, now, will it?"

Alim frowned. "It's possible that, by trying to develop one, they happened on the other. Do you think you can get both processes from Stringer?"

"Hey, don't worry, I have a plan."

"Which includes us."

"Yes. But we do it my way. After all, I'm the one who got the job offer. Stringer's expecting me to say yes."

He crossed his fingers at the white lie. He was pretty sure Stringer would call him to offer him a job, although not for working on the dust.

"And in exchange for the dust formula and the retrovirus, you want immunity and a job."

"Yes."

Alim stared at him for a second then extended his hand, a slight smile hovering on his lips. "You've got it, Dr. Lockwood."

"Good. Here's the plan."

TORVER WAS STARTLED AWAKE. HE OPENED HIS EYES, AND LASLO'S FACE LOOMED SO CLOSE he could see the spidery red veins on each side of his nose. Laslo had him by the shirt and was shaking him.

"What did you do to my son?"

"What?" Torver tried to clear his mind sufficiently to figure out where he was. His lab. He must have fallen asleep. "What time is it?"

"I said, what did you do to my son?"

"Is he dead?"

Laslo let go of the front of Torver's shirt. "No. He's better. The doctor says the disease is regressing." He smiled without humor. "According to him, it's a damn miracle."

"Hmmm. I thought it would work a little faster."

"His mother and I should have been there when you gave Zelimir the retrogene. What if it hadn't worked?"

Torver shrugged. "Then he'd be gone. I asked your son what he wanted me to do. It was his decision to make."

"No, it wasn't. He's just a kid, you tech-head."

"He's also the one who was getting eaten alive." Torver frowned. "What's the problem, anyway? He's better."

"It's more complicated than that."

"Why, because if you'd been there you could have got your hands on some of the retrogene, so you could break it down later?"

"I paid for that research, damn it."

"And I'd say you got your money's worth."

Laslo glared at him for a moment. "What are you going to do with it?"

"It's already taken care of. Demetria and I discussed it."

"She knew about your research?"

"Only at the end, before they took her. Ironically, she didn't care about herself, only about the millions who could die because of my discovery." He waved his hand in a vague motion. "What can I say? She's a stickler about issues like making genetic weapons. She believes scientists have a social responsibility. I promised her I wouldn't put this weapon in the hands of someone who could misuse it. Like you, for instance."

"I'm not Stringer."

"That's true. But what could you do with an illegal piece of research except sell it on the black market? Demetria's right—eventually, it would end up in the wrong hands, for the wrong purpose."

"This would never have happened if you'd stayed away from her like I asked you."

"You mean I wouldn't care that she's in Stringer's hands because I wouldn't have known her?" Torver nodded. "Doesn't say much about me, does it? Or about you. It doesn't matter. Demetria and I met outside of work. I didn't know until a few days ago that she was the statistician you'd hired."

"Then why in hell is she so important to you?"

Torver shrugged. "She's my sister."

*"What?"*

"Yep." He looked directly into Laslo's eyes. "A long-lost one, I grant you, but a sister nevertheless."

"What did you do with your research?"

"Nothing. Yet." Torver tapped the side of his head. "It's all in here." And on a small encrypted disk in his pocket, but Laslo wasn't going to know that.

The door opened, and they both turned. A small, dark man stood in the entrance.

"Mr. Radic, your son would like to speak with you."

"Thank you, Doctor." Laslo turned to Torver. "Come."

Zelimir was sitting up. On the far side of the bed sat a woman with long, straight hair and a serene countenance, whom Torver guessed was Laslo's wife. At the foot, the now-awake nurse was rearranging the covers. Zelimir smiled.

"Hi, kid." Torver stopped beside him. "Feeling better?"

Zelimir glanced at the nurse then back at Torver, who shook his head slightly.

"Yeah," he said, his voice soft as if it hurt to speak, "better." He took his father's hand and squeezed. "Thanks, Dad."

Laslo nodded and blinked quickly several times. He was about to speak when Mahoud burst into the room.

"Laslo, you have a comm waiting. I think Dr. Lockwood should be there, too."

Radic nodded then stroked his son's cheek. "I'll be back. Take care of him, Jelena."

Torver looked across the bed before he turned to follow. Jelena Radic smiled at him then mouthed, *Thank you.*

He nodded and hurried out of the room.

"We'll take it in my office," Laslo said.

DEMETRIA FELT DAZED AND LOST. SHE HAD NO IDEA WHAT TIME OF DAY OR NIGHT IT WAS, OR how long she'd been Stringer's prisoner. When she came out of her vision, she'd found herself in a windowless room the size of a closet, its only furniture the cot on which she lay.

She spotted a piece of what looked like old paper beside her. Her heart skipped then contracted painfully. Her prosthesis, out of its nourishing solution, had dried into a wrinkled, sallow strip. She ran her fingers lightly along the edge of her face where it had connected. It felt swollen and was painful to the touch. Her jaw and neck also felt thick and raw. She opened her mouth experimentally. Only her right side obeyed her. She could barely see out of her left eye.

Despite the pain, her stomach rumbled. The sound made her notice the smell of coffee and something else. Soup. She peered at the door with her good eye and noticed the tray on the floor. Someone had come in and left food out for her. Her body quivered as if the aroma, overpowering in the small room, were passing through her pores like an electric current.

Slowly, she unfolded her body from the cot and placed her feet on the floor. Her ankle was swollen. Her arms ached and had a swath of burn blisters. Her hands were raw and cut in several places. Where did those come from?

*The buildings in my vision.* The blood like acid, the breakneck descent along the pole, the DNA forest. Images that kept changing, as if their appearance and their reality were different. She stared at her hands. It was the second time she'd retained physical evidence of an experience in a vision.

She puzzled over that for a moment then remembered feeling Torver before she'd lost consciousness. Those DNA helixes inside the building. Maybe Torver needed to see something in her vision. She shook her head, more to chase away the hope that Torver was looking for her than to drive out her rambling thoughts.

She picked up the tray. The soup smelled delicious and hot. The sight of the thick tofu slices and chunks of carrots and celery made her even hungrier.

Her eyes clouded and the soup turned red and bubbled and hissed. Startled, she nearly dropped the tray. She placed it very carefully at the end of the bed and sat at the opposite end, staring at it. The blood in her vision had superimposed itself on the food. A warning? Or just illusion born out of exhaustion and pain?

Stringer's face popped into her head, and with it a question. *Why would he feed me before killing me?* Her gaze fell on her prosthesis. The jostling on the bed had turned it to dust on the mattress. Dust. It reminded her of the reason Vincent had died. His data. Maybe Stringer had put some kind of truth drug in the food.

The soup lost its appeal.

She sat on the cot and leaned her back against the wall, closed her eyes. The left side of her face throbbed; she ached all over. It was difficult to think through the exhaustion. She should try to devise ways to escape, but all she could do was sit there, emotionally numb, and wait.

She didn't know how much time had passed when she heard the door to her cell open. Argus stood in the entrance.

"Come with me."

Demetria got up without a word and hobbled after him to Stringer's office. She was pleased she didn't stumble once, even when he marched her up the stairs or when he pushed her inside the crimson room.

"Ah, Ms. Greyson, how are you this morning?"

She glanced towards the red velvet drapes, but no light came through. "What time is it?"

"Quite early. I trust you had a good rest?" Stringer studied her face for an instant. "Does it hurt to talk?"

His fake concern threatened to make her sick. She swallowed down the bile that burned her throat, walked to one of the chairs and sat down.

"What do you want?"

"Argus tells me you didn't eat. I thought you'd be hungry. Pain always gives me an appetite. You didn't like the soup? Perhaps a sandwich? Cup of tea?"

Demetria nearly told him that she suspected he had drugged the food, but she changed her mind. There were more aggressive ways to administer a drug and she didn't want to give him an excuse to use one.

"Hurts too much," she said.

"Ah." Stringer looked pleased. "Well, it's time to use the comm and call your friend Dr. Lockwood. I hope for your sake, Ms. Greyson, that he'll be co-operative."

She thought he looked as if he hoped for the opposite. Argus grabbed her from behind under her armpits, pushed her to the side of the desk and held her there.

"We have a connection." Stringer slanted a smile at her. "It's your show, Ms. Greyson. I hope you'll make your dear mother proud."

As usual, Laslo sat at his desk. Torver positioned himself to his right, while Mahoud stayed out of the comm line of vision.

Torver immediately recognized the fat man from Demetria's lifepath. He was smiling broadly, which pushed up his jowls and made two thin slits of his eyes.

"Mr. Radic, Dr. Lockwood, good morning. I surmise you know who I am."

"Stringer," Radic said.

"Excellent, it simplifies matters. So nice to meet you, Dr. Lockwood, even if it's not in person. I was hoping we could have a nice chat in private."

"Don't count on it," Laslo said.

Stringer shrugged. "I'm calling to offer you a job, Dr. Lockwood. I'd like you to come work for me."

"To do what?" Torver said.

"The same thing you've been doing for Mr. Radic. You'll find that I can pay you much better."

"I doubt it."

"You'll find added incentives, too." Stringer glanced to his side. Demetria appeared beside him.

Torver gasped. Demetria's left eye was swollen shut. The muscles along the left side of her face and her neck were puffed up, almost black, patches of crusted blood lighter brown against them. The line where her prosthesis had attached was purple and red, in some places still oozing clear fluid. The front of her sweater was brownish-red from dried blood.

But her right eye was clear and fierce, and she held her head high. Torver's rage settled into stark determination.

"Hi, Demi," he said.

"I told you to stay out of my head." Her voice was firm. She was yanked away.

"You've made your point, Stringer," Torver said.

"If you want an exchange," Laslo said, "I'll trade you Gerry Sinclair for her."

Stringer chuckled. "Oh, no, keep him, please. He's my gift to you. It's Dr. Lockwood I want."

"Well, you can't have him."

Stringer stopped smiling. "Dr. Sinclair was very thorough in documenting his use of your laboratories to make my dust, Mr. Radic. It would be a shame if that information fell into the wrong hands. Your good name in the community would be somewhat sullied." He tut-tutted. "Not to mention you'd become a favorite among our law enforcement groups."

Torver put his hand on Laslo's shoulder. "It's not your problem anymore, Radic." He nodded at the vidscreen. "I'll work for you, Stringer. On one condition."

"Yes, yes, you'll want me not to kill your girlfriend."

"I want more than that. I'll need her to finish my research. That's how I got involved with her in the first place. She's the only one who can do the biometrics modeling I need to test the retrogene. So, you'd better not drug her. Or kill her."

He saw the brief look of annoyance that flitted across Stringer's face. So, he'd been right. Stringer had planned to dope Demetria, or even use her as a test subject. He shuddered internally at what brain dust could do to her. She'd never be the same, probably would lose her incredible analytical abilities.

"He's right," he heard Demetria say from the side.

He could tell she hadn't taken any dust yet. She was as crabby as ever.

Stringer turned his head in Demetria's direction. "If you insist on taking part in this conversation, Ms. Greyson, I'll have to ask Argus to silence you." He turned back to the comm. "I don't think I believe you, Dr. Lockwood."

Torver shrugged. "Why do you think Radic here wants to exchange her for Gerry? Without Demetria, I can't finish the research. Period."

"I guess we're at an impasse, Stringer," Laslo said. "We both have half of what we want."

Stringer picked up a vidstill from his desk, contemplated it for a moment then turned it around to show them a picture of Laslo with his family. "I've often thought having a family would be nice, you know, maybe have a son like yours, Mr. Radic. But children are so prone to accidents, it would've broken my heart if something happened to one of them. So here I am alone, with only Argus for company."

Torver saw Laslo pale. He felt suddenly impatient with the charade. "You've made your point, Stringer. I'll come, and Radic will let me go, as long as you abide by my condition."

"Fine, fine!" Stringer sounded like a petulant child who had just lost a favorite toy. "I want you here in an hour."

"I'll need five. I have a lot of material and data to pack up."

"I'll give you three. Argus will expect you at the Lickspittle Bar then. Otherwise," he grinned, "I'll have to start amusing myself with your girlfriend."

Laslo slapped the comm line off. "I'll kill that bastard," he said. "Nobody threatens my family."

"You brought it on yourself, Laslo," Torver said. "What did you hope to gain by bargaining with him?"

"You're not going there."

"It's none of your business what I do."

"Going into Stringer's compound is the same as giving him the formula, can't you see that?"

"He won't get it out of me."

"You're the one who mentioned drugs first," Laslo said, his voice hoarse. "He'll use them on you."

"Not if I can help it. I have a plan."

"You care to share it with us?" Mahoud said.

Torver turned to the chief of security, who'd remained silent and invisible during the exchange with Stringer. Exhausted from faking a calm he didn't feel, he walked around Laslo's desk and slumped into one of the chairs. He rubbed his eyes with the tips of his fingers and yawned.

"You'll need to call in the two Mungers snooping around your plant."

"No way." Laslo straightened and flattened his hands on his desk.

"Maybe we should hear what Lockwood has to say first."

"I may go along with this so-called plan of his, but anything that involves MGRC is out of the question. I won't jeopardize my business."

"You already did that when you hired me," Torver said.

"This is different."

"Why, because it's not your son's life that's at stake?" Torver got up from his chair and leaned on the desk, his face only a few centimeters from Laslo's. "You owe me, you sonofabitch."

"Yes, we do," a calm voice said behind him. Torver whipped around. Laslo's wife stood just inside the office.

"Jelena," Laslo said, "this is none of your business. Go back to our son."

"I just made it my business, Laslo. I hope our son never learns how heartless his father is. How can you not do everything to save this young woman?"

"You don't understand, Jelena. I could go to prison."

"Your son will live. I remember you saying it was worth the risk of being destroyed. Have you forgotten that?" She straightened. "Either you help Dr. Lockwood, or I'll go to MGRC myself."

Torver gave her a half-smile. "You and Demetria would get along very well," he said to her.

"You don't have a choice, Laslo," Mahoud said. Laslo threw him a dark look but said nothing. "Let's hear your plan, Lockwood."

"When I speak to the Mungers, I'll keep close to the truth. I'll say that Vincent Francis sent his data to Demetria. She asked me to help her interpret the information, and I found out someone was trying to modify dust to increase addiction by tampering with the genetic structure."

"Why would she call you?"

"We're friends."

"Okay," Mahoud said, "Ms. Greyson asked you to help her with Dr. Francis's data. Then what?"

"We were about to go to the authorities when Demetria was kidnapped. I came here to get some help from my boss. Stringer contacted him and said that he wanted me to finish the research for him in exchange for Demetria's life."

"Hmmm." Mahoud rubbed his five o'clock shadow absently. "Close enough to the truth. It could work."

"How about Sinclair?" Laslo said.

Torver grinned. "You could always give him back to Stringer. Free of charge."

Laslo grunted. Mahoud paced a few lengths then stopped.

"I can't penetrate Stringer's perimeter," he said, "but with their equipment MGRC can. You're giving them an incentive to do so."

"Yes."

"And in the meantime, what will you do?"

"While Stringer thinks I'm working on the retrogene, I'll plant Francis's data into his bionet. Added to Gerry's research, it should give the Mungers more than enough to convict them. If I can, I'll try to disable his security system."

"You won't be able to do that. I suspect only Argus and Stringer have the code for it. It's programmed into their Identicodes."

Torver's smile was grim. "We'll see."

Mahoud frowned, and considered him for a few moments. It was clear from his stance he knew Torver hadn't told them his entire plan. The security chief hesitated another few seconds then shrugged slightly.

"Call up the Mungers, Laslo," Torver said. "I'll need at least an hour to prepare. I'll have to bring some credible data with me to Stringer's, especially if Gerry is there with me to verify them."

Torver was placing the last of his supplies in a slim briefcase when he heard the drone of a cyber-chair. Zelimir stopped in front of him as he was sealing the case.

"Slidin' chair, kid."

"I'll use it until I get new feet."

"How fast can you go in it?"

"Pretty fast. Are you going to kill those bad guys?"

"No."

"Are you going to give them my disease, then?"

Torver raised his eyebrows. "You're a pretty smart kid. A bit ghoulish, though."

"Well, are you?"

"No. I'll give them something worse."

"What's worse than what I had?"

"A little something I concocted. They'll pray they could die." He ruffled Zelimir's hair. "Wish me luck, kid."

## Chapter Thirty-three

"READY?" MAHOUD DIRECTED THE QUESTION OVER HIS SHOULDER. Torver nodded and hung on to the rig's hand-holds. The hover-rig was faster than the bus, and they needed to make time if they wanted to get to the Lickspittle at the prescribed hour.

It was Mahoud who'd insisted on piloting the rig for Torver.

"You made a deal with MGRC, didn't you?" he had said as they strode to the stables.

"Why do you say that?"

"I lost Alim for half an hour. I bet he was with you. Besides, the Mungers were too easily convinced. You ask them to mobilize their forces to storm a drug underlord's compound and they don't even make sure your story's watertight."

"Laslo made the difference."

"Laslo can be very convincing when he plays the concerned employer and outraged citizen. Even if they'd believed him, they don't involve civilians in their operations. They should have said 'thank you very much' and disappeared. So, what's the deal?"

Torver grimaced. "I told them Stringer had the retrogene and the modified brain dust formula, but neither works at the moment. I also mentioned that Demetria had the key to the research, so it was in their best interest to get her back at the same time as the research. In exchange for delivering the two genes, they get Demetria out and I get a job with MGRC."

"I could tell them what you're really planning to do."

"You could. Then we'd both lose." Torver stopped in front of the closed stable doors and faced him. "Why are you helping me?"

"I work for Laslo."

"He got what he wanted out of me."

Mahoud crossed his arms over his chest. "What happens if MGRC buries your research? Or worse, starts using it?"

Torver shook his head. "I know one person who won't let them."

"Demetria Greyson."

"She's a formidable woman."

Mahoud waved the door opened. "So maybe I'm helping her. What's your plan to get rid of Stringer?"

To Torver's relief, Mahoud's team and MGRC contingent rejoined them at that moment, preventing the man from asking more questions.

A few kilometers down the road, after Mahoud had split from the rest of the group, they'd met up with Tomás, who was carrying Gerry Sinclair behind him, tightly handcuffed to the sidebars. Torver glanced at Gerry. The man was pale as moonlight. Everyone had been deaf to his pleas not to turn him over to Stringer. It seemed his descriptions of Gerry's past activities had been relayed to Mahoud's team, who Torver suspected were also escaped clones. Since the clones from the Clone Revolt had been subjected to accelerated growth, they probably hoped Gerry got his own. As for Laslo, by handing back Gerry he'd ensured his secrets would be kept.

And what about me? Torver thought. What did he feel for Gerry? Demetria's battered face appeared in his mind, and his resolve hardened. Gerry was the direct cause of Demetria's pain. He deserved what he got.

"There he is," Mahoud said. "That's Argus, leaning on that limo."

Torver stepped down from the rig and slapped Mahoud's shoulder. "Thanks." He picked up his briefcase and slipped it under his arm.

"Good luck." Mahoud grabbed his sleeve to stop him. "Be careful with those patches, okay?"

Torver raised an eyebrow, chuckled. "I will." He continued on to the other rig where Tomás waited, a hand banded around Gerry's arm.

Argus did not move while Torver crossed the empty street, Gerry and Tomás in tow.

"We're returning your property," Torver said.

Argus merely opened the door and let Tomás shove Gerry inside. Tomás backed away to let Torver into the car. Argus entered after them, slammed the door and sat facing them, a plasma gun in his hand. The car began rolling immediately.

"How's Stringer, Argus?" Gerry asked. "I hope he recognizes the efforts I made on his behalf. He will need my services, now that Lockwood has agreed to work for him. He'll need watching, you can be sure of that. I have some ideas on how to proceed—"

Argus bent forward. Gerry stopped, his eyes wide. Argus pinched Gerry's neck at the shoulder. He slumped, unconscious.

"Thank you," Torver said with a half-smile.

"Asshole talks too much. Gets on my nerves."

The drive to Stringer's compound was short. The door of the car opened from the outside. Argus signaled Torver to get out, then followed him.

"Bring the other one inside," Argus directed the man holding the door handle.

Torver climbed the stairs to the front door. As soon as he passed a certain point, a sharp alarm sounded. Argus placed a hand on his shoulder. Torver stiffened.

"You brought a weapon," Argus said.

Torver slowly dug in his pocket and brought out a plasma gun by the barrel. He handed it to Argus.

He smiled as he passed the front door—the sound of the alarm was the signal to MGRC agents that he was inside. That siren blast and the few seconds it took to hand over his weapon would have given MGRC time enough to study the defense system.

He stopped in the entrance hall and whistled. "Nice."

"Upstairs."

He climbed the stairs and ambled along the long, narrow corridor until Argus detained him. His heart pounded, and his nerves were stretched to breaking.

Argus motioned him inside. Torver peered around the dim room until he located Stringer.

"Dr. Lockwood. I like punctuality in a person. You're obviously not the absent-minded professor type."

"Depends on the situation. I don't hear anything when I'm working." He dropped his briefcase on the chair in front of the desk.

"Yes, of course. You also brought me a gift, unwanted as it was." Stringer grinned in Argus's direction. "Put Gerry in with the remaining Termite."

"Oh, and, Argus," Torver called out, his eyes boring into Stringer's, "bring Ms. Greyson back with you."

He moved into Stringer's lifepath and came out almost immediately, shuddering. The path had a slimy quality to it that repulsed him. Even Gerry's had been cleaner.

Stringer threw him a dark look but said, "Bring the woman, Argus. Have a seat, Dr. Lockwood."

"I'd rather see the lab you promised me."

"Excellent. You'll start right away, then. I mentioned your discovery to a few organizations that could use your research. They're interested, to say the least. I've arranged a special auction for tomorrow night."

"That doesn't give me much time."

"I have every confidence in your abilities. I think we should have a little demonstration as well. You can use Dr. Sinclair and the last Termite."

Torver's last qualms about what he was about to do to this man disappeared.

"I can do that," he said, "only once the retrovirus is put together. For that, I need Demetria."

It was a good thing he had no intention of producing anything for Stringer because he knew the fat man would get rid of him and Demi as soon as the technique was documented, sold and tested.

He turned around when the door swished open. Demetria entered, her head high, then stopped in her tracks when she saw him. Torver walked over to her and folded her into his arms. She was so stiff he thought he might break her. Then a shudder passed through her body, and she slumped in his embrace. Her arms twined around his waist and she hugged him fiercely.

"Hi, sis," he whispered in her ear.

She took a great breath and pushed away from him.

"I told you to stay away from here."

"No, you told me to stay out of your head. Not the same thing." He raised his hand and traced the edge of her skin with light fingers. "You look awful."

"Thanks."

"You wanted Ms. Greyson, Dr. Lockwood, and you have her. I suggest you start right away."

"No!" Demetria said. She grasped his arm. "What have you done? You're not going to give him the formula, are you?"

"It was that or let you die."

"I can't believe this. After all we've gone through? What about your—"

Torver grasped her shoulders and shook her. "Enough! I did what I thought was best." He looked straight into her good eye and felt the pull. "I don't want to lose you."

He felt her push him away from her lifepath. She frowned.

"Perhaps I can persuade your girlfriend to help you, Dr. Lockwood?"

Torver glanced over his shoulder. Stringer had an expectant look on his face.

"She'll do what I tell her to do. After all," he said, his voice hardening, his eyes boring into hers, "I certainly wasn't attracted to her pretty face, was I? Come on, darling, you knew what you were getting into when you decided to get involved with me. You're too intelligent not to know what the deal was."

She stared at him for a moment, her defenses still up. Then, suddenly, he was inside, looking at the twisting strands of her lifepath. He was kicked out as abruptly.

"Yes, Torver," she said, her voice subdued, "I knew what the deal was. I'll help you, but it's the last time. When we're out of here, we go our separate ways."

"How touching." Stringer sneered. The walls separated to reveal the gleaming surfaces of the laboratory. "There's your lab, Dr. Lockwood."

Torver let his hands drop from Demetria's shoulders and went inside.

"Good. All I need is here. I have to set up. Demi, bring me my briefcase, would you?" he said, his tone abstracted.

"Tea," Stringer said. "This calls for tea."

"Whatever," Torver said. "Set up your terminal here," he said to Demetria. "I want you to do some probability modeling of series X102 and 103, decomposed to the alleles and fanned out. Got that?"

"Yes." She threw him an amused glance. She knew he was talking perfect nonsense, but he hoped Stringer would be impressed by it. All he needed now was to let her in on his plan. He just hoped she wouldn't put up a fuss.

Stringer's assumption they were lovers had been a bonus. Going along with it had given him the means to tell her he was here under false pretences and to ask for her help. He knew she'd understood when she'd let him inside her head for a moment.

Demetria busied herself setting up the holonet.

"I wish I had my EP," she said. "I work so much better with Dympna."

"You'll have to make do without her." Torver opened his briefcase and took out a set of small disks. "Set up an interface between these and your bionet then do the analysis I asked you. I want it up and running in two minutes."

"Two minutes! You're kidding."

"Do it."

He heard Stringer chuckle behind them. Torver was glad they had their backs to him when he saw Demetria's eye widen at what appeared on the vidscreen. He knew she recognized Vincent's data and was wondering how he'd gotten it. Time enough later to explain he'd made copies.

"By the way," Stringer said, "when the authorities come to save you, they'll find a few added surprises they wouldn't expect. I love the effect of plasma on a body. It makes it burn and sizzle. The smell of grilled meat is wonderful. Did you know our ancestors used to cook meat that way—I mean, by grilling it?"

Torver silently swore. He hoped Mahoud and the Mungers were up to Stringer's traps.

"I wish you'd stop talking, Stringer. I can't concentrate."

"THE CREW'S IN PLACE?" ALIM ASKED OFFICER MARTIN. HIS FACE WAS LOST AGAINST THE dark clothing he wore. Mahoud now knew why Alim favored white.

Martin nodded. "It's much too quiet for my taste. We haven't seen any of Stringer's men for the past forty-five minutes."

"I agree," Mahoud said. "Last time I was here, I saw at least three people on the roof and movement in and out the door."

"They might have extended the motion sensors' perimeter," Alim said. "That way they don't need the men."

"Did you figure out the secsys protocol?" Mahoud said.

"We're still working on it."

"I wish I knew what was going on in there," Mahoud said. He paused to make sure he had the facts straight between what he was supposed to know and what Torver had told him. "Stringer might decide to force the solution out of him."

"Stringer will try the easy method, first," Martin said. "Dr. Lockwood's supposed to cooperate."

"Okay," Alim said, "their security is breached. Here's what we'll do. We move in slowly until we're in sensor range. We neutralize the sensors, ram in the door and swarm the building."

Mahoud frowned. "I don't like it. Doesn't feel right. Too easy."

"We know what we're doing," Martin said.

"Let's do a test," Mahoud suggested. "Send someone out, see if the motion sensors are working."

"You're saying that if they're not..."

"It's a trap."

"But if they're operational we've given ourselves away."

He shrugged. "We're expecting a fight anyway."

Alim thought about that for a second then nodded. He motioned to one of his men and instructed him to stroll past Stringer's house. The man started down the street. Three plasma rifles followed him past Stringer's house.

"Satisfied?" Alim said.

Mahoud shook his head. He still had that feeling of wrongness.

Alim gave the order to move forward. The crew, a mix of MGRC-enlisted skirmishers and Mahoud's people, crept towards their goal, eyes peeled on the roofs and the motion sensors. Mahoud peered down the street. He raked each building with narrowed eyes, his anxiety increasing with each step they took.

Suddenly, he saw a flash of light at sidewalk level. Not on the roofs, he realized, in the basements.

"Down! Everybody down!"

He saw the flash of a plasma beam, heard a scream, then another.

"They're in the basements," he yelled. "Use your smoke guns."

The next minutes passed in a flurry of movement. Martin fell beside him, smoke wafting from her upper arm. Mahoud threw himself down beside her just as he felt a beam graze his back. The pain was searing. Martin checked the damage.

"It's a minor wound. My right arm's useless, though. Take my smoke gun. I can shoot plasma with my left hand."

He grabbed the gun from her useless hand. A few of the men had succeeded in throwing smoke grenades into the basements, but the element of surprise definitely belonged to Stringer's men. He saw the flash of a plasma beam aimed away from him. He spotted the shooter, saw his advantage. To hell with smoke guns, he decided.

He picked up his plasma rifle and crawled to the wall of the building. He marked the shooter, took his time to aim, pulled the trigger. One down. He just hoped Torver was doing his thing in there.

Under a barrage of plasma beams, he crawled from one small spot of cover to another until he saw his chance to drop another of Stringer's men. A few minutes later, he got another. *How many of them are there?*

Paving sizzled beside him. He searched for the origin of the beam and saw a basement window he hadn't noticed before. The barrel of a rifle was pointed directly at him. Its owner was smiling.

# Chapter Thirty-four

DEMETRIA HAD SET UP AN IMPRESSIVE-LOOKING MATRIX. "WHAT DO YOU WANT ME TO do?" she whispered.

"Later," he murmured back. "I want to finish here first."

He completed entering the data he'd brought with him into Stringer's bionet then picked up the stacks of discs and motioned to Stringer. "What do you want me to do with these?"

"Just leave them on the counter. Argus will take care of them."

Torver nodded. "Are you set up?" he said to Demetria. He bent over her, as if to verify her work. *Can you find a way to get close to Stringer?* he typed on the keypad. The words appeared on the vidscreen.

*Think so.*

He pointed at two colored patches he'd placed behind the bionet plate. *The red one on Stringer's skin,* he typed. *5 seconds.*

*Red. No kill?*

Torver stared meaningfully at her mangled left side. She frowned. He typed *No kill.*

"No, that's not what I want," he said, his tone impatient. He deleted their conversation in one swipe. "Use the chromatin substance and extrapolate. We'll see what we can get."

"How long until you have a result?" Stringer squirmed in his chair.

"I don't know," Torver said, his voice still impatient. He turned to Demetria. "Can't you find a way to amuse him so we can work quietly?"

Demetria threw him a disgusted glance. "I don't know what I saw in you." She picked up the patch as she straightened and turned to face Stringer. "I may have something to help you pass the time."

Stringer looked intrigued. "What?"

"Yesterday I remembered some old home vids of my mother playing the piano. They're with my EP at home. I could retrieve them for you."

Stringer's features turned greedy. He mopped his face with his handkerchief.

"They must be worth a fortune."

"I don't know. I suppose so. I'll need your comm to access my library. The lab bionet is working to its full capacity."

"Impossible."

"I do all my statistical analyses with the help of an EP. This bionet is barely powerful enough to do the job."

"Get those vids, Demetria," Torver called out. "I need you here now."

"Well?" she said to Stringer.

"All right. You can use this console."

TORVER WATCHED AS DEMETRIA WALKED AROUND STRINGER'S DESK AND STOOD BESIDE him.

"It'll go faster if I input the codes myself," she said. "Oh!" She stumbled. Her hand landed at the back of Stringer's neck.

"Don't touch me," he growled. He pointed the plasma gun he had on his lap. Demetria pushed away a few inches and raised both her hands.

"Don't shoot, please. I tripped on your carpet. I swear."

Stringer's face changed, took on a wondering expression. "I feel strange." He lifted his gun. "What did you do to me?"

"Nothing. I just tripped."

"And stuck a little patch on the back of your neck," Torver said, hoping to distract Stringer's attention away from Demetria.

Stringer's head lurched in Torver's direction. "A patch?"

"Yes, a little patch, filled with my own brand of surprises."

He didn't see Demetria move. All he heard was the gun skittering away in the direction of the velvet drapes. She ducked behind Stringer's chair and, in one swift motion, pulled him away from his desk and whipped him around.

"I think he had time to call Argus."

"Take the blue patch, stick it on Argus. I still have a couple of things to do here. Can you manage?"

"Don't worry about me." She ran over to the wall beside the door and flattened against it. The door opened, and Argus loomed in the entrance.

"Argus," Stringer called out. "Careful. She's waiting for you."

Stringer's man advanced inside the room, gun at the ready. Demetria let him come in then jumped up and landed on his back. Before he could react, she slapped the patch on the side of his neck.

Argus reached back, grabbed a chunk of her hair and pulled. Instead of resisting, she used her feet on his hips to propel herself forward. The sudden movement surprised him, and he let go. She fell to the floor and rolled back to her feet.

Argus threw a punch. Demetria ducked just in time. She crouched low and waited, knowing his size would be a disadvantage in the small room. Argus charged her and slashed down. She rolled away.

"Is anything supposed to happen?" she called to Torver.

"Soon, I hope," he yelled back.

Somewhere, a siren erupted. Argus, distracted by the sound, turned his head towards it. Demetria saw her chance. She leaped forward and lashed out a kick at his knee. To her surprise, she heard the bone crack. Argus cried out and toppled to the floor. He put out a hand to break his fall. She heard another crunch. Argus crumpled, moaning.

Torver rushed to the door and closed it.

"I've locked the door, but it won't hold for very long if someone decides to break it down."

"Am I dreaming, or is he shrinking?" Demetria said, pointing to Stringer.

"What...?" Stringer swallowed. His voice was a mere whisper. "What did you do to me?"

Torver glared at him. "I tailored my retrogene technique just for you, using the old cloning accelerated growth technique—an idea that came from Gerry, by the way—except it's acting in reverse. Your system is now over-metabolizing. It's burning all your fat. When it's done with the fat, it'll start burning off muscle tissue. Even walking or talking will burn off more. The only way you'll be able to counter the problem will be by eating more than your system can burn." He paused, smiling. "That's a lot of eating. I guess you won't have time for anything else, Stringer."

Stringer just stared at him with horrified eyes.

"What about Argus?" Demetria asked.

"I inserted a gene that made his bones brittle. Any kind of shock will cause a break. He'll have to spend the rest of his years in a very sedentary state. Unless someone finds a way to reverse either defect."

"How could you tailor the genes to them specifically?" Demetria said.

"I copied your auth code and used it to find their gencodes in MGRC genebanks."

"That's illegal. MGRC—"

"Won't ask questions. They'll have Vincent's data, plus everything they need to convict Stringer and Gerry. I made sure of that." He smiled. "Trust me, I'm good at manipulating secrets."

Someone pounded on the door. They called Stringer's and Argus's names. He crossed to the velvet drapes and picked up the plasma gun.

"How are we going to get out of here?" Demetria said.

"The Mungers should get here soon. I hope."

She shook her head. "No, they won't. Stringer suspected you'd bring MGRC. He installed a brand-new encrypted security system behind his regular one. It acts like a privacy bubble. It's impenetrable. If MGRC does succeed in breaking down the code, we'll probably be dead by the time they get here."

"Damn." The pounding on the door intensified. Torver turned to Stringer. "Where's the encryption key for the security system?"

Stringer smiled, lifted a hand and tapped the side of his head. His arm fell away, and he closed his eyes, still smiling.

"He's not lying," Demetria said. "He bragged to me that he had a phenomenal memory for numbers. The starter string is in his head."

Torver pursed his lips. "Did you see him code in the string?"

"Yes, but I wasn't paying attention. I—"

A louder thump made them both jump. The thermoplastic door began to show small spidery tears. Torver strode around the desk and tapped a key on Stringer's desk. The lab walls began to close.

"Let's go in there. It might give us a few more seconds."

They slipped inside the narrowing opening.

"What good is hiding in here? We can't lock the doors from inside."

"They might get sidetracked by Stringer and Argus." He placed his hand on her shoulder and looked her in the eye. "At least long enough for what I want to do."

"What?"

"I want to go into your lifepath and see if I can retrieve the string."

She grimaced then shook her head. "You won't be able to remember it."

He searched around him then picked up a tablet and stylus. "I'll say it to you. You can write it down."

Demetria gaped at him. "We can't communicate when you're in my head."

"I can watch your visions. I've influenced your actions before, and all this without you knowing. Maybe I can talk to you in a vision, give you the numbers."

"I told you, I have no control over these visions."

"You can use your vocal scanning, can't you? If you're conscious that I'm in your head, maybe you can hear me, too, in some way. You'll have to find a way to transfer the information I give you in your vision to reality." He paused, cocking his head to listen to the cracking sounds. "Do you have a better idea?"

She stared at him for a moment then sighed. "I'll try."

She sat cross-legged on the floor, breathed deeply a few times then began scanning. Her hands held the tablet and stylus so tightly her knuckles were white. Torver placed his hands over hers, willing her to relax. She gasped, opened her eyes wide.

"It's working," she whispered. "Torver..."

## Chapter Thirty-five

THE NOISE WAS DEAFENING. DEMETRIA SPUN ON HER HEEL AND GAPED IN astonishment. Hundreds of mechanical clocks surrounded her, some hanging on the walls, others sitting on tables or counters. As she became accustomed to the din around her, she began to sort out the clack and clatter of some, the rattle, clang and whirr of others. Each clock sounded different.

*Time. We're out of time.* She felt panicky. Was that the only message she'd get from that vision?

She heard a knocking that wasn't part of the clock sounds. Someone behind the door, there, between the two grandfather clocks. She heard Torver's faint voice on the other side. *Come on, Demi, Let me in.* She hesitated. What if it wasn't real? She could open the door and find Argus, ready to kill her. She remembered the welts on her arms from her last vision. She could get hurt here and she'd feel it in reality.

A clock behind her whirred. She turned just as it bonged. The face of the banjo clock lit up. She approached it. The clock had only two numbers, eleven and three. She touched the eleven. It shone briefly then disappeared. She touched the three. The same thing happened. A bell pealed. She turned to the illuminated face of a round wall clock. The letter A, an ampersand and seven. When she touched the symbols, they faded.

She suddenly felt elated. One, one, three, A, ampersand, seven. Another clock rang, and three numbers stayed on the face. Torver was giving her the numbers. She hoped that, by touching them, it really meant she was writing them down. Otherwise, all her vision meant was that they were running out of time. Fast.

IMMEDIATELY, HE WAS INSIDE. HER LIFEPATH APPEARED DIFFERENT, BRIGHTER. TORVER ran his gaze along the thread and focused on a point close to him. Nothing happened. He tried again. Nothing.

"Come on, Demi," he muttered. "Let me in."

As if she'd heard him, his body caught up with his consciousness, and he was in front of Stringer sitting at his desk. He saw the drug lord tap keys in order. Too late. He collapsed the image and backed up.

A feeling of urgency spurred him on. He blinked, realizing it wasn't his anxiety he felt but Demi's. He stared at the lifepath. There was one problem he hadn't anticipated when he'd proposed this scheme. He'd be able to see the numbers, but how could he rattle them off when Demetria was caught in a vision? He'd have to be looking at both scenes at the same time.

He remembered his idea of tying a knot in her lifepath as a marker. Maybe he could do something similar—bring the scene with Stringer parallel to her vision. He could speak out the numbers, and hopefully, she'd hear him in her vision. It had to be that or nothing. They were running out of time.

"Okay, let's do this." He focused on the thread again, and Stringer's bulk appeared. He grabbed the thread just before its opening and pulled, walking backward. Behind him, some kind of racket was getting louder. A moment later, he saw Demetria, surrounded by clocks. He grabbed the edge of the lifepath where her vision began. Both scenes stayed up.

Using his eyes like a vid lens, he zoomed on Stringer's fingers. Quickly, he repeated aloud every number and letter the fat man tapped into his pad. The air filled with the sound of bells. He ignored them, focused on the interminable sequence of numbers. Then he was out.

He shook Demetria. She blinked and focused on him.

"Did you get the numbers?" he asked.

"I don't know." She looked down at the tablet in her hands then smiled. She showed him the code.

Torver laughed. Demetria rushed over to the bionet and began entering the string of numbers, letters and symbols she'd jotted down.

"I'd never seen clocks with letters and symbols before. It was weird." A cracking sound exploded from Stringer's office. "Let's hope this works."

A PLASMA BEAM ZINGED FROM BEHIND MAHOUD. THE GRINNING GUNMAN WHO'D HAD HIM in his sights blinked and looked down in surprise at the hole in his chest then fell backwards.

Mahoud flattened against the wall. Martin came up beside him.

"Thanks," he said.

"Any time. Let's go."

"This is ridiculous." He ducked a beam and ran a few meters. "We haven't made any headway. Why isn't anyone inside by now?" He waited for an answer. "Martin?"

He turned to check if she was behind him. She was still leaning on the wall where she'd come up beside him. Her eyes were opened wide. A small hole sizzled in the center of her forehead. He turned back, forced himself to push down the anger. You lose your edge when you're angry, he told himself. Remember that.

He was very close to Stringer's compound by now. He advanced another step and came up against an invisible barrier. He pushed with his hand. It didn't move.

"Alim," he called into his comm. "There's no point in this carnage. Stringer's got some other kind of barrier set up."

"I know. We're working on it."

"In the meantime, we're getting slaughtered."

"Just a few more minutes. Then we'll see."

Mahoud swore, pulled back into an alcove.

"Torver Lockwood," he said to the wall, "you'd better do your part, you jerk-head. I don't intend to die here."

"I'VE GOT IT," DEMETRIA SAID. "THE SECURITY SYSTEM IS DOWN." SHE TURNED AT THE sound of the lab walls opening. "A moot point, maybe."

Torver grabbed her arm and pointed to the steel table in the middle of the room. She nodded, and they overturned it. Torver was glad Stringer hadn't thought of bolting it to the floor.

They dove behind it. He tightened his grip on the plasma gun.

"Give me that," Demetria said as she grasped the gun. "Even with one eye, I bet I'm a better shot than you are."

She lifted her head above the table and pulled the trigger. Someone screamed.

"I thought you didn't want to kill people," Torver said.

"I don't. I'm aiming for a more sensitive part of their anatomy."

Torver winced. He heard shouts and a scuffle, then nothing.

"Maybe MGRC made it inside after all," he said.

"We'll wait here a bit longer."

"Fine with me."

"Did you give your retrogene research to MGRC?"

"They'll find it in Stringer's bionet, with a few pieces missing. Unfortunately, it'll take me years to study it and figure out whether I can fix it. Which I won't be able to do, of course. Neither will any other scientist."

Demetria shook her head sadly. "So, there's no hope for Laslo's son."

"That's not what I said."

She stared at him then smiled. "The vision helped, then."

"It did."

Someone called out. Torver recognized the voice. The door of the lab opened wider to reveal Mahoud and Alim.

"Took you long enough," he griped.

"Everything okay here?" the MGRC inspector asked. His gaze went from Demetria's face to Torver's.

Mahoud jerked his thumb towards Stringer and Argus.

"What happened to them?" Alim demanded.

"They got a dose of their own genetic tampering. It all happened in self-defense, I assure you." He turned to Mahoud. "Any big problems?"

"Nothing we couldn't handle." Mahoud smiled. He was holding his arm and was limping. "Glad to see you're alive, Ms. Greyson."

Torver motioned them inside. "You'll find all the proof you need in there. If you don't mind, I'd like to take Demetria to a medic. She needs to have her face seen to."

As they went down the stairs, Demetria stumbled. Torver propped her up.

"Come on, Demi, only a few more stairs. Then you can sit down."

"I need to sit down now."

"Fine." He sighed. "I'd carry you, but you're the physical one in the family."

They sat huddled together on one side of the stairs, his arm around her shoulders, while what seemed like an army trundled up and down in a great rush.

"It sounds strange, doesn't it?"

"What?"

"Saying we're family."

He said nothing for a moment. "Strange, but good."

"Yes." She leaned her head on his shoulder. "Torver?"

"Hmmm?"

"What are you going to do now?"

"Oh, I have a project that's close to my heart. I think MGRC will want to get in on it. I'll be working for them, now."

"You'll hate it."

"Maybe. You haven't asked what my next project will be."

Demetria sighed wearily. "Okay, I'll ask. What's your next project?"

He set her away from him, put the tip of his fingers under her chin and turned her face towards him.

"Seamless skin regeneration."

She stared at him for a moment. Then she laughed.

He got up and pulled her after him. "Come on, sis, let's go and grow you some skin."

They continued downstairs and through the verdant hall to the front door. An MGRC skirmisher blocked their path.

"Medic's over in that corner," he said, pointing to a spot to his right.

"She needs more than first aid," Torver said. "She needs to go to the Health Center."

"We'll take her," Alim said behind him.

Torver turned around. The inspector was followed by two MGRC agents.

"As for you, Dr. Lockwood, I am hereby placing you under MGRC protection. You'll come with us."

"We know what your protection means," Demetria said.

Alim glanced at her then returned his attention to Torver. "Your abilities and knowledge are too valuable for MGRC to risk." Alim gave him a half-smile. "Add to that a maverick personality...we'll provide you with an environment that will facilitate your research and give us peace of mind. You'll have everything you want."

"Except freedom."

"Who has that, these days?" Alim gestured to one of the agents. "Take Ms. Greyson to the Health Center."

Torver grasped Demetria's waist. "So you can make her vanish, too? I don't think so."

Mahoud appeared from the side. He looked angry. Tomás, Souko, Bibi and Taps positioned themselves around Alim and his agents.

"We'll take Demetria to the Center, Torver," he said. "I'll make sure nothing happens to her." He glared at Alim. "Now or later."

Alim only raised an eyebrow and shrugged.

Torver stared into Demetria's eyes. For a moment—a long, satisfying second—she let him inside.

"You have my picture," he heard her say.

He stepped out and nodded grimly. Alim smiled and waved him through the front door.

Torver glanced behind him. Demetria stood tall and straight, her mangled face proudly visible to all. Mahoud and his people surrounded her in a semi-circle. He was struck by the fact that, somehow, he'd acquired allies and friends. It felt almost as strange as gaining a sister.

Demetria would make certain he wasn't buried somewhere forever. Mahoud would help.

He stared at Alim and grinned. The MGRC would soon let him go. After all, despite his newfound conscience, he still had his weapon of choice. He wouldn't have any compunction about manipulating people with their secrets to gain his freedom.

He turned and walked back to Demetria. "I do remember my promise, and I'll keep it. Take care of my apartment until I come back, will you?"

She cupped his cheek with her hand. "I will."

He leaned over, kissed her right cheek and smiled. "I'll come visit you."

Demetria's right eye widened. He knew she understood he was talking about walking her lifepath.

"We'll see," she said. "I might even let you in."

He nodded and strolled back to where Alim waited. He gave himself two, maybe three weeks before he was back in his apartment with his mouse and Demetria living above him. He grinned, then laughed. Without its knowledge, MGRC had acquired formidable opponents. The countdown towards its demise had just begun.

END

# ACKNOWLEDGMENTS

This story could not have been written without the help and support of the following people:

Peggy Loyer, who not only tracked my syntax errors with the zeal of a tornado chaser but also helped me stay consistent and never let me get away with anything;

Jim Luce, who scolded me when I didn't write my best, and who gave me more than I can ever repay;

Robyn Williams, who always presented me with a fresh perspective on my writing;

Dr. Gary Shutler, who took time out of his busy schedule to suggest a better scientific line—any scientific implausibility, wild imaginings and misinterpretations are strictly my responsibility;

Elizabeth Burton, editor extraordinaire, who put the finishing touches to the story without cramping my style.

Thank you all.

# ABOUT THE AUTHOR

M. D. BENOIT is the author of the Jack Meter Case Files, an SF mystery series. The first two, *Metered Space* ("...mystery, humour, suspense and sheer out-of-this-world fantasy..." Neil Marr, BeWrite.net) and *Meter Made* ("...a fast-paced, hardboiled, non-stop, seat-of-your-pants, action-packed SciFi mystery..." The Science Fiction Review) were received to great acclaim. The third book in the series, *Meter Destiny*, is scheduled for publication in 2007.

M. D. discovered science fiction and mystery through her father's bedtime stories, which were always full of gadgets, dark doorways, and disappearing people. She lives in Ottawa, Ontario, with her husband and her cat (who is really an alien in disguise). She has a masters degree in psychology from Saint Mary's University, Halifax, Nova Scotia, where she lived for eight years before moving to Ottawa.

She is currently hard at work on her sixth manuscript, *Entropy*, and a fourth Jack Meter Case File, *Meter Parents*.

## ABOUT THE ARTIST

BOB HOBBS—Moor Dragon—has been a professional illustrator for over 30 years. His work has graced the published short stories of such celebrated authors as Ursula K. LeGuin, Larry Niven, Algis Budrys, Yves Maynard, Alexander Jablokov, Lawrence Watt Evans and more. and has appeared in dozens of magazines such as *Amazing Stories*, *Tomorrow SF*, *On Spec* and *Talebones*. His illustrations have appeared in *Drawing and Painting Fantasy Worlds* by Finlay Cowan, *Healing Magick* by Levanah Bdolak and *The Star Trek Concordance* by Bjo Trimble, to name a few. He has also done game-related work for such companies as Wizards of the Coast, Flying Buffalo and Steve Jackson Games.

His creations have been exhibited in such venues as the Park Avenue Atrium in New York City, The DragonCon convention art show in Atlanta, the Rhode Island School of Design Museum and the U.S. House of Representatives in Washington DC. His original works are owned by several celebrities including *Sopranos* actress and *Playboy* model Kelly Kole, B-horror movie queens Lilith Stabs and Debbie Rochon as well as actor James Marsters from *Buffy The Vampire Slayer*.

Bob currently lives in Huntington Beach, California.

Printed in the United States
73549LV00002B/367-408